THE FIREBIRD'S TRAIL

PART 1
OF THE FIREBIRD TRILOGY

By

Louisa Dwyer

DEDICATION

For Sam, for everything.

CONTENTS

ACKNOWLEDGMENTS

With my great thanks to Mike Taylor who brought
the Upper Face to life.

PROLOGUE

The Burning City, First Year of the Dancer, summer.

The Old Man of the Sands, as he was affectionately known by his subjects, sat neatly on a cushion of deep turquoise-dyed silk, topping a small wooden stool. Before him had been laid a low wicker table, upon which rested a wooden board and a carefully arranged series of small, polished stone blocks.

The puzzle was truly devious. It challenged the logician to save his counter by deconstructing a wall of thirty irregular shapes into a bridge across a line denoting a river. The player was allowed only fifteen moves in which to effect the conversion and the nature of the blocks rarely allowed the builder more than six moves before any construction became so unstable as to collapse.

For three days he, the King of all the Desert, had devoted the greater part of his evening to studying the problem. However, it had, more often that he would have liked, crept into his thoughts during the daylight hours. So bad was the distraction that he had almost allowed a concession in his barter with one of the wretched merchant people who had come to trade spices at his palace.

He narrowed his eyes and smiled thinly. It was an excellent riddle. And he would master it, even if it took him a whole season. And besides, it was *important* to keep one's mind sharp. He had not survived so many cycles of the seasons by going soft in the mind.

The Old Man of the Sands really did have a lightning-quick mind. This was accompanied by an equally quick temper and even quicker wit. These traits he often deployed with intentional succession and overlap which gave him the position of power in most interactions.

The Old Man of the Sands was also really *very* old. People across the Six Kingdoms had long speculated about the number of his accumulated seasons and tried and failed to have their sources verified. He had certainly seen at least fourteen hundred cycles pass, for these were well-recorded by the Kingdom Scribes. However, beyond this, speculation was wild.

A few of the more gregarious pilgrims to the Sand Kingdom had even dared to ask the wiry old King. This had invariably been an error of judgement on their part. Such people had left the Sands with the knowledge only that the King was not disposed to wasting his time settling the bets of small-minded persons.

In fact, the King of the Desert had no idea how old he was and, more to the point, had no interest whatsoever in even attempting to work it out. Apart from anything, it would dull the inexplicably long-debated gossip in the taverns of the Northern and Western peoples which kept his fame alive. Who was he to deprive them of their fun?

The Old Man of the Sands was a firm believer in fun. Moreover, given the certain knowledge that he was indeed very, if not a *precise* sort of old, he must use his remaining time to put his mind to higher tasks such as the engineer's test before him. It was simply a matter of priority.

His internal monologue was rudely interrupted by a knock at the door and the leathery, tanned face of the King scowled up at the poor server whose bad luck it was to have to break the reverie of his master.

With tragic emphasis he raised himself laboriously from his low seat and exclaimed with wide eyes and clasped hands, 'By the stars, one hour is all the King of the Sands requires to rest his old bones!'

The young server was never quite sure how to take the enigmatic temper of His Majesty which, more often than not, seemed to give his lord more pleasure than pain. After only momentary reflection, he elected to bypass addressing the King's indiscernible outburst in favour of delivering his message and attempting to make a hasty retreat.

Bowing, he informed his master, 'Your Majesty, a young man requests an audience.'

The King fixed him with a hard stare before learning back and stretching his arms behind his head. He relented with rolling eyes. 'I live to serve my people, do I not?'

Seeing the confusion and worry in the hapless servant's features, he sighed and with a slight flick of his hand said resignedly, 'Send him in.'

His visitor was not an expected suppliant, but supplication was certainly in his demeanour. The King had anticipated a departing merchant. Either that or an overexcited official, keen to allow his King to be the first to know of some important completion or development of one of the many building, conservation or investigatory projects of his kingdom.

However, the dark hair, tall and broad build and clear blue eyes marked his visitor as not of his own Desert People, but as a man of the Forest. The ornaments of his sash recognised him to the King as one of the deputation from that desolately cold and damp country in the Western Lands who had come, four seasons ago, to study the arid plant life of the Sands.

At least his time in the Desert had given him a little colour, for the first time that the King had met him, the man had looked so pale that he had wondered whether he was ill. The Forest people lived an outdoor life and were not generally milk skinned. Perhaps he had some Snowseal blood in his veins. Or perhaps had had merely been sea-sick from the voyage across the Middle Sea.

The King considered his respectful low bow and searched the face of the earnest man of, perhaps, two hundred and fifty cycles of the seasons. He recalled that the poor fellow had a pronounced stammer, no doubt one of the many disagreeable side-effects of children having to grow up in all that damp and shadow of the Forest.

Nonetheless, the Master of Horticulture in the city of Hijake had written most favourably in his seasonal reports of the Forest man's expertise and conduct. The King had been given the impression that he was a popular and respected personage within the region.

Recalling (with great satisfaction for he had so very many things to remember) the name of this man, the Old Man of the Sands addressed him airily as if instant recognition had dawned at the moment of his entrance.

'Gretan, Master Botanist of the Forest People, you disturb my peace. For what reason do you journey from your service to your King and your people in Hijake to my chambers in the Burning city? Are you dissatisfied? Have you come to petition me to settle some complaint?'

Gretan internally shrank in the face of such interrogation, for the King of the Sands had his formidable eyes widened and his hands open and outstretched. They seemed to imply a provocation to the kind of verbal duel which he was not only extremely unlikely to win but, more importantly, could not be further from his intention in seeking the audience. It was a bad start.

Rallying himself, he managed, 'I have n-no complaint, Your M-Majesty.'

The Old Man of the Sands slowly cocked an eyebrow, casting him a quizzical look before relaxing his pose and slowly sauntering back to his stool, neatly sitting himself again like a self-satisfied cat.

'Then,' he said slowly and quietly, 'you had better state your *intention*.' The last word was emphasised with a carefully enunciated intensity. Gretan had the distinct and uneasy feeling that the King already knew it.

Collecting and drawing himself up into the best stature he could manage, Gretan took a breath and steeled himself to make his request to the Keeper before him.

'Your Majesty, I c-come before you as K-Keeper of the soul of Jazya of the People of the Eastern Sands. I wish to p-present my suit and beg your p-permission to c-court her who is loved by you as K-Kin and King.' He bowed low again and slowly raised his eyes to meet those of the man before him.

Gretan's heart was thundering but at least he had managed to get the formal request out without too much spluttering. Now that he had formed the initial part of the traditional request, the ball was in the King's court. He smiled internally at the mental pun.

The Old Man of the Sands let a very long silence pass before nonchalantly stretching his legs and, seeming to consider them with interest, asked, 'Which daughter of mine is Jazya?'

The King was extremely pleased by the look of horror that the Forest man tried to mask as he quickly replied, 'Sire, your twelfth daughter, Horticulturalist of the Gold Class, Manager of the Hijaki irrigation system, Overseer of the New Gardens project—'

'—Ah yes. Now I remember,' the King interjected, adopting a guise of thoughtful recognition. The suitor before him regarded the old man before him uncomfortably, unsure as to whether he was conversing with a fool or being made one.

'It is good to know,' the King continued, 'that when you speak with passion at least, you do not stammer your feelings. Indeed, you own them without reserve or hesitation.'

He looked hard at the stunned Gretan and carried on in more formal tones, 'And what gift do you bring me as measure of your sincerity and judgement of her Keeper?'

Gretan, encouraged by the continuation of the age-old formula, which at least implied that he was not to be rejected outright, did his best to force his face into something resembling a smile. 'Your Majesty, there is a great p-poem among my p-people composed by the honourable Irwince of Highturth.'

Stars, thought the Old Man of the Sands, appalled, recalling the vast length of the verses. In his long life he had been subjected to a full rendition at least twice. The tedium he had experienced was enough to lodge it firmly in his memory, if only to try to ensure at all costs, that he might avoid a third sitting.

The language and form of the piece were indeed quite beautiful but the subject matter was all trees and streams and the serious, dark elegance of the Forest. It made him shiver just thinking about it. Here in the heat of the vast desert plains the people knew that poetic forms should not eat into whole hours or encourage deep contemplation.

Everyone who dwelt under the open and relentless desert sun knew that verses should be short and amusing. A few stanzas were more than enough for tired feet on hot sand to soak up before needing to move on from the glare of the blistering sun of the day. And as for the sharp fall in temperature that accompanied a desert night, did a caravan of travellers not prefer to break a long journey by taking turns to delight the others with a short verse of mirth to warm their companions with laughter?

The People of the Forest were far too serious.

He studied the keen young man before him. No doubt he had endured a miserable season labouring over the words that he might avoid stammering through each verse. Yes, he reflected, it was the Forest way to appeal to a Keeper in such terms as demonstrated a personal trial as a symbol of the extent and sacrifice which they were prepared to make for their love. Very noble, the King considered, without enthusiasm.

Well, what was he waiting for? Gretan stood before him, quite mute. Was he waiting for some sort of permission to begin? Ye Stars, the sooner he began, the sooner it would be over. The King prompted, impatiently, 'Well?'

'*Well*, Sire,' the young man replied, reusing the King's own word and frowning slightly. He considered the floor, laid with rich carpets, before continuing thoughtfully. 'I had m-memorised and p-practised the poem most c-carefully, Your Majesty. On occasion I have b-been able to recite almost a *third* of it without stammering.'

To the Old Man's surprise, the latter comment was delivered with an altogether quite different tone of voice; self-mocking and dry, the King thought.

Gretan continued, now warming to his theme, and gazed directly at the grizzled form before him who had suddenly graced him with a look of interest.

'However, I then b-began to think that Your M-Majesty is so very well-seasoned that he has n-no doubt heard the tale b-before. M-Moreover, I daresay he will have heard it performed by a g-great speaker, one that does n-not fall over his words.' He paused, gauging the reaction of his listener. He could not be sure, but he thought he saw the very smallest curve of a smile forming on one side of the Old Man's face.

'And I thought that I should n-not ask you to suffer such an inferior p-performance. And so...' He got up and picked up the small satchel that he had placed at his feet upon greeting the King and, hurriedly lifting the flap, removed a bundle about the size of his arm from within.

He walked up to the Old Man of the Sands who was sitting, quite straight, piqued with curiosity, his eyes fixed upon the package. Gretan made a neat bow and held it out to him in both hands.

'And so, I g-got you this instead,' he finished.

The King snatched the object held out to him with the quick lightness of a panther swiping at its prey. He was aware that his action betrayed his eagerness to understand it, but he loved surprises and could not quite contain the thrill of anticipation. He turned the gift around in his hands, feeling its weight and examining the rough sacking sheets that wrapped it. He saw the unmistakable crude sturdiness of the Sea People in the cloth and rough brown twine that fixed it. He deftly untied this and peeled back the coverings.

He beheld with genuinely aghast elation the dark blue-green, crushed-effect glass bottle which he set on his little wicker table. He had not come across this treasure for a very many seasons.

'Sea Fire!' he exhaled, his voice having taken an airy and awe-filled quality. He looked down upon the bottle as if it were a priceless artefact.

The grin he wore was truly something to behold. It lit up his ancient features, revealing a row of almost perfect, white teeth and his eyes glittered like two dark jewels. Tearing his glance from the gift back to Gretan, the King broke into a short cackle and hopped to his feet.

'Gretan of the Forest People, how did you come to acquire such a jewel? Do the Sisters of the Seas themselves not jealously guard the secret? Ha! Why, it is banned in four of the Six Kingdoms!' He waggled his forefinger at Gretan's face. 'Your King would certainly not approve.'

The latter comment evidently seemed to add to the Old Man of the Desert's delight, for he turned back to clasp his prize once again and his grin widened further still. Cradling the opaque vessel, he swivelled on the balls of his feet and met the Forest man's eye and in his most dryly imperious tones appraised the young man. 'You have chosen well. And your gift was made the better for your trick in its delivery.'

Continuing in a softer, more careful voice, still with a smile on his lips, the Old Man of the Sands said, 'Your gift is found acceptable to me as Keeper of your heart's desire. State the nature of your love and what you may offer so that I may consider your worthiness to court that which is precious to me.'

Gretan couldn't help breaking into a gratified smile and proceeded to tell a loving father about his own daughter. The Old Man of the Sands was not truly listening, but waited with patience for him to finish extolling her virtues and complementing them to his own.

When the suitor had exhausted his carefully prepared repertoire, the King came close and patted him lightly on the shoulder as one might indulge a small child. He appeared tired now and wandered over to a pile of cushions, where he seated himself, cross-legged. Slowly and carefully, the King recited the final traditional form of phrase.

'Gretan of the Forest People, your request to court Jazya of the Sands is granted. Present your token so that all may know her heart is sought.'

Gretan felt within the inner pocket of his light tunic and brought out the beautifully incised feather-shaped metal clip that was the mark of love sought, but also of love gained among the People of the Six Kingdoms. He carefully fixed it to the heavily laden, plain but pristine sash that was draped from the shoulder to the knee of the King. The pin was to join two others in bronze, the mark of permission given by a Keeper for a suitor to court a loved one. Above were the two silver feathers marking the marriages of the old King himself. Silver feathers denoted that, in each case, he had outlived his wives. Gretan's eyes hung wonderingly for a moment on the pins in bronze.

Following his train of thought, the King said quietly, 'You have no need of despair, Gretan. Twenty daughters have been born to me by the two Souls who in turn courted my own heart. Many come to see if the rumours of their Crafts and beauty are true. Alas for them! For, by the time they think themselves ready to return and confirm the tale, they find they cannot depart without first seeing whether they might win one for themselves.' He leant forward and said kindly, 'The two feathers in bronze on my sash are not for Jazya and pose no threat to your suit.'

Gretan smiled shyly and bowed again, stepping backwards towards the entrance to the King's chamber as was the respectful, old way of departing from the presence of the of the ruler of the Sands. The King internally prayed that the Desert gave him strength to endure such a tedious gesture.

As Gretan reached the threshold, the King called out one final time to his unsuspecting would-be son-in-law.

'If she will have you, you will take Jazya West to be one of your people. You will relieve me of one of the far too numerous women of my blood who daily seek to better my health and comfort and, in so doing, I am sure are bringing me to an early demise.'

'My Lord,' Gretan replied his assent with a nod. Though he did wonder at what the King considered to be *early*.

'But you must be married here in the Sands.' The King went on. 'For I cannot travel to your cold Western land of endless trees where an old man used to the warmth and refinements of the East such as I, would surely catch cold and die.'

'Yes, My Lord,' Gretan nodded once again, smiling. 'But all this is only *if* the Princess accepts me.'

'Indeed.'

And with that, the King closed his eyes and Gretan left, hurriedly.

The King heard the padding footsteps of the server on the threshold of the entrance to his chamber. They came to a halt as their owner peered in to find his King slouched in slumber. The Old Man of the Sands waited for the soft click of the door to his chambers being closed before slowly opening one eye to a mere squint. After double-checking that the coast was clear he sprang up from his cushions and tip-toed across the room like a cat-burglar back to his stool. The puzzle demanded his attention, and he demanded its challenge.

'I wonder if a little Sea Fire might catalyse my thinking,' he mused quietly to himself.

It turned out that Sea Fire did not aid the solving of the logician's game. But the King of Sands enjoyed a most interesting night.

CHAPTER 1

Forestfyth, Fifth Year of the Dancer, midsummer.

Almost five hundred people had gathered in Forestfyth for the Winter Dance. The Nearage had relieved the parents of younger children of their responsibilities for the evening, themselves not able to join the celebration until they had come of Age. These young adults could be seen with their young, excited charges at the windows of the disparate wood and thatch houses of the Forest, admiring the townsfolk and those from the wider surrounding area who were arriving in their finery.

The celebrants gathered in the great clearing before the Palace gates. Everywhere lanterns and flowers had been hung and they lit up the faces of the chattering crowd in the warm evening light.

Silence fell as their King and his sister took their places on the half-moon shaped raised platform at the edge of the large square which served as a market and meeting place for the rest of the time.

Jazya watched them in fixed interest step up to greet their people. She and Gretan had travelled from their home in Highturth for the first time since her arrival in the Forest to attend the summer festival in the capital at the invitation of King Aislyth.

'People of the Forest, welcome!' the King cried, his deep, booming voice carrying just a touch of the long vowels of the Forest Folk. This was greeted by a loud and enthusiastic cheer.

'Like you I am anxious to stretch my legs in dance on this wonderful summer evening.' There was a quieter yet pronounced approval of this comment too. After all, their King was quite the dancer and more than a few dared to hope that he might ask them for their hand.

'However,' he continued, 'I wanted to take a moment in this season of beauty and richness to welcome some new faces who come to enrich our community further still.

'Firstly, I give you Master Gretan of Highturth who stays for this celebration period in our city. Two years ago he brought home new wisdom from the East. He has applied his learning well and I have invited him here to honour his irrigation efforts in the Western basin which have been an unqualified success.' There was a polite round of applause.

'Maser Gretan was no more empty handed than empty headed when he returned to us,' he continued, a twinkle in his eye. 'No indeed! For he also brought to the Forest Kingdom an Eastern treasure. May I present Princess Jazya of the Sands, his wife!' Raising his hand in a wave to the embarrassed pair, the King led his people in a more cooing and enthusiastic ovation.

Gesturing slightly beyond them, the King beckoned another couple to him. 'Let me also introduce you to our new Tutor of the Nearage who has left the Plains to return to the Kingdom of her father and share her Craft with the young men and women of our city. Welcome Ravar, now woman of the Forest once again!' The crowd clapped and admired the remarkable, silver-haired, slender young woman smiling her thanks.

'The personage standing at her side begged me to abstain from a formal introduction, but her secret will out in the end and I had hoped that she might grace us with her talents tonight.' Faces turned curiously to the shorter woman at Ravar's side. 'She travels as Soul Friend and assistant in the School of the Nearage to Master Ravar. Her name will no doubt be no familiar to many. You are most welcome in our Kingdom, Amalin of the Plains.'

The crowd erupted into 'oohs' and expressions of delight as those unaware were quickly informed that Amalin of the Plains was a celebrated Master Musician, widely acknowledged to be one of the best of the age.

The King mouthed an apology at the woman who, with her striking companion, was already being accosted by a host of admirers and well-wishers. He met his sister's look of mock censure before chuckling himself and nodding at the players to strike up a tune.

Ravar and Amalin could not have looked less alike. Amalin had the timeless beauty and colourings of the riders of the Plains with large green eyes and red-chestnut hair. Her companion was taller, with pale skin and the unmistakable long, straight hair that marked the people of Snowseal in the Frozen North. It was silver-white with the distinctive moon-like quality that made it appear to glow in the last of the summer evening light.

However, the Forest part of her parentage was given away by the dark blue, rather than lilac eyes that were currently sparkling with laughter. Her Soul Friend was clearly struggling to remain irritated by whatever she had said to mock her and, despite her best efforts, she broke into a helpless giggle and clutched her friend's hands to support her crumpling frame.

Jazya had never seen such juxtaposed or unusually lovely women and walked over to them to introduce herself.

Before she could do so, the rich tones of King Aislyth sounded from behind her.

'Princess?' he asked, waiting for her to turn to face him. 'Would you give me the honour of joining me for the Second Dance?

Jazya beamed. 'Sire, I assure you that the honour would be mine.' She turned the Second Dance pin over to show its gold side on her sash.

However, as he did likewise, she added in a more strained voice, 'But Your Majesty? I am no longer of the People of the Sands. *You* are my King now and I your subject. The only Princess in this Forest stands at your side.' She made a small bow to Istreeth whose eyes danced, but was otherwise inscrutable.

The King looked bemused. 'Jazya, you are, of course, most welcome in my Kingdom but surely you do not reject the land of your birth and Blood Kin?'

'No, My Lord. But I embrace that which is now my home.'

The King frowned slightly, trying to understand her meaning. 'But you are still the daughter of my brother in rule. May we of the Forest not honour you with your title as is your birth right?'

Her brow wrinkled and she gave a slight sigh. 'I hope you will not, Your Majesty.'

'But—' the King persisted.

He was cut off, mid-protestation, by the intervention of Lady Ravar's eloquent, carrying voice. She had been following their dialogue and had understood Jazya perfectly, even if the King had not.

'Perhaps,' she said, 'the Lady Jazya hopes that in her new Kingdom she will become known for her *own* qualities and Crafts—' She, in turn was stopped, mid flow, by a firm squeeze of her hand.

'Ravar!' Amalin implored in a hoarse whisper.

As it dawned upon Ravar that she had not only cut into a conversation, but had also interrupted the King, her hand flew to cover her mouth as if she could retrospectively gag herself. She lowered it to apologise, remonstrating with herself to mind her tongue and own business.

'Please!' said Jazya, smiling and reaching for the mortified Tutor's hands. 'Do not apologise, for you spoke the truth of my heart precisely. It is a vanity, but I do not always wish to be remembered as the daughter of the King of the Sands…'

Somewhat reassured, Ravar turned to Aislyth, saying, 'And yet I should not have cut across my King. My apologies, Your Majesty.'

The King bent forward, looking carefully into the graceful, strange features of the Master Tutor. Seeming to make up his mind, he turned to Jazya and broke into a smile.

'Of course, now I understand, My Lady. I should like to amend the terms of my former offer. I would be delighted to escort My Lady Jazya of the Forest People, newly a subject of my Kingdom in the Second Dance.' She grinned and bobbed in a neat bow.

He swooped his tall frame away from her and caught the eye of Ravar before she could find distraction in some other conversation. He leant forward conspiratorially.

'Master Tutor, you have been here but hours and already you have dispensed some wisdom in the city of Forestfyth.'

'I am sure I did not mean to tell Your Majesty how to behave,' said Ravar, pained.

'And why should you not, when your King is so foolish that he had failed to see the Lady Jazya behind her royal title? My Lady, I am glad for your enlightening me.' He waved his strong, long arm, indicating their surroundings. 'Here under the trees we speak our hearts freely. Would you not similarly coach your Nearage to speak their mind?'

'No, Sire,' Ravar brashly replied, without hesitation.

'No?'

'No. I would ask my students to consider the minds of others and contemplate their response accordingly.' Her blue eyes held those of Aislyth evenly.

'Just as you spoke up for Jazya,' said the King.

'Just so.'

'Hm,' the King exhaled to himself with an amused expression.

As if noticing her for the first time during the conversation, Aislyth looked to Ravar's side, where stood Amalin. She had been quietly following the interaction, eyes narrowed with interest.

'My Lady Amalin, may I have the pleasure of the Fourth Dance?' Amalin replied in the affirmative. And then, without taking the time to adjust the fourth pin of his sash he returned his attention to her friend, saying, 'And My Lady Ravar, will *you* give me your hand in the Fifth?'

'If you are game, Your Majesty,' Ravar replied, raising her eyebrows a fraction.

The King paused, his eyes flashed and he set his teeth in a grin. He gave a single laugh, turned and walked away. However, as he did so he could not resist glancing back to favour her with a look of a competitive man having accepted a challenge.

*

During the First Dance, Ravar and Amalin stood at the side watching the slightly unfamiliar styles and continuing to make the acquaintance of many of the inhabitants of the city. The most memorable was the Lady Fiance. Fiance was a woman of enormous proportions, high volume, and fiery opinions. She was also a Master Cook, kind, warm and wickedly funny. Although she fancied that this new pair of women had been appallingly underfed by the Plainspeople, for they were so *terribly thin,* she quickly approved their capacity for laughter and self-deprecation. Thus, the Soul Friends were accepted into her vast circle of friends, colleague and cronies.

However, it was Ravar's penchant for relating amusing personal experiences that truly won her to this essential and pivotal clan within the Forest City's society. Her retelling of the 'advice' that the Elderwomen of the Plains had imparted to her and Amalin before their departure to the Forest realm had had them in stitches. Within minutes, the dire warnings of Forestmen turning themselves into wolves and tree sprites that whispered spells to move the very trees and lead the traveller to ruin, were being repeated around the clearing.

The King danced with his sister, as was his usual way in the First

Dance. They were Soul Friends as well as siblings, able to share their most intimate feelings and emotions by placing their hands to each other's hearts. As Blood Kin, they would have been able to do so in any case, but in adulthood, their love and loyalty had become such that their bond transcended ordinary family ties.

They moved naturally and with familiarity enough that they could talk with ease. The King was somewhat distracted by the happy sounds of his people surrounding the women from the Plains. Following his gaze, Istreeth teased him playfully.

'Two beautiful and unattached women have arrived in your Kingdom, brother. All are drawn to them and even you cannot help but to stare.'

'Sister, I do not *stare!*' he said with mock hurt.

'Who could blame you if you did?' said Istreeth. 'Tell me, my discerning brother, has one beauty and Crafts enough to tempt a man of your picky taste?'

The King frowned and leant closer to his mocking sister, saying seriously, 'It is not a matter of taste. Have I not told you that I am for a different tale?'

The princess rolled her eyes and sighed. 'Yes, many times, brother.' Her hand released his to trace the golden interwoven band that laced his fingers and wrist. Under his shirt the pattern snaked up his arm and behind his shoulder to his neck.

This was the rare and unmistakable mark of one whose living story had been told by a Bard of one of the Hidden Places. Were it not for the few across the Six Kingdoms who returned, changed in mind as well as body, the Peoples of the Upper Face of the world might not have credited the existence of the near-mythical locations.

It was said that the Hidden Places called men and women whose lives would have meaning and stories for those in a later Age. Only those called might find their way to either Eslebard in the West or Satria in the East and hear a little of their own destiny. Istreeth's brother had been one of these.

Aislyth had heard the call at just one hundred cycles of the seasons and returned later that year bearing the mark of a Master Bard in addition to the undulating circular rings snaking up from the fingers on his left hand. The mark was distinctive, yet far from garish. It looked as though molten gold had been ironed into his flesh.

The people had hailed him as one with a great destiny and it had formed part of the decision of the Council of Elders to make him heir to the Forest Kingdom in the later years of his predecessor's reign.

It was now the fiftieth year of her brother's rule and the Council had been confirmed right in their decision. Aislyth was a just adjudicator, quick-minded and hard-working. He had a powerful way with humour and was famed for his ability to pass on the tales and traditions of the Six Kingdoms. He was popular with his subjects and, only in his third century, was likely to be their King for an exceptionally long time.

Nonetheless, the experience of hearing a part of his Living Tale had changed him in one respect which had made the heart of his sister heavy. In addition to his status and Crafts, King Aislyth was tall, dark and widely held to be devilishly good-looking. Unsurprisingly, many had sought Istreeth's permission to court him. However, it was with sadness that she had long since given up considering consenting to such requests. For although Aislyth's heart was not of stone, nor was it unfeeling and appreciative of beauty, it was closed. He was adamant that his destiny to marry was tied by the mark on his arm and would not be drawn further on the subject.

She regarded him fondly and resolved that she could at least press the idea a little further.

'But it appears that Amalin of the Plains' beauty is famed with good reason,' said Istreeth. 'And is there not something truly striking in her snow-topped companion?'

'Aye, sister. See how our people even so early in their acquaintance gather about and listen and laugh and depart smiling.'

'A great Musician is said to possess a Siren's power,' observed Istreeth, dryly. The King nodded but was silent. He had not been thinking of Amalin.

After the Second Dance, which saw Ravar and Amalin take to the floor in earnest with some of their new friends, the music slowed and atmosphere calmed.

The Third Dance was always reserved for those Soul-Bonded by friendship, marriage or blood. Amalin and Ravar embraced joyfully and shared their first impressions of the Forest and its people. Both professed to be happy in their new home and with the warmth of the welcome they had received.

'And will you play, friend?' asked Ravar, knowingly.

'Yes,' Amalin replied, softly. 'Though not until the Last Dance.'

Ravar answered with a smile. 'And do you look forward to your dance with King Aislyth?' she asked.

'Do you?'

'I have not quite the experience of dancing with Kings as someone I know.' Ravar's eyebrows rose and her eyes danced. 'Stars, he has not yet even heard you sing!'

Amalin's voice *was* that of a Siren. She only had to join in a harmony part four summers ago and the King of Marketdawn had bowed for her hand. In Eagle's Mount, Amalin was *always* obliged to take the First Dance with King Brehain. Ravar was glad of the move to the Forest Kingdom for many reasons, not least because she did not relish the prospect of having to turn down a request from the King of the Plains to court her Soul Friend.

Amalin did not blush, for she knew Ravar spoke true.

'He is very handsome,' said Amalin, glancing across at King Aislyth. 'And a good man, I think. Did you know he bears the mark of Eslebard? A Living Tale… I have only ever met one other who heard the call.'

'Yes,' Ravar nodded, 'the Grandmaster of Rivermare. *And the horses of the river understood every word he spake,*' she intoned, with seriousness.

'The tales of his work are already well learned and told. I wonder what we might one day sing of the King of the Forest,' Amalin mused.

*

Elsewhere within the dancing ring, King Aislyth was again partnered with Istreeth and they made an elegant pair in the Dance of Souls, slowly travelling the floor. This time they were silent, hands to hearts. The King was thinking of Istreeth's mocking. He could feel it still in her through the Soul Embrace.

He looked upon her fair features and wondered that she had never spoken of her own desire regarding marriage. He felt chagrined that he had never asked. He had never received a request as her Keeper, though he felt this was more to do with her ability to make her interest, or lack of, abundantly clear to a would-be suitor. No doubt, if she found her match, *she* would be the one to offer the suit.

The feast followed with special thanks given after dessert to Lady Fiance and her assembled team of Bakers and Cooks who had contributed most of the excellent fare. As the meal was drawing to a close, Ravar had spotted a young man at her table, looking a little over-awed, though clearly enjoying himself. She walked down the side of the long table and took a seat beside him. It was customary for folk to mingle, and no place settings beyond the King's own table were fixed. Even in the case of the latter, the companions might move around after the first course.

'Good evening, My Lord,' said Ravar before bowing. 'May I introduce myself? I am Ravar, newly of the Forest.' She smiled encouragingly.

He returned her bow immediately. 'Yes, My Lady, of course I know who you are.' Looking abashed, he quickly replied, 'That is – I mean King Aislyth introduced you to us all. I am Hathsurst and very pleased to make your acquaintance.'

Nodding at his sash, empty excepting the pins for the Dance and the embroidered emblem of the Forest denoting his fealty, she said, 'You are newly Come of Age, I see. My congratulations to you. This is your first Dance?'

The young man nodded. 'Thank you. I took the sash at the start of the season and returned to my family home in the Forest City to learn my first Crafts.'

'You passed Nearage at Highturth?'

'Yes, My Lady. Until now there have not been Nearage enough to form a Final School. Too many of the previous generation were lost to the sickness.' He lowered his eyes sadly.

'I know,' said Ravar, quietly. 'I myself was brought up in the Plains after Westarm fell to its grasp. My parents sent me away with the other children when they first felt signs of the sickness themselves.'

'I am sorry, My Lady,' said Hathsurst, with feeling.

Ravar brightened. 'But that was many years ago. Thank the Stars the people of the Forest flourish once more and a Tutor is needed for the Nearage again. And you? What Crafts are you embarked upon mastering?'

Hathsurst swelled a little and said proudly, 'I have a desire to become a Healer, Lady.'

'A noble and challenging path, encompassing many Crafts,' said Ravar, with approval. 'From which Master do you learn?'

'Why, from Doctor Eduerd, Lady,' he said with obvious gratification. Remembering Ravar's recent arrival to the town, he elaborated, 'My Lord Eduerd is a Master Healer of very great learning. I am most fortunate and grateful to have been accepted as his pupil.'

'Perhaps he feels equally pleased to have taken on an able and hardworking student?' mused Ravar, kindly.

Hathsurst smiled. 'Lord Eduerd is an excellent teacher, My Lady. In part, I think this is because he still sees himself as a student, though he has mastered many Crafts. He is forever reading or writing or testing some new idea. He corresponds with scholars from every Kingdom. It is his aspiration to find the Way of the Mathematician.'

Ravar, who had already favoured all that she had previously heard of this Eduerd's qualities, found her interest was truly piqued. 'One who openly seeks a High Way? Your Master is someone I should like to meet. Does he dance tonight?'

Hathsurst shook his head. 'No, My Lady, he lives towards the border and divides his time between the Forest City and Woodsedge of Marketdawn. Tonight he dances with those people of the latter, which is the home of some of his Kin and his Soul Friend.'

'In that case, I look forward to making myself known to him in the coming season. Do you think he would give a little time to speak to my Nearage about the healing arts? I am keen for as many of the Crafts to be represented as is possible as part of their education. Only by gaining insight from those who proffer or have daily use of such skills may the young know their import and pleasures.'

'I will ask my Master, Lady. And I am certain he will not refuse,' said Hathsurst.

'My thanks.' Eyeing the top of his sash again, Ravar said lightly, 'I see you are not engaged for the Fourth Dance. Neither am I. Perhaps you would take my hand?'

Hathsurst, hearing the Musicians' introductory notes, pulled her to her feet before she might change her mind and won many an impressed and envious glance from his Kin.

Amalin was in the hold of a very different sort of man. The King was strong and confident, leading her own accomplished steps with facility. He quizzed Amalin about her musical endeavours and accomplishments, interested as keen Musician himself.

As a Master of the discipline, Amalin would have been required to reach gold in three disciplines and the King enquired as to her chosen forms. When Amalin revealed that in addition to voice, lyre and flute, she had attained gold in the grand harp, he was quite taken aback. Such instruments were so difficult to make, let alone play, that as far as he was aware, there were only two such devices in the whole of the Forest

Kingdom. It disappointed him to think that his new subject might not ever be able to grace Forestfyth with the opportunity to hear one played. Perhaps Waterfyth might be persuaded to loan theirs to the capital for a season.

Amalin found King Aislyth good company and an excellent partner in the Dance. She was unsurprised to see that he bore the pin of a Master Dancer on his sash, so easily did he guide and move her, despite the form being unfamiliar to one so newly come to the Kingdom. However, she caught the King, more than twice, looking past her to the floor beyond, where Ravar laughed alongside a very young man whom she had not met.

Seeing he was found out on one of these occasions, Aislyth apologised, 'I am sorry, Amalin. Your friend is so uncommon in the Land of the Forest Folk. Her eyes betray Forest Blood, but she must have Snowseal Kin to own such hair.'

Amalin was not offended by his distraction. Ravar had to put up with the reaction of those unfamiliar with her own gift for music when she first graced them with a song. And in turn Amalin must contend with the hypnotic draw of the dark-haired peoples of Western Kingdoms to her friend's silver-white tresses. Not only were they of an iridescent quality, especially noticeable in the dark such as now, they were thick and long and always beautifully woven. She hazarded the last thought with a little pride, for the artist behind this feat was none other than herself.

'Her mother was of those people, Your Majesty,' she explained.

'Did the Lady Ravar ever know her?'

'She did not. She was too young when she was evacuated,' said Amalin.

'Like so many,' said the King. 'Well, she found family with you I think? Your Kinship is obvious to all who see you together.'

'Aye, My Lord King, we grew up together,' said Amalin. 'My family made her their own and I made her my sister. We are of the same schooling and Nearage Tutor and even share some Crafts.'

'And after you came of Age and specialised in different areas you and the Lady Ravar became Soul Friends, that you might never truly be parted in life,' the King finished her account for her, with warmth and understanding.

'Something like that,' said Amalin, smiling to herself.

The King ended the Dance with a flourish, lifting Amalin lightly from her feet as though she were as light as a fallen leaf and setting her back down in a twirl. 'I am sure we will converse again before long, and perhaps sometime play a little music together?' he said, as the players ended their piece.

Amalin proffered her hand to accept his parting kiss. He clung to it when she offered no immediate reply, grinning. 'My Lady, you *will* play for us tonight?'

*

Ravar and Amalin sat out the common, informal dancing and found seating at a table set back from the dancing area where they could talk without having to raise their voices.

'How does the third King to take your hand compare, friend?' asked Ravar, brightly. 'How does a Man of the Forest fare against a Man of the Plains?'

Amalin laughed but raised an eyebrow, coyly admitting, 'King Aislyth is probably one of the best Dancers with whom I have ever taken to the floor.'

Agog, Ravar squealed her delight and mimicked her friend's own earlier words, 'Well, after all he is *very* handsome.'

Amalin let Ravar enjoy herself before reminding her, 'Well you are to dance with him next, Ravar. You can judge for yourself.'

'Indeed, I shall,' said Ravar, still smiling. 'I look forward to knowing better the man who has made such an impression upon you.'

Amalin rolled her eyes slightly. 'You misunderstand the nature of my interest, Ravar. And besides, I think our King may be looking forward to the Fifth Dance with more than a little anticipation. After all he spent much of the Fourth looking at you.'

Ravar sighed. 'It is the hair.'

'Yes,' Amalin agreed. 'It has been some seasons since we came to a place where you were sufficiently unknown for it to draw such attention.'

Seeing her friend deflated, she took her hands and said jauntily, 'I could always cut it off?'

'Alas, it would grow back!' Ravar returned, regaining her humour. 'But perhaps when I am bent and grizzled as the Old Man of the Sands, my hair will not have to turn to grey to look as all others' of advanced years. Perhaps then I shall finally have peace!'

They proceeded to take the mime forms of doddery old women, half blind and deaf, shouting at each other about their grey hair. 'Whaaaaaat?'

shrieked Ravar, pretending to crane her ear toward a giggling Amalin. Before long they had descended into a ridiculous charade and, because of this, they had not noticed the approach of a tall, fascinated figure.

The King of the Forest cleared his throat and the women, still incandescent with laughter, turned to make their bows, the embarrassment only making them giggle harder.

Aislyth found it infectious and it was all he could do to restrain himself from enquiring as to the joke. Instead, he made a low bow to Ravar, signifying his call to take her place with him for the Fifth Dance.

Regaining her composure, Ravar was taken aback by the stature of the man rising from his bow before her. At this close range she was struck by his height against hers. Her head reached only his upper torso and his broad, muscular body totally eclipsed her slender frame. She could not deny that there was something deeply attractive about falling into its shadow. As she took his extended hand, she felt an unexpected thrill as his strong, warm grip enveloped her fingers.

The Musicians had begun the introductory bars and the dancers took their places on the floor. Ravar, who had been internally berating herself for being so meek and flattered by the touch of her partner, was forced into an extended silence as he took her waist into his other hand and drew her close into hold. He had a way of maintaining absolute control of his strength so that she was totally obliged to follow his lead, yet masking it with a gentleness so that she never felt dominated.

As the dance began, Ravar could see what Amalin had meant about dancing with the man. Although unfamiliar with the twists and slow turns that characterised the dance-forms of the Forest Dwellers, she was somehow never allowed to put a foot out of place.

In fact, the King had the effect of making Ravar feel light and graceful. She had the freedom to truly enjoy the athletic and twirling sensations, to watch the night stars spin as the King sent her in spirals. She felt as though she might fly on into the sky when he lifted her by the waist as if she weighed nothing and raised her aloft in a half circle, her hair streaming in an arc behind her.

As the Musicians transitioned to the second half of the ballad, the tempo slowed and Ravar beamed at her King, exhilarated.

Aislyth found he could not help but reciprocate in kind, so thrilling was the flushed, smiling visage of his beautiful counterpart. A born dancer, the King was never one to sit by while others took to the floor. However, rarely had he taken so much pleasure from pairing his steps with an unfamiliar partner. The Lady Ravar seemed to bend with the music and to his arm, compelling him into forming the next move each time. And her eyes were lit up like such bright stars that they danced in their own right.

The King overcame his awe-filled smile with a grin. 'Well, My Lady, I am so very glad to be dancing with you this night. I will say you appear most happy and at home among the Forest Folk.'

'I am, Your Majesty,' said Ravar, without aplomb.

The King cocked his head slightly and said in a stage-whisper, 'Then, you do not fear I might turn into a wolf and come at you in your sleep?'

Ravar threw her head back and laughed. 'Then my stories of the tales of the Elders of the Plains have made quick work in reaching your ear, Sire!' She squinted slightly and brought her face a little closer to his as if looking for something before adding, with mischief, 'I have heard that wolves have excellent hearing…'

The King rumbled a deep laugh.

'You really are quite uncommon, My Lady Ravar,' mused the King.

Ravar nodded sagely. 'In the Plains I am described as a patchwork horse, for this breed too was a slurring of the artist's palette. As you see my eyes betray the woods but I have ice in my hair. Yet most of my life I lived in the open sun of the Plains.'

'My sister is the Master of paint and brush and she would be able to give a better commentary on your colourings I daresay. However, I was not speaking of your external aspect.'

Ravar regarded him carefully. His deep blue eyes seemed to be searching her own. At length he spoke again, quietly and thoughtfully like a Grandmaster evaluating a great work. 'Words pour from you like a waterfall, even without your leave, yet I wager that they always hit their mark. You can read the faces and minds of those before you and yet all you choose to do with your power is to undo them with laughter. You present your challenge in such a way that no person can resist meeting you in the duel, and yet you can still play like a child.' He paused for a moment, reflecting, then smiled again. 'Yes, Ravar, I believe you to be most uncommon.'

And with these words, the King made a very slow, significant bow before turning to applaud the Musicians and Ravar was left in silent surprise.

*

It was Amalin who ended the summer festival. In the interval before the Final Dance she had made herself a place among the awestruck band and spent some time admiring their instruments. She was full of admiration for the lead fiddle player who she recognised as of the Gold Level at once.

Expressing her delight in his skill openly, Amalin was introduced to Lethan, a Carpenter by Craft, but whose love of all things musical might match her own. She had turned the body of the polished wood in her hands and professed that she had never seen such a beautiful instrument. It was with unabashed pride that Lethan told her that he had crafted it himself.

Lethan, in turn, was astonished to learn that Amalin had never taken up the instrument among her arts and even more surprised, and not a little intimidated, when she begged him to teach her. However, he would not dream of refusing such a request which promised the prospect of being able to play with such a beautiful and talented Master on a regular basis.

Ravar had refused several requests for the Last Dance with the enigmatic explanation that she was sure that there would be little dancing. She stood near the Musicians and gave her friend a smiling nod.

Amalin held back as the other players began their piece and the dancers glided gently around the floor for the calming end to the night. It was only after a quiet of sorts had descended upon the people of the Forest, drowsily swaying in the embrace of those with whom they danced or watched, that she picked up her flute.

Amalin closed her eyes and the airy soft tones of the Master Musician echoed through the trees and washed over the people like a spell.

Although Ravar was far from immune, she had been prepared for the enchanting effect of her Soul Friend's Craft upon those unaccustomed to her mastery. She watched as the feet on the dance floor fell still and all eyes and ears became trained on the woman playing at the centre of the stage. Even the other Musicians had lowered their instruments and, by the time Amalin brought her hypnotic melody to an end, she opened her eyes to a split second of a world around her quite frozen before it erupted into deafening applause.

The people of the Forest that night fell asleep with music in their hearts. Some dreamt of dancing, others of those they loved. One dreamt of fire.

CHAPTER 2

Forestfyth, Fifth Year of the Dancer, summer's end.

Ravar had opened the School of the Nearage only days after her arrival. The first task was to renovate and prepare the rather dilapidated building complex which had suffered due to lack of regular use.

Its design was the same as all schools of the Nearage: a series of smaller rooms surrounding a larger central hall. The former could be used for the study of Crafts, or be set aside as hosts to longer projects. The larger space, was the most frequented by Tutor and students, being the assembly place for performance, the arts, discourse and debate.

Aided by a number of willing Craftsmen assigned to the task as part of their compulsory Service to the Kingdom, the necessary repairs had been speedily affected and lessons had begun.

Due to the long life-span that the Peoples of the Upper Face enjoyed in the Third Age, time was taken to ensure that all children received a wide-ranging and advanced education. Attending formal schooling from the age of seven, pupils were taught at staged Schools of the Young until they were nearing physical maturity, usually around the age of forty. They would graduate as Nearage provided that they had displayed proficiency in core areas of knowledge and a willingness to put adolescent passions and occupations behind them in favour of studying the higher arts. Only Master Tutors of Nearage were able to proclaim the students in their charge as come of Age, marking them as full citizens of their Kingdoms. For many young men and women, it took at least a decade before they received the sash that signified this graduation.

Ravar's students found her an exacting task-master with a knack for always finding ways to raise the level of challenge, while instilling an urge to please her and rise to it. They never ceased to be amazed by the beauty and variety of her calligraphy and composition, or her memory and recital of poetry and the Written Works. However, by far Master Ravar's most admirable Craft was her way with words and ability to improvise and outmanoeuvre any opponent in debate. She seemed to be so advanced in the many Crafts of the Mind that her students wondered how long she would be satisfied as a Tutor of the Nearage. Would she not feel the lure of one of the Higher Ways that would take her from the Forest City's Final School?

Their other teacher, Master Amalin, was also quickly beloved of her pupils by virtue of her infectious enthusiasm and humour. She habitually took the last class of the day and the Nearage did their best to emulate her understanding and manipulation of music, composition, linguistics and dance.

The two teachers revelled in their respective tasks and equally threw themselves into the challenges they had embarked upon outside the classroom. On the days where they gave Service to the Kingdom they had become more familiar with the characters of the city community who enlightened them about the rich heritage of Forest, its tales and traditions.

In the evenings Amalin worked to master the viol she had acquired from the Carpenter's workshop and took lessons from the ever amiable Lethan, who would guide her hands and accompany her on his own similar instrument.

Meanwhile, Ravar gave great pleasure to the Keeper of Books of the city library by avidly attempting to read her way through the vast collection. Her passion and recommendation had seen a surge in interest among the townsfolk and the old building came to life with those seeking its secrets entering and departing, so that it breathed as a living being.

Into the late hours the Soul Friends would talk, sometimes deeply, sometimes lightly, often with friends but on other nights preferring to enjoy the company of one another alone.

*

It was during this happy beginning to her new life in the Forest, that Ravar stood at the centre of the Assembly room inviting the Nearage to study a magnificent painting she had placed on the wall behind her.

'Nearage, it is time to put the theory you have been studying to the test. Therefore consider the artwork before you and speak your minds.

What does this image signify?'

The fourteen young men and women, standing in a semi-circle before her took their time to ponder the picture before attempting a response. They had learnt that rash ideas, not fully formed, would be crushed under the soft blows of their Tutor's counter questions and arguments.

She did not rush them, pleased that their early desire to please her by speedily volunteering their opinions had passed, in favour of the more considered rhetoric that she held in higher regard.

One of the Nearage stepped forward, indicating his desire to speak.

'Sethays, speak and we will listen,' said Ravar.

'I ask the Assembly to consider that this Artist has sought to capture the nobility of the Great Oak,' the young man began. 'This tree, on account of its longevity and capacity to house life, both within and without, even beyond its death is the honoured symbol of our Kingdom. The Artist has caught the sense of its proportion and grandeur so that the beholder might respect its majesty and consider its place within the culture of our people.'

Ravar nodded, thoughtfully. 'Sethays, you advocate that the Great Oak has nobility by virtue of its place within the Forest and the hearts of that people who dwell within it. It is a good opening argument. Who will challenge?'

Another pupil stepped forward and spoke. 'I put it to the Assembly that nobility is not in the ignorant nature of a thing, but arises from how it is held in the minds of those capable of making the distinction. Therefore a tree may not be noble in its own right.' Ravar nodded acknowledgement and ranged around the other faces. She gestured that the floor was open to a third speaker. One stepped forward.

'If the Assembly is measuring nobility…' The young woman cut off suddenly. She was staring at the doorway behind Ravar and had clamped her mouth firmly shut, for she had just noticed that the high-arched opening was almost filled by the smiling figure of King Aislyth.

'Continue,' commanded Ravar, without turning her attention from the speaker.

'But – My Lady,' the student stammered, 'the King—'

'The King honours the Nearage by calling to enquire of their progress in the arts of the Six Kingdoms and my students answer the enquiry with silence and reticence? A fine testament to your skills and my teaching.' Ravar cast a disappointed look around the room.

The students were astonished that their Tutor could even know of the King's presence from her vantage point and equally horrified that they might be failing to do justice to their mentor, in whom they had the highest confidence and respect. The student who had broken off straightened herself, returning her eye to that of her Tutor with an almost fierce strength of resolve. She recommenced her point.

'If the Assembly is measuring nobility then it suggests that such a virtue is a quality to be bestowed by the sentient. However, that does not preclude it being bestowed upon that which is not. Moreover, I ask the Assembly to consider that we are discussing not the tree, but an artist's portrayal of it. Therefore the more pertinent question is how we might discover the Painter's intention.'

Ravar aimed the smallest hint of a smile at her brave student and the flicker of a wink.

A loud, slow clapping emanated from the doorway and all of the Assembly, Ravar included, turned their attention to him and gave a courteous bow.

The King treated them to the same and a proud smile. 'Nearage of Forestfyth, I apologise for interrupting your debate. But I will say that I am most impressed by the manner in which you form and conduct your words and the quality of the arguments I have heard. You benefit from excellent teaching I think?' The King sidled his eyes in the direction of Ravar.

The Nearage were at great pains to agree, smiling and nodding fiercely, with earnest comments about how much they had learnt from their Master. Ravar smiled tightly but cast them a hard look that silenced them once again.

The King addressed Ravar directly. 'Forgive my intervention, My Lady, but the last speaker of the Assembly raises a good point. I wonder if the Nearage would enjoy the opportunity to put their questions about this Artist's creation,' he waved at the painting, 'to the Painter herself?'

The students nodded earnestly, turning to Ravar to silently put to her their request.

Ravar answered, evenly. 'Your Majesty, your suggestion is most welcome, *if* the Craftswoman of the brush may be persuaded.' Crafty smirks betrayed the fact that she and the King appeared to share something of a private joke.

'Then I will ask her,' said the King, still with a twinkle in his eye, 'for I happen to be acquainted with the lady in question. I wonder if the students might recess for a while so that I may discuss their progress in more detail with their Tutor.' The students obeyed the King's implied command by filing quickly out of the room, excited and keen to talk to each other about what had just happened.

The King walked closer to Ravar and spoke with feeling.

'No wonder you were drawn to the teaching Crafts, My Lady Ravar. In a matter of weeks I see such an impressive change in the Nearage of our city. You are a most gifted Tutor.'

Ravar was moved by the praise, but loyally asked him to acknowledge the great contribution that Amalin had also made to their learning.

'I had in no way meant to diminish her role, My Lady, only to express my thanks and admiration for your own,' replied the King.

Ravar made a small bow of acknowledgement which helped to hide her shy, pleased smile.

'Thank you for your offer to speak to Princess Istreeth about the possibility of coming to see the students,' she said. Indeed I wish many more of those Craftspeople of the higher levels would spend some time at the School to share their arts.'

'If you desire it then I shall make it so,' declared the King, shrugging. 'I can have time allocated within the Kingdom Service rotation.'

'Oh – no!' exclaimed, Ravar. 'Please, do not do that. The Nearage must hear from those who have a genuine wish to pass on the passion and pride that their Crafts bring them. The best lessons come from those who speak in the hope that others might follow. If we compel people to speak of their skills as a form of Service, it becomes a chore and the purpose of the exercise would be lost.'

The King looked thoughtful and nodded his head in a light bow to her. 'My Lady you are, of course, quite right. But I believe there is yet still something I may do to help. Would you object to my appealing in the morning gathering for volunteers who wish to pass on a little of their knowledge and experience?'

Ravar smiled again. 'I would be most grateful.'

'Good, then it is settled,' said the King. 'I apologise, once again, for descending upon your classroom unannounced. I confess I was more than a little curious to find whether the rumours of the good work taking place here had been exaggerated. I am now quite sure they are not.' Ravar could not help the blush that appeared on her cheeks. 'I am equally certain that I should very much like to return here before long. Tell me,

Master Tutor, may I visit your School again?'

'You do not need my permission to visit a School of the Nearage in your own Kingdom, Your Majesty,' said Ravar, cheerfully.

'Ah, no I suppose not, though my sister would scold my poor manners,' the King replied, smiling again. After a moment's contemplation he continued. 'But, My Lady, you misunderstand the meaning of my request. I ask not as your King but as a Craftsman wishing to learn from a Master.'

Her mind whirring as she processed the unexpected sense of his words, Ravar eyed the heavily laden sash of the man before her and found the symbol she was searching for: the mark of the Craft of the Teacher, a stylised form of a human figure reaching out to another, smaller form. The King's token was woven in bronze.

'You seek to be of silver?' asked Ravar, seriously. As a Master of her Craft it was to be expected that those seeking to improve in that field, might request to follow and observe her practise of the art. Aislyth's was far from being the first application, and she had granted many, though it was the first time she had been asked to be Master to a King.

'I consider that bronze is a poor level for one such as I who seeks the Way of the Bard,' the King replied. 'Will you accept me?'

'I will,' said Ravar solemnly, and without hesitation. 'But I warn you, Sire, that *all* who stand in the Assembly are expected to speak, and as *equals*.' She raised her eyebrows a fraction, posing the question.

The King met her eye without discernible emotion, saying simply, 'I look forward to it.' And, with that, he bowed deeply to Ravar and strolled from the room.

*

Later that week, Ravar was overseeing the students' calligraphy when the School was graced with another unexpected visitor. There was a knock at the doorway and he stepped into the small workroom.

Looking up from a desk where she sat next to one of her pupils, Ravar saw a Man of the Forest that she had not met before. He was tall, slim and immaculately dressed in a simple, but clean blue and white long tunic over dark hose. He was wearing long, leather walking boots and carried a satchel over his shoulder.

'Good morning,' he said with an elegant bow, before stepping forward. 'Are you the Lady Ravar?'

Ravar studied the fine features of the man before her. He had bright, wide blue eyes set in a chiselled face and a mop of black curls, longer at the top, but cut short at the sides. He was clean-shaven and his warm smile revealed a row of straight, white teeth. He was very handsome, to be sure.

'I am Ravar, the Tutor of the Nearage, My Lord. I am afraid you have me at a disadvantage, for I do not know you.'

The students, who had abandoned concentrating on their tasks in favour of watching this exchange, erupted in delight to inform her. 'Why, it is Master Eduerd the Healer, My Lady!'

Eduerd waved a greeting to the room followed by a frown which clearly commanded the pupils to return to their studies. They at least made a show of doing so, though several of them were whispering, while flashing approving sideways glances at the attractive Doctor.

'I am told you might be interested in some introduction to the Healing art for your Nearage students, My Lady?' said Eduerd, politely. Ravar noted that he spoke with perfect diction and with no noticeable accent. She smiled, recognition dawning that this must be the Doctor the young man at the winter dance had mentioned.

She replied enthusiastically, 'Why yes, we would very much like that, My Lord Eduerd.'

'Just Eduerd, please. Though the same does not go for all of you,' he added, casting a stern glance at the Nearage pupils, some of whom giggled. 'Then, tell me when to start. I come to the city twice weekly on my rounds so I will fit around you if you can fit around me.'

'I am certain we can. You live, I believe, in the Eastern Forest towards Woodsedge?' asked Ravar.

'You are well-informed,' he said. 'I split my time between the fringes of the Forest and Marketdawn, for I am fond of both.' The Healer's eyes darted around the room, taking in all about him with a sort of energetic thirst. He moved over to examine the script of one of the pupils, who glanced nervously up at him, trying to gauge his reaction.

'You are improving your calligraphy! Excellent! It is one of the Crafts I hold most dear.' Eduerd turned to Ravar. 'My Lady, if you are ever in need of ink or pigments for your School, you have only to ask me. I prepare those used by both the Palace and Library but I would take great pleasure in knowing they are used by the Nearage in pursuit of learning.'

'That is most Kind, Eduerd,' Ravar replied. 'It seems the students are to benefit twofold from your association.' Ravar's eyes sparkled as they were wont to do when she was truly pleased and Eduerd felt as gratified to have learnt her pleasure as might one of her students.

At that moment, Amalin entered the room, looking for her friend to discuss the afternoon arrangements. Taking in the Doctor in a brief top-down visual survey, she shot Ravar a look of surprise and exaggerated approval, no doubt purely based upon his notable physical attributes.

Giving her friend a quick, slightly pleading look of disapproval, Ravar said, 'My Lord Eduerd, allow me to introduce to you my fellow teacher and Soul Friend, Master Amalin.'

'Of the Plains?' Eduerd gasped. He made a very low bow and said, 'I am very honoured to make your acquaintance. I am afraid I lack musical ability, though I am extremely fond of listening to those with talent.'

Amalin narrowed her eyes. 'I am glad to hear it, My Lord, or we should not get on well.' Her stern look creased into a grin. Her smile was catching and Eduerd returned it.

With a glance out of the window, the Doctor patted his bag and said that he must go, but that he looked forward to seeing both women and the students again soon. Under her breath, Amalin remarked to Ravar that she believed everyone would look forward to the occasion. Although Ravar rolled her eyes, she had to admit that she would anticipate the good Doctor's return with enthusiasm.

*

Throwing herself on the long, padded seat that lined the curved sitting room in their shared cottage that evening, Amalin exclaimed, 'Are *all* the men of the Forest so *very* easy on the eye?'

Ravar laughed. 'Not *all*, friend. Though our workplace does seem to attract handsome men. Of course, I believe that Lord Lethan comes purely on your account.'

'Perhaps,' smiled Amalin, coyly. 'Though I think that the King came on yours.'

Ravar strode across the room and picked up a book to hide her discomfiture. 'Do not be ridiculous, Amalin. He is a good ruler who cares for the future of the young. And he seeks to further his own Teaching Craft.'

Amalin clucked her tongue. 'If you say so. But now we also have the dreamy Doctor Eduerd promising to make a regular appearance. Stars, he is even more handsome than Lethan!'

Ravar cocked an eyebrow to herself more than her friend. 'High praise indeed, from you… He is certainly popular among the townsfolk. And did you see his sash? I do not think I have met many of his age with such accomplishments.'

'Trust you to have noticed the one part of his person that any other would have been far too distracted to notice,' said Amalin, flatly.

'I think I will visit the library tomorrow afternoon,' said Ravar, ignoring Amalin's provocation. 'If the students are to learn some of the Healer's arts then I should not like to appear completely novice.'

'In front of the students or Master Eduerd?'

CHAPTER 3

Forestfyth, Fifth Year of the Dancer, early leaf fall.

Ravar read through the complex timetable that had been delivered to her personally by Ralgan, the Chief Scribe of the Palace, in delight. As a result of the King's appeal, his team had been most busy; ascertaining convenient times and timescales, enquiring as to suitable seasons for various Crafts and liaising between volunteers and the staff of the School.

The fruit of their labours came in the form of a packed rota from the forthcoming week until the end of winter, in which the Craftspeople of the Forest had put themselves forward in droves to give part of their time to the School.

Masters of Tailoring, Earth, Art, the Banquet and Agriculture were to work with her pupils over the coming months, with the promise of more Crafts represented in the New Year. There was even a regular evening space allotted for Bardic tales. With these added to the sessions already begun by the good Doctor, Ravar's pupils would enjoy a veritable feast of learning about the paths open to them when they came of Age.

As the image of Doctor Eduerd crossed her mind, Ravar swelled. She had been quite transfixed by the Healer's first two lessons. He had a way of speaking honestly and with feeling to the young, always offering a practical application relating to his chosen topic and encouraging discussion and reflection. He was a great asset to her school and she herself had learnt much.

The first area of the Healing arts upon which he had decided to focus related to the medicinal plant-life that was native to the Eastern Forest.

He spent time going through the most common local examples and how they might be identified, cultivated, harvested and used. Ravar was glad of her own studies into the field which allowed her to participate and occasionally elaborate during the lessons.

As for Eduerd, he too had taken enjoyment from his work at the School. A lover of learning himself, he relished being surrounded by like-minded people. Although much his junior, the Nearage seemed to share his thirst for knowledge and improvement, and he often found himself contriving reasons to stop by unannounced, so that he could listen in on the discussion of the Assembly. Most of all, he took advantage of any opportunity to converse with the Lady Ravar.

Eduerd considered her to be a truly exceptional woman. She was so young, yet so gifted in the Crafts of the Mind. The Tutor seemed to have an unquenchable desire for further study too. Had she not openly professed her recent efforts, he would have guessed her a much further seasoned student of the art of healing. She appeared to possess an endless capacity for reading and absorbing the knowledge and wisdom of those around her.

Most impressive of all was watching Ravar put her Gold Level rhetorical skills to use. Her prowess as a speaker was quite without equal and the Doctor found himself completely spellbound on the rare occasions that she allowed herself the centre stage.

Eduerd also had to admit to himself that the Lady Ravar was also, without question, by far the most beautiful woman upon whom he had ever laid eyes.

Eduerd had travelled widely but he had never come across the striking combination that her unusual lineage had given her. Even if had he done, he doubted any could have been so graced with the perfect sloping features of her body, or the pearly skin that set off the high, flawless features of her face.

Ordinarily Eduerd would have fended off such distractions from his real aspiration, that of scholarship and the pursuit of the Way of the Mathematician. However, somehow his interactions with Ravar served to further that learning and ambition. He found in her a great mind, in whose high level and often taunting challenge, his own flourished.

At the start of the autumn season Eduerd had offered to assist Ravar and her students in planting up the gardens which were to eventually surround the School. Divided into four distinct genres, one was dedicated to plants and herbs which had healing applications.

Gretan the Botanist, with whom Ravar was evidently acquainted, had come all the way from Highturth to give careful instruction to the Nearage about the plants' installation and care. Eduerd himself would oversee the Nearage's adherence to Gretan's directions and had great plans for how the crop might harvested and put to use in the following year.

As the day's work was coming to an end, Eduerd was chatting with Lethan, who was not just a friend, but also one of his Kin. Although not blood-related, the two men were part of a small circle of friends, comprised of an eclectic assortment of like-minded Forest and Market folk. These were the men and women whom Eduerd considered his family, as was the way of most people in an Age where blood relatives were scarce.

There were few secrets between the Eduerd and Lethan, who had known one another since childhood. In the absence of his Soul Friend during the past cycle, the Doctor had come to rely on the Carpenter to help fill the void. This was despite the fact that Lethan and his absent friend could not have been more diametrically opposed.

'Will you dine with us at my home tomorrow evening, friend?' said Eduerd. 'Desledair is returned to Woodsedge and will stay with me this this week. I know he will be most desirous to see you.'

'Desledair is home?' Lethan smiled with surprise and delight. 'No wonder you are in such good cheer! Of course I shall come, though I do not believe that he is so anxious for *my* company. Or have his travels converted him into a socialite?'

Eduerd, who likewise knew of the Lord Desledair's general dismay when required to attend any public gathering, chuckled. 'No, I suspect such a thing would be quite impossible. But it will only be a small party for supper.'

Lethan smiled easily and ran his hand through his fine, long hair. 'Have you invited Fiance?'

Eduard laughed. 'What do you take me for?' His eyes widened in dread as he muttered, 'If Fiance were to hear we had had a party without her...'

He did not need to finish the sentence because Lethan was thinking the same thing. Returning to his usual upbeat disposition, the Carpenter clapped his friend on the back, saying, 'I am so very glad Desledair is back.'

'Stars know I am too,' said the Doctor, with feeling. 'There is much I would speak with him about.'

Lethan nodded, appreciatively. 'Four seasons is long time for Soul Friends to be parted. But I trust that his venting project was a success?'

Edward nodded. 'The thermal vent system is now extended to the Eastern District of the city. He drew a deep breath and added softly, 'He has been awarded the mark of Snowseal.'

Lethan's jaw dropped.

'I believe,' continued the Doctor, 'that our friend is quickly becoming the most eminently thought of and sought-after architect in the Western Kingdoms.' Eduerd smiled at the floor, proud of Desledair's accomplishment.

'Deservedly so, from what little *he* allows me to gather,' reflected Lethan.

Eduerd pursed his lips, nodding. 'Yes… he is certainly not one for boasting.'

Returning to practical matters and the original invitation that had provoked their conversation, Lethan asked, 'I take it you will be here again tomorrow to finish the Healer's garden?' The Doctor nodded. 'Shall I stop by at the Fourth mark to pick you up? We can walk together.' Eduerd gave his assent and raised a hand in farewell as Lethan departed. He caught sight of the Carpenter bowing and pausing to greet the Lady Amalin who was on her way in. Eduerd had seen them spending a lot of time in each other's company. There seemed to be something beyond merely professional respect between them. He grinned.

The light was fading in the School grounds and Ravar called the students over to the open area at their centre, where a bonfire had been carefully laid.

'Tonight, you are most fortunate,' she told them, as they gathered before her. 'A Bard has offered to share with you the traditions and stories of the Forest by fire-light.'

There were murmurs of excitement from the group. The art of story-telling was one of the many strands of the Way of the Bard, one of the three great Paths of the People of the Six Kingdoms. As children, like all Forest Folk, they had been brought up on a rich diet of traditional songs and stories that told the history and legends of their world and ancestors. The most talented Bards, much revered, were gifted in the art of Fireplay. This ancient ability allowed a story-teller to manipulate flames, shadows or even the stars themselves to create images and movement to enhance a tale.

'Who is the Bard, My Lady?' one student asked excitedly, amid the chatter.

'I do not know,' said Ravar, truthfully. The slot on the timetable from the Palace had had no name to it. She silenced the Nearage with a quiet but firm instruction. 'Kindly light our fire and then we shall take our seats so that we may be ready to receive our guest.'

Minutes later, all were quietly seated around the fire, waiting in anticipation as the last of the light disappeared and the flames danced higher toward the sky.

It came as a shock to them all when the Bard, clad in a traditional long, white cloak, took his seat before the fire, because Nearage's storyteller was none other than King Aislyth himself. Ravar was well aware that he carried the brass lyre-shaped pin on his sash, making him as a Master Storyteller. Yet she had never suspected that he might be the Bard to share his gift with the Nearage.

Standing before the fire, he breathed in deeply the scent of burning wood and, smiling, intoned the formal greeting to his audience.

'Welcome, people of this circle, to the light of the fire and the community of this gathering. Listen with open minds and open hearts.'

The rich voice of the King reverberated through the crackling of the flames and the Nearage sat, wide-eyed, waiting for him to begin his tale. Ravar felt the hairs of her neck stand on end, so compelling was that voice of the Bard, her King. His imposing figure appeared quite transformed in the firelight, his pale robes making him appear ethereal against the dark.

The King addressed his audience directly, speaking in a soft rhythmic way, as if singing without a melody.

'It is a great pleasure to sit before a new Nearage class of Forestfyth. Our people are to be renewed by a generation coming of Age to replace those lost to the sickness that swept our Kingdom in years past. Heavens be thanked that the People of the Forest flourish once again.' He smiled, perhaps a little sadly, before gently adding, 'Happy are we to live in the Third Age.'

The King paused, letting the silence draw in before commencing his tale. His voice rose, stirred by painful emotion.

'Alas for those who came before us, who lived through our fall from grace! For the

Second Age was a time of suffering. Bitter contest and suspicion had grown between the Kingdoms and the Second Era would close in bloodshed so great, that half the Souls of the world were lost in its fury.'

The King took a long breath and spoke in less forceful terms.

'Some say the Great War began when two Soul Friends fell in love with the same woman. Sensing a rival for the match in the Soul Embrace of the other, each man closed his heart to his friend and courted the maiden in secret.

When she realised the damaged but undeniable connection between her suitors, the woman called them together. She told them that she was unable and unwilling to accept either man, lest their weakened bond were severed forever. She left them and that place to seek her own heart, hoping they might reclaim that of each other.

But the Soul Friends were left bereft by her parting. Each blamed the other for their loss, believing them at fault for the secondary bid that had driven her away. The Soul Friends parted as enemies, seeking to detach themselves far from the object of their ire.

Each man being gifted in learning and guile, they found places in the high courts of distant and foreign Kings, where no one would be able to hear the counter-tale of the other.

'At opposite ends of the Upper Face and parted by the Middle Sea, their hatred and bitterness grew. For, by being parted so long and by so great a distance, the bonded Souls became even more weak and corrupted. The inability to meet in the Soul Embrace meant that they never felt the sorrow weighing the heart of the other that might yet have reconciled their love.

Instead, their biting animosity poisoned the hearts of those around them, adding to the growing enmity between their respective nations. Word spread in both kingdoms of the supposed treachery of the other, harboured by a wicked, alien King, and many became lost to black and destructive imaginings.

Further darkening the People of their Age was to live in time where a great and prolonged drought swept the Western lands. The famine that inevitably followed caused suffering on an unimaginable scale. Parents wept for the misery of their children as hunger held them to ransom. Whole towns ceased to be as their inhabitants became wanderers on an endless quest for food.

The traders of Marketdawn could not supply adequate resources from the Eastern Lands to meet the need of those in the West. But the twisted hearts of the once Soul Brothers saw opportunity to have their revenge on the other, and whispered in the willing ears of their crowned masters.

The brother in the West fanned the suspicion that the Peoples of the East intentionally held out relief in the hope that the West would fall. Perhaps, he said, the

Eastern King coveted the rich resources and pasture across the Middle Sea.

'In the East the second brother laid before his ruler ornate maps of the vast, rich plains of field and tree beyond the ocean. He filled the King's mind with images of a sovereign who might straddle an empire, a foot in both East and West.

'It was not difficult to sway the hearts of Kings who, in the Second Age, took their places by right rather than worth. And equally, in the wider climate of suffering and greed, their peoples were quick to follow their commands. Thus followed the terrible war that would be waged until near all the Kingdoms were setting each other alight.

'The Eastern armies struck first in the West. Hundreds of thousands of Souls were killed in the slaughter. The meagre crops rotted, abandoned and untended as swords and fire swept orchard and prairie.

'The trading nations of land and sea were caught in the cross-fire and allied themselves with the Peoples of the West. They lent their ships and technology to retaliate against the Eastern aggressors, augmenting the fury and capacity for destruction. The world was locked in arms for thirty seasons, each more damaging than the last.

'The worst of the conflict took place on the Middle Sea, where Carpenters who had striven to make trees soar on the waves would see their creations turned to transporters of Souls to a fiery death. Cannons flashed with explosives that soared like comets. They struck the bellies of the Sea Peoples' fine ships and drowned the lives within them in the bloody turmoil of the waves.'

The King stepped forward and blew into the flames of the fire, casting embers into the air. Ravar saw in its heat the fury of the battle, and heard the screams and clashing of metal in the blaze. The Fireplay brought history to life before the eyes of the listeners and burned its cruelty into their minds.

The King lowered his arms and stepped back from the fire, giving his circle time to let the image sink from their gaze, before continuing.

'The ocean was a blanket of the dead and the dying. Doomed and desperate, only at the end and too late, did so many realise the pointlessness of the struggle that was so consuming the world.

'It was in these churning waves that two men, clinging to the hope of life, made a common bid for a piece of floating debris. They fought for hold of its buoyancy but as their hardened hands pushed one another away, their palms met with the beat of the other's heart.

'Although as men they were long beyond recognition, their tortured Souls were not. The longer part of a lifetime's heart song was sung between them. They saw with terror and remorse what their unshared hurt and resentment had helped bring to the Peoples

of four Kingdoms. They left the field of battle, sick in mind of death through conflict, grieving the folly of their hate.

'Unfortunate wretches, for the momentum of war was too great for two broken men to quell. Seeking rest from the relentless struggle, they sought the last refuge of peace on the Upper Face. To the Frozen, barren lands of Snowseal they journeyed and appealed for sanctuary from the Kingdom's lilac-eyed King.

'Now this ruler had a gift for seeing into the depths of men's hearts. When they stood before him and he looked into theirs he saw them as catalysts of suffering. He wished to cast them out from his land, the last place of solace for those who would chose a frozen waste over the wasteland of war.

'However, his young daughter, wise beyond her years, sensed his intention. She took into her hands one of each of the Soul Brothers and stood before her father invoking her right to speak in their defence.

'The King was dumbfounded. For his daughter had never before interjected in the proceedings of his court. She was his pride to be of a scholarly, higher nature, confining herself to the library and teachings of her Master.

'The King appealed to her, speaking in open dismay, "Daughter, you do not know what I have seen in the Souls of these travellers. They are the kindlers of hatred and bloodlust between men."

'But his daughter spoke with the force of the wind. "And Father, you do not see what I see: two Souls lost and broken, yet reformed in the eye of the storm."

'She folded her cloak back over her shoulder to reveal her sash and there was an awestruck intake of breath from all in the chamber. For they beheld the mark of the Advocate, fixed to her breast.

'An Advocate may bend and turn the mind of a Mathematician, or direct and inspire the song of the Bard, so what hope did the King of Snowseal have, but to concede to his daughter's wisdom? Her father bowed to one who had sought and found one of the three High Ways.

'This daughter of Snowseal would be the greatest *Advocate to have walked the Upper Face.*

'Hers were the interventions that cooled the already war-wearied hearts of Kings and Kin. She brokered the first peace accords that put an end to the prolonged destruction of the lands and flesh.

'She spent the rest of her long lifetime travelling to the far corners of each Kingdom. She preached the beauty and bounty of peace.

'She would call for leaders to rise by the will of the people, rather than by blood line. The Peoples of our world began to elect those who had demonstrated by their Crafts and deeds that they sought to serve their Kingdoms, rather than covet their

crowns. A new generation of future-minded rulers took to the thrones and worked to forge new links in infrastructure and trade with their neighbours.

She advocated law and custom that would safeguard against the consequences of that which threatens the hold of two Souls bonded. From her our ancestors learnt a new way of courting, one that depended on the person closest to the object of desire to act as Keeper of that Soul. He or she would be charged with considering the wisdom and potential outcome of any would-be courtship and, as the sole guardian of that heart, be positioned to jealously guard it or lovingly give it dependant on the offer.

'Keepers took feathers to their sashes so as to display their consent openly. From there on, no man or woman would ever be ignorant of a rival in affection and would have the freedom choose to stand down or bid humbly for love, accepting the potential strength of an alternative offer.

'As the Peoples of our world adopted these traditions and changed to lives of greater harmony, they also developed a greater understanding of the bonds of love, Kin, community and Soul.

'Their lifespan grew.

'They passed on the memories of the shadowy days of war and suffering to later generations so that they might never undervalue the sacred path that Souls might travel.

'Children became fewer, more preciously valued and the privilege of a deeper, generous love.

'Thus, our careful ways represent all that we have become higher, and strive to become higher still. May the horror of war always remind us of the strength of the love between men. May we never be blind to its power, or take for granted the traditions which keep it in peace.

'Listeners, the tale is ended. Go in peace with it fixed in your hearts.'

The Nearage left the circle in silence one by one, each making their bow to their Bard as they departed. At the end, only Aislyth and Ravar remained. The King searched her face.

'Thank you, Your Majesty, for the gift of your tale,' she said, finally. 'You have given us all much food for thought and that is the mark of a Tutor. Come again soon and challenge your students to make of it what they will. It is in this way, My Lord, that you may tread the path of Silver.'

With that, she rose, made a solemn bow and departed, leaving King Aislyth alone.

*

Eduerd had walked home at a fast pace that evening, anxious to have his home warm and prepared to receive Desledair. As he approached his unusual abode, overshadowed by the skeleton of a long-dead tree and surrounded by neat beds of herbs and plants, he exhaled shortly, for he could see the lights already glowing from within and smoke rising from the chimney.

The door of the cottage swung open and there stood his friend, smart and haughty as ever, treating Eduerd to a self-satisfied smirk.

'I see you have made yourself quite comfortable, Desledair,' said Eduerd, exasperatedly.

'Indeed I have,' his friend replied shortly. 'I was not inclined to sit on your doorstep, waiting for hordes of Glow Flies to descend upon me in the cold.'

Eduerd stepped forward and pulled his guest into a tight embrace while Desledair only slightly rolled his eyes, before stepping back and looking closely into his face.

'My friend, I am so glad you are back,' he said with warmth.

Desledair gave a fraction of a smile. 'I, too, am glad to return to your company.'

Simultaneously, they reached their hands to the each other's hearts and took in the emotion and strange understanding of the other's past cycle of the seasons. Although they had maintained a regular and detailed correspondence in writing, each knew their friend's labour and reward so much more fully through the Soul Embrace.

Moving his hand to his friend's shoulder, Desledair spoke softly. 'It seems there is much of which you did not speak in your letters, Eduerd.' Seeing the hallmarks of a protest in Eduerd's demeanour, he continued, 'I know, I know! You have told me of your admirable new endeavours and associations. But I wonder if even in your own mind you have recognised their effect. Come inside. We have much to talk about.'

CHAPTER 4

Forestfyth, Sixth Year of the Dancer, early leaf fall.

The following day Eduerd took a seat on a large, protruding tree root and set down his foraging bag. The autumn brought with it a wealth of fungi, many of which had medicinal uses. On this occasion however, the varieties he sought were hailed for their culinary use.

Although it was pointless attempting to meet the exacting standards of a Master of the Banquet such as Fiance, he was determined that he would provide a more than acceptable supper for his guests that evening. He would allow himself a short rest and then force himself to make his way back to his cottage and begin his preparations.

Staring into the trees with no particular focus, he caught sight of a burgundy-clad figure moving between the trunks. As it came closer he saw the clearer shape of a slowly moving walker in a hooded, loose cloak. He could not make out the face, for it was lowered, lost in a book. However, as she came nearer still, he was confirmed in his surmise that it could be none other than Ravar.

She seemed quite oblivious to his presence, so engrossed was she in the text. He wondered that she never seemed to stumble over the uneven terrain or walk into a tree.

He called over to her by name, causing her to look up, looking surprised. 'My Lady, do you even read as you walk?' he said. 'You will exhaust our library before long!'

Ravar, having initially smiled cheerfully in recognition, grinned shrewdly. 'I think not, My Lord Eduerd! Though I shall make it my life's endeavour to attempt the feat. And if I succeed I shall have to learn to barter and see what I may obtain from Marketdawn.'

'Then I shall help you, My Lady!' said Eduerd. 'Stars know you will need it! I am obliged to trade in the rural market of Woodsedge and those merchants would sell sand to the Peoples of the Desert.'

'I am not so sure,' said Ravar. She held out the book that she had been reading so that Eduerd could see its spine.

Eduerd read its title aloud: 'Verses of those who search for the Oasis.' He frowned, cynically. 'Desert poetry?'

'Yes!' Ravar laughed. 'Not that most would consider it such. But you should read it, my good Doctor, for it is most outrageous!'

'Yes?'

'Yes! And terribly funny.'

'The People of the Sands evidently know a thing or two about having a good time,' Edward stated, rather than asked, as if he already had some notion of this.

Nodding sagely, Ravar said, 'They must think us frightful bores... I think I should like to travel to the Desert Lands and prove them wrong.'

'As would I, though I have my own reasons,' Eduerd said seriously. 'Their knowledge of the heavens is second to none. I would forego many a luxury to study the stars with the astronomers at the towers of Xyn.'

Ravar studied Eduerd, whose expression had taken on a glazed, starry quality of its own. 'You make a study of the night sky, My Lord?'

Eduerd shook his mind back to the Forest and the hooded woman before him. 'I confess it is the Craft above all that I hope to Master. There is something beautiful in the difficulty of plotting the trajectory and measuring the movements of the moon and stars. So much of our world is under their influence, from the tides, to time-keeping, to the seasons themselves. Indeed it is this Craft which gives the Peoples of the Six Kingdoms our only clues about the Southern Face of our planet. Perhaps one day we will learn to soar into the very heavens and fall down again beyond the burning rim that bands our world...'

'Your passion is infectious,' smiled Ravar. 'Perhaps one day you would share some of your learning with me?'

Eduerd sprang up with a thrilled expression. 'My Lady, it would give me great pleasure. But in this discipline, your much-loved books alone will be quite inadequate. You will have to join me in stargazing aloft in the trees.' Eduerd had come close to Ravar now and was holding her captivated with his bright, dancing eyes.

Ravar, finding with difficulty, a little poise, arranged her cloak unnecessarily and nodded gently. 'I shall look forward to it. For now, I must head back before darkness falls. Good evening, Eduerd.'

'Good evening, My Lady.' Eduerd bowed and watched her turn and walk back in the direction from which she had come, opening her book once again and inclining her head to read from it.

He stood motionless for several minutes, an unreadable look upon his features. His mind whirred in a series of strange thoughts and emotions. Self-censure battled with a disturbing sort of exhilaration for some time until, brought back to reality by the echo of Ravar's comment about nightfall, Eduerd realised that would have to run home, so much had he been delayed.

*

Lethan had arrived at Eduerd's house in the woods early that evening, greeting Desledair with warm affection and breaking open a bottle of Forest Warmth, the more powerful of the brews of their people. While Eduerd attempted to fend off their encouragement to join them in a cup, in favour of being able to serve some edible supper, the other two friends indulged themselves.

This happy scene was interrupted by the front door of the cottage crashing open with great force and the radiant, ample proportions of Fiance appearing triumphantly at the threshold. She made a beeline to Desledair, who was always astonished by the speed and alacrity with which this formidable woman was capable of moving.

He was subjected to an embrace so mighty that the air was knocked from his lungs, followed by a highly critical examination of his face, physique and attire.

'The seal of Snowseal!' she cried in delight, pawing at his sash and carefully studying the beautifully crafted brooch with its Snow Cat emblem. 'Why, you shall surely be considered a Grandmaster before soon! Of course, that is no surprise to any of us in here, for we are all of good taste and have long recognised your talents.'

Her expression turned darker as she gripped him by the tops of his arms, frowning.

'But you must not take such long commissions again, for your absence has all but wasted you away. Stars, you are become so *thin!* Thank heavens you are returned to civilisation where we can fatten you up again. Eduerd, I hope you have some hearty fare for us tonight for Desledair is much diminished.' She cast a disparaging glance at the kitchen area, where pots were bubbling.

Desledair was a man of medium height with neat, short hair and an immaculate beard, trimmed with precision of a gem cutter. His Soul Friend's elder by 300 years, his jet-black hair was laced with a smattering of silver, more pronounced in his beard. However, his eyes and brows retained their original rich colour in full. Desledair actually took great care to maintain a healthy physique and had not gained or lost any significant amount of weight in at least 150 cycles.

'Do not fuss, Fiance,' said Desledair grumpily. 'Or I shall make sure my next commission is for twelve seasons at least!'

'I shall fuss over my Kin if I want!' cried the Lady Fiance, with severity. 'Who else will keep an eye on all you men who do not take care of yourselves?'

'Fiance, you always accuse us of wasting away!' Eduerd laughed.

Turning on him, she pointed at the Healer with an accusing finger. 'And you would do better to spend less time in this little cottage so far from town, for you are *also* turned to skin and bone these last few seasons! You must attend more of the Forest celebrations and less of those inferior Marketdawn rabbles. In the Forest we know how to provide a decent feast.' She folded her arms and set her expression, daring anyone to disagree.

Eduerd glanced at Desledair who was sipping at his Forest Warmth with a look of relaxed delight that the focus of Fiance's criticism had been directed toward another target. Realising that he would get no support from him, Eduerd cast a plea for help in Lethan's direction. Trying to stop himself from laughing, the latter loyally and gallantly intervened.

'Well Fiance,' said the Carpenter, 'the good Doctor has been coming to the town more often of late on account of his lessons at the School of the Nearage. Indeed, I understand from the Lady Amalin that you yourself are to share some of your culinary secrets with the students soon?'

Disarmed by the easy charm of the Carpenter, Fiance relented into a reluctant and slightly muttered reply that at least the future generations would be capable of feeding themselves properly.

The meal was good, as was the conversation. Fiance's gossip and jokes had the party in hysterics within minutes and even Desledair joined in with a spontaneous rendition of a raucous Marketdawn song as the Forest Warmth ran lower in the bottle.

Lethan, his tongue loosened by the potent drink, had slipped into a slightly wandering account of his musical forays, extolling the many virtues of Amalin of the Plains. This was much to the delight of his present company, who teased him relentlessly about his obvious infatuation. Lethan did not even try to deny it and merely agreed that she must be quite the woman of any man's dreams.

Drawing his chair back and stretching his legs, Desledair sighed and donned a face of despair. 'Stars! I am gone for just four seasons and I return to find that all my Kin are victims to love and are become quite insensible. I fear I shall have to retire lest such a disagreeable state is infectious.'

'*Everyone?*' countered Fiance, quickly. She surveyed the company suspiciously before deigning it more necessary to defend her own presence of mind.

'I can assure you, My Lord Desledair, that *I* am not love-sick or insensible.' She smoothed out the rich, colourful folds of her dress primly and straightened into an imperious poise, making her look like a queen on a throne. 'I have been forced to turn down many an earnest suit.'

This was in fact true, and her Kin in the room well knew it. Fiance might be loud and feisty and downright terrifying, but she was seemingly irresistible to many. Especially those governed to a larger extent by their stomachs.

'Unfortunately,' she continued, 'I have *very* exacting standards and I have yet to meet the lucky bachelor who will be favoured with my acceptance.'

'Perhaps you must extend your search further afield, Fiance? And cast your net in higher circles?' said Eduerd, a little malevolently as the others pictured her hunting and netting her prey.

'Perhaps I shall,' said Fiance, considering this a perfectly sensible suggestion. 'Perhaps I shall travel to foreign climbs and court myself a King.'

Lethan, in his inebriated state could not help but laugh. 'A fine array of choices you will have there, Fiance. If we discount those married already you may choose between a wild, horse-jumping bandit of the Plains who cares for nothing but sport, the Market King who would probably charge you for the honour of his hand or the two thousand-year-old King of the Sands!'

While the others stifled their laugher, Fiance considered this seriously and frowned. 'I would not care for *sport*...' she muttered to herself.

Desledair rose, addressing the woman cheerfully. 'Well, Fiance, I am glad to hear that you, at least, are in full control of your faculties. Therefore, with the assurance that you will not bend my ear with romantic notions on the way, I shall offer you my arm and escort you to your home.'

Fiance could have purred like a cat, sliding her arm into his and smiling ingratiatingly.

'Ah Desledair, you *are* still in possession of the charm of a gentleman. Perhaps you are still salvageable after all, if we can get you fattened up a bit. When we reach my cottage I shall give you one of my pies.'

Desledair threw the others a look which said that he clearly considered that such a prize made him the victor in his wrangling with Fiance that night.

After long and fond farewells, Desledair, who was glad of the walk, despite the good Lady Fiance's concern for his frame, said to Eduerd that he would let himself back in on his return.

As the door closed the two remaining men returned to the polished wood table that was elegantly positioned in the alcove of his seating area, always referred to as the 'Den'. Eduard took a seat close to Lethan and gently clapped him on the shoulder.

'Friend, aside from our mocking, it gives us, your Kin, great joy to see you so alive and taken by the Forest's new Songbird,' he said.

Lethan smiled to himself and sighed. 'I must confess that I am quite lost to her.'

'Then you must apply to make your suit,' said Edward, seriously.

'And would it be accepted? I am not even a Master of my Craft and there must be many who have already tried and failed to win her hand or she would be long since married.'

'I think you underestimate the Lady Amalin, who would surely not settle for a mate based on the contents of his sash.' He continued, kindly, 'I have not been blind to the attention she pays to *you* during my time at the School.'

Lethan gave him a grateful smile. 'Thank you, Eduerd. I must swallow my cowardice and start to think of my request if I am to prove myself a serious contender for her heart.'

Eduerd sat back, grinning. 'Indeed. You face a first hurdle in finding a gift that the discerning Keeper, Lady Ravar, will find acceptable.'

Lethan gave his friend a sly look. 'Yes. The Lady Ravar… I believe, my Eduerd, that *you* might be better positioned to know that which might turn her mind.'

Eduard was a masterclass in maintaining composure in the face of such a ruse but Lethan knew his friend too well. He leaned forward, saying, 'For you have taken *much* time to know the Master Tutor of Forestfyth better, have you not?'

Eduerd cleared his throat slightly. 'She is a very accomplished young woman,' he hedged, defensively.

'Accomplished, yes. And ambitious in the Ways of the Mind. Qualities I believe you have always held in high regard?' Lethan's eyes danced with mischief.

Eduerd narrowed his eyes a fraction, refusing to be drawn, so Lethan continued airily.

'And is she not a little beautiful in a strange sort of way?'

'She is *wildly* beautiful, Lethan,' Eduerd spat before he could stop himself. 'You would have to be blind not to—' Catching himself, he gave an angry sigh and looked hard at Lethan. It was bad enough having to deal with the cynical mockery of Desledair which had continued this morning after their long conversation the night before. Now Lethan too, seemed to have unmasked him.

'We need another drink,' Eduerd said.

*

Some weeks later, Ravar and Amalin had been woken shortly after dawn by a loud rapping at the door of their cosy home. Still yawning, Amalin joined her friend in the entrance room, where an animated Fiance was excitedly telling them that her sister had decided to accept the suit of Falthson, a Grandmaster Carpenter from Highturth. In three weeks' time they would be married in the women's hometown of Forestfyth and all were invited to what promised to be a heady celebration.

The wedding was to coincide with the Autumn Feast, where all the townsfolk came together to share the bounty of the harvest and fruits of their labours. There would be common dancing, music and the awarding of honours to those progressing through the Levels or achieving Mastery in their Crafts. Children were always welcome at the leaf fall Dance and enjoyed the rare privilege of an evening within the Palace and its grounds.

The women embraced each other in turn, both Ravar and Amalin congratulating the glowing Fiance in her part as Keeper, which had set the ball rolling in making the match.

'I very much look forward to meeting the man so worthy of both you and your sister's affection,' beamed Ravar to her substantial friend.

'You will not be disappointed, my dear Ravar,' Fiance, assured her, 'for you will find him a *fine* figure of a man! Of course, he must be, for he has shown himself to be of excellent judgement in courting my dear sister.' Amalin had to force herself not to giggle.

After promising that they would both be in attendance, the two women left their excited caller to hurry off to the next household with her news and began to make ready for their day at the School.

'Lethan will be pleased to see Master Falthson in the city,' Amalin said, thoughtfully.

'Oh?' said Ravar, conversationally. 'I suppose he must be thinking of submitting a piece for his approval.'

'You mean a *Masterpiece*? No, surely not... He would have told me if he was considering such an undertaking.'

'Perhaps not,' replied Ravar. 'I think he would be reluctant to make such a boast to you of all people before it had been judged and accepted.'

'What? What do you mean *me of all people?*' exclaimed Amalin. 'Why?'

Ravar laughed in surprise and smiled patronisingly at her friend. 'If you do not know, Amalin, then I do start to despair of you a little.'

'You think he would be concerned about my judgement of the level of his art?' said Amalin.

'My Lord Lethan is highly accomplished by any measure, my friend,' said Ravar, gently. 'But he sits in the shadow too often, of not just a Master, but one who is already hailed as one of the great Musicians of her time. It can be rather intimidating.'

'Ravar, you do not speak for *yourself*, surely?' asked Amalin, worried.

Ravar hugged her. 'No of course not. But you are my sister and my Soul Friend and I know that you see me as your equal.'

'I do not want Lethan to think of me as anything other than an equal,' said Amalin, her brow furrowing into a frown.

'I know you do not,' replied Ravar, gently. 'Have you considered, in fact, what you *do* want him to be to you?' She smiled warmly and kissed Amalin on the cheek before rising and leaving her without expecting an answer.

*

It would turn out to be an important day at the Forestfyth School of the Nearage. All its pupils would gain new knowledge and understanding, and all its teachers would learn something of themselves and each other.

Eduerd had arrived for the early lesson in possession of a sealed bucket. To the fascination and dismay of the class, it was filled with Yondil Worms. These were the dull-coloured, segmented invertebrates that were farmed and distributed throughout the Forest and Marketdawn by the Kingdoms' central Administration.

Although most of the Nearage were familiar with the slow, uninspiring creatures as a concept, few had ever seen one up close, or thought to look. Eduerd placed several on the desks in front of small groups of students for them to study.

They were long, fat and grey. Ravar had to bite her lip to stop herself from laughing at her pupils' underwhelmed expressions. Catching her eye and flickering a wink, Eduerd addressed the Nearage.

'Who can tell me something of the Yondil Worm?' Several students raised their hands. Gesturing for one to speak, Eduerd listened carefully to the rather monotone and bored-sounding reply.

'My Lord, the Yondil Worm is heralded for its expeditious ability to break down decaying matter. In the Forest Kingdom they are added to compost and cess pits where they cause the waste material to decompose at a faster rate. The end product may be transported to the Plains or the Northern Basin where it is used as fertiliser in agricultural employment.'

'Very good,' the Doctor said and clicked his tongue. 'But I am not here as a Master of the Crop or to speak to you of the trade and administration of Kingdoms. Tell me then, why have I brought them to your school today?'

There were looks of hard consideration as the Nearage searched their minds for the answer. Doctor Eduerd did not ask trick or rhetorical questions; he required a response.

After giving his audience fair opportunity to speak, but no ideas being forthcoming, Eduerd sat down on a high stool and brought his palms together. He formed his next question slowly and carefully, as if the question itself had great meaning.

'What would be the implications for our people, were the Yondil Worm to become absent from the Forest?'

The students now took it in turns to state various consequences: the composting process of plant matter and sewage would be lengthened; the fertiliser could not be collected and redistributed so regularly; the longer putrefaction would be characterised by a stronger smell which would attract flies and necessitate privies being located further from living spaces.

'Good. Continue to follow the terms of the hypothesis. Consider the wider implications,' Eduerd prompted.

'Agricultural return would be diminished, My Lord,' suggested one student. The Doctor nodded.

Another voice added that, 'This would lead to more limited distribution of food crops. The inner towns of the Forest would suffer, being unable to support their populations only by what was available from the Forest floor.'

'Yes,' said Eduerd, gravely.

'My Lord?' enquired one young woman, stepping forward to speak with resolution. Receiving a nod of acquiescence, she was handed the floor. 'The Peoples of the Forest, already weakened by limited access to fruit and cereal crops would fall victim to the water and insect-borne diseases that come of the long stagnation of corroding waste.'

Eduerd smiled at his keen-minded scholar while her peers breathed a sigh of satisfied understanding. A few nodded a silent congratulation to their friend.

Resuming the mantle, Master Eduerd held forth on the need for a Healer to be responsible for educating his patients and ensuring that they followed advice regarding preventative measures, in addition to relieving immediate maladies.

Ravar, seeing that all were listening and making careful notes, slipped into the Assembly Hall, where she picked up a book and stood, silently reading and gesturing in practise for her lesson on the physical forms of rhetoric that afternoon.

She was surprised to be caught unawares as she turned. She was sweeping a parallel movement of arm and head, signifying a speaker's intention that their audience shifted from one mode of thought to another. As she turned to the side, she noticed her spectator.

'My Lord Eduerd, you gave me a shock!' she said.

'I am sorry,' he replied, earnestly. 'I have always been under the impression that you have a sixth sense for an additional presence in this hall and assumed you were ignoring me until your exercise was complete.'

'Oh, yes…' Ravar frowned a little, accepting the truth of this. 'I must be losing my touch! Where are the Nearage?'

'I have sent them out to add the Yondil Worms to the School's compost pits and asked them to study their behaviour. They are to track their movement and distinguish from this their preferences in terms of light, moisture and warmth.'

'Excellent. I commend you, Doctor. You have, in one morning, stretched our young minds across many disciplines.'

Eduerd smiled his gratification, before noticing that Ravar was unconsciously rubbing the back of her neck and twisting it to one side. The healer in him took over and he stepped forward to meet her eye. He used the gentle command of one who expects a truthful response to ask, 'My Lady, you are in pain?'

Reluctantly, Ravar admitted that the left side of her neck and shoulder were troubling her and the discomfort had grown worse in the last few days.

Without emotion, Eduard said, 'Show me.'

Ravar scooped the masses of her shining, silver hair and sent them cascading over her right shoulder. The Doctor moved around her, carefully examining her long, graceful neck. To his experienced eye, the raised, aggravated muscles were obvious.

He scolded her in measured tones. 'Too much time spent bent over a book, My Lady. You hold your heavy tomes far too low. And you favour bearing the weight with your stronger arm, forcing you to incline your head at an angle.'

Ravar could not argue with Eduerd's impeccable diagnosis and was suddenly aware of careful, strong fingers plying the skin of the sore area. Eduerd applied and released pressure down the line of inflammation with careful, rhythmical movements.

After a time she felt the muscles relax a little and dropped her shoulders as the tension decreased. It was only after this relieving sensation that she became more aware of her present situation.

Eduerd stood so close behind her that she could hear his steady breathing. The heat of his hands radiated into her skin and she could sense his practical concentration on his task. Feeling suddenly self-conscious, Ravar filled the silence by thanking him, for she could feel the difference. She found that she did not go so far as to imply that he should stop.

Ravar's soft thanks had broken Eduerd's focus too, which had up until that point, been one of automatic practise. He had been a healer for long enough to dispense with asking permission to ply his skill in such a way as to alleviate pain or discomfort.

Suddenly, he became acutely aware of his hands on the body of the woman before him. Her skin was like silk and as her shoulders had relaxed, the soft lines of her elegant form that he had so long admired drew his gaze and distracted his attention from the task at hand.

Berating himself that, as a Healer he should not think in such a way of a patient, he tried to focus on the movement and anatomy, with only limited success.

From her vantage point, Ravar could see Amalin and Lethan strolling past the entrance to the room. Amalin had caught sight of the scene and had stopped to stare, round-eyed and drop-jawed. This was followed by an outrageously exaggerated leer at her friend, before bundling Lethan, also gaping, away out of sight. Ravar internally grimaced. Amalin would have a lot to say about this tonight.

Moments later, yet another person came to the doorway. King Aislyth was due to take the afternoon class as a follow up to the previous night's Bardic Tale. He had arrived in good time to get the feel of the round Assembly room and think over his plan for the lesson.

What he had *not* expected, was his most treasured new subject to be standing before him in the caressing hands of the handsome Healer. Something burning and instinctive rose up in him, shocking his conscious mind with such ferocity that it was all he could do to clench the scrolls he held like talismans, to keep himself rooted to reality.

As Ravar stiffened, Eduerd looked up and took a hasty step back from her and bowed to his King. Feeling compelled to offer an explanation, he carefully told His Majesty that Ravar had sustained a neck injury.

King Aislyth felt the surge of unbitten bile wash away and guiltily forced a smile. He bowed in return.

'Then I am very glad that she has availed herself of your excellent services, Doctor Eduerd. Master Ravar, I am sorry to hear you are pained.'

'It feels a little better now, Your Majesty,' Ravar replied, hurriedly. She turned to Eduerd and thanked him, whereby he wished them both a good day and went out.

A little awkwardly, Ravar repeated the conclusion that had been reached about the detrimental impact of her reading habits.

'Then you are a victim of your own Craft, Master Tutor!' smiled the King. 'Well, as you will never, I am sure, be able to curtail your penchant for all things written down, you shall have to find a better way of sponging up knowledge. After all, I cannot have a half-crippled teacher serving the Nearage of this town.'

Ravar's eyes sparkled laughter. 'I shall think on it, Sire.'

Some time later the Nearage could be heard waiting outside the Assembly room and Ravar called them in to take their accustomed places in a wide circle. The King stood at its centre, greeting the pupils by name as they filed in.

'Today I want you to put your books and notes out of the way,' he instructed. His deep voice echoed around the hall and the Nearage unceremoniously flung their bags and implements to its edges.

'Last night at the fire you heard the story of the Seven-Tailed Fox and the weight of his pride. The fireside is a place to listen and see a tale come to life in the mind's eye but today I have asked the Lady Ravar for use of the Assembly. By daylight we hope to consider and challenge the meaning of such stories and bring their lessons to life in our own realities.

'To liven our debate and focus your thoughts, I wish today to judge the tale against another. From either your studies or memories of the tales of our people, who among you know the story of the Chained Songbird?'

Several students tentatively raised their hands.

The King drew his arms out invitingly. 'Then which of you will stand among us and remind us of her story?'

The young men and women around him looked from one to another with horrified expressions. The King stepped back into a place within the line of the circle and motioned to the centre of the floor.

At length Elpeen, the oldest of the female students, stepped forward, to the amazement of her peers. She was breathing slowly and deeply, fighting for control over her nerves, but raised her eyes and cast them evenly at each face in the circle in turn. The last face she met was that of the King himself, who nodded slowly at her as a sign to begin. She spoke slowly and with a soft, melodious voice.

'A Queen of Snowseal once travelled to the Sky Kingdom, for she wished to see its towers that pierced the clouds and feel the grass of its stepped gardens beneath her feet.

'Climbing the mountain paths, the Queen was amazed at the rich colours and sounds of the alpine life all about her. But none was so breath-taking as the Songbird's call, which echoed through valley and danced up and around the steep cliffs. The Queen would watch the Songbird soar in the morning haze, a kaleidoscope of colour on the wind. The Queen would hear her melody in the evening sun as she dived into the green thickets to roost.

'The time came for this daughter of the ice to return to her Kingdom. She did not regret the call, for the harsh heat of the Sky Summer burnt at her silver skin and blinded her lilac eyes so that she longed to be once more in the strange, muffled whiteness of her home.

'But the Queen could not bear the thought of the awaiting silence of her palace in the far North, to where no Songbird could fly. She thought of the dawn being unsung and the day brought to an end without music.

'And so this Queen of Snowseal laid a trap for the Songbird, and caught and caged her, collaring her with a golden chain. She took the poor creature with her to the frozen city, that she might forever grace her people with her chant.

'The People of Snowseal came to listen in awe to the beautiful sad refrains of this prisoner of the Ice Palace. But as time passed her tune became so mournful, that the Queen had to shut her away.

'Up in the High Tower of the Castle of Ice, the Songbird looked through the window and dreamed of returning to the skies. Although she could not help but sing, her song had become one of misery and solitude. Even the Queen could not bear her sorrow-filled carol, but neither would she relinquish her once-loved prize.

'She ordered her servants to tend to the Songbird, so loath was she to be in its presence. The servers would hurry their ministrations so as to lessen their time in the company of a creature whose song filled them with woe. The cycles passed and many had forgotten the desolate existence of the captive in the tower.

'Until one day the elusive Snow Cat, prowling the deep drifts in search of prey, heard a haunting song howling with the wind. Curious as all felines are, he sneaked into the Ice Palace and padded silently up through the empty spire. He found the Songbird faded and weak, her feathers turned to grey. She turned her dulled eyes to him and tried to sing but could only utter a few melancholy notes.

'The Snow Cat would have devoured such an easy quarry, had he not felt in his *heart her sadness. He saw the heavy chain that fell from her neck and wondered at the cruelty of the Queen of the Ice, for it was a selfish thing to trap such a treasure and then lock it away from the pleasure of the world.*

The Snow Cat picked the lock of the chain with his claws and lifted the heavy mantle from the Songbird's neck. When the Songbird knew that she had been unbound she took a feather from her crown and placed it at the Snow Cat's feet, saying, "Take this and wear it as a token of the love that I will bear for you always because you have set me free. I will return to the skies and sing for you with all the joys of my life. And the Peoples of the world will know my song and your kindness. May they remember that an act of compassion can live forever."'

As Elpeen finished her tale, the Nearage broke into a round of applause but Ravar was looking between her student and the King, as if she had seen something the others had not.

'Well, I am impressed, Elpeen!' cried the King, clapping himself. 'Perhaps you are destined for the Way of the Bard? You might learn Fireplay yet!'

The young woman blushed and returned to the edge of the circle, where her friends patted her on the back in congratulation for such a performance.

Raising a hand to settle the floor, the King said more soberly, 'Two tales, then, of compassion we have heard. Are these tales such an easy lesson? Speak.'

Stepping forward, a student said, 'The Assembly will recognise that both tales speak of, and to, the Soul. The Seven-Tailed Fox relinquishes the very part of himself that has won him admiration for the lives of his Blood-Kin. The Snow Cat unwittingly makes his suit and wins the feather and love of another forever.'

Another student added to his friend's surmise: 'In the Third Age we seek to improve ourselves through the Crafts and Ways of our Peoples. However, these tales serve to remind us that the ways of our *hearts* are not a matter of careful practice and application. The weight of our goodness will be tested by the decisions we make in the instant that they are required of us.'

Warming to the theme, a third student issued a challenge: 'Does the Assembly acknowledge that both heroes ultimately gained as a result of their kindness? Perhaps they acted in the hope of the love and affection of those they saved?'

'A cynical view from one so young,' commented the King.

'But one that requires answer, Your Majesty,' countered Ravar, quickly.

Understanding the cue, the King addressed the room once again. 'The Assembly has been asked to consider the virtue of altruism itself. I would have you pair with another classmate and prepare your arguments in time for our next meeting. There we shall engage in formal debate by the procedure already laid down by Master Ravar.'

With that, the students quickly found their partner and left the room, understanding the dismissal.

'Ye Stars, My Lady Ravar,' the King said wistfully. 'To present a tale, unprepared, in such language... If ever Elpeen, once she is of Age wished to explore the Bardic craft, I would gladly have her sit at my fire.'

'You underestimate the influence your mastery has already had on her, I think,' replied Ravar. This was high praise and the King acknowledged it with a bow.

'The students will be in their workrooms planning their arguments,' said Ravar, after a short silence.

'Of course!' said the King, flustered. He should be overseeing them. Ravar chuckled slightly as he hurried out of the Assembly.

After he had left Ravar remained standing, gazing at the room and reliving the events that had just taken place there in her mind. The Mastery of the King in the Way of the Bard had actually provoked a proactive attempt to emulate his skills. Moreover, despite the two-fold factors that might intimidate one from such a public risk, his royal status and level of Craft had not deterred his pupil.

Ravar recalled her own training under the Grandmaster Tutor in Eagle's Mount. She found herself echoing some of the words of her great mentor in her own thoughts, and took these with her as she made her way home.

She was only jolted by this careful consideration, when Amalin burst through the door that evening. She had had to endure the late class at the School, meaning that she was prevented from grilling Ravar about the scene she had witnessed in the Assembly room for many hours longer than she would have liked.

'Well!' she said beadily, pointing an accusatory finger at her friend. 'You have a lot of explaining to do!'

Ravar pulled a face and sighed. 'It is really nothing to get excited about, Amalin. He was just fixing my neck.'

'Oh, is that what you are calling it?' Amalin replied, howling with laughter.

'Yes, because that is what happened.'

'Not from where I was standing. I could see *both* of your faces!' Ravar grimaced at Amalin's glee.

'Actually, what was exciting was in the lesson that followed,' said Ravar, hoping to move her friend on from this vein.

'The next lesson? But that was taken by the King.' She looked unimpressed. Then, suddenly she pricked up and launched into another tirade. 'Oh! Something happened with the King? Did he wear you down with his *sensual, commanding* voice? Ha! I know you hold him in superior regard, ever since you danced back in summer!' she trilled. Then, waggling her finger at Ravar she continued, teasingly. 'And he really is *very* dedicated to our school. He is forever within our walls. Perhaps you encourage him?' Amalin was almost hopping from foot to foot.

'I am serious, Amalin,' Ravar pleaded. 'The man has a gift for teaching. I have thought of little else since coming home. It is not the romantic notion that you would suggest.'

'Ah, but to you what distinction is there between the two?'

CHAPTER 5

Forestfyth, Fifth Year of the Dancer, high leaf fall.

The Autumn Dance with its accompanying wedding being only days away, Ravar had travelled to Woodsedge with Fiance at first light, to barter for the necessary extra ingredients required for the feast. She had left the School of the Nearage that morning in the capable hands of its other Tutor, who had taken it upon herself to arrange for a different sort of lesson for the students.

The Nearage filing into the classroom were surprised to see so many familiar and eminent faces together waiting for them. The Lady Amalin had greeted them at the door, leaving a vacant chair at the front of the room. Beside this were three more chairs but these were occupied.

Doctor Eduerd, Armick the Tailor and Princess Istreeth all sat before them.

Taking her seat alongside her fellow Masters, Amalin smiled at the class and introduced the day's lesson. 'Good afternoon, everyone. We are privileged today, to be in the company of some of our city's most highly accomplished Craftspeople. I have asked our guests to join us to speak to you about the types of Craft and levels of Mastery to which you might one day aspire. Each of us sitting before you has achieved the highest level within an art, though we all still have yet to fully embrace the Higher Ways. May I welcome first, Princess Istreeth, who will speak to you of the nature of the different Crafts and how one might ascend through them.' At this prompt, the woman in question stood up and took a step forward.

'Good morning to you all,' said Istreeth in a quiet, commanding voice.

The Nearage smiled. They had been very taken with the Princess in their previous meeting, when she had come to speak to them about her painting of the Great Oak. Although she had been more reserved in the tone and emotion of her words than some of their other teachers, they had been fascinated by the way she had taken them through her work. She described the artist's craft as a series of journeys: from inspiration, through conception and application of skill, to polishing, placement and reflection.

Istreeth, seeing with satisfaction that she had her audience's full attention, began.

'Regard the sashes which, as you know, those who are of Age wear from shoulder to knee.' She paused while her audience's eyes flitted between the elegant cream bands of their teachers.

She resumed, 'While the top portion is reserved for marks of love, friendship, honour and the Dance, the lower half reveals the marks of a person's learning.

'Beyond their service to the Kingdom, all may choose to embark upon one or more of the rich array of Crafts of the Six Kingdoms. There are three broad categories by which such endeavours are classified.' She walked over to cast a hand up and around the physical structure and decoration of the room.

'Firstly, one may choose a Craft of the Hand and work with materials such as paint or clay. You have those Craftspeople to thank for your homes, your library, your school.' The Nearage nodded, appreciatively.

'Secondly, there are the Crafts of Care. These include the tending of crops, livestock, children and the sick.' Istreeth inclined her head towards Eduerd, who returned her nod in acknowledgement.

'The final classification relates to the Crafts of the Mind. These are extensive and range from Teaching to the Bardic way.

'Those seeking to learn a Craft,' Istreeth continued, 'must study under the tutelage of a Master. They may pursue this at three levels: Bronze...' She pointed at her badge denoting the way of the Engineer, woven in soft, brassy brown thread. The Nearage craned to see it.

'Silver,' she went on, 'is awarded at the next level, for those who can prove their Craft has impact upon the world around them.' This time she gestured to the patch on her sash denoting the Athlete.' The design was modelled on the constellation that formed one of the ten signs of the Long Calendar who gave their names to a five-hundred-year cycle.

'Gold,' she said, with emphasis, 'is for those who demonstrate *excellence* of understanding and application across all areas of an art.' She gestured to the golden Dancer sewn to her sash. All eyes fell upon the shining thread.

In a tone which reminded the students of that adopted by her brother at the fireside, Istreeth intoned the final part of her explanation. 'Once a Goldman of a Craft, that person may seek the ultimate Level by kneeling before a Grandmaster. If accepted, the pupil may enter into a higher training that may take a *very* many years to complete. For, only when they can prove they are competent to raise others to the Gold Level and can produce a work that may be considered a Masterpiece, will the highest accolade, Mastery, be awarded.'

Istreeth gently unpinned the large, polished metal brooch that denoted her own accomplishment at this level and handed it to a student to pass around the group. They handled it as one might a fragile and precious object, crowding close together to admire the design. Upon it were overlaid compasses and set square, revealing the Princess to be a Master of Geometry. Eventually handing it back to her, a little awed, the Nearage returned to their places.

With a polite nod, Istreeth indicated that she would now hand over to Armick.

The slight, pointed features of the town's pernickety Master Tailor lit up in a bright smile and he stood, stepping forward towards the young men and women before him. He took a cheerful intake of breath before gesturing at Istreeth and speaking.

'Nearage, you have had the great honour of examining the Master's mark from the sash of Princess Istreeth. I have no doubt that, in her case, it will not be her only such mark.' Istreeth maintained a practised poise in the face of the compliment.

'However,' Armick said with relish, 'you will have noticed that the Princess made reference to one whom we would call a Grandmaster.' The Nearage thought of the few personages they knew of this rank. The most famous was the old Grandmaster Dethir who lived in the Palace tower. Rarely surfacing from the library or his observatory, he was something of a curiosity to the young. Their elders afforded him the upmost respect, bowing in respect on the sporadic occasions that he was seen in town or at the seasonal celebrations.

'Such individuals,' Armick continued, 'are not awarded the title by virtue of the Masterpieces they have created, but by the virtues of those who will kneel at their feet, to seek their wisdom. For they are the very trainers of Masters, themselves being men and women who seek the Higher Ways.'

'The Peoples of the Six Kingdoms acknowledge these Ways as the ultimate aspiration of each Soul in its path. They hope that through this level of application and understanding, they might make their own contribution to the ushering in of a Fourth Age of men.' The Nearage hung on his every word, eyes like saucers.

'Three forks lie before those who walk this road.' Armick used a hand to indicate each direction in turn. 'To the left lies the Way of the Mathematician. This is the culmination of all Crafts of the Mind and Hand, that through great wisdom, humanity might better its understanding and place within the vast universe.

'To the right,' continued Armick, 'a traveller of the Way might elect to take the path of the Bard. This route encompasses all the Soulful Crafts of the Mind, such as Music and Storytelling, that we, as a common People, might know greater joy and fulfilment.'

More carefully and quietly, the Tailor completed the triad. 'The Middle Path is the Way of the *Advocate*.' He gave the final word slow emphasis. 'It is the most difficult Way of them all because the Advocate may use all of the Crafts of Mind, Hand *and* Soul for the betterment of the human heart. It is the ultimate Craft of Care. The Advocate's Way, is the Way of all the Peoples of our world. It is through such persons' interventions and guidance, which we may reach a higher state of being.' He let the silence in the room last as the magnitude of his words sank in.

A pupil, daring to break the stillness, stepped forward enquiringly. 'Do you seek one of the High Ways, Master Armick?'

Armick smiled at the student and said pleasantly, 'At the moment I hope to better some of my lesser Crafts.' Cocking his head to one side slightly, he added, 'I also hope to inspire others to take the needle and thread and learn to shape beautiful garments.' He raised his eyebrows at his class. 'That is why I have spent these last weeks showing you some of my secrets!'

The Nearage grinned. They had enjoyed his sharp eye for detail and their share in his construction of his creations. Armick appeared to be thinking hard, a frown overshadowing his usually placid face.

'But there *is* one among us today who can boast such an ambition. For I think Master Eduerd would make no mystery of his desire to find the Mathematician's Way.' He looked across to where the Doctor sat next to

Amalin and Istreeth. He hoped he had not spoken out of turn and gave him an enquiring look.

Eduerd cleared his throat and answered softly. 'No, indeed, it is no secret, My Lord Armick.' He cast a sideways glance at the other Masters in the room, feeling a little vulnerable under their gaze.

'But I would stress how early and young I am in my endeavours,' he said quickly. 'I may study a lifetime and never reach the High Path I seek. At present I can only hope to attain mastery in as many of the disciplines of the Mind and Hand as my efforts and abilities will allow.' He took a deep breath, smiled and added, 'And this is both my toil and my recreation.' The whole room smiled with him. It was difficult not to when treated to such an aesthetically pleasing visage.

'However,' said Eduerd with a mock-apologetic smile, 'I am not here to talk of the Higher Ways. Actually, I am to be the one to speak to you about Kingdom Service.' The Nearage looked a little disappointed. They all knew that their adult family and friends worked at least one day per week, sometimes inconsistently and averaged out over the course of a year, directly for the Kingdom Administration.

In fact, the Doctor taught them a lot in his short lecture. Few had grasped the variation in work tasks available from sorting Kingdoms Post messages, to repainting signs on roadways. He also explained how such tasks were allocated and how the Councillors tried to ensure that citizens were matched to their tasks according to skill and some regard for preference. Many were also unaware that Kingdom Service was unique to the Western Continent and that the Sky Kingdom in particular operated a very different and complicated system to ensure that common needs were met.

When Eduerd had finished taking questions Amalin rose from her seat once again to bring the formal part of the lesson to a close. She spoke with the elegance demanded as host to her esteemed companions, but as always this was accompanied with an underlying warmth.

'I want to thank our guests for speaking to us all today.' The Nearage smiled and nodded their agreement.

'After the midday break,' Amalin gestured to the clock on the far wall, 'each Master has agreed to let you study their sashes and familiarise yourself with some of the symbols of the Crafts. You will also be able to ask them about their experience of the nature and demands of each level they have obtained. In the meantime, I believe that Lady Fiance has left the necessary materials for you to be able to prepare a good lunch for our guests.'

*

Ravar arrived towards the end of the afternoon session, flushed from the journey on horseback through the woods. She was delighted to see the classroom so alive with questions and discussion. After greeting each of the adult speakers, she went over and clasped Amalin's hands by way of thanks for her organisation of the day.

Amalin had given time to her own study of the sashes of the other Masters in the room. She could not help but agree with Ravar's previous assessment that, for so young a man, Eduerd's accomplishments were exceptional. It was no wonder her friend, also of a determined way when it came to intellectual pursuits, was so taken with him.

She considered with seriousness the potential for a Soul Match between them. However, Princess Istreeth interrupted her thoughts by joining her and Ravar at their vantage point in the far end of the workroom. She took a breath, before carefully making her request.

'Lady Ravar, as we have all been reminded by the day's lesson, the Peoples of the Six Kingdoms strive to better themselves in the Crafts that build and better our world. Therefore I hoped that I might ask you about the requirements to which I might work, in order to attain Bronze in the Craft of Teaching?' She made a careful bow.

Ravar's eyes widened in recognition, before smilingly replying, 'Istreeth of the Forest, I would be glad to be your mentor, if that is what you wish?'

Istreeth betrayed the smallest sign of a smile. 'It is, Master Tutor.'

Ravar nodded solemnly. 'Then come to the School as you wish and learn as we all do. A teacher of the Bronze Level is characterised by their ability to engage their charges in their learning. This teacher is able to challenge each pupil in such a way that there are noticeable improvements in their knowledge and skill. A teacher sets the example, but judges carefully the difficulty and areas of study so that no mind may be discouraged, nor allowed to coast.'

Istreeth bowed again and glided away to say farewell to the other Masters, for the school day was drawing to a close.

Armick diverted from his course to the door to approach the two women. It was clear he wanted something.

Ravar cast him an enquiring look.

'Ladies, I have a request of you both and I will not take offense if you wish to refuse it,' he said, evenly.

Ravar looked at Amalin and then back at the Tailor. 'Master Armick, we are all ears!'

He smiled. 'Very well. If it is your wish that I might continue in my instruction of the Nearage into the winter season, I wonder if I might offer them the prospect of selecting and tailoring your outfits for the masked Solstice Ball?' He looked from one to the other, nervously.

'We would be honoured, Master Armick,' said Amalin for both of them. As he took his leave, she grinned at Ravar, who grinned back. Under her breath, Amalin whispered, 'Thank Heavens, for I was already starting to dread having to make something!'

'I do not mind dress-making, though I will be very glad to wear something made by my own students,' said Ravar.

'I wonder what they will choose for us,' said Amalin, excitedly.

'As long as it is better than that awful horse with the tail that kept falling off you made one year, I will be happy,' said Ravar.

Amalin grimaced. 'Yes, that was one of my poorer efforts,' she admitted.

'*One* of them...' said Ravar.

Before departing, Eduerd also lingered, though with the purpose of speaking to Ravar specifically. Sensing his intention, Amalin busied herself with tidying the room.

Ravar looked up into his face with such warmth that he almost forgot the purpose of his enquiry.

Finding his voice, 'Lady Ravar,' he said merrily. 'I trust your excursion with the Lady Fiance was a success?'

'Of course, My Lord Eduerd.' A mischievous smile in her eyes, she said conspiratorially, 'I think our mutual friend could be capable of giving the Merchant King himself a run for his money!'

Eduerd laughed. 'Yes, we would all do well to learn from her in that respect.' He paused, then said more prosaically, 'I have been asked, on account of my Kinship with her family, to conduct the marriage ceremony of her sister.'

'Then I congratulate you on such an honour,' Ravar said, with feeling.

'I do hope that I will have the pleasure of your company at our table at the feast?' he asked, a little shyly.

'But you will be seated on the High Table, Eduerd, if you are to perform the rite,' Ravar pointed out.

'Indeed. But the Lady Fiance was most insistent that you would join us.'

'She did not mention it to me this morning,' mused Ravar.

'I daresay she had many things on her mind,' replied Eduerd, meaningfully. Ravar laughed.

'You are quite correct, My Lord, but when does she not? Very well, I would be honoured to dine at the table of the happy couple and among friends.'

As he left, Amalin, who had been unashamedly listening in from the other side of the room, raced to her friend's side.

'You are to leave me alone to dine with the top cats, Ravar?' she exclaimed, mockingly.

Ravar raised her nose to the sky and with haughty sarcasm replied, 'Yes. I find I am quite going up in the world, Amalin of the Plains.' She waved a regal hand as if to dismiss her Soul Friend, saying, 'You shall have to content yourself with a meal in the company of lower personages such as *Lethan* and alike.'

Amalin wore a mask of dismay and said solemnly, 'I shall endure the hardship with good grace as best as I can, My Lady.'

Giggling like adolescents, the two women closed up the School and made for home.

*

In the private chambers of the Royal Household, Istreeth found her brother in the unusual state of partial undress, being carefully scrutinised by two of Armick's assistants. Given that he usually hated 'wasting' time on such things, she was surprised to find him in good spirits, chatting with the two Silver-Level Tailors about the form and material of the nearly finished garment that they had prepared, for what must be a final fitting.

Although it was still pinned in places, Istreeth highly approved of the long dress coat. Rich blue with a gold trim, it was fastened at one side with elegant buttons that matched the stitching. As they buttoned up the high collar that sat flush with is neck, she gazed admiringly at both the workmanship and the effect it had of enhancing the attractive figure and features of the King.

'It suits you, brother,' she said, causing a slight flush of embarrassment in Aislyth.

'How do you manage to sneak around so, that I never see or hear you coming?' he said.

'Good deportment, I daresay,' Istreeth replied dryly. 'And do not try to change the subject. I was bestowing you with a rare compliment.' The siblings locked each other in a stalemate gaze.

The King relented. 'Well, if you must know, as I am to give the groom away at the Autumn Feast, I thought I might try to look the part.'

'Oh, this is for the *groom's* benefit,' Istreeth said. 'I *see*.'

Her brother sighed, irritably. 'And what,' he said, almost not wanting to know the answer, 'is that supposed to mean?'

Istreeth adopted a look of shocked innocence, but could not help herself. 'Only that I have never known you to take such care as to present yourself so particularly at a formal occasion. It makes one wonder whether you have an ulterior motive for wishing to show yourself at your best.' She enjoyed her brother's attempt to hide his guilty expression. However, she turned on her heel towards her own quarters in the palace before he had a chance to think of a retort, smiling with satisfaction.

CHAPTER 6

Forestfyth Palace, Fifth Year of the Dancer, the Autumn Feast.

The wedding ceremony had been a splendid affair. In the face of hundreds of their people, and in the open air of the Palace Grounds, Falthson had been taken as a husband by his wife under the auspicious glow of the autumn sun.

Amalin and Ravar had wept at the moment when, guided by the hands of King Aislyth and Fiance, the happy couple had joined in their first Soul Embrace.

The feast that had followed had been magnificent, its crowning glory a splendid cake, decorated by none other than the Lady Fiance herself. Eduerd had won her eternal favour by declaring that if he were a Grandmaster Cook, he would have declared it her latest Masterpiece.

At the High Table, Ravar had become acquainted with the much enduring Desledair. Fiance seemed to have made it her mission to ensure that the man ate as much as was humanly possible, endlessly refilling his plate with ever more rich delicacies. Ravar had leant over and facetiously asked him, upon finishing yet another course, whether she should alert the Cook to his present state of affairs.

Desledair's look of horror and contempt was quickly replaced by a wry grin when he realised that he was being teased.

'Alas,' he said, sullenly, 'I seem to be the primary object of Fiance's desire to ensure that all the men of the Kingdom achieve the stature of her much-esteemed new brother-in-law.'

Ravar laughed. The Grandmaster Carpenter was an enormous man.

No wonder Fiance held him in such high regard.

'It is very good to make your acquaintance, Lady Ravar,' Desledair smiled, 'for I have heard much from Eduerd and have been quite desirous to discover whether his reports are to be believed.'

Ravar pulled a face. 'I am not sure what Lord Eduerd has told you, but I shall deny every word on principle.'

'I am glad to hear it,' said Desledair, approvingly. 'Alas, my poor Soul Friend is of a dangerously romantic disposition.' He smiled ruefully. 'It is all I can do to try to rein him in.'

'You are not succeeding so well then!' grinned Ravar.

'No indeed. I fear he is quite the lost cause,' said Desledair, drolly.

Ravar cast her eyes upon her companion's sash. Lord Desledair was highly decorated, bearing the Seals of both Marketdawn and Snowseal and those denoting Mastery of *two* disciplines. 'You are, I daresay, a man of much greater grounding than our Healer friend,' she said. Desledair nodded, nonchalantly.

'And yet,' Ravar said thoughtfully, 'I can see why you and Eduerd are Soul-Bonded. My Lord Eduerd must admire and envy your achievements.'

As if noticing the contents of his sash for the first time, Desledair stared down at it with raised his eyebrows, before saying easily, 'Ah, but I have a few centuries on him. He will, no doubt, exceed by own efforts in time. We of Marketdawn,' he continued, 'are not so obsessed with the finer arts of learning. I find greater pleasure in the practical application of those skills I have acquired.'

'Do you reside in the capital?' Ravar asked.

'Stars, no! I live in Woodsedge, keeping the demands of my brother and the racket of court at arm's length.' Desledair sighed, 'Having said that, my next commission is one from him that I cannot refuse, for he has asked me to oversee the improvements to the city's drainage system. It will be far from elegant, but it is a service to the Kingdom whose importance I shall not ignore.'

Ravar's mind was working hard, digesting the implications of all that Desledair had just said.

With sudden comprehension, she blurted, 'Why, you are then… the Merchant King's brother! Your Highness, I had not—'

Desledair cut her off severely. 'Do not use that irksome title in the one place I might enjoy a night's entertainment unmolested!' He looked around anxiously in case anyone had heard her.

Ravar mimed zipping her lips shut, but whispered pointedly, 'Very well, My Lord. Your secret is safe with me, though I have just spied Fiance eyeing your empty plate. So I fear that you will not remain unmolested for long.'

As Ravar rose, chuckling, to join in one of the common dances beside her famous friend, Desledair turned his attention to Eduerd, whose gaze was locked upon the pair. More precisely, it was fixed on the silver-haired half of the duo.

Treating his friend to a pitying glace of disapproval, Desledair waved a hand over the Doctor's eyes and eclipsed his view with his own dark stare. 'Heavens, man, do not stare so!'

'Sorry, friend. I cannot help it,' Edward confessed.

'Yes, well I am reluctantly forced to admit that I can begin to understand why,' admitted Desledair. He continued, grudgingly, 'She is marked by both brain and beauty, and is not a little pleasingly cynical in humour.'

Eduerd regarded his Soul Friend in amazement. 'Then,' he excitedly, 'you approve?' He searched Desledair's features, appealingly.

'Not that such a thing has ever mattered to you before, Eduerd, but yes. For what it is worth, I believe you would do well to seek such a match.'

Eduerd beamed from one side of his face to the other. He clasped Desledair hard, in full knowledge, but unconcerned, that this would annoy him. Releasing him to observe his inevitable scowl, he said, 'Then I am resolved. I will go to the Lady Amalin once my preparations are complete.'

Desledair made an indecipherable sound. 'Then we had better get up and dance, Eduerd. Or everyone will think we are a fop and a stooge who lurk at the table, when all others are engaging in the pleasure of the music. Such a reputation is not one that will win you a bride.'

'Nor you!' Eduerd pointed out. Desledair winced and deigned not to reply.

King Aislyth had certainly not skirted the dance floor. He and Istreeth had partaken continuously in the complex routines of the communal dances that were traditionally performed at the Autumn Feast.

Gasping for breath, the Princess reined in her brother, as he made to take his place for another set. 'Brother, please! I cannot keep up with your endless zeal for the dance! I must rest, just for a minute!'

The King laughed, heartily. 'Are you so much my elder, dear sister?' He stood, his own chest heaving from the exhilaration and took her by the shoulders, saying, 'Very well. If you so desire it, let us take a break for a while. In any case, I am parched!' Walking together back to the High Table, Istreeth watched as her brother flung himself into his seat, one hand still tapping to the tempo of the music, while the other grasped for his goblet.

This drained, the King exhaled in hearty satisfaction and gazed around at his people before him. Lady Amalin was dancing with Fiance's group and laughing at some no doubt unseemly joke. He searched for Ravar among the dancers, but caught sight of her cool, radiant hair at the edge of the floor. She was crouching down examining a toy that a small child had presented her. She was conversing seriously with this little boy, who was nodding his head and earnestly telling her something which he obviously deemed of vital importance. Behind him, several other little ones were craning forward to follow their friend's discussion.

Istreeth turned in the direction of her brother's eye and sighed. 'The Lady Ravar is much in demand tonight,' she said, softly.

'When is she not?' the King replied, without taking his eyes from the scene. 'See how even the children come to her.'

'She is well-loved by the People of Forestfyth,' Istreeth agreed, gently. 'I confess I, too, have fallen a little under her spell. She is an excellent teacher of the young and adults alike. I hope to learn much from her.'

'It is not just her prowess as a Tutor, Istreeth,' the King replied, sighing. 'She has a gift for putting people at their ease and then drawing them close with laughter. Did you see her at the meal? People hang on her every word. Why, she even had the cantankerous Lord Desledair chuckling.'

'Lord Desledair is not *cantankerous*, brother,' Istreeth corrected him, admonishingly. 'He is just graced with a little reserve. Not all of us so enjoy the limelight.'

The King was too taken up with his own thoughts to tackle his sister on such a rare occasion as this where she had decided to defend the virtues of another that she barely knew. Evidently Ravar had sent the children on some sort of mission, for she had pointed in the direction of the east garden and they had scurried away resolutely. Immediately she had turned back to the dance floor, she was intercepted by Doctor

Eduerd and Lord Desledair who were pulling her, unresisting, into their group. Aislyth shook his head as a horse might shake off flies. He must try to get a grip on himself.

Istreeth had been regarding her brother with ill-ease. She had never known him to be so stupidly stubborn. But then again she had never known him to be remotely interested in a woman this way, let alone so completely infatuated, since he had come of Age. She must try to speak to him properly, but now was not the time.

Instead, she joined her brother in watching the dancing, where she was surprised to see Lord Desledair, just as her brother had said, beaming and throwing himself into the jig. His arm was linked with that of the Lady Ravar and they were clearly sharing amusement at Doctor Eduerd's expense.

The Architect was in fact, very full, very happy for Eduerd, (who was almost effervescing whenever he took Ravar's hand in the common dance), and not a little drunk. Nevertheless, as a Dancer of the Silver Level, he managed to conduct himself with impressive lightness. Unknown to him, he was being much admired by some of the unattached persons of the Forest.

Fiance had also finally abandoned the dining table and was in her secondary element, her sash revealing her as being matched to Desledair's own ability. It was a shame that the Autumn Feast was the only seasonal celebration that precluded formal dances for, they had many times in the past, made an elegant pair. This was in spite of their vastly opposed physique.

'Ah, My Lord Desledair,' Fiance extolled when a turn brought the pair next to one another. 'You see what good a decent meal has done for you?'

Desledair grimaced. 'My Lady, please do not talk anymore of food. I feel quite sick.'

'Nonsense! All the ladies are in admiration of your dancing and you have a spark in your air tonight.'

Glancing around, with a dismayed expression he said, 'It is not *my* spark, Fiance. It is that of Eduerd which has merely rubbed off on me. Surely you have noticed the stars in his eyes tonight?'

Fiance, briefly taking in the Doctor's electric aura, nodded vigorously. 'He is besotted, isn't he? I do not blame him, of course, for I very much approve of the Lady Ravar. Although she is in need of a few more breakfasts, she has excellent taste in breads and is very sensible about things that *matter*.' Desledair thought that their ideas about what mattered might differ a little.

Fiance continued, excitedly, 'And would they not make for a handsome pair? Stars! Think of what children they might produce!'

Desledair threw his head back in exasperation. 'My Lady, I think you are getting a little ahead of yourself! He has not even asked Amalin her permission to make a suit yet.'

Fiance rounded on him. 'And *why* should the good Lady Amalin not consent? Our Eduerd is as good a prospect as any. Why, I know of *several* young women who might think of approaching your good self as his Keeper.'

Desledair laughed openly. 'Calm yourself, dear lady, for of course *I* agree with your assessment. But Fiance, the ways of the Soul, as you well know, are each person's own. We can only support Eduerd in his bid and even if Amalin will give him her blessing, it is the Lady Ravar's heart that will open or shut the way.'

Fiance limited herself to pulling a face by way of reply.

*

After a time, Ravar and Amalin had retired from the dancefloor to catch their breath amid strong protestations from their dance group. Downing a cup of water, Amalin gasped with relief.

'Lethan *is* talking to Grandmaster Falthson.' Ravar nodded her head in the direction of the side of the dance area, where the men in question were engaged in a serious conversation.

Discarding her cup and peering forward, Amalin observed that her friend was quite right. The Grandmaster seemed to be gesturing technical instructions indicating the dimensions of some large object and Lethan was nodding thoughtfully and jotting down notes in a small notebook.

'I wonder if they are discussing his Masterpiece,' said Amalin, wishing she was near enough to overhear what was being said.

'Unlikely. A Craftsman does not take advice in such matters – you know it yourself. For it would hardly be an original work if he is taking direction,' replied Ravar.

At this moment, both men turned and looked their way. After doing their best to look otherwise engaged, both women cast their eyes back to find them once again deep in discussion, the Grandmaster curving his arm around in a swooping gesture.

'More curious by the moment,' mused Ravar.

'*Very* curious,' frowned Amalin.

*

At the close of the night the People of Forestfyth gathered before their King for the final part of the festival.

'My subjects, we are gathered tonight in celebration of the harvest and all the bounty that is the reward for our toils.' The King's booming voice carried across the crowd before him and a merry cheer arose from their masses.

'At this time we also congratulate those Craftsmen whose labours have reaped their own rewards. Are there any Masters tonight who wish to come forward and tell us of the achievements of their pupils?'

Armick the Tailor walked forward to the dais and made his bow to the King before turning to address the crowd. 'I wish to recognise in the presence of our city, the talent and efforts of my assistant, Heleys.' A young woman at the front of the crowd blushed as all turned to look at her. Armick regained their attention, saying, 'The tailed jacket I wear this evening is her own work.' The spectators let out an impressed murmur as he held out the embroidered sides for them to admire.

'Such workmanship,' he continued, 'is of fine enough quality that I am pleased to don it myself!' Ripples of polite laughter echoed through the crowd. 'I therefore ask the Lady Heleys to step forward and receive the mark of Gold in the Craft of the Needle.'

Heleys stepped forward, humbled and delighted to kneel before him. As she rose, he presented her with the beautifully embroidered emblem and pinned it over its replica in silver. He smiled and guided her round back to the crowd to receive her applause.

Two more presentations followed in the Crafts of Earth and Childcare and the recipients of their new emblems received their due ovation in turn. The King was about to step forward once again, to bid his people goodnight, when one last voice commanded silence with its clear and formal tones.

'People of the Forest. There is one more honour that must be bestowed tonight.' The onlookers turned towards the voice, which emanated from Ravar, looking resplendent in her long, powder-blue gown. She stepped up to the platform and faced the interested crowd.

'The Second Level in the Way of the Teacher is characterised by one who is able to inspire a proactive desire to emulate their own skills. Such a Tutor raises the student to ambition which is not cowed in the face of a superior skill or the critical minds of their peers. It is therefore my privilege to present His Majesty, King Aislyth, with the mark of silver.'

And so it came to pass that the King of the Forest knelt before his Master to receive her commendation. As she fixed it to his sash, the silver stitching of its design shone in the moonlight. It had an eerily familiar quality that many could not place, as if the thread glowed of its own accord.

*

As the last revellers left the Palace, many unsteady on their feet, King Aislyth and his sister seated themselves at the immense hearth of the Great Hall, where the fire was burning low.

Istreeth delicately reached an arm around her brother's broad back and leant her head on his shoulder. He was holding his new mark, gazing at it with a strange intensity.

Sighing, Istreeth stood and paced the fireside. 'Brother,' she said, tiredly, 'I do not understand the conflict that your Living Tale brings to the way of your heart.' She waited for him to meet her eye before continuing. 'However, you cannot hide the depth of your feelings from me. I know them every time our Souls embrace.' Raising her hand to maintain him to silence, she went on. 'Aislyth, you cannot deny that the Lady Ravar has won your affection. Indeed, I do not need the benefit of hand to heart to see with my own eyes how you light up in her presence, or how your gaze follows her in all that she does.'

King Aislyth wore a pained expression and ran his hands down his face, pulling his features downward, before slowly shaking his head.

'I do not deny it, sister, for I know I cannot hide it from you. I confess that she is near all I think of each hour of the day but at night I have such dreams...'

'Dreams?'

'Oh, you would not understand! I do not understand what they mean in any case.'

'Then act upon it and make your suit!' Istreeth appealed. 'You cannot—'

'Istreeth it is not so simple!' cried Aislyth. 'The Songstress of Eslebard does not trifle with a man! Her story is *living* after all. What she told me...' He faltered a moment. After some time, he met Istreeth's concerned expression. She sat down at the fireside, patiently.

More steadily, he said, 'It makes no sense to me either, Istreeth. I am caught between adhering to the Way I have chosen as a Bard, and following the strength of my heart as a man.' He gave a huff of frustration. 'But unless I flee to the very ends of the Upper Face and take up home with the Old Man of the Sands, I will be forever tormented by the Lady Ravar! For even when she is absent, I see and hear and feel the marks of that she had left behind. Everywhere I look there are children and Nearage carrying out her will. In the town square I hear her laughter in the stories retold by others. In the gardens the Craftsmen of Earth and Plant discuss her wisdom. Stars, even the Yondil Worm farm is not safe! For when I arrived this morning a young woman was avidly questioning their Carer in pursuit of some project she intends to present to her Tutor!' The King slumped and drew a long, sad breath.

'Heavens help me, sister. She leaves a train of light and laughter wherever she goes.'

Istreeth took a poker to the glowing coals at the base of the dying fire. She drew it along their angry bed, sending small red sparks flying. 'Like a trail of embers,' she said slowly, pleased with her foray into a little Fireplay.

No response being forthcoming from her brother, she looked up to find him wide-eyed, open-mouthed and fixated on the hearth she had just stirred. '*A trail of embers,*' he repeated gravely, to himself.

'Do not look so surprised, brother,' she said irritably. 'I have not heard you hold forth in the white robe so many times to have failed to learn a little of the Craft.'

'Oh, sister,' he said, rising to crouch before her and take her hands softly in his. 'You surely have the makings of a *Master* Bard, for you know not the power of the words you have just spoken.'

Now very confused, Istreeth frowned and subjected her raving brother to a cynical appraisal. 'Perhaps, you should go to bed, Aislyth. For I think you have imbibed too much Forest Warmth this evening.'

The King clasped her in a tight embrace before pushing himself back and smiling dazzlingly at her. 'Try as you like you will not vex me tonight, dear Istreeth. For you have exposed me for a fool and given me sight of what I was blind to see before!'

'I... do not understand,' she said, still uneasily.

'Then understand this,' he said with conviction, gripping her by the shoulders. 'You are right that my heart is for the most excellent and beautiful Lady Ravar! Until now I have been so stupid as to fail to see what lay before me. But now, I understand how the two roads that have brought me here meet.'

'Then… Then you will apply to Amalin for permission to make your suit?' Istreeth asked, cautiously.

'Oh yes, sister! Oh yes, I will.' He grinned to himself, his eyes dancing.

Istreeth sighed. 'I am glad to hear it, brother,' Istreeth said noncommittally, for she was still regarding him in bewilderment and disapproval. 'Tell me, now that you have finally seen the light, have you even considered in what manner you will present your petition?'

'Yes,' said the King seriously. 'In the only way I know how.'

CHAPTER 7

The Burning City, Fifth Year of the Dancer, early winter.

The King of the Sands silently skipped around his private quarters. He triumphantly pointed at an invisible opponent on the other side of his favoured wicker table, then knelt down on the floor in front of it to inspect his victory once again.

Before him stood a perfectly symmetrical bridge made of just fifteen polished stone blocks. He had positioned them so that they overpassed the line symbolising the river on the board, and left the remaining wall, from which the pieces used to construct the bridge had been taken, both stable and elegant.

With some trepidation, he picked up a small weight from the set of scales he always used during negotiations. He wavered slightly, keeping his hand that held the smooth, round disc suspended above the little crossing.

He dared himself to do it. He carefully placed the leaden circle at the centre of the bridge and cackled with delight as it stood firm. The King hopped to his feet once again and scurried over to his bed of cushions where he sprawled himself and aimed a gleaming smile at the ceiling.

'Come!' he responded to a knock at the door. The Kingdoms Post messenger hastily made his way over to his King, made a quick bow and presented him with a pile of letters. The Old Man of the Sands grimaced at its size, but the young man who had delivered them turned his load at an angle so that the King could see the format and handwriting of that which had been placed at the top.

It was a thick, brown packet with the hallmarks of Forest and Market Kingdoms. The sophisticated scrawl in distinctive burgundy ink was none other than that of his daughter Jazya. He gave an involuntary gasp of pleasure, sprang to his feet and snatched it from the collection. Without so much as an acknowledgement to the Post messenger, he turned and scurried over to his table, where he unceremoniously swept the blocks to one side. Both bridge and wall collapsed, sending small stone pieces tumbling to the floor.

Ignoring the mess entirely, the Old Man of the Sands broke the seal of the large envelope. It contained a number of thicker sheets in addition to the usual low-quality cream paper that the Forest People considered satisfactory for written correspondence. The delivery man quietly placed the rest of the stack on a side table and crept out. The King read the letter.

Father, with my great thanks for your many letters and all love and kind wishes in return to you and my sisters.

The winter in the Forest has now begun in earnest. Everywhere one looks people are clad in thick woollen cloaks and fires blaze in every hearth.

Although many of the trees have lost their leaves, I find that I still enjoy the beauty in the intertwined shapes of the empty branches. I enclose some sketches of these that I have made under the tutelage of an Artist of the Gold Level, here in Highturth.

The King of the Sands swelled with pride as he leafed through his daughter's charcoal sketches on the stiffer leaves beneath the missive.

Everyone here is already excited about the Winter Dance. In the Forest communities the solstice festival takes the form of a costumed ball and this year's theme has been set by King Aislyth as 'creatures from the ancient tales.' We are all spending every moment of the rest days with a needle and thread as there is great competition for the winter wreath, the prize awarded in each town to the man or woman judged to have created the best outfit. You will be glad to know that my choice is the Sly Salamander and that Gretan has constructed a great hump for his interpretation of the Stubborn Camel!

The King rumbled a small chuckle, picturing his son-in-law in such ludicrous attire. Good, he thought. Gretan's return to the woods had not dulled his sense of humour. He read on.

I have been spending one afternoon a week with the pupils of our Young School, who are learning about the different Kingdoms. They can't imagine a sea of sand and believe I am trying to deceive them when I describe our lizards and camels! I am also due to visit the Final School in the New Year. Our resident Tutor has been inspired by the efforts of the Lady Ravar in the Capital, who has introduced a rolling programme of guest speakers and short courses about the Crafts to her curriculum. Stars know what I will have to say about fauna that would be of interest to Nearage, but I shall try my best. I thought I might start with something unusual such as carnivorous plants – what do you think?

He thought it an excellent idea. With the unique insight of one who had sired so very many offspring in an age where children were so few, he considered that he had a fair idea of what made the young tick. In his experience, all juveniles, from babes to adolescents – or even Nearage – could be easily fascinated, provided you applied one of the three key descriptive criteria: strange, beautiful or horrible.

Have you solved the Engineer's test yet? You said in your last letter that you felt you were close to cracking it. If so, and if you are ready for a new challenge, I have come across a Woodland knot puzzle that I believe you will enjoy. Send word and I will have instructions and a set made up or, if you cannot wait for a parcel delivery, I shall send a diagram of manufacture direct to the Masons in the Burning City.

Please kiss all of my sisters who reside with you and remember me to them. Remember also the love I bear for you and drink a little less Sunbiter, for it worries dear Zankira, dreadfully.

Your fond daughter,

Jazya.

The King smiled, then grimaced, then growled. So, his youngest daughter had enlisted even the distant Jazya to intercede against the dangers of imbibing too much of a good thing. The Old Man of the Desert was quite defeated. If he could not escape the nagging of his female relations, even when he had sent them to the other side of the Upper Face, then there was not a glimmer of hope for a carefree life.

A gong sounded indicating the eighth hour and the King steeled himself to getting up and making his way to the Palace Hall. The main order of business that day was taking receipt of the annual gifts from his counterparts in the other Five Kingdoms. It was not a prospect to which he looked forward.

The ceremony and long, gushing explanation that accompanied the presentation of each gift was always a most drawn-out and dull affair. Even worse was the fact that most of the other Kingdoms' ideas about presents were quite different from his own. He could count on his fingers the number of Masterpieces and rarities that had arrived at the Palace which he hadn't positively disliked and even fewer that served any useful purpose.

That was, if you discounted those from Snowseal since the accession of Queen Liis. Now there was a woman with sense. Although he had never met or corresponded directly with her, the King of the Desert held her in rather higher opinion than his other brothers and sisters in rule.

For a start, there was the fact that she *had* never tried to induce him to travel to Snowseal to see her. And, equally importantly, she seemed to desist from sending embassies to the Sands unless it was absolutely essential. This may have been, in part, because the land of ice was necessarily cut off from the rest of the Kingdoms for a season, when the seas were too dangerous to cross. However, the King considered that this too, was a favourable aspect of Snowseal. If only the Sands were so impassable, he might too afford a little welcome respite.

The Old Man of the Sands reflected that, in reality, their Kingdoms were not so very different, other than in temperature. Perhaps the People of Ice too, had had to develop some rational thought and humour in order to be able to cope with life in their own desert.

After enduring three predictably tedious hours in which he had been presented with an ugly gold statue, a passable wooden gilt table and some sort of firecracker rocket whose secrets he would be interested to know when he lit it later that night, the King was fatigued and longing for the comfort of his chamber. There were still two benefactions to go and, with a weary wave, he instructed his keen herald to marshal in the deputation from the Plains.

With great pomp a trumpet sounded, and in came six leather-clad, bronze-skinned men and women, towing a ludicrously decorated, agitated stallion. The animal was the largest of its kind that the King had ever seen.

'And what,' he said, with a look of unconcealed horror, 'is this?'

A courtier rushed to his side to inform him. 'This, Your Majesty, is a horse.'

The King had to restrain a sarcastic reply. Instead, he settled for, 'I see.'

'This stallion, Sire,' the earnest man persevered, 'is the finest of its class, bred by the great horse-tamers of Plainsmeet.' The Plains People swelled, visibly.

'Is it indeed?' the King mumbled, suspiciously. He looked over the beast, noting the way it skittishly stamped its hooves. He eyed it with dislike, sure that it felt the same way about him.

'And what does it eat?' asked the King, innocently.

'Grass, Your Majesty,' came the reply before, realising the obvious issue, adding rather lamely, 'and hay…'

'And how much load does it bear?' continued the King, warming to his theme.

The courtier looked strained. 'It is not a beast of burden, Your Majesty. It is for riding. The Stallions of Plainsmeet are remarkable for their speed.'

The Old Man of the Sands was quite sure that they were. He was also quite sure that nothing could compel him to ride such a creature anywhere. Even if it did not throw him from its back within ten minutes out of sheer spite, it was likely die of thirst half the way to the nearest oasis on any worthwhile journey.

What, the King thought despairingly, *am I do with the poor animal?* It was so clearly unfit for life in his realm and could not be put to any purpose of utility. Through the narrow slit window to his side, he considered the hot, sandy and shadeless expanse that would be its home.

By a sort of dark-humoured joke of the universe, he could also just make out the unmistakable silhouettes of a group of camels in the distance. If ever there was a more striking contrast, the King could not think of it. Camels were eminently sensible and admirable creatures. Not that they were sensible in themselves, of course. Most of the strange-featured, unkempt animals were of a nonchalant and lazy disposition. However, they were perfectly adapted for a desert climate, had remarkable endurance over long distances and were strong, if stubborn pack animals.

Heavens! the Old Man of the Sands thought. He would much rather have *any* old camel than some fancily groomed, uneconomical purebred *horse*, which was just as unimpressed by the situation as he was. He looked at his strange little audience of anxious courtiers, frowning

Plainsfolk and equine ill-temper.

'I think that such a *fine*,' the King forced the word through slightly gritted teeth, 'horse would benefit from a younger, fitter master than a geriatric such as I. Let it be sent to my daughter who dwells on the coast of the Sky Kingdom, for she is a Horsewoman of the Silver Level. Let the People of the Skies covet the marvellous skill and generosity of the People of the Plains, who have presented a Princess of the Sands with such a gift.'

The King was pleased with himself, not least because all in the room, perhaps even the horse, seemed to be delighted by his order. The Plains envoys felt honoured, his courtiers appreciated his skilful diplomacy. They also could not conceal from him the slight slackening of shoulders betraying their relief that none of them would have to be responsible for the welfare of the huge, inapt animal.

As the deputation were fawningly ushered out of the hall, the King allowed himself a fraction of hope and optimism. He felt sure that the representatives of Snowseal would continue the recent tradition of concise, acceptable illustrations of good will.

As the door to the chamber was held open, he was delighted to see that Queen Liis had not disappointed. A single, white-cloaked woman, wearing a careful headdress to protect her ashen skin, was walking towards his throne, holding but a small, cloth-wrapped parcel. The emblem upon her sash marked her as an Ambassador. Such people were only given this lofty status if they were personally trusted by their sovereign to speak for their Kingdom.

She bowed gracefully before the aged King and smiled simply up at him. 'Greetings from Her Eminence Queen Liis, Your Majesty.' The King smiled, and bowed obligingly. 'The Queen asks you to examine the sample inside this packet, Sire.'

The King took it gently and unfolded the loose material to find his wrinkled hands affected by the almost sensually soft white pelt of a Snow Hare. It was so light that he barely felt its weight in his hands, and so pure white in colour that it dazzled the eye.

'The Queen,' the Ambassador continued, softly, 'is aware that your daughter has lately become a resident in the Forest Kingdom, where seasons reign in alternating ascendancy.' The Ambassador smiled kindly. 'She did not want Princess Jazya, unaccustomed to the climate, to suffer from the bite of the Northern winter. Therefore she has had a shawl of this fur made for Her Highness and to be shipped forthwith by your assent.' The pale woman's lilac eyes had a penetrating quality.

The Old Man of the Sands radiated delight. 'Tell your Queen that I am much gratified by the consideration given to one who is beloved of me. I would have Her Majesty send such a beautiful garment to Jazya of Highturth without delay, for she has written to me only this week of the descending cold.'

He pressed the small package back to into the hand of its agent. 'Please see that this pelt, too, is put to good purpose,' he said warmly. The Ambassador made a parting bow and glided out of the room.

'Ha!' The King's singular laugh echoed around the room. An advisor who had watched the events of the day with increasing discomfort, breathed a slow sigh of relief. It had been a good judgement to place the party from Snowseal at the end of proceedings, for it had, in recent years, been the only episode of the ceremony that did not irk his King.

Deciding to strike while the iron was hot, he approached the Royal dais and made an obsequious bow. 'Sire, have you resolved what the Desert Kingdom might send in return to the Royal Houses of the North and West?'

The King of the Sands surprised his advisor by saying, 'Yes,' with alacrity. Without waiting for the question, the King elaborated, 'The Desert Kingdom will send envoys to those Kingdoms, each in possession of a camel from the Royal Stables.'

'Camels, Sire?' repeated the advisor, looking uncomfortable and unhappy.

'Yes, man, camels!' the King confirmed, irritably. 'I find that too many of the Kingdoms seem to concern themselves with trinkets of no value or beasts of bad character and characteristic.'

Airily and smiling slightly, he continued. 'Therefore, let us send them a gift of true worth which may prove its usefulness a better asset than some showy bauble. In any case, a camel is *required* by my daughter as part of her difficult task in educating the Younglings of the Forest.'

Still dismayed, the advisor bowed. 'Yes, Your Majesty.'

'However,' the King continued, 'as for Snowseal, a whitewash is no place for such an animal.' He rounded on the discomforted man before him, adding, 'And it shall not be levelled at *my* door, that I sentence creatures to be incarcerated in unsuitable realms. No, I should like a copy of the Logician's puzzle in my quarters to be created and sent to the good Lady of Snowseal. I am of the certain belief that she is most deserving and capable of rising to its challenge.'

Frowning and helpless, the advisor bowed his obedience.

The Old Man of the Sands subjected him to a glance of distaste before hopping down from the richly decorated throne and skipping through the large, heavy doors.

Through them, his courtiers peered and saw him scurrying like a scuttling insect across the sand. He seemed to be heading in no particular direction, for all that could be seen on his horizon were the outlines of a caravan of camels, distorted by the heat. They exchanged troubled but resigned glances as they moved off to effect his orders.

The King of the Desert lay in the sand, hot from the day's rays. The camel next to him broke wind. The King did the same, closing his eyes in a happy doze.

CHAPTER 8

Forestfyth, Fifth Year of the Dancer, winter.

Istreeth waited for the Nearage to close the gate before returning to the Assembly Hall to speak with Ravar.

It had been a strange last month. At home it had felt lonely. Aislyth had been quiet and absorbed, spending most evenings at the fireside and disinterested in company. He had seemed indifferent even when a deputation from the Kingdom of the Sands had hauled a great hulking, awkward-looking creature into the Palace Square. It had immediately set about eating much of the ornamental shrubbery, causing pandemonium among the Palace Staff. The only accompanying note to this rather late and unusual gift had stated that Jazya required its use in Highturth and so Istreeth had suggested that this instruction might be followed straight away. Normally the King would have found the whole debacle hilarious but he just shrugged and smiled distractedly.

Things felt rather odd at the School too. This was because, despite the ongoing popular classes with Armick and his assistant, the rest of the teaching had fallen back to its Tutors.

Most of the other regular visitors had been otherwise occupied: Fiance's introduction into the art of cooking had been suspended while her team began preparations for the winter banquet; Master Eduerd had been away in Marketdawn for almost four weeks and the King had confined himself to appearing only for his fortnightly night tale. Even Lethan had an important project at the Carpentry workshop which had precluded him from being able to join Amalin's music lessons. The School had felt strangely mundane and empty.

The Princess on the other hand, had spent as much time as her duties had allowed, shadowing Ravar. She had grown quite proficient as Chair of the Assembly and had begun her own discreet workshop course that introduced the basics of two-dimensional art forms. She was proud of having been acknowledged as a Teacher of the Bronze Level in such a short time and had no intention of lessening her efforts.

She held this in mind to give her confidence as she came into the presence of her instructor.

'Master Ravar?' Ravar looked up from a book and smiled. 'I wonder if I might put an idea to you?'

Ravar made a point of putting down her tome to show the Princess that she held her full attention.

Istreeth cleared her throat and spoke with careful precision. 'It occurs to me that the Nearage would benefit from a break in the routine into which we have, by necessity, fallen during the past month.'

Ravar held her gaze evenly, and gave a single nod as a sign for her to continue.

'I have been thinking about the skill our Nearage are beginning to show in the formal spoken arts of the Assembly. Given the short time they have been receiving training, I believe we may consider their abilities unusually proficient.' Ravar said nothing but continued to listen, with interest.

'However, I am conscious that those of Age have responsibilities beyond the lofty affairs of Kingdom and the pursuit of the High Ways,' Istreeth continued. 'Much of their lives will be dependent on the ability to communicate freely and informally across Kin, culture and Craft.'

Ravar's eyes flashed keenly. 'And you have a suggestion as to how we might better prepare them in this field?' she asked.

Istreeth nodded. 'As part of my endeavours to improve myself in the path of the Tutor, I have given a little time to watching the schooling of the Young.' Ravar lit up, unaware but pleased that Istreeth should have taken such an initiative.

'As the nature of their curriculum is weighted towards the acquisition of knowledge of the Six Kingdoms and their customs,' she continued, 'I have noted the skill that teachers of the Young must deploy to ensure that their delivery is varied and engaging. It struck me that it would be an excellent challenge to put to our Nearage, if we could find a suitable topic, to ask them to plan and deliver a small series of lessons for some of the children of the city.'

Ravar smiled. 'It is an excellent idea, Istreeth! What better and more discerning audience for our Nearage to try to enthuse?' Istreeth beamed. 'Tell me,' Ravar went on quickly, 'do you have an idea as to an apposite theme?'

Istreeth bit her lip before replying, 'I did wonder, given that the whole town is in a state of excitement about the Winter Dance, whether we might use that very event as the guiding premise?'

'A good idea,' Ravar replied without hesitation. 'Please make the necessary arrangements. I shall look forward to following the Nearage's progress.' *And yours*, she thought. Istreeth beamed, bowed and left the room.

Ravar listened to the echo of steps fade into the distance and looked around the empty Assembly Hall. Istreeth had been right, the Nearage needed a change. Things seemed rather dull at the moment. Not that she hadn't been enjoying her work or the company of her colleagues at the School. And it was hardly as if she wasn't busy. She and Amalin had been working in the central Administration as part of their Kingdom Service and had spent their rest days renovating their cottage and dining with friends. The remainder of their spare time was spent indulging their own respective intellectual and musical pursuits.

And yet, it *had* felt strange these last weeks. Everyone had missed the frequent calls and conversation at the School of those additional people who had become so much part of its character and appeal.

'Ready?' called Amalin from the corridor.

Joining her friend, Ravar surprised her by stopping her and reaching for her heart. Amalin reciprocated at once.

When they parted Amalin stared carefully into Ravar's face. 'We are a silly pair, you and I,' she said, smiling sadly. 'Are we so moderated by their absence, even when we have each other?' Ravar wore an unreadable expression somewhere between guilt and annoyance.

'Do not deny it, Ravar, for you know I feel it too. If it makes you feel better, I did hear from Fiance that Eduerd is due to return to the Forest next week.'

'You did?' said Ravar quickly, betraying more enthusiasm than she would have liked. 'I do wonder what has kept him so long from his Kingdom.'

Amalin frowned. 'He did not tell you?' Ravar shook her head but looked at her friend enquiringly. Amalin waved the unspoken query aside. 'I have not the first idea, but I had imagined he had told you of his plans.'

'No,' replied Ravar, sullenly. 'He said only that he was travelling to the Market City and envisaged his business taking some weeks at least.'

'Fiance said something about him ending his stay at the house of Widow Frensith. Any idea who she is?'

Now it was Ravar's turn to frown. 'The Widow Frensith? Are you sure?' Amalin indicated that she was and unhappy to see Ravar's expression darken further. Ravar felt a small chasm forming in the pit of her stomach, but swallowed hard and enlightened her friend.

'I have met her, Amalin.'

'You have?'

'At Woodsedge with Fiance. She is a woman of incredible wealth and astonishing beauty. What she does not control with her purse, she certainly manages with her charm. Even Fiance was a little in awe of her.'

'Surely not!'

'She *was*,' said Ravar, seriously.

She went on, as if thinking aloud. 'What business can Eduerd have with such a woman? She trades in luxury goods from the Eastern Kingdoms and I cannot think any of her merchandise relevant to the Healing arts...' She trailed off, her brow creasing.

'Maybe he wasn't there to buy medical supplies,' suggested Amalin.

Ravar looked up sharply. 'What do you mean?'

'I *meant*, Ravar, that Eduerd practices countless Crafts which might require imported materials,' said Amalin, edgily.

'Such as what?'

Amalin grew short, throwing her arms up as she spoke. 'Stars, I don't know! Perhaps Eduerd just knows her! After all, Desledair is a Prince of Marketdawn and would be acquainted with most important personages. They probably met through him.'

Ravar was wearing an uncharacteristically sulky expression. 'Maybe Eduerd is quite taken with the widow and is paying her court.'

Amalin whirled round on her friend, suddenly understanding Ravar's strange behaviour. She took her hand gently and kissed it, saying, 'Oh Ravar, is that what has you so het up? Do you fear the good Doctor directs his affections in a direction you would reserve for yourself?'

Ravar looked away, flushed. Then, fighting for control and finding it in honesty, said, 'I confess there is some truth in what you say.'

'But I have only just told you of Eduerd's association with Widow Frensith! You cannot cook up a bleak imagining based on such a crumb of information. Where is Ravar, the shrewd analyst?' Amalin tapped the side of her friend's head.

Ravar sighed and massaged her temples. 'I do not know, friend. In fact, I really don't know what's wrong with me at the moment. Everything is making me irritable.'

'Aye, it has been a weird month or so,' agreed Amalin. Then more upbeat, 'But Eduerd will be home soon and we have the Winter Festival to look forward to. Let us hope some of those rather absent men might be in the market for a dance!'

Ravar gave a reluctant nod and looked at her wise friend. She smiled. 'Yes, Amalin, you are right. I think that all the People of the Forest could do with a good dance.

*

Some days later, Istreeth was very proud of the Nearage, who were giving their first class to the children of the local School of the Young. Having given them a few pointers, the Princess had left the planning largely up to her students. She was glad to see that they had obviously thought most carefully about the content and manner of delivery of their lesson.

After introducing themselves, each of the Nearage speakers had taken seats on the soft-rugged floor with the little ones, who ranged from seven to ten years old.

Instead of holding forth straight away, the Nearage had encouraged the children to share what they already knew of the Winter Dance and wait for questions to arise. These, they had anticipated in advance and had prepared some longer explanations and activities.

Ravar watched the lesson unfold with a mixture of pride and delight, though her gratification was directed more at her Bronze Level student whose critical and creative eye had led to the inception of the morning's occupation, than those pupils carrying it out.

She observed with interest as two of the Nearage, having been asked about the order and meaning of the set Dances, produced a large sheet of paper and a charcoal stick. They laid the page in the centre of the room and the little ones stood to be able to see it better.

Elpeen was sketching the outline of a sash. The children smiled as they recognised its form and one exclaimed, 'Dance pins!' as she added six thin strokes to the side of the upper part of her sketch.

Sethays gave a querying glance to his peer and took her affirmative response as leave to explain. 'Those of Age attending a Dance may wear six such pins from the day before the celebration. Each pin represents one of the formal Dances. They will be pinned with the bronze side facing outwards, indicating their availability to those who might seek their partnership.' He cast around at the young faces in the room. 'Now, who can tell me what happens next?'

One child's hand shot up in the air. 'If someone accepts they turn their pin around to gold,' she said.

'Quite so!' smiled Sethays. 'From the time that the pins are displayed, those wishing to secure a dance with a particular person may ask for any of the first five Dances. And the Sixth?' He waited to see if anyone would answer.

Seeing that no ideas were forthcoming, he explained. 'Well, the Sixth Dance cannot be reserved before the night itself.'

'Why?' a small girl asked.

'To keep things exciting!' he replied. The children grinned.

Now Elpeen took over. She took a narrow stick and pointed to the upper part of the sketch. She drew a line grouping together the top three pins. 'Who can tell me the meaning of these Dances?' The children were keen to oblige.

'The first is the Dance of Honour,' one said.

Elpeen smiled. 'Yes. Traditionally it is offered to the individual that the proposer holds in the highest regard. A suitor will try to secure the First Dance from the man or woman they hope to marry, but another person might simply wish to show his love and respect for a parent or sibling.'

'My dad says that King Aislyth always dances with his sister,' supplied a young voice, authoritatively.

'Indeed. Now, what about the Second?'

'It is a way of saying thank you,' said a boy, shyly.

'Excellent! The Second Dance is one of thanksgiving and respect. Royal Houses often devote this turn to visiting Ambassadors from other Kingdoms. A more common example might be that of an apprentice begging the hand of their Master to show their gratitude and admiration.' The children nodded their understanding.

'And the Third?' asked Sethays.

'The Dance of Souls!' chorused the little ones.

Sethays smiled. 'You are quite right! The Third Dance is for those bonded by blood, marriage or friendship. The dancing and music take a slower form so that all partners can remain hand to heart.' Istreeth and Ravar met each other's eyes and smiled. They both knew the magic of this Dance.

A curious child leaned over the sketch again and asked, 'What about the final three Dances?'

A few nervous glances passed between the Nearage. Having never actually attended a formal dance, they found that theory and second-hand anecdotes didn't really adequately prepare them for the question. Several pairs of eyes appealed to their Tutors.

'I suppose they signify something known only to those who share the dance,' supplied Ravar, smiling. She sent half a wink in Istreeth's direction, who supressed a smile.

One of the Nearage cleared his throat. 'Having discussed the meaning of the Dances, we now wondered if you would like to learn a few turns yourselves?' There were high-pitched squeals of delight which increased in magnitude as they caught sight of Amalin, who had arrived at the School of the Young to help provide the music for their moves.

Ravar slipped out at this point, intending to visit the library. She might also call upon Fiance, to see if she could elaborate further upon Eduerd's likely day of return.

*

On her way through the winding paths of the Forest City, Ravar heard the distant sound of a man singing the ancient Ballad of Summer. The vocalist possessed an exquisite voice. A bass, she thought, though Amalin would have known for sure. The song's words were quite beautiful, calling upon the constellations to bring eternal summer to the Forest. The verses had been set to an enchanting melody in a minor key. She slowed her pace to catch part of the refrain.

Heavenly stars, give me summer everlasting,
Where days always outlast the night.
All of my life give me sunlight forever,
Bathe my Soul in summer's bright light.

Ravar felt a shiver surge down her arms. The lyrics may have been simple, but in the command of that low voice, they were enrapturing. The singer reached the chorus once more, though he had adapted the content.

Queen of my heart give me summer everlasting,
For you are the sun of my life.
My darling, so fair, I will love you forever,
Give you all of the joys of my life.

Ravar was touched by the adaptation of the familiar words of the traditional marriage vows. Whoever had inspired the singer was either already, or soon to be, courted. A lucky woman, she thought.

Ravar breathed in deeply, taking in the rich scents of the cold undergrowth and walked on. She was so absorbed in her thoughts that she practically collided with Lethan, who was looking up at a tree, rather than the path in front of him.

'Oh, I am so sorry, My Lady!' he spluttered.

'Please, Lethan, I am not hurt. It is my fault for I was not paying attention,' Ravar reassured him. 'Was that you singing?'

Lethan's relief was quickly overtaken by puzzlement. 'Singing?'

'I heard someone singing the Ballad of Summer,' Ravar said, sheepishly. She realised she had blurted out the question before she had even said hello.

'Not me,' said Lethan, unfazed. 'Though the King has been known to sing among the trees and he does favour the old songs.' Ravar considered the deep voice she had heard. It was possible, she supposed.

'Well he had a fine voice, and had it been you, I would have paid you a compliment,' she said, mildly. 'As it is not, you shall have no such praise! However, it *is* good to see you. We have missed your company in the orchestra at the School. I hope you will find time to re-join us before long.'

'Yes indeed, Lady,' Lethan said in earnest. 'I shall be in attendance this week.'

Ravar was glad, but before she could say anything, Lethan interjected.

'Actually, I walked this way in the hope of meeting you. I was told you were teaching at the Young School today?'

'Yes and no. It is actually the Nearage who are teaching under the Princess' supervision.'

'And you are there to watch her,' Lethan said with a knowing smile. Ravar reflected that the Carpenter's cheerful, relaxed manner masked a mind that missed little.

Speaking as though she had not heard him, Ravar continued, 'I am indeed just come from the Young School. Amalin is still there and would, I am sure, like to see you.' She was hopeful that she might at least do some service to her friend.

'Thank you,' he replied, 'but as I said before, My Lady, it is you who I sought.'

Ravar hid her surprise. 'And now you have found me, My Lord,' she said, expectantly.

'Yes!' He laughed, a little nervously. 'Are you walking back to the School of the Nearage? I shall walk with you.' He held out his arm and Ravar took it. Despite not intending to go that way, she wanted to see what this was all about. She had a sneaking, hopeful suspicion.

Arriving at the main entrance of their destination, Lethan drew himself up with obvious effort. He treated Ravar to a wide smile and spoke quickly before he lost the courage to do so.

'Lady Ravar, I would speak with you of an important matter, if you are not otherwise engaged?'

Ravar eyed him carefully. 'Will you step inside, then?' she asked, gesturing toward the main door.

Inside, Lethan pulled a chair out from underneath a table in the workroom and offered it to Ravar. She accepted it with grace and laid her hands carefully in her lap. She looked up at Lethan, who had remained standing.

He said, solemnly, 'Lady Ravar, I have asked you to speak with me today as Keeper of the Heart of the Lady Amalin of the Plains. I appeal to you for permission to make my suit to the woman, whom my Soul desires.'

Such formal language seemed strange on the lips of Lethan. Even so. Ravar's heart leapt, and she had to control her instinct to embrace the nervous Carpenter, whose strained countenance was now searching her face. However, she knew the order of procedure and was determined to do it justice.

'Lethan of the Forest, do you have a gift to present to the Keeper of that heart which you hold so dear?' she asked, gently.

By way of answer, Lethan stepped forward and offered her his hand. His big blue eyes were excited and anxious all at once. Piqued, Ravar placed her hand in his and found herself being led from the room and along the corridor. Halting outside the Assembly room, Lethan turned to her. 'Forgive me, My Lady, but I am aware that your love of books has afflicted you?'

A little mortified, Ravar thought back to the scene some months ago, when Amalin had dragged Lethan from this very doorway while the Doctor was treating her neck.

'Yes…' she said, unsure of where this was leading.

Lethan drew her into the room, where, at the end stood a magnificent, wooden lectern, the likes of which she had never seen. Ravar gasped.

The workmanship was exquisite. The frame was carved from deep oak into the shape of the twisting trunk of an ancient tree and polished to such a high shine that it reflected the light from the narrow high windows of the room. From the trunk which was carved to look just like knotted bark, elegant branches grew up to shoulder height. The twisting forms flared out then curled in to support a wide stand, upon which a book or notes might be placed.

Ravar walked over to it and ran her fingers over its smooth, organic curves. 'It is magnificent, Lethan,' she said, almost at a whisper.

Lethan looked more relieved than pleased. He hastened to explain its features. 'The base is lined with felt so that it may be moved with ease in this hall should you wish it out of the way.' He demonstrated by gently pushing it and it slid without resistance across the floor.

'The height is made to complement your own, My Lady,' he continued. 'Standing, you should never need to stoop and your hands will be free to rest or be animated as you please. If you would rather be seated I will make up a tall stool from the same material in the coming weeks, for I have drawn up the design.' Ravar waved her hand to stop him from speaking further.

'It is my habit to stand, Lethan, as you know.' She approached him and this time made no effort to keep the warmth from her voice. 'Lethan of the Forest, your gift is acceptable to me as Keeper of the heart of Amalin of the Plains. State the nature of your love and that which you offer her to persuade me of your sincerity and suitability.' *As if such declarations are necessary,* she thought, happily.

Lethan looked pained. He glanced at the floor, hesitating for a moment before huffing and answering in his characteristically more free and informal speech.

'Lady, I do not have your skill for rhetoric and way with words so I shall not make an attempt to persuade you in this manner.' Seeing Ravar nod slightly, a smile on her lips, he gained a little more pluck.

'Ravar, believe me when I tell you that to me, Amalin is—' He seemed momentarily lost for words, before they spilled out with gushing emotion. 'She is every star in the sky, every note that I play, every tree in the Forest!' His eyes gleamed. 'She is everything to me and I am never as happy as when I am in her presence.' He wavered giddily on the spot as he continued, almost in a daze.

'Her Mastery as a Musician hardly needs affirming, but Amalin's tune plays to my very Soul and I am a better man for it. Is not every Soul that hears her? Why, the Great Musician of the Sky must long for her notes! She makes me long to further my own Crafts and ambitions simply so that I might find a rightful place in her shadow. And I do not simply speak as a man bewitched by her music, for I find inspiration in her humour, her kindness and her beauty. I would play forever her ridiculous games that have us all remember what it is like to be a child! I would…'

He paused, regaining his calm. He had the feeling that he had made his point. Lethan fixed Ravar with a more serious gaze and continued. 'As for what I can offer such a one as your Soul Friend, I confess I cannot claim to provide a Royal Seat.' He shrugged slightly and explained himself. 'I have heard that such advances may have been previously made.'

'They may have been contemplated but fortunately I have never had to consider such a request,' Ravar said, blandly. 'You, on the other hand are here doing just that. So tell me, My Lord, what life do you offer to my Amalin?'

Lethan replied soberly. 'I am a simple man, as you know, My Lady. I am Forest through and through. I offer her my home and a life among my people, while she may always carry her title as Plains if she wishes. To the Lady Amalin I offer a warm place as part of my family and Kin. You know many of that number and trust you understand the welcome she would receive.' Ravar nodded, thinking of Eduerd and Fiance.

'I offer her all my love and, I hope, much laughter. I promise to strive all my days to make her happy, no matter the darkness or difficulty life may bring. I offer her the very best of myself, in the hope she will give just a little, to me.' He ended there abruptly, his teeth clamped tight.

Ravar stepped forward and took this good man who had proved himself worthy, in her arms. What more could she wish for her closest and dearest friend than someone prepared to give so freely with his honesty of emotion?

Parting enough to smile up at his easy good looks, she said, 'Amalin is your muse then, Lethan? This Keeper opens the way.'

Lethan's eyes brimmed. 'Thank you, My Lady.' He smiled, shook his head slightly. 'But she is not my muse.'

'No?'

'She is the music.'

*

While Ravar was thus engaged, Amalin bid Istreeth farewell at the Young School and headed for the town centre. It was her intention to go to the Palace complex to see if Ravar was still at the library. Finding that she was not, Amalin was considering whether to make for the School of the Nearage or home, when she was hailed from across the market square by none other than the striking Doctor Eduerd, leading a large, black horse.

The animal was laden with saddlebags and its master was in riding gear. Amalin realised with surprise that he must have come to the town directly, rather than stopping at his cottage on the way.

'Greetings, My Lady Amalin!' He smiled as she walked closer. His voice was always so crisp and well-spoken. He did not have the local twang of the Forest People, more that of the wealthier merchants of Marketdawn. He bowed smartly.

'Hello, My Lord Eduerd,' she returned, somehow managing to make her own bow look sly. 'We had not expected your return until next week.' She thought of how thrilled Ravar would be.

'I did not realise that it was a matter of speculation,' Eduerd said, relaxed but bewildered.

Amalin ignored the statement in favour of getting down to the business that mattered. 'I am sure that Ravar would be happy to see you, My Lord. She has missed you, for the School has not been the same for your absence.'

Eduerd shifted, awkwardly for a man so usually composed. 'Indeed, I look forward to seeing her next week when I shall resume my lessons.' *Next week*, thought Amalin, *is five days away.* Had she been wrong about his feelings? Surely he would want to see Ravar before then.

'Will you not accompany me back to our house and join us for a drink or some supper?'

'I thank you, no, My Lady. I have much catching up to do, not least see to my apprentice who has been holding the fort while I have been away. Please do send my best regards to Ravar, though.'

Oh, best regards, she thought. Hardly likely to bring much joy. Amalin tried to hide her disappointment.

'However,' the Doctor drew closer to Amalin, meeting her eye with seriousness. 'I would be very glad if you would join me for dinner tomorrow night?'

Amalin beamed. 'Why yes, Eduerd, we would love to. I am sure that Ravar—'

'Just you, My Lady,' Eduerd interrupted.

His penetrating blue eyes locked hers with meaning. Amalin processed this and suddenly the whole conversation held a different meaning. She bit back a big smile and gave a dignified reply. 'I am taking the last class of the day tomorrow. Will you pick me up from my house at the nineteenth hour?'

'I will look forward to it.' Eduerd took her hand, kissed it and made off.

So will I, thought Amalin. She watched his toned form mount his horse with a lightness that would have been acceptable to a Plainsman. As he rode away she thought over what had just passed, trying to be sure of her theory. It was not the usual custom to invite an unmarried person unconnected by blood or kinship to one's home, unaccompanied.

However, one reason for an exception could be that such privacy was required in order to make an appeal to a Keeper.

Amalin raced home to find Ravar reaching their gate just as their cottage came in sight. Although she was bound by tradition to say nothing of what she suspected was in the offing, she was dying to at least tell her that Eduerd was returned.

Ravar, too, was alive with excitement and had not anticipated having to deal with her Soul Friend so soon. She had intended to take a few minutes to wait outside the door and compose herself.

'Well met, Ravar!' Amalin exclaimed, happily. 'I have good news for you!' They embraced.

'As have I for you, friend.'

'Well I will go first,' Amalin declared, darting to the kitchen area to pour them both a cup of Forest Warmth.

'Steady on!' protested Ravar.

'Well you will celebrate with me when I tell you that I have just seen Master Eduerd in town!' she exclaimed.

Ravar blinked. 'He is back already?'

'Yes!' Amalin cried, smiling eye to eye. 'Clearly the Widow Frensith's charms do not have such a hold on our good friend as you feared.' Amalin giggled, sidling up to Ravar with a cup.

Ravar did not match her jollity, but said, 'Is he still in town? You should have invited him to dine with us.'

'What do you take me for? I *did* make the offer but he said he was too busy. In any case I — *we* will see him next week.' Amalin suddenly clenched her jaws shut and, most uncharacteristically, seemed to have nothing else to say.

Ravar regarded her friend carefully. Had Amalin bitten something back? Sensing the scrutiny, Amalin seized the moment to change the subject. 'Anyway, what is *your* news?'

Ravar's eyes lit up like diamonds as she sat down gracefully on the sofa before her, a smile breaking through supressed lips.

Amalin's eyes widened in fascination. 'What?' she demanded, excitedly. When Ravar said nothing, she crawled along the long seat toward her.

'What?' she cried, this time at higher pitch and volume. She took her Ravar by the shoulders and playfully shook them.

Ravar pushed her back softly. She felt round for the fastening of her cloak which she had not taken off since entering the house. As she undid it, the dark cloth fell away from her shoulder, revealing the sash beneath. She touched her hand to the upper part and Amalin caught the glint of bronze upon it.

Amalin made a huge gasp and stared at it with eyes like saucers. 'It is... you have...'

Ravar let out a snicker. 'Finally I have silenced you, friend! I should accept applications to court you more often!'

Amalin picked up a cushion and threw it at her. 'Is it...?' She stopped herself. Ravar could not tell her and she should not ask. 'Sorry, don't answer that.'

'I would not have done so in any case. However, I would not have given my leave lightly. You know that.'

In the long, happy silence that followed, Amalin lay her head in Ravar's lap, fingering the bronze feather pinned to Ravar's sash that hung above her. Ravar's heart swelled at the happy glow emanating from her treasured friend.

CHAPTER 9

Forestfyth, Fifth Year of the Dancer, winter.

The next morning Ravar was humming the Ballad of Summer as she dressed. Amalin came in to tie her hair. She chose a shining gold ribbon, working it into small plaits that linked together loosely to form a lattice over the free, straight locks beneath.

Amalin hummed the harmony of the song with her until her work was done. 'We are mid-winter and it seems everyone is still pining for summer,' she reflected, standing back to admire her own handiwork.

'I don't mind the winter,' said Ravar.

'That is because you never feel the chill.' It was true that Ravar hardly ever felt cold. The counterweight was that she had suffered through some of the hotter summers of the Plains.

'Have you been out with the King?' asked Amalin.

Ravar was thrown by the question. 'The King?'

'He has been singing that song all week,' said Amalin.

'Then it *was* him that I heard in the woods,' Ravar said with a little awe.

'He has a wonderful voice, does he not?' said Amalin, admiringly.

'Magnificent,' agreed Ravar.

'*Magnificent,* Ravar?' Amalin giggled. 'I had thought you over your liking for our handsome royal, but I must have been mistaken!'

'Do not start, Amalin,' said Ravar, tiredly.

'Ha! Oh, try and stop me now, friend! Why, isn't he coming tomorrow evening to sit at the fire? Perhaps you should ask him to sing!'

'He is taking the evening class as you say,' Ravar said, evenly. 'However, I shall not see him, for Princess Istreeth has invited me to dine with her at the Palace.'

Amalin snorted her disappointment that the opportunity to tease her friend had been cut short. Remembering her own pending dinner date, she enquired as to Ravar's plans for that evening.

'I told Fiance I would assist her in the kitchens. Do you want to come?' said Ravar.

'Oh, I am meeting with the other band members to go over some of the music for the Dance,' she improvised.

'I hope you are not intending to sit out the formal dances, Amalin. *Some* might be very disappointed to miss a chance to pair with you.' She tilted the feather on her sash with her finger so that it reflected the light.

Amalin had already considered both the pin and Ravar's point at length. 'Only the final one,' she conceded. 'But Lethan is, after all, likely to join me in the orchestra.' They both giggled.

*

Before closing up the School at the end of the day, Amalin arranged herself neatly. She had chosen a simple, fitted maroon gown that fell at the knee, but adorned herself with a bronze necklace and earrings. Although she knew that her appearance was not of any significance to Master Eduerd, she thought that it was important, if her notion of what was in the offing was correct, to dress well for the occasion.

The Doctor was waiting at the School gate as she let herself out of the entrance of the main building. Amalin internally rejoiced in her preparation, for he was formally attired in a silver and dark grey long waistcoat over a white shirt and dark leggings. His smart, black coat was draped over his arm, for he had walked from his cottage and was warm from the exercise.

Darkness had already fallen by the early evening at this time of year, but Eduerd knew the route like the back of his hand and led his guest by lantern through the woods with confidence. He was glad that although cool, the weather had not yet turned wet and their progress was swift. He had exhausted just about all the small talk topics he possessed, when his cottage came into view.

Amalin stopped, staring at the rounded wooden silhouette, light breaking out through cracks around the door and from the windows. However, it was not the house itself which had frozen her in her tracks, but what surrounded it. A halo of Glow Flies circled the house so that it appeared covered by a giant, golden dome. She turned to the Doctor, a look of thrill about her.

Eduerd smiled and explained. 'I am afraid they are a vanity, My Lady.' She frowned incomprehension. 'About you,' he continued, 'you will see my little garden.' Amalin looked about her. It was certainly not little. He wandered over to a bed that lined the path to his main door, crouched down and beckoned Amalin to join him. 'See this.' He pawed at a plant at his feet.

Amalin looked down in the glowing light and observed an unremarkable-looking small shrub. As she was never one for mincing her words, she said, 'I am afraid, My Lord that, to me, it just looks like a weed.'

'Ha! Well you are right, My Lady. It has no discernible value of which I am familiar. However, the Glow Flies love it.' Amalin gazed around the beds and caught sight of the same small bushes planted at regular intervals around the plots. She smiled.

'Does the light not keep you awake at night?'

'Ah, no. Thankfully they seem to switch off, for the most part, by the twenty-third hour.' He unlatched the unusually carved, stout door and opened it for Amalin. 'Will you step in?'

Inside, Amalin was struck by the enticing smell of cooking, intermingled with herbs and the scents of dried flowers and spices which were neatly arranged on dozens of small shelves in the kitchen. The house opened out into wings on either side. She could see a laid table in the room that led off the kitchen and a spacious seating area beyond it. Eduerd waved toward the latter and she took a seat on a comfortable leather armchair which was draped in a very soft blanket.

'Welcome to the Den, My Lady. I hope you are hungry,' said Eduerd, handing her a cup of warm, spiced Forest Brew.

'Whatever you have left cooking certainly smells good,' Amalin replied. 'The Den? That is the name of this house?'

'Just the room in which we are seated,' said Eduerd, looking about him fondly. 'It is not of my naming. My Kin are responsible for that. Lord Desledair cannot understand how I tolerate such a location and form of abode, but even he admits to being happy and relaxed in this room.'

Amalin most certainly felt that way. She wondered what Ravar would think when she saw it all. The house was remote and strange and beautiful. The whole place was lined with books and potions, maps and devices. It resembled a museum crossed with a library. In fact, it bore a remarkable resemblance to Ravar's study, so she was bound to like it.

After a delicious supper, over which Eduerd described some of his travels to the East and the pair compared amusing stories from their respective experiences of the people and places of Marketdawn, the table was cleared and Eduerd refilled their cups.

Amalin decided it was time to get down to business. 'My Lord, it has been a most pleasant evening sharing your company,' she said carefully. 'However, I do not believe you are in the habit of entertaining single persons in your home on a whim.' Eduerd saw the sparkle in her eye. 'Why do you not dispense with the niceties and get to the point of your asking me here?'

Eduerd put down his cup and looked at her. 'Very well, My Lady.' He was not surprised by her directness, having regularly encountered it at the School. And with Desledair for a Soul Friend, he was quite capable of facing and matching it head on.

'As I am quite sure you have already guessed, I wish to appeal to you as the Keeper of the heart of Lady Ravar of the Forest.' It felt odd using her full title. However, it was protocol he was not prepared to ignore this time.

Amalin regarded him brightly, internally jumping for joy. She had known it! 'You would offer your suit, Lord Eduerd?'

'I would, My Lady.'

She raised an eyebrow. 'And what is your gift?' This was so *exciting*!

Eduerd marvelled at her bluntness. Clearly Amalin was enjoying herself. He exhaled, pursing his lips. 'It is behind you.'

Amalin swung round to the polished sideboard at her rear. Upon it was a large, ornate book. It was in dark-blue dyed leather, stitched in silver thread. 'This?' she asked, taking it carefully. Eduerd nodded.

The tome had a pleasant weight about it, with thick binding and pages. The cover had been imprinted with a hot iron to form the image of the constellation of the Musician. Amalin ran her fingers over the uneven surface, admiring the inlay, also in silver.

'I confess I had to seek a professional for the binding, but the illustrations and calligraphy are my own,' said Eduerd, as she opened it at random.

She was overwhelmed by what she found within. The double page spread before her was beautifully decorated with a repeating dolphin motif. On the left, an immaculate musical score filled the page. To the right were verses of the Song of the Lost Mariner. As she thumbed through the other pages, all intricately illustrated, she found traditional music and lyrics from across all six Kingdoms.

'I fear you will know many of the songs already, My Lady,' said Eduerd, apologetically. 'However, I did manage to persuade an eastern merchant to impart some of the songs of the Far Sands which I hope will be new to you?'

'Indeed they are,' Amalin murmured wistfully, still gazing upon the pages. To her mind, each was a work of art. 'It is a magnificent tome. Ah!' she exclaimed, almost in a whisper. 'Now I know what you were doing in Marketdawn all that time.'

The Doctor smiled, shyly. 'Do you find my gift acceptable?' he asked.

Amalin broke free of her trance. 'Hm? Oh yes! It is the loveliest thing I have ever possessed!' Her smile lit up her face. 'Now, Master Eduerd,' she said, without pause, 'you must state the nature of your love and what you have to offer to be worthy of the sister of my Soul.' With that, she placed the book closed on the table and sat back expectantly.

Eduerd did not reply at once. Instead he looked directly at her, his face calm but serious and straightened in his seat. Amalin did not hurry him. For one thing, she was not averse to taking in his crystal blue-eyed stare and, for another, she thought that she had a fair idea of what he was going to say. At length he rose from his chair and said mysteriously, 'Do you mind heights, My Lady?'

'No-o…' said Amalin, intrigued but cautious. Whatever she had expected, it was not this.

'Then, come with me,' he said.

Amalin followed Eduerd up a right-angled staircase to the upper floor landing, where Eduerd reached up to open a trapdoor in the roof. He unfolded a collapsed wooden step-ladder that sat against the wall below it and set it beneath the hole. Through it, peeped the twinkling night sky.

Without hesitation, the Doctor nimbly climbed the ladder, only turning back to the fascinated Amalin when he had cleared the gap. He reached down a hand and she scaled the steps to clasp it, his strong arm pulling her up into the cold of the night.

Up on the roof, Eduerd folded a cloak around her shoulders, but she barely noticed. From this vantage point, she realised for the first time, why he chose to live in this remote part of the Forest.

The dead tree whose base formed the backbone of the dwelling must once have dominated the surrounding area, for the nearest great trees were some way off. This, combined with the extensive cultivated areas surrounding the cottage, meant that it sat within a rare clearing in this part of the Eastern Forest. The view of the stars was without parallel in Forestfyth, where even comparatively open areas such as the Palace Grounds might be overshadowed by smaller trees and follies.

Amalin gazed up at the bright moon and stars, and exhaled slowly. She relaxed, letting her eyes adjust to the darkness so that more and more of the jewels of the heavens came into sight.

'Can a woman of the Plains climb?' asked Eduerd, a little maliciously, breaking into her thoughts.

'Climb?' This time he had really taken her by surprise.

'The best view is from the arms of the old tree.' With that, Eduerd began to scale the branches behind them, leaning down once again to offer Amalin his hand.

She followed him carefully, though even to her, the knotted arms of the once fine Broadbirch presented no great challenge. They settled, their backs against the trunk, on two arms that protruded from the trunk just apart from one another at disjointed levels.

There was silence between them for a few minutes, while they took in all that shone above them, but Eduerd was the one to break it. 'You asked me to state the nature of my love and what I have to offer, My Lady. Well, here you see the first thing I learned to love.' He swept his arm across the night sky.

'The Heavens have always held my fascination. Who cannot be attracted by their beauty, their mystery, their elegance? Understanding the movements of the moons and planets is considered, by many, to be one of the most challenging disciplines and I have made it my life's ambition to master the art. In fact, since I can remember I have had a burning desire to better all of my Crafts of the Mind in the hope of walking the Higher Way.'

Eduerd paused, turning to Amalin. He spoke again, this time with quietly burning intensity. 'Ravar is the only person I have ever known with whom I believe I could share that journey.' He paused again, before continuing. It was almost as if he were thinking aloud.

'In truth I do not believe I have, or will encounter again a mind like hers… so sharp, such capacity for learning. I do not doubt that she could master any discipline. I am, in fact, quite sure that she is capable of outstripping many of my best endeavours.'

Suddenly, he grinned. 'She has all this and yet she is also able to make all in her company smile. Even Desledair likes her! She is all that is desirable in conversation, both high and low, even if the beauty of her features were not already enough to bewitch all who behold her! Stars! What I would give to walk together through the world for just day in her Soul's embrace…' He trailed off.

'And what *do* you give, Master Eduerd?' Amalin prompted, seriously.

Eduerd faced her once again and spoke evenly. 'My Lady, I offer her only what I can. I offer her this.' He spread his arms about him, encompassing the view, the gardens, the cottage and the tree. 'I offer her my strange existence at the margins between Market and Forest. I offer her my arm in the quest to seek the secrets of all of the Kingdoms, to traverse the sands and snows and mountains of every realm. I offer her a partnership in the highest ambition, and my pledge never to dominate or fawningly serve. I offer the Lady Ravar my heart as a man. From me, she would know the love and warmth of my Soul and body. She and her Kin will always be at home in the Den, and she would share with me this place beneath the stars.' He stopped. 'Tell me, Lady, is it enough?'

Amalin did not look *at* him, but through him, as if she were straining to see something far in the distance. At length she intoned gently, 'It is enough. Lord Eduerd of the Forest, I open the way for you to make your suit to Ravar of the Forest. Present your token so that all may know her heart is sought.'

Eduerd smiled with his eyes as he passed the bronze feather brooch across the drop below to the Keeper that had accepted his bid.

The silence of deep thought remained between them even as he escorted her home.

*

'That was a late rehearsal,' commented Ravar, as Amalin came through the door, throwing her cloak and hat messily at the stand. Predictably they slid along the main pole to form a crumpled heap on the floor. Oblivious to this, she hopped over to the seating area, where Ravar was huddled up with a book and collapsed into the opposite end of the long couch, flinging off her shoes and settling her legs up on the soft cushioning.

'Yes, well I may not have been entirely honest with you earlier,' she said, grinning.

Ravar looked up over her book and, catching her friend's expression, let it slide gently to the floor. She leaned forward, eyes narrowed. 'Amalin? While I have been toiling in the kitchens with Fiance, what is it that *you* have been cooking?'

*

Both women were in good form the following morning and their little house was filled with humming and laughter as they dressed and prepared for a day.

A Kingdoms Post messenger arrived with a letter from Amalin's parents addressed to them both and they reflected that sooner or later, they would have to write and share their news. There was also a short card from the Palace, reminding Ravar of her engagement to join Istreeth for supper, over which they might discuss the plans for the School of the Nearage in the coming year. It seemed a little unnecessary, as Ravar was not one to forget an invitation. Perhaps it was just the nature of the formal procedures of the Palace.

'You do not mind seeing the students out and settled for their Bardic Tale, do you?' she asked Amalin.

'Certainly not, though I am sorry that you will miss it.' It would be the first that her friend *had*, ever since her first experience of the King in his element. Ravar actually looked slightly disappointed, despite her overall excitement and hopeful suspicions regarding her friend's latest adornment to her sash. Amalin rolled her eyes. 'Heavens, Ravar, cheer yourself! There will be many more tales, I am sure!'

'Sorry,' said Ravar, recognising the truth of this. 'I will be back late this evening, I should think. Don't wait up.'

'Pah! As if I would, just to hear you spout endless educational ideas that you have formed with the Princess. You two are incorrigible.'

*

Ravar had been dismissed by her own students during the morning lesson with Master Armick as they were going to discuss the Winter Dance costumes. This gave her some unexpected free time and she went to make up a brazier in one of the other workshops that would be in use in the afternoon. She might never feel the cold, but there were always loud complaints from the Nearage if the winter chill invaded their classrooms.

She was startled to find it already occupied by Eduerd who was seated, reading through some notes. As she jumped, he looked up and became a picture of gentlemanly concern as he realised he had been the cause of her fright.

However, Ravar did not give him a chance to apologise, exclaiming, 'My Lord Eduerd, you are back! I am so glad to see you!' Remembering her manners, she quickly bowed and was favoured with a smiling reply in kind.

'Thank you, My Lady. I am sorry to have neglected my duties at the School for so long.' Ravar considered that she would have much rather heard that he had some pleasure in seeing her again, than a reference to failing in his *duty*.

'Well, I hope that you have no more prolonged adventures beyond the Forest planned in the immediate future, My Lord. The students missed you.' *Stars, now I am doing it,* she thought.

Eduerd seemed to sense something awkward in the tone of their conversation and did his best to remedy things. 'No indeed, Lady, I am fixed for the rest of the winter at least. I do hope we shall be able to share some time and conversation soon, for the People of Marketdawn have worn me down with their endless bartering and talk of trade. I have missed having an intellectual to spar with.' He treated her to a smile. This was more like it.

'Master Eduerd!' came a shrill cry from behind them. Three Nearage students had come to fetch materials from an adjacent room and had overheard the Doctor's voice. They now hung at the door, excitedly, welcoming back one of their favourite teachers. Before long, the full contingent had arrived and were animatedly telling them of their activities in his absence.

Eventually Armick the Tailor appeared, wearing a forgiving grin. Nonetheless, the Doctor scolded them lightly. 'Get back to your lesson, all of you, or Master Armick will not want to give you his time again.'

There were shrieks of protest from the Nearage. 'He cannot abandon us, Master Eduerd, for we are engaged in a top-secret operation,' one said, overdramatically. The others laughed.

'Top secret? Well now I am intrigued.'

The same student grinned, admitting, 'It is no secret really. We are making costumes for Master Amalin and Master Ravar to wear at the Winter Dance.'

'But they are not allowed to know what we have chosen and made until the day,' another student added, quickly.

'I see,' said Eduerd, nodding sagely but flashing Ravar a wicked look.

'Are you coming to the Forestfyth Dance this year, Doctor Eduerd?' another student asked, boldly. Several of the other Nearage turned to hear his answer. He often attended the seasonal festivals in Marketdawn, but they had enjoyed his company at the Autumn Feast and, although their age prevented them from attending the winter celebration, were keen to know if he would join the Forest People once again.

Ravar realised that she had not even considered the possibility that Eduerd would not be there and so she too awaited his response with anxious interest.

'Well, I had thought to visit my Soul Friend at the Market Hub…' Eduerd said thoughtfully. Ravar's heart sank. The pin on Amalin's sash, then, could not be from him. For surely he would wish to secure a dance with her if he had. Her mind whirred, but her thoughts were interrupted as he continued, jovially.

'But now that I hear that the only way to find out the nature of your tailoring efforts is to attend the Dance in Forestfyth, I suppose I shall have to alter my plans!' The Nearage exchanged looks of triumph. Ravar was attempting to work out whether the Doctor spoke in earnest or was playing with his audience. He certainly had a gleam in his eye. She tried to not think about whether he might also be playing with her.

*

As Ravar and Eduerd were parting company at the School gate, the imposing form of Fiance hailed them from a distance. Without bothering to make a formal bow, she embraced both of them in her cushion-like arms and smiled brightly.

'Ah Doctor, Ravar, are you done with your toils for the day? You must both come and dine with us this evening. My sister and her husband have come to stay and I wish them to be treated to a good supper. You must come and make up the numbers for I have cooked pies and puddings and there will be meats and soup and all things good.' She looked at the pair critically a moment, before adding, frowning, 'And it looks as though you both could do with a hearty meal.'

Eduerd was treated to especially severe scrutiny and she said accusingly to him, 'Too much work and gallivanting around *Marketdawn.*' She spat the last word as if it were a highly distasteful destination.

'It will be my pleasure to join your table, Fiance, for I have no plans,' Eduerd said easily. Fiance preened herself and two sets of eyes turned to Ravar. The young woman apologised, explaining her prior engagement with the Princess. Ravar did not catch Eduerd's reaction, for Fiance gave a disappointed snort and grudgingly conceded that it would be highly improper to reject a royal invitation.

Having satisfied herself that Ravar's excuse for missing supper was acceptable, she then proceeded to give an account of her high opinion of Princess Istreeth whom she had known since childhood. This was barring her, 'propensity toward moderation', which had resulted in her growing into such a, *tiny little thing*, despite being of the same blood as the acceptably proportioned King.

Ravar received such declarations in good humour, though she did wonder at the implication that she might have *considered* cancelling her appointment in favour of attending Fiance's supper. She consoled the forthright Cook that she was looking forward to the delights of the feast at the Winter Dance and that upon this occasion she intended to eat her fill.

'And Eduerd has just decided to attend with the Forest Folk this year, too, Fiance,' Ravar added, 'so you will be able to ensure that all your friends are sufficiently well-fed.'

Fiance regarded her with approval, before pulling a face, saying, 'Of course Master Eduerd is attending in Forestfyth! Why he has been fussing over his costume for weeks!' She cast a disparaging look at the Doctor. 'And I daresay the formidable Widow Frensith struck a fierce bargain for those pelts?' Eduerd winced at the giveaway but Fiance was oblivious.

'I am sorry that she lost poor Lord Frensith, Stars shine with him, so early into their marriage,' she said to herself thoughtfully. 'Still, I am glad that after I rejected his suit he did not set his sights too much lower, for I approve of a woman who knows her own mind. See you this evening, Eduerd!' She bowed quickly and strode away.

As she bustled off, Eduerd and Ravar shared a moment of silent laughter, before saying their own goodbyes.

*

At the Palace, the Princess approached her brother who was once again at the fire, turning the flames with his hands. 'You will become some sort of sickly night creature if you do not spend a little time outdoors, Aislyth,' she said, disapprovingly.

'I have been walking in the Forest most days after my midday meetings, sister,' he growled in defence. He stepped back from the hearth, picking up his white Bardic robes. 'When do you expect the Lady Ravar?'

'In an hour or so,' she replied. 'I will endeavour to keep her entertained as long as I can, as you have requested.' She sighed, a little impatiently. 'Am I to assume that you are finally going to speak to Amalin?'

Without looking at her, the King donned the long, white garment, saying only that he was off to the School to give them a tale. Istreeth made no effort to hide her exasperation as he kissed her cheek and strolled towards the door.

CHAPTER 10

Forestfyth School of the Nearage, Fifth Year of the Dancer, winter.

Shortly after the King set out from the Palace, Amalin had ensured that the fire was lit and the students were seated quietly. The weather had held so she had decided to make up a fire in the grounds and it was not long before it had taken sufficiently that they were all benefitting from its warmth.

The King arrived, his white gown overlaid with his sash making him easily visible as he approached. He greeted the Nearage warmly and they reciprocated in kind, though tempered by their respect for his office. Amalin wondered which of these held them in greater awe – his Royal status, or his immediate authority as a Master Bard.

She bowed. 'Welcome, King Aislyth. The students are looking forward to your tale.'

The King made a great, formal bow in return, much to the surprise of both the recipient and her audience. With eyes that sparkled in the darkness and charm radiating through his voice and demeanour, he took her hand and said, 'My Lady, will you stay for my tale? Tonight I am not inclined to give a lesson. The story is simply a gift.'

The last word resonated with Amalin, so recently in receipt of a gift of an altogether different sort. However, since she was already long since won by the charismatic allure of the King of the Forest, with his talent for music and making others smile, she did not attach any significance to it.

She reflected that, although he had not quite the carefree spirit of

Lethan, whose easy nature and upbeat philosophy so matched her own, King Aislyth was strong and kind and clever. She liked him and respected the way he threw himself heartily into and well beyond the demands of his position. His present invitation and the very fact that he gave up an evening so often to the Nearage of his city were prime examples of this.

She smiled and said, 'Thank you, Your Majesty. It would be my pleasure.' She seated herself at the opposite side of the fire and the King took a stand, looking through its spiralling flames around the group.

'Tonight,' he began slowly, a hint of a strange smile forming on his lips, 'I wish to tell you the story of a foolish King and a magical creature.' The Nearage exchanged excited glances and their Bard waited for calm before beginning. He forwent the usual formal introduction in favour of launching into the beginning in his slow, expression-filled tones.

'*A man once ruled over a great kingdom. His people brought him happiness and he delighted in the treasures and hidden secrets of his realm.*

'*Furthermore, he knew that he was generally held to be a fair and good King. He strove every day to live up to expectation in this respect, and beyond. He took pleasure in the pursuit of his Crafts and in the company of his Kin, both of these being most dear to his heart.*

'*Alas, the King whose life many might have considered one to be coveted, was never truly fulfilled. The truth was that his Soul desired to find its match and he had reigned a long time, not alone, but lonely inside. He knew he had the capacity to give great love and find his joy in another but, despite several most flattering offers, had chosen to remain unwed.*

'*This King was not excessively hard to please. Nor was he so self-absorbed that he could not deem any interested parties worthy. Indeed, he presided over the weddings of many of his subjects and Kin. When he did so, it was with the sad envy of a man who would have so liked to have himself known the pleasure of the Soul Embrace of those willingly bound.*

'*In fact he was held back by a strange prophesy he had received as a younger man. On the journeys of his youth he had come across an ancient teacher, whose enlightenment and bearing recognised her to him as one who had truly found the High Way of the Bard.*

'*In his youthful ambition and thirst for knowledge he had begged her to look into his Soul and tell him a little of what he might hope to one day become.*

'*The Bard had not needed to look hard to find an answer, for a woman so possessed with the Way of the Soul could see all of the roads that might branch ahead of the young one before her. However, she chose to tell him only one secret of the many she knew. It was not one that he had particularly sought and, with hindsight, a truth* he found little benefit in knowing.

'The Sage took him by the hand and put her lips to his ear. She whispered to him that she saw the way of his heart and that he should not look for a mate among the fragile bodies of mortal women. She told this man that he was destined to fall in love with none other than a Firebird, whose sly and terrifying ways would capture his Soul forever. When he tried to question her further, the Bard banished him from her presence and he was forced to leave with more uncertainty than when he had come.

'Although he did not understand such a strange foretelling, so many years later the King was still haunted by her words. He gently shunned the affections of many a beautiful and accomplished suitor until his Keeper, with sorrow, closed the path to spare any more persons the sorrow of rejection.

'It was long into the man's reign that a strange woman came to reside in his realm; an eccentric and perplexing personality whose uncommon traits turned even the head of her King. Although he tried to fight such an earthy desire, the King became deeply troubled by the way she crept into his thoughts. Unable to help himself, he felt drawn to her company and found that he never tired of residing within the circle of her warmth.

'As time passed he began to forget the words of the seer to his youthful self. Unbidden, in his mind he formed happy imaginings of the life they might lead, bound together. And yet, at night, his sleep was troubled by the terrible thunder of blazing fire. In his half-remembered dreams he could not shake off the burning melody of a Firebird's call and it drove him close to madness as his days and nights battled within his mind for supremacy.

'The prophet's words had become a curse which held him chained back from that which any other man might have sought. The King was weary with love. And he was heavy with the grief that he held for the same emotion, so prohibited he was from acting upon it.

'Then, one evening, he sat at the High Table beholding his people as they caroused at the seasonal Dance. He saw their happy faces and twirling bodies as they took to the floor and in another life could have been satisfied. As it was, he was not because everywhere he glanced there lay a reminder of the mortal woman who called to his heart.

'No matter in which direction he looked, always a token of this woman was there. It seemed to him that she left behind in all that she touched a light of humour, or wisdom, or the crackle of some emotion. For she was there in the giggle of the courting lovers. And her smile shone from the eyes of the old and astute. Her words rose forth from the lips of the sagacious minds of the learned and shrewd and even the children bore the sparkle of her eyes in their laughter.

'At the centre of the floor the woman was surrounded by the people who loved her *now as one of their own. As she danced by the light of the great fire, the King looked about and saw her trail blazing among them and setting his Kingdom alight.'*

The King stepped forward to the fire and conjured from the blaze the form of a dancing woman, her dress composed of the curling flames. The Nearage gasped, astonished at the Mastery of his Fireplay. He held the flickering form and she seemed to dance for him as he continued to speak.

'As the sparkling scene before him was reflected in his eyes, suddenly, the King's whole being lurched like a ship on a stormy sea. And in that moment he held his head in his hands and laughed, for only then did he realise that that he had been deceived. Finally he saw the true path of the woman before him. It was a trail of glowing embers that were born from her very feet.'

The King stirred the ashes, just as Istreeth had done at the Palace, so that the dancing maiden image in the fire appeared at the centre of the glittering coals. He lowered his voice to a slow, rumbling whisper and the Nearage leaned forward to hear his words.

'And as he beheld his love once again, he knew that the woman before him was no woman *at all, but the* Firebird *in disguise! The clever creature had cloaked herself in a magical veil to trick the foolish King!'*

An intake of breath was heard from all the young spectators.

'So it came to pass that the King knew that he had found his Soulmate at last.'

The King cast his arms into the fire itself and pulled the light from the body of the image of the woman, flinging it sideways so that her dress extended into flaming wings. He sent the image up with the heat so that it soared above them and was gone.

As the Nearage stared up, open-mouthed in wonder at its disappearing form, he stood back, lowering his head, and was silent. The story was at an end, and the young men and women sensed the strange dismissal, each of them bowing to their Bard until only he and Amalin remained.

Amalin stared into the deep eyes of the King which were lit with a fire from within. Nothing had prepared her for the real nature of the tale that had just been articulated. This she knew to have been for her understanding alone. As the thoughts raced through her mind she was forced to accept the inevitable conclusion that the King's tale was his own.

The King regarded her gravely and intoned his request without waver across the flames.

'Amalin of the Plains, I seek the heart of Lady Ravar of the Forest People, whose Soul is bound to yours. I have presented my gift in the form of the truth of my own Living Tale. It is shared with my audience tonight but recognised to you alone beyond the Hidden Place of Eslebard. Do you accept it as a worthy token? It is given to you out of the respect I bear for the one whom the object of my love has already chosen as her Soul's companion.'

Amalin breathed unevenly, her heart beating hard in her chest. Had she seen this coming? Had she known of the ferocity of feeling from the very ruler of the whole Kingdom? Did Ravar? If he was certain of the meaning of his Living Tale then it was tied to *her!*

She stood and walked around the fire, where the vast figure of the King stood, awaiting her response. She reached out for his left hand and used it to draw his long, tanned forearm before her. The golden swirls of the mark of Eslebard glinted in her shadow as she eclipsed the fire. She looked up into his steadfast face. There were many things she wanted to ask, but for now there was only one thing that she must.

'King Aislyth, Lord of the Forest, I am honoured to accept your truth as your gift. The nature of your love has been told in your tale.' She raised her forefinger solemnly and held it up to his face. 'But tell me, Your Majesty, what do you *offer* that I might consider your request to present your suit?'

The King brushed the mark on his arm softly and then drew it to his side. He spoke with force and seriousness, his low tones boring into her.

'My tale was one of passion and perhaps a little pretention, but I would speak to you, Ravar's Keeper, as a man and leader of men.' He paused and spoke again with conviction. 'In Ravar I know that my position among the People will be of no consequence and that she would not fear to deny my suit. Yet, I would see my people raise her to share that throne. I would do this, not to exalt her above all others as some gift of my affection. Rather, I would have her by my side to rule the people who have come to love and respect her already. I would have her wisdom guide the judgement decisions made on their behalf.'

'You would ask the Forest to make her Co-Regent?' exclaimed Amalin, wide-eyed with shock.

'I would make the woman who knows the better ways of the Kingdom and her People a Queen! Tell me that the Forest would not demand it!' he said, fervently. 'Lady Amalin, I know that she desires a Higher Path, and I see such a path that she could forge for *all* who would follow in her wake. I see what we could achieve together in pursuit of bringing our people to a better height.'

Amalin felt a shiver run down her arms. *Ravar, ruler of a Kingdom,* she thought.

'And I, as Aislyth,' the King continued, 'would give her a warm and music-filled home among my family and Kin. I offer her my love and service as an *equal,* where title and position are no object. Step inside my Palace of a morning or evening, My Lady, and join in our table and pleasure in the company of our community. I would give her that part of me which is not for my subjects, but reserved for the Dance, the fireside, in games and merriment.' His voice rose to a crescendo.

'Let her take her place in my circle and grow in its nurture and love! Let her converse with the scholars whom I welcome to my home as my friends! Let her skate on the ice with my sister on the cold winter mornings and know that she is free. Let me present her to the monarchs of every realm as the light of my life and our People! Let our heirs fill the world with the goodness our love will instil!'

His tirade came to an abrupt end as he stunned even himself by his words and the dreams he had betrayed.

Amalin walked over to a bench and sat down. Her mind was reeling through the implications of what the King had said. A ruler, a family, *children!* Why was it that Amalin had never thought about Ravar as a mother? The King had seen this fate and yet she had thought only of Ravar's own personal ambitions and desires.

How did she marry her decision to allow Eduerd to court her friend with this counter-proposal? She knew that Ravar favoured the Doctor, but had her friend had any notion of the alternative life that this other great man might offer? There was a stark contrast, if not in the fervour of the intention, in the manner of marriage they offered. It was a choice between the exclusive and intellectual mystery of the joining of mind and body, against a productive and outwardly loving public union, whose fruit might also be great.

And that was just it, she thought. It was a choice. Ravar's choice. And Ravar should have it, if the King was prepared to be a rival in suit. She looked up guardedly at his, now slightly strained, face, for she had kept him waiting all the while.

'Aislyth of the Forest, I will open the way to you to court my Ravar, but before you place your pin on my sash, regard it with care and know your position.' She undid her cloak to reveal her sash and the bronze feather that already glinted at her breast.

The King's eyes widened as he beheld the ornament. It silenced him for some moments before he came to her resolutely and pinned its likeness below it.

'I am glad you are not cowed in the face of another suitor, Your Majesty. *But*,' and her tone became ice, 'tell me directly that you will honour the *choice* that Ravar now finds before her and accept that she has the right to deny *either* or *both* the claims on her Soul.'

Startled, but profoundly moved by what she had just said, the King bowed low to her. 'I give you my promise that I shall accept the judgement of Ravar in this and all things, My Lady.'

Amalin inhaled slowly, narrowing her eyes to be sure of his sincerity, before pursing her lips. 'Then good luck to you, my King. And spare a thought for this Keeper, for I anticipate that I shall have a turbulent time ahead.'

*

The King went directly to his chamber, entering the Palace by a side-door so as to avoid anyone who would disturb his thoughts. He took a seat on the worn yet richly embroidered chair he favoured at the fireside and stared into nothingness, trying to picture his way forward in the knowledge that Ravar was the object of desire of another.

He was not keeping track of time and so when, some time later, Istreeth leaned her head through a crack in the door, it took him a moment to realise that it had grown late.

'Is she gone?' he asked.

'The Lady Ravar departed some time ago, brother,' she said. 'I awaited your return until I came to the conclusion that you must already have slipped in. Now I find you staring in the dark, looking as though a tragedy has befallen you. What has happened?' Istreeth was troubled.

The King sighed and pulled his Soul Friend into his lap. He took her hand and pressed it to heart and she made a faint noise of alarm as she felt the emotion stirring within him.

She frowned slightly. 'Brother?' she questioned. 'You have made your request to give your suit?'

'Aye, Istreeth,' the King replied tiredly.

'And?' she demanded.

'And the Lady Amalin has accepted my plea.'

Istreeth leapt to her feet, smiling. 'Then, brother, why do you not dance for joy? Is this not what has held you so distant and brooding these last weeks?'

'There are now *two* feathers on the Lady Amalin's sash!' the King barked.

'Two...' said Istreeth, softly.

'Yes, dear sister, two,' the King said, despairingly. 'Do you know who else vies to stand beside her?'

Istreeth remained still and thoughtful. 'I do not, brother. However, why is it that this news comes as either surprise or hardship? Is Ravar's affection not such a prize that you believe no other would seek it?'

'No, of course not!' he growled.

'Then,' she replied, curtly, 'take a hold of yourself, Aislyth of the Forest People, and *fight* for her love! Do you shrink so feebly in the face of a competitor?'

'Amalin would not have opened the way to a lesser man,' he replied, sulkily.

'Is your own desire so paltry that you believe the battle already lost? I confess I had not taken you for one to be so easily defeated.' She gave him a look of disfavour.

The King looked stunned for a moment, then growled again. The noise rose from his belly until it became hearty and strong. 'Istreeth, you are right!' he shouted, a booming laughter replacing the rumble. 'Stars, how is it that I am reduced to such a weak wreck?'

Istreeth regarded him more approvingly and kissed him lightly on the cheek. 'Of course I am right, brother. I suggest you get some sleep and tomorrow morning consider what needs to be done.' She stood and walked towards the door but stopped at the threshold. She turned back and said, 'I have had a very pleasant evening, by the way. For what it is worth, I should like such a woman for a sister.'

*

At the cottage of Amalin and Ravar, the atmosphere was tense. Ravar had been escorted home by a Palace attendant and found that Amalin had awaited her return. Immediately sensing that something was awry, she had demanded that her friend came out with whatever was on her mind.

After a lengthy disclaimer that Ravar would need to understand that she had not made the concession lightly, Amalin had shown her the secondary brooch on her sash.

Ravar had known better than to pry extensively, though it was made perfectly clear to her Soul Friend that she was quite unhappy with the circumstance. Ravar had been slyly hopeful that the first might have been presented by Eduerd, who had promised to spend time with her since his return and for whom she herself could not deny a growing affection.

Even if she was now right in her suspicion, she would have to contend with another's advance. She racked her brain to think of who it might be, going over the single persons of her acquaintance and worrying that she might have given a wrong impression through her words or actions.

Surely Amalin knew the direction in which her heart leant? Why would she allow another to court her Soul Friend, unless the proposal was so very convincing or out of the ordinary? She had to swallow her anger when, in the sea of sensations of the Soul Embrace, she had felt the certainty and peace of Amalin's resolution. Nonetheless, she struggled to make sense of it and Ravar was not accustomed to being presented with a problem that she could not solve.

CHAPTER 11

Forestfyth, Fifth Year of the Dancer, the day before the winter solstice.

The King had risen before dawn, decked himself in his finest everyday clothes and made for the house of Ravar and Amalin in the darkness. Ever since Istreeth had given him such a talking to, he was absolutely determined that he would give his all to his suit.

He had called at the School nearly every day to offer his services and prove himself a man of conviction. He had joined its orchestra for practice, baked a sweet loaf for the teachers to share and even been shunned from Armick's lesson, where he hoped to glimpse the form of Ravar's costume for the Winter Ball. Had he been successful, he might have tried to adapt his own to complement it. As it was, the Nearage had chased him out, saying that it was a surprise.

And now the much-anticipated event was only a day away and he would be damned if he did not secure Ravar's first Pin. So, he settled himself on a tree stump opposite the gate and clapped his hands to warm them as the sun peeped over the frosty horizon.

Within the cottage, the two women were sleepily donning their sashes, Amalin affixing the Pins of the Dance to Ravar's with care. Ravar had been somewhat calmer in the days that had passed following the revelation of a second suitor, as things had remained very much in the ordinary.

The Doctor seemed to have made good on his promise and had called by the house as well as the School in the last week. His visits had been of a social, rather than professional nature and she thought that she had detected a note of affection in his conversation and attentions. Although she had hardly dared reciprocate, lest she were mistaken about his intentions, Ravar had lowered her guard sufficiently that she felt they were able to converse more as close friends than mere acquaintances or colleagues.

Things at the School were also much improved. Lethan had come to *all* the afternoon lessons that Amalin took and the music workshops in particular had been the better for his presence, marked by the sound of duelling strings. This had been much to the delight of all concerned, Ravar included as she watched how happy it made Amalin.

In addition, Master Armick had reported that he was extremely proud of the efforts of his class and on the last day of term the Nearage had informed their Tutors that their costumes were complete. The finished articles would be presented to the women on the morning of the Dance.

Finally and most happily, the presence of both King Aislyth and his sister in so many activities had made for a merry and stimulating end to the semester. They made a great point of publicly teasing each other and leading competing sides in discussion, team challenges and games of logic. The King had suggested, as was customary in the last week before the seasonal break, a number of light-hearted topics for debate. These included such examples as whether the addition of a tail or webbed feet would make a more desirable augmentation to the human form. The bizarre arguments and laughing discourse that had followed had had everyone in stitches.

As Ravar started to prepare breakfast, it was Amalin who threw open the front door, carrying two clinking buckets to be filled at the well at the far side of their little garden. The King who had been humming to himself jumped up from his repose on the wood stump and hurried to meet her.

'Good morning My Lady Amalin!' he cried, heartily.

Putting down her load, Amalin sauntered towards him, a crafty smile spreading across her face. She bowed.

'And a very *early* good morning to you, Your Majesty. How long have you been lurking there?'

'Ha! Only a short while, My Lady,' he grinned. 'Is the Lady Ravar risen?'

Amalin flashed excitedly. 'Why yes, Sire, she is! I shall fetch her.' And with that, she skipped back into the house before he could stop her.

Ravar came out behind Amalin looking slightly bewildered. Seeing the personage before her she smiled and came forward to make a small bow.

'Good morning, Your Majesty. To what do we owe this pleasure?'

The King made a deep, elegant bow. 'My Lady I called in the hope that I might beg the honour of the First Dance at the Winter Ball tomorrow night.'

Ravar was quite taken aback. She glanced at Amalin who was making no effort to hide her merriment and returned her gaze to the tall, earnest features of the King.

'Why, I…' She faltered only briefly. 'I would be most honoured, Your Majesty.'

King Aislyth beamed, took her hand and kissed it, before turning his first pin to gold. He turned swiftly to Amalin. 'My Lady, I hope that I might also have the pleasure of your company in the Second?'

Amalin responded by eagerly turning her own second pin.

'Until then!' boomed the King. He bowed to each of them and turned on his heel with a spring in his step.

'Well, Ravar! How about that! Tomorrow we shall once again dance with our King!' Amalin cooed.

'Amalin,' Ravar said slowly. 'What is this about?' She attempted to check the giggling, hopping form of her friend, taking her by the shoulders and peering into her eyes.

'I don't know what you mean!' said Amalin, her tone all innocence.

'The *First* Dance, Amalin? The Dance that our King always takes with his sister?'

'Hm,' Amalin said nonchalantly. 'Perhaps she has been otherwise engaged.'

'Already? At this time of the day?' Ravar narrowed her eyes at her.

Amalin broke from her grasp and trotted back inside, singing. She ignored all attempts by Ravar to speak of the matter any further and Ravar was left to think about the King in a wholly new light.

About an hour later, the pair were ready to make their way to the town square. The day before all seasonal celebrations was a rest day, as were the five that followed them, and they had decided to go into town to see if Fiance could spare a break from her kitchen to join them for lunch.

As they were closing their front door behind them, they were met by two more handsome callers, this time in the form of Lethan and Eduerd, whose cheerful greetings were happily reciprocated. Lethan was the first to speak. He stepped closer to Amalin and flashed her a big smile.

'Lady Amalin, may I be so bold as to ask for your hand in the First Dance tomorrow night?' He asked.

Amalin did not hesitate in her reply. 'You may and I would be delighted!'

'Well,' he said, chuckling, 'that was easy! Lady Ravar, I wonder, as I appear to be on a roll, if I might also ask you for the Second?'

Ravar smiled warmly, understanding the implication at being asked for the Dance denoting honour and thanks. As she turned over her second pin, Lethan saw that she now sported the first *three* in gold. He turned uneasily to his friend, whose eyes were rooted to the same target. He wore an unreadable expression, but Lethan knew that he must be as surprised but also very disappointed.

Nonetheless, Eduerd rallied and stepped forward to Ravar as Lethan moved aside. He treated her to a sighing smile and spoke gently, his crisp enunciation cutting through his frustration. 'I see that you are already engaged for the early Dances, My Lady. I confess I had thought a morning visit might have given me the opportunity to ask for an earlier slot. However, I would still be most pleased if you would agree to take my hand in the Fourth?'

Ravar felt her heart sink. She had also nursed a hope that a request for the First might be in the offing. She did her best to convey her sincerity in her happiness to accept the offer and Eduerd gently turned the pin on her sash himself. As he did so, there was a moment of stillness when he looked directly into her eyes. In the next second he had stepped away and the moment was gone.

'Lady Amalin,' he continued, 'I see that you too are heavily engaged already.' He really was amazed and annoyed that he and Lethan should be considered late to the game. They had risen at first light to make their way together with a view to avoiding this very possibility in mind. 'May I at least have your company in the Fifth?' he said dryly.

'You may, Master Eduerd. We cannot wait,' she replied, matter-of-factly. 'Now, we are for town. Will you walk with us?' The men acquiesced without hesitation, but it was a strange mix of thoughts that ran through the minds of the four friends as they walked.

Eventually, Ravar got a hold of herself enough to attempt to make conversation.

'Will Lord Desledair be joining us tomorrow night?'

'Alas, no,' Eduerd replied. 'He is obliged, much against his will, to celebrate at the High Table of the Marketdawn festival.'

Ravar laughed. 'Oh, poor Desledair! I suppose his brother has insisted that he must perform some of his royal duties.'

Eduerd grinned. 'Indeed. And Desledair believes that the Market King has placed the esteemed Widow Frensith at his table in some bid to match-make between them.'

Ravar pulled an exaggerated expression of mortification. 'Oh dear! And do her many charms not have any appeal to him?' From what she knew of him, they most certainly would not.

'Most definitely not!' he replied, emphatically. Ravar laughed.

'Have you and Amalin finally been let in on the secret of your costumes?' he asked.

'No, the Nearage have been completely tight-lipped on the subject. Let us hope that they have chosen well and we are not destined to be two of the Three Witches of the Sea or Yondil Worms!'

Still chatting amiably, the four reached the Square which was buzzing with children, carts, a few travelling merchants and the bustling comings and goings of Palace workers who were hauling decorations and food towards the Great Hall.

Ravar caught sight of Istreeth looking over a ledger presented to her by a Scribe for approval. Nodding her assent, she saw Ravar and waved in greeting. The party made in her direction and once the formal greetings had been made, Istreeth exclaimed with raised eyebrows at the many already turned pins of their sashes.

'Heavens, you make me feel quite inadequate, with only my Third Dance secured!' Seeing that Eduerd sported the only empty early slots of the company she turned her attention to him. 'Master Eduerd, as I find myself in the unusual position of being without a partner for the First, I wonder if you would take it with me? You would spare your Princess the humiliation of having to sit it out.' She made a rueful smile.

'It would be my great honour, Your Highness,' he responded at once.

Istreeth exhaled shortly. 'Good! I shall look forward to it. Perhaps I shall not look too much of a lonesome old woman after all,' she said dryly.

'Who is a lonesome old woman?' boomed the piercing tones of a familiar voice. Fiance had appeared from nowhere and was determined to be part of the conversation.

'Princess Istreeth is in need of dance partners, My Lady,' supplied Lethan, a twinkle in his eye.

'Nonsense!' Fiance said flatly. 'I heard Master Armick saying only ten minutes ago that he intended to ask her for the Second Dance in thanks for the beautiful mural she painted for his workshop. And, in any case, she will dance with the King in the First and Third.'

'Not so,' Istreeth interjected. 'My brother is taken to courting and so I have had to find another partner to grace me in the First.'

'What?' Fiance cried, aghast. 'The King is *courting*? I knew nothing of this! Who, pray tell, has finally won his heart?' When no one replied, she pursed her lips. 'Well it is about time, if you ask me,' she continued, haughtily. 'The Kingdom wants him to be happily settled down. Ah me, those poor wretches that he turned down early in his reign. We all thought he must have a heart of iron.'

Ravar had remained silent throughout Fiance's spiel, though Eduerd and Lethan were quite as fascinated by the subject as their friend. Amalin rescued the conversation from what could have taken an awkward turn by saying that she and Ravar had to run some errands before lunch and that she hoped Fiance might join them later. Fiance grumbled that she could not leave the Palace kitchen unsupervised but promised to dine with them soon.

She then demanded Eduerd's Second Dance pin, proclaiming that she did not need an excuse to dance with one of her Kin, and hang any old-fashioned notions of thanksgiving. Lethan was also required by her in the Fifth as, in the absence of Lord Desledair, she would need a *man's man* to take her through her steps by that point in the night.

No one really knew what was meant by this but, as Fiance seemed utterly certain, they did not question it. The Cook seemed to suddenly remember that she had left her kitchen unattended, made swift farewells and raced her wobbling bulk back to it in case it might burn down in her absence.

'Until tomorrow night then,' said Eduerd as Ravar and Amalin headed off to complete their 'errands'. She risked a glance back in his direction as she walked away and was gratified to see that his gaze had remained in her direction.

CHAPTER 12

Forestfyth, Fifth year of the Dancer, winter solstice.

The Nearage had arrived, quite unable to contain their excitement. Ravar and Amalin had been asked to sit and their pupils flocked before them to present the boxes containing the costumes that they had made. Under the indulgent oversight of Master Armick, the ladies opened the lids and admired the beautiful colour and quality of the material within.

Amalin lifted the suit of iridescent blue feathers from her box and squealed with delight. The back of it fell away to form a long tail in deep turquoise blues and greens. Underneath it, she found an equally magnificent headdress that sported an elegant crest of long blue feathers, laced with silver trim and beads.

'Look in the box once more!' came the shrill cries from her audience. She reached within and found a large, ornate stiffened fabric necklace, embroidered in silver loops that fell from the choker in a long train.

Amalin shrieked her pleasure. 'I will be the Chained Songbird! Oh, you are so clever – how did you ever create something so wonderful? Thank you all!' She jumped to her feet and embraced them all one by one. As the noise fell, everyone turned their attention to Ravar, who had paused in her own foraging to see what her friend had found.

The sound of nervous breathing and anticipation filled the room.

Obligingly, Ravar pulled up the bodysuit from within her own box. It sparkled with more gold sequins than she had ever seen. The tail was even longer and more dazzling than that of Amalin's costume. Glistening gold strands swept the floor as they flared out from a central spine.

Gasping, she then took her own headdress from the box. It was in shimmering gold, the mask emerging from the headpiece picked out in thousands of glistening tiny beads of blazing oranges, reds and yellows.

'Can you tell what it is yet?' one of the Nearage asked, almost hopping from foot to foot.

Ravar continued to delve into the box, to find two exquisite long arm pieces, from which fell a waterfall of gold-painted feathers sewn together in the unmistakable form of vast wings.

Ravar still did not understand but it was Amalin who said, with an odd smile and whispering voice, 'Stars, they have made you the Firebird...'

Ravar did not have time to react before the room erupted in applause as the Nearage congratulated Amalin for successfully guessing the design.

It took some time for the women to usher the students and their Master from the house. They had showered them all with praise and insisted that they thanked Master Armick for devoting so much time to this project. He received such compliments magnanimously and encouraged his entourage out of the door.

'Well, I have to say that I am quite overwhelmed by the beauty and standard of our garments,' said Ravar. 'However, beyond the concept I have to say I am unfamiliar with the Firebird's Tale. Where did they get such an idea?'

The muscles in Amalin's jaw were working as she clenched her teeth, totally unprepared for how to explain. 'I believe you will have to ask our resident Master Bard, Ravar.'

Ravar looked puzzled. 'The King? He told them the story?'

Amalin supressed a sigh. 'Aye, he did. Now, let me think how I am to tie your hair so that it will not interfere with your costume.' Amalin fussed sufficiently that Ravar could not enquire further. *Heavens*, she thought. Tonight, King Aislyth was in for quite the surprise.

*

As the bell in the North Tower of the Palace tolled the seventeenth hour, the guests began to arrive at the Great Hall. A blazing hearth roared at each end of the vast room and every pillar and surface was richly adorned with ribbons, fir cones, berried branches and painted decorations.

Welcoming every attendee at the door were the King and Princess. The former was attired in the green, gold and red feathers of the Early Rooster, a great red comb crowning his head. His sister donned soft white down, interspersed with black spotting, and a high mask and headdress that gave her the pointed features of the Old Owl.

Much clamour was made as people arrived, comparing and admiring each other's outfits. Choices ranged through the full span of mythical birds, animals, sea creatures and spirits of the old tales of the Kingdoms. All were especially keen to impress the critical eye of Grandmaster Dethir who would be judging the winner of the Winter Crown.

He himself wore an elegant plaster cast mask, from which long white whiskers bristled. He was perched on a stool, around which trailed a long, soft tail. However, he hardly needed the costume to resemble a Snow Cat.

Although impervious to bribery, the Grandmaster did not go so far as to refuse the many offers to procure him drinks or fetch those people with whom he professed a desire to speak.

'Your Majesty!' he called out to the King, who was still standing upon the threshold. The tall rooster bounded over to the much-revered Dethir and bowed. This was acknowledged with an impatient nod of the head.

'By my count nearly all have now arrived, Sire,' the Grandmaster stated abruptly. 'Therefore for what purpose do you persist in hanging around at the main door? Are you waiting for some special envoy?'

The King did not like either the hint of malice in the Grandmaster's voice, or the twinkling of his eye. He was certain that the old man was mocking him but completely uncertain of by which means he seemed to be aware of how to do so. He cleared his throat.

'No, My Lord, but your arithmetic and memory are good enough to know full well which of our community have not yet made their entrance. I am sure you would agree that, as King, I have a responsibility to ensure that all are welcomed to the party.' He grinned. He would not be so easily embarrassed by the old Tutor.

The Grandmaster allowed himself a small guffaw. 'Oh yes, it is most important that a Host pays attention to the care of his guests!' Then, looking beyond Aislyth, his expression changed. 'Great heavens, now there is something to behold,' he said quietly, almost under his breath. The King reeled round to see what had so affected the Grandmaster.

There in the entrance way Amalin and Ravar were a blazing collage of colour. At the shrill behest of a crowd of admirers, spearheaded by Lady Fiance, Amalin tuned to the side to take a deep bow and treat everyone to a full display of her crest.

However, it was Ravar's turn to show off her attire that made the

King's heart skip a beat. For, as she raised her arms and twirled around, he saw the sparkling spread of her golden wings and her body glide under their arc. He had to shake himself to be sure that he was not hallucinating because, before him, he beheld the living, moving form of the fiery creature from his dreams.

'Well, brother,' said Istreeth, quietly in his ear, breaking his trance, 'did you in fact somehow manage to find out what she was going to be tonight? For you are well matched, as two birds together.' He looked at her and she smiled mischievously.

'Believe me, Istreeth, I had no idea.' Istreeth only half credited this, but heard him muttering under his breath something about how only a Firebird might hide behind her own mask.

'Well the Nearage have excelled themselves, as has their Master,' said Istreeth. 'I am glad that I shall be taking the Second Dance with Armick, for I shall have a chance to commend his efforts. Ah!' she exclaimed, spotting Master Eduerd and Lethan also coming into the hall.

Lethan had crafted the pointed ears and cheeky, laughing visage of the Tree Sprite into a full-face mask. He was dressed in clothing made to replicate the natural greenery of the Forest, right down to his green, felt shoes.

At his side, Eduerd was a stunning image. His own elegant frame and handsomeness somehow perfectly married with the expertly tailored silver and white pelts that made up the main body of his costume. His eye-mask was also made with real fur, with dark black lines running over the eye slits and continued in black face-paint beneath the mask to his nose. The long pointed canine ears, again of fur, seemed to sit naturally among his dark curls and his own piercing blue eyes only served to make him a more convincing fox. Finally, from his right arm hung seven fine, soft and bushy white tails that swished lightly as he raised a hand in greeting.

Istreeth smiled like a little clever monkey. 'It seems that I shall be dancing with the bearer of the Winter Crown.'

The King had to admit that the costume was quite something and, before he knew it, Grandmaster Dethir was on his feet and striding toward the Doctor, a look of grudging approval upon his face.

'You dance with Lord Eduerd tonight?' asked the King. He had been so taken up with his own plan of action for the evening that he had not enquired as to which persons Istreeth had elected to turn her pins for.

'Yes, in the First,' she confirmed, 'then Armick and after the Soul

Dance, the Lady Seldan before finishing with Master Ralgon. I do not think I shall dance in the Sixth, for there are too many suitors who will be desperately vying for a second turn tonight. I should not like to have to pick a way across the floor in the midst of such drama.'

'You have a veritable line-up of Master Craftsmen, sister. But perhaps you favour one partner a little more specially, to honour him with the First Dance?' He cocked an eyebrow but was swiftly brought to earth as Istreeth rolled her eyes with genuine irritation and batted away his comment with the sweep of her hand.

'As if I could be interested in a man who spends so many hours engaged in the gruesome arts of Healing. Why, he must have to interact with an endless horde of callers night and day. I should think the poor man never gets a moment's peace. Indeed, I cannot imagine a more irksome existence.'

'Oh, I see,' responded the King, thinking that he personally should like a profession which introduced him to so many people. 'Yet, he is a most handsome man, is he not?' he persisted.

'Dreadfully handsome, brother! And *very* charming. I shall not find my First Dance a trial, certainly.'

While the siblings were talking about them all, the four friends had met and were busy admiring and discussing each other's costumes. Lethan's jaw had dropped like a stone upon seeing Amalin thus attired and when Eduerd laid eyes upon the sparkling Ravar he was left quite speechless. However, neither reaction could quite match that of Ravar as she stared up into the beautiful features and workmanship of the Doctor's attire.

'Great Stars in the Heavens!' Amalin swore through a smile of distant greeting. She whispered sideways to Ravar, 'Is your man *a fox* or what?' Receiving a sharp jab in the ribs did very little to rein her in from a detailed commentary of how Eduerd's various physical virtues were quite augmented by his costume. Ravar did not need to be told. Neither did any of the other guests in the hall.

The two men had made a beeline, so far as they could, for Ravar and Amalin. They had bowed and kissed the women's hands in the highest formality of style and the women made their elegant bows in return.

'My Lady, you are quite transformed,' exclaimed Eduerd, warmly. 'I am so used to your silver that I had quite no idea how well you might look in gold.'

Ravar was glad that her half mask and gold make-up would do

something to cover her reddening cheeks.

'My Lord Eduerd, *everyone* stares at your costume,' Ravar replied. 'I shall have to persuade your friend the Tree Sprite to fulfil his part in the myth or I fear so much adoration may go to your head!'

Eduerd laughed. 'Well Lethan, will you keep me in line?'

Lethan only half heard his friend as his eyes were locked with those of Amalin, the pair not even making conversation. 'What? Oh! Yes, of course, Eduerd. I shall demand a tail every time you are in danger of losing your head.'

'Oh? And what will you do with so many fox tails?' asked Amalin, grinning.

Lethan wrapped his arms around the shoulders of the two women, adopting the high-pitched trickster voice of the Sprite. 'Why I shall weave a soft nest and lure the two most beautiful birds of the Forest to it and feed them to my Kin!'

As they laughed, Eduerd said that in that case he had better be on his best behaviour.

In fact, Eduerd had every intention of being on his very, *very* best behaviour. After their call on Ravar and Amalin the previous morning, he and Lethan had discussed the second feather on the latter woman's sash at length. Lethan claimed he had no idea of the identity of the second suitor, though there was something uneasy in him that led Eduerd to think that his friend might have at least a suspicion.

Eduerd could not claim to know everyone in Forestfyth well and he was certainly unsurprised that Ravar was the object of another's affection. He had thought that Ravar showed him a little favour, but he also doubted that the crafty Lady Amalin would bestow her blessing upon any old acquaintance. *Stars*, who was this man? He was bound to make himself known tonight. Indeed, it was surely he who had won Ravar for the First Dance.

His thoughts were interrupted by the approach of the Princess. He bowed to Istreeth and kissed her hand as she treated him to a small smile. 'Good evening, Lord Eduerd. I hope that I shall at least be able to match you in dancing tonight, if not your costume.'

'I have no doubt of that, Your Highness.' As he spoke, the introductory notes and bars of the music were sounded to give the dancers notice to find their partners and come to the floor. Looking towards the band, Eduerd raised a finger in the air as if pointing at the sound.

'Your timing is perfect!' he said.

'Well met, Lord Eduerd!' boomed the voice of King Aislyth who had come up behind his sister.

Eduerd bowed, but before he could add his return greeting, he rose again to find his King making a deep, formal bow to Ravar and extending his hand. Her eyes sparkled even more than the mask around them and she took it in hers, letting him lead her to the dance floor.

As Istreeth in turn took Eduerd's hand, he followed her to the dancing circle almost in a daze, his head spinning with the realisation that his competitor could be none other than his *King*. The King of all the Forest. *Stars fall*, he swore to himself.

Horrifyingly, as he turned it over in his mind, it made some sense. King Aislyth had spent a lot of time at the School with Ravar and the Heavens only knew how much more beyond. From what he could make out Ravar respected and liked him enormously, for they shared a gift for teaching and the spoken word. It was just that Eduerd, like the rest of his subjects, had become used to his King's seeming disinterest in the ways of the heart.

The Doctor was not oblivious to the man's obvious charm and talent, and he could be considered a handsome man by any definition, but it was a well-known fact that his Sister no longer accepted approaches from any suitors. Of course, Eduerd was forced to accept, if anyone was able to move him, it was Ravar. Had she not had the same effect upon his own heart?

Istreeth was such a fine dancer that she was able to carry her distracted partner, but it had not escaped her notice that his thoughts were elsewhere. 'Master Eduerd, please assure me that *you* are not so interested in my brother's love-life that you are made dumb like most of the other dancers.'

Eduerd looked about him, nearly everyone's eyes were on the King and Ravar at the centre of the floor.

'I am truly sorry, Your Highness,' he said, bashfully. 'However, it is not your brother's affection that concerns me, but how it is received.' His mouth fell a little as he saw Ravar lean in towards the King, a wicked smile on her lips.

'Oh...' Istreeth's brow furrowed as she glimpsed his expression. 'Then, the second feather... It is yours?' *Of course it was,* she thought.

'I make no secret of it as of tonight,' he sighed. 'Though I will admit that I would rather not be up against your brother.'

Istreeth shared part of the sentiment. While she was fiercely loyal to Aislyth she liked the Doctor. One or both were to be heartbroken in the end and she would not wish it upon either.

'Well, we mustn't let them outshine us in the dance,' she said, more cheerfully. 'I am not of the Gold Level for nothing, and I have as my partner the beautiful Seven-Tailed Fox! Come, let us steal a little of the limelight!'

Ravar and the King had spent the first minute of the dancing in silence. Once again, she was vying for control of her senses as his expert skill manoeuvred her body and made her feel as though she had melted to air. The King of the Forest felt as though he were in one of his haunting dreams, watching the Firebird taunt and bewitch him. Only this time, the Firebird was in his arms, beautiful and smiling.

It was Ravar who broke the silence, leaning forward so that the King could feel her warmth close to his face. 'I have a question for you, Your Majesty,' she said, with a sly smile.

'Ask away, Firebird,' he replied, smiling back.

'Yes, *Firebird*,' she repeated, with emphasis. 'That is just it. I know of the creature but not of its tale. Amalin says you put it into the Nearage's heads to pick it for my costume. What story did you impart to have affected them so?'

The King made a noise something akin to a growling purr as a puma might make as he considered his answer.

'All tales of the Firebird are the same,' he said at length. 'Her power and cunning deceive the slow witted.'

Ravar was far from satisfied. Before she could tackle him further on the point though, the King's eyes widened, looking over her shoulder. They flashed with laughter and a little fire of his own as he exclaimed, 'I do believe my sister means to show me up for abandoning her to find another partner in this dance!'

He spun Ravar around to see Istreeth and Eduerd twirling quickly around the edge of the floor and drawing the admiration of the onlookers and other dancers.

'Well, I'll not have that from her this night!' the King said with electric defiance. 'Or no one will believe I am a Master of the Dance!'

With that, he swept Ravar from her feet and held her aloft with one hand. In the other, he held hers and lifted it in an arc so that her wing appeared to spread and carry her in flight. With astonishing reflex and strength he moved her as he might craft the fire to carry a story. Several other dancers halted in their steps to watch as the King appeared to make his golden bird fly about him, her slender body arching and twisting and turning through the air.

When the Dance was finally over, Ravar accepted the kiss at her hand as they parted, but her Soul was still soaring like a bird, wings licking the sky. She declined to join the common dance and found a quiet spot outside the main hall to catch her thoughts. So that was how it felt to be under the command of a Master of the Floor. Her legs trembled at the recollection. And this man sought to give her his hand in marriage as well as the Dance.

*

'Ravar, there you are!' It was Lethan, looking relieved. 'I know I shall be a poor substitute partner after your acrobatic show in the First, but will you still allow me to take you for a turn?' He grinned.

Stars, it is the Second Dance already? Ravar thought. She forced herself, unsteadily, to her feet. 'Of course, Lethan.' Taking his arm, she managed to ground herself a little in his cheerful presence. 'I suspect it will be even more an anti-climax for you! How did you enjoy your first spin with Amalin?' He blushed, but beamed.

'Very much, My Lady!'

Amalin herself was, not long afterwards, enjoying the benefits of dancing with a Master, though to her it was nothing compared with the feeling of Lethan's embrace. She could still feel it. The King had a strange look in his eye but she was the last person to be afraid to poke the bear.

'So, Your Majesty, you have your Firebird at last!'

He fixed her with a severe look. 'Was it your doing?'

Amalin gave him a look of incredulity. 'It most certainly was not! Why, it was no one's doing but your own! If you had not given such a tale to the Nearage, they should never have thought of the design.'

'Hmm…' he accepted.

'Do you not like her so well in this form?' she asked, accusingly.

'Do not taunt your King, Lady Amalin,' he grinned, warningly.

'I shall tease the man who hopes to win my Soul Sister all I like,' she said mischievously, 'for he cannot afford to lose my favour.' She flashed him a triumphant smile and he cast his eyes to the heavens for support. The Heavens ignored him.

*

'Well now, Doctor, that was quite a show you made with the Princess before!' raved Fiance to her partner elsewhere on the floor. 'We were all most impressed!'

'Aye, until we were overshadowed entirely by the King and Ravar,' Eduerd replied, grumpily.

'Oh, it is like that, is it?' Fiance remonstrated with him fiercely. 'So Ravar has a second suitor and you think that the best way to win out over him is to whine and grizzle while he laughs and jokes with her Soul Friend.' Eduerd followed her pointed finger and saw the King and Amalin in hold, doing exactly what she had just described.

'Can I win out over such a man?'

'Stars, Eduerd! What is *wrong* with you?' she cried. 'There is no more accomplished or handsome man among all the Forest Folk as you, if only you would own it and use it to your advantage. Perhaps you will do better after some food, for I do not like you a jot when you are for nothing but feeling sorry for yourself.'

Eduerd, suitably chastised, donned a sheepish smile. For once the Lady Fiance was right that food would, at least partly, help. After all, he would have a chance to talk to Ravar who would no doubt sit among his Kin, while the King was stuck at the High Table.

The Dance of the Souls was a calmer affair for most, Eduerd and Lethan sitting it out and comparing notes, while Ravar and Amalin enjoyed the second-hand sensations of their respective First Dances. The King and Istreeth also had a chance to catch up.

'It was a good move to ensure that you took Ravar in the First Dance,' the Princess acknowledged, shrewdly. 'Your rival may be handsome, but no man's hand could compare with that of a Master. In fact, I will acknowledge that I believe you excelled yourself tonight, for I have not before known you to so transform the movement of your partner. The Desert Dancer would have been impressed.' She squeezed his hand encouragingly.

The famous Desert Dancer's identity was a great mystery, the man turning up out of the blue to seasonal celebrations and taking the parties by storm. By some trickery he was able to ensure that no one could ever quite describe his face, though the common memory of the way he led the Dance remained for seasons after and kept the magic of his tale alive.

The King nodded, pleased and flattered by the compliment, before all of what she had just imparted sank in. Istreeth had referred to his 'handsome' rival. 'You know who he is?' he asked, quickly.

'I do. And I shall not be the one to tell you for I am sure you will see for yourself in good time.' Her words had the edge of finality about them.

The King sighed. 'I must seek the final Dance with her.'

Istreeth nodded. 'I think that would be a good idea. Why did you not ask Ravar while you had the chance? We will be quite taken up with our Kin and visitors from the Plains over supper.' She referred to the Ambassadors that had come by invitation as part of the annual act of thanksgiving the Forest bestowed upon the South.

'Indeed and I cannot shirk that responsibility.' The tradition marked the Forest People's indebtedness for the Plains Kingdom taking in so many of their children when the plague had struck during the middle years of the last Athlete. The King was berating himself for neglecting to ask Ravar, but it was difficult to think of such things when he had been busy trying to dance the best Dance of his life while simultaneously doing his best to keep control of his mind. That latter had proved difficult while the woman he desired more than anything in the Six Kingdoms had been smiling in his arms.

The Feast that followed was a merry time for Ravar and Amalin, who were surrounded by two of their admirers and those men's shared Kin. These persons of course included Fiance and her own close friends, among whom were several parents of Nearage students. Proud mothers and fathers were full of compliments and high regard for the teachers. They also invariably shared Fiance's flare for hilarity and there was much outrageous talk and laughter at the table.

Additionally, Ravar was glad to finally get a chance to speak with Eduerd properly and they were so engaged in a complicated conversation about the form of some sort of telescope tower in the Desert, that Amalin rolled her eyes and pronounced them a lost cause to the rest of their group.

After a whispered conversation where several heads nodded fervently across the table, Amalin and Lethan agreed to play with the band during the Fourth Dance. They headed over to the Orchestra, where they found King Aislyth had also taken up a bow and was seated behind a huge bass. Somehow, he managed to dwarf it. The Musicians smiled with delight that yet more players were to join them.

'Something slow and melodic?' Lethan made his suggestion a request. Only Amalin caught his glancing wink at his friend, the Doctor, standing across the Hall.

As the strings began the soft notes of the 'Winter Romance', Eduerd took Ravar's hand in his. Waiting for her eyes to meet his, he said softly, 'Lady, I have waited longer than I would have liked for this moment. I have never so looked forward to a Dance.'

Ravar had to catch her breath in the face of such an open declaration. And, although he could never be the dancer of the ability of the King, it felt curious and exciting to be in his arms. The music was made infinitely more beautiful when Amalin added her voice to it and a second singer joined his voice in harmony.

Ravar and Eduerd did not speak. They had had plenty of time for that over the meal. Instead, they let the music fill their ears and enjoyed the simple pleasure being close and their slow movement around the floor. To Eduerd it was the most perfect few minutes of his life. He was profoundly sorry when the song came to a close and he was obliged to relinquish Ravar to Ralgan, the Chief Scribe who had come over to talk to her before the Fifth Dance.

The King, on the other hand, had watched the dancing pair from the Bandstand with open dismay. It did not take genius to recognise the same feverish admiration in the good Doctor as he no doubt exuded himself while with Ravar. *Damn!* he thought. He even liked the man! And he knew that Ravar did too, for they were forever trying to best each other at the School. He had often come across them sitting in the garden conversing at length. She also, he thought ruefully, attended most of his classes.

Thank Heavens she was now with Master Ralgan, who was one of his own closest friends, thought the King. No doubt Ralgan had asked Ravar on account of her excellent service to the Palace Administration. Indeed, the King could not remember ever receiving such a favourable report from the perfectionist Scribe.

His friend was almost certainly aware of his feelings towards the Tutor, despite his efforts to conceal them. Hadn't Istreeth's pointed comment about his being distracted at their last Kin breakfast been met with knowing looks all round? Well, he was glad for that. After all, Ravar had danced with Lethan earlier and he and Eduerd were thick as thieves. *I really must secure the Final Dance,* he thought.

Eduerd's mind had followed a similar course. After gently thanking Amalin once again for allowing him to pay court to Ravar during the Fifth Dance, he resolved to find Ravar and ask for the Sixth.

During the long interval that preceded the final dance of the night, Ravar was talking to a group of Forest folk at the back of the Great Hall. One with a bird's-eye vantage point would have observed that two men were making a beeline in her direction from opposite ends of the room. Both the King and Eduerd were striding towards her, oblivious of the other but sharing the same intention.

However, in the event, neither were to achieve their aim as, moments before they arrived, Grandmaster Dethir stepped up to Ravar and made a crooked bow.

'My Lady, may I take your hand in the Sixth Dance?' he asked, without preamble.

Ravar had to do a double-take. The much-revered Grandmaster had not even donned Dance pins that night and it was generally assumed that he was not up to much in the way of dancing, walking as he did, so heavily reliant on a stick. Nonetheless, it was a great honour and one that she would not have dared to refuse.

'Thank you, Grandmaster, yes.'

'Good. Lady Amalin, I trust that your Musicians may be relied upon for something *slow* for the last turn?' His tone left no room for anything other than obedience. Amalin made straight for the orchestra.

Ravar's two suitors arrived just in time to see her turn over her lowermost pin and had to make some rather awkward small talk with her nearby companions to hide their original purpose for being there.

Inadvertently, the King found himself standing directly next to the Doctor. He took a breath and made himself extend his arm and clasp that of Eduerd's, bracingly.

'A good evening to you, Master Eduerd.'

'Your Majesty,' said Eduerd, and bowed.

The King looked strained, then his face relaxed with a small sigh.

'Please, do not address me as such in this conversation, for I speak to you now as just one man before another,' he said. Eduerd looked mystified and the King continued. 'The fact is that we court the same woman, do we not?'

After a barely perceptible flinch, Eduerd met his eye and said, 'I believe all the Kingdom now knows it.' He pointed a thumb back over his shoulder, to where Fiance was among a large cluster of people, taking it in turns to look in their direction and speaking in hushed voices.

The King looked unhappily at them, then clapped Eduerd on the shoulder. 'Indeed, My Lord. That is why it is important that we make a good show that there is no animosity between us. For my part, this is the truth.' He sighed. 'Stars, if the Lady rejects us both at least I will have someone with whom I can share the pain. And, if she takes you for a husband, well…' He sighed again. 'Then I shall endeavour to be pleased that she finds happiness with a good man.'

Eduerd was quite taken aback, and not a little ashamed that he had not thought to extend the same sentiment himself. The King was a better man than he.

'Thank you, My Lord Aislyth.' The name sounded odd on Eduerd's lips. 'I do hope that at least one of us might make her happy. And if not, I shall bring the Forest Warmth to your table and we shall drown our sorrows together.'

The King chuckled and made a parting bow and they each felt a sense of relief that the conversation was over.

The opening notes eventually came and Ravar made her way to the edge of the floor, partly supporting her elderly partner. She studied his lined, wise face. In it she saw a great certainty and natural authority, of which she had previously only experienced glimpses on the rare occasions that she had previously spoken to him. In fact, Ravar had probably interacted more with him than most of the community, for he was often to be found in the Library, where he had his own corner, equipped with a desk and comfortable-looking leather chair.

'Do you know why I asked for this Dance, Ravar?' he asked her. He tone was that of a Tutor, full of intent.

Ravar was not one to be cowed, but she did not know the answer. 'I do not, Grandmaster. But I am sure that you will tell me?'

'Ha! You are impetuous. But what more could be expected of a Firebird? You are more like your costume than you know.'

He leaned closer. 'I asked you for the dance,' he continued, 'because there are two very good men here tonight who wanted it far more badly than I. Such a scenario is unremarkable but, unfortunately for them and for you, the status and popularity of your personages mean that all the Forest are watching the play.'

'Oh,' said Ravar, frowning uncomfortably as she thought about this.

'Tell me, My Lady, do you seriously consider both suits?'

There was no point in trying to evade the questions of such a man and so Ravar gave him an honest answer. 'Truthfully, before tonight I should have said no. But now, I hardly know what to think.'

'Mm,' the Grandmaster grunted, shortly. 'Then you must be careful until you make a decision to favour either or none. Many will be eager to speculate or influence the outcome.' Before she could interrupt, he silenced her by raising his forefinger.

'You do not have to tell me that such interference will have no effect upon you, *Master* Tutor.' He smiled as if enjoying a private joke. 'But consider what you shall do, when and if you take a husband.'

'Do?' said Ravar.

'Yes, Lady, what you will *do*. What is it that you desire beyond your current position?'

'Do you ask whether I seek a Higher Way?'

'I ask *which* of the Higher Ways you might seek.'

Ravar was stumped. Such a question could not be simply answered.

'No, do not try to answer the question now, for I doubt you have given the matter enough consideration. How much longer does this go on for? My poor feet ache!'

*

Amalin and Ravar fell into bed together that night, exhausted, heads spinning with images and memories of the Dance. 'Are you happy?' whispered Ravar, drowsily.

'Yes! Are you?' But Ravar was already asleep.

CHAPTER 13

Forestfyth, Sixth Year of the Dancer, late winter.

As was the usual practice of suitors paying court, the men pursuing Ravar and Amalin had had extended to them invitations to meet and dine with their Kin. Lethan's family mostly lived in the communities of the Western Forest, but he had invited his brother to stay and, being of the same Kin-circle in any case, had suggested jointly hosting an evening party at the Doctor's house.

It made much sense. Firstly, the courted women could be chaperone to one another. Secondly, the burden of Fiance's bossing and direction would be shared between the two suitors and thirdly, even Desledair could not object to the prospect of a combined social occasion that meant he would not have to endure a second such engagement.

The evening at Eduerd's house had been a roaring success. Fiance had, to the great relief of the hosts, insisted on catering and had produced enough food to feed a small army. Ravar and Amalin had been delighted to find out that Lethan's brother shared his sibling's easy manner and humour. Music also evidently ran in the family and his strong voice was warmly welcomed as he joined it to others in the inevitable songs that came of having so many keen Musicians among their number.

In addition to this, Desledair could not have been happier to have escaped Marketdawn for a few days. In fact, he was so genuinely glad to be out of the company of Widow Frensith that he was prepared to put up with any amount of nagging from Fiance. She had never been able to get away with so much gentle scolding and so was in a sort of ecstasy of her own.

Also in attendance were Hathsurst, recently invited into his Master's inner circle, so well did they like each other as well as work together. Eduerd's smartly dressed counterpart from Woodsedge, Doctor Keldair and her husband Credain, a much-respected Midwife, had also joined the party. The final guest to arrive was the dark-humoured Bathvess, a childhood friend of Lethan and Eduerd, who worked at the city forge.

In such biased company, the women could hardly fail to conjure the happy image of many more such cheerful occasions as this, should they favour the suits of their hosts.

Even through the more critical eye of a Master Tutor, it was good to know that, were Ravar to consider a life with the Doctor, she would be so easy and at home amongst his Kin.

It was Desledair who took her arm in the merry group walking home to the city. He himself was staying as a guest of Fiance as Lethan was to stay in the spare room of the cottage that night in order to assist Eduerd in clearing up the following day.

It was strangely comforting to be in such close proximity to a man who was free with his cynicism and mocking of his friends. Ravar wondered whether she felt so much the better because she was no longer being given the hard sell, however kindly the others had meant. She liked Lord Desledair very much. How sad for Eduerd that the man was so frequently commissioned so far from his home. Ravar had never parted company from Amalin for more than a few nights at a time.

'I gather the King of the Forest also seeks your hand, My Lady,' said Desledair, without emotion.

Ravar almost tripped up. 'That is so, My Lord,' she managed.

'I have met the man on several occasions and have always generally believed him to be a decent sort,' he mused. 'I do not envy your position, for I daresay each man would catch you a star if you so desired.' He raised his eyebrows and gave her a faint smile.

This seemed to be it, as far as he was going to say any more. It was awkward and she really did not know what to say. Eventually Ravar swallowed hard and attempted to change the subject, before she caught the laughter in her guide's eyes and realised he had scored the point. Desledair chuckled as she rolled her eyes.

'I see I have not lost all my skill, for I have an orator of the Gold Level lost for words,' he said, smugly. 'Of course I would rather that you made my Soul Friend happy, but I am the last man to be desirous of interfering in such matters. I will confine myself to confessing that I am relieved that Eduerd has, at least in one respect, shown himself to be a man of good taste.' He smiled at her and his eyes twinkled. Ravar reflected that Desledair could be quite the charmer when we wanted to be.

*

The King's offer had taken a very different form. He had invited Ravar to attend breakfast at the Palace on the first rest day of the new year. The formal request was handwritten and delivered in person. Ravar had been very curious as to what the early-morning meal might entail.

On the appointed day, Ravar had been greeted at the main entrance by Istreeth, rather than the usual attendants. The Princess led her into the western wing, which served as the private quarters of the royal household.

Instead of some grand dining room, Istreeth had relieved Ravar of her cloak and led her down into a vast, semi-subterranean kitchen. Inside were an odd collection of important personages. It was strange to see these people outside of the context in which she knew them, magnified tenfold by the fact that they were all clad in aprons and merrily working dough, beating eggs or spreading flour on surfaces. Every one of them was at least quite messy and either humming, singing or talking animatedly.

The King himself was wearing an elaborate but wonky chef's hat, a big white apron and wielding two large pans which he set on a huge stove. 'Good morning, Lady Ravar, and welcome to our gathering! These are my Kin.' He spread his arms to encompass the whole company. 'We meet on the first rest morning each week to share a good breakfast and some fun while we are free of our duties.'

Gesturing around the room, he said, 'Master Armick and his better half the Lady Estha you know.' The couple smiled their greetings. 'The same goes for Grandmaster and Lady Falthson,' the King continued, and the well-endowed couple waved flour-covered hands in the air. 'And here is Ralgan, my very good friend, who you know from the Palace Administration.' Ravar ginned at the good-looking Scribe, for once devoid of the stern face he wore at work. 'And finally, these young ladies are Fethain and Lamsyth, his two impossibly beautiful daughters.' He winked at them and they produced two gap-toothed grins. 'They take after their mother who is away in Woodsedge visiting her father.'

Ravar waved at the two curly haired girls who could not be more than a few years apart and said hello. They stared wide-eyed at their unusual guest. 'You have nice hair,' Fethain stated, shyly.

'Thank you!' Ravar beamed. 'But I wish I had yours for mine will not curl.' Fethain shared an approving look with her sister and smiled.

'These excellent persons are some of our extended family,' the King said happily, reaching an arm around his Istreeth's shoulder, 'and today you are part of it.' Ravar cast her eyes around the room, brightly. 'Which means,' he continued, 'that you are in need of an apron and a task.'

Istreeth obliged by fetching a battered blue overall and handing it to an amused Ravar. The King reached out a long, outstretched arm to each woman and pulled them over towards the stove where oil was now sizzling in the large, shallow vessels.

'Ah, now, ladies are you ready?' said the King. And with that, he seized a bowl of batter from a chuckling Armick and poured a generous amount into each pan. Ravar was then schooled in the art of frying and throwing her pancake. After this she was compelled to adjudicate between fiercely conflicting views as to the best toppings while others took their turns at the hot plates. In fact, she had the chance to test each recommendation as, no sooner had she finished her plate than she was hauled up to the stove again.

Istreeth admonished Ravar for addressing her by her title as she was among friends and Ravar saw the Royal Household in a new way, namely that of just a household. Everyone joked and teased and roared with amusement. Even the usually so poised Princess stole and ate the berries that Falthson had just neatly arranged on his pancake while he reached down the table for the cream. Having been threatened with a good tickling in return for her treachery, she ducked her small form under the table and escaped, helped out at the other side by Armick's giggling girls.

The cleaning up was a long affair as, between them, they had made a terrible mess. The task was lightened by them taking it in turns to sing choruses of the *Tallest Tree in the Forest*, a playful chant with an ever louder refrain, to which they all lent their voices.

When all was clean and tidy, a debate emerged as to what game they should play.

'Riddles?' suggested Ralgan.

'No! We cannot play riddles with Lady Ravar among us!' cried Armick. 'I have heard her in the Assembly and she will defeat us in a trice!'

'Charades, then?' suggested the King.

'With the prop box!' added one of the girls, excitedly.

'Charades it is,' Istreeth said, looking around at the nods of assent.

The following hour saw a rolling pin become a ship's mast, clothes affixed to the King's head to become flowing locks and Armick donning a saucepan, the handle becoming his beak – to name but a few of the performances.

By the time the King dropped her at home, Ravar was quite exhausted from laughing and still so full of breakfast that she doubted she would be able to eat supper, let alone any lunch.

Less happily, upon his return to the palace, the King's excellent mood took a turn for the worse. A messenger anxiously summoned his attention as soon as he came within view of the gates and he was quickly ushered into his private meeting chamber. Inside, one of his highest-ranking Councillors was waiting.

Seeing the urgent expression on the man's face, the King hurried to close the door to ensure their privacy. 'Well? What has happened?' he demanded.

'Sire, a contingent of Sea Guardians has arrived at the Palace.' The man licked his lips and continued quietly as if worried that he might be overheard. 'They are in pursuit of a pair of dangerous felons who they believe have come to the area.'

'Felons?' exclaimed the King, alarmed. 'What is their crime?'

The Councillor looked pained. 'Illegally boarding and taking passage on a vessel, theft and *violence*, Your Majesty.'

'What? Are they mad? The Sisters will have them cast adrift! How have they not yet been apprehended?'

'When they were discovered as stowaways they overpowered the sailor who found them, braining him with a club, Your Majesty,' said the Councillor. 'By the time the crewman awoke, the ship was skirting the coast and the pair were seen running from the shore for the woods. The poor man was quite grievously injured and I am afraid that the crew were more concerned with finding him medical assistance than chasing down the perpetrators.'

'Yes, of course,' the King muttered, nodding. His brow furrowed as he took it all in. Though far from non-existent, serious law-breaking was a fairly rare occurrence in the Six Kingdoms. Violent crime such as this was even more uncommon and tended to be the result of sickness of the mind or youthful aggression amongst minors which could be managed within the local community.

'How long ago was this?' asked the King.

'Two days ago, Sire.'

'And where were they last sighted?'

'On the northern coast roughly halfway between Northarm and Westarm.' The King considered this. Assuming they were hoping to make their way inland, perhaps westwards towards the denser areas of the Great Forest where they stood a better chance of evading detection, they would likely make their way predominantly through the Highturth region.

'Send word to the Governor of Highturth as a matter of urgency,' he said.

'Yes, Your Majesty.'

'I will write to the other governors as soon as I have spoken to the Captain of the Sea Guardians. Please have messengers of the Kingdoms Post ready to ride within the hour.'

'I will make the arrangements straight away,' the Councillor replied.

The more detailed account of events did not make for easy listening. The description of the two men, dark-haired, slender and between one and four centuries was hardly going to narrow things down. This was especially the case in the Forest Kingdom, where the account could match a great number of its male population.

The Seaman who had been attacked was recovering slowly, though it was thought that there had been no lasting damage. Unfortunately, the man had not heard his attackers speak by which means it might have been possible to identify them as bearing the accent of a particular region.

According to the Guardians, the miscreants were not believed to be in possession of large packs, as these would have been sighted, even from afar. However, the ship's quartermaster had reported some missing food rations and two blankets. The men would likely be cold and hungry, for the woods supplied little of warmth or sustenance at this time of year.

Stars, the King thought, *they must be desperate.* What could drive them to such a miserable flight? The penalty for stowing away would certainly involve a hefty fine or spell of service, but this could not possibly have been reason enough to physically attack the man who found them. And now they were on the run, compounding their crimes yet further.

Later that morning Palace runners were sent to herald the announcement that all Forestfyth Citizens were to attend an extraordinary midday Assembly in the City Square. Messengers were sent even, and especially, to the remoter hamlets and dwellings of the Capital Province, so that one of Doctor Eduerd's mid-morning callers was a uniformed Guard on horseback urging him to make his way to town.

The Doctor had saddled his horse as soon as he had seen to his last patient and ridden fast to ensure he made it in time. As he dismounted, Eduerd saw that a great crowd of anxious people had formed outside the Palace gates, extending well beyond the limits of the main square. In time, The King emerged from the Palace complex and took a stand on the central dais. He held up a hand to signal for quiet.

'People of the Forest,' he said, seriously. His deep voice carried well and all before him were still, listening curiously. 'I have received a report that two fugitives, pursued by Guardians of the Sea, have absconded into the Northern Forest.'

There was a quiet hum of shocked murmurs but he held up his hand again. 'It is not my intention to unduly alarm you, but for reasons unknown these two men are somewhere within our realm and are considered to be dangerous. While I do not believe they can have made it as far south as here I urge you all to be alert and exercise caution. Therefore, please ensure that your families and Kin do not venture abroad alone. I also ask you to report any missing produce, especially food, to the Palace Guard immediately. Finally, if you see someone you do not recognise please do not panic or take the law into your own hands. Leave the place immediately and make for a well-populated area where you may report your sighting in safety.' The King let his instructions sink in for a few moments.

'At this time I am needed to make arrangements for our own search and information-gathering efforts. I ask you not to burden the Palace Administration with questions and to allow them to do their jobs. Indeed, they will, I have no doubt, be working very hard until this affair is resolved. Please offer them your support and understanding.'

With that, the King stepped down from the platform and marched back into the Palace, leaving the volume of the crowd to rise exponentially as everyone turned to those near them to speculate about what they had just been told. Eduerd heard several voices muttering that they must write to friends and relatives in the Northern Provinces at once.

Ravar and Amalin had listened to the announcement with concern, but were practically minded. Passions tended to run a little higher in the competitive, athletic culture of the Plains and so there had been occasional incidents in their previous province during their early lives which called for intervention by the Kingdom Authorities. With level heads they quickly discussed the fact that the new term at the School for the Nearage had already commenced and they would need to ensure that arrangements were made for the students' safe commute.

Ravar would also have to ask Lethan to postpose a short series of lessons about the Forestry and Woodland management that had been planned for the winter season, as these were due to take place in the Eastern Woods. It was a shame, because this was the best time of year to show the students how the deciduous varieties might be trimmed or harvested, when the branches were most visible.

There was also bound to be wild scaremongering and overexcitement among the young men and women in their charge. Ravar suggested that she would tackle it head on, allowing a sensible discussion in the Assembly on the first day to include them in decisions taken for everyone's safety.

*

In the event, the panic died down much more quickly than anyone in the city had expected because, after two full weeks, there had been no further news or incidents relating to the two escapees.

The King suspected that the unfortunate men had probably succumbed to the hardship of the Forest winter and would be discovered, too late, by some poor wanderer in the spring. One unit of Sea Guardians would remain at the capital until the end of the season as a precaution, but he had ordered organised searching to cease.

The puzzling thing was that, despite the cooperative efforts of the authorities of both Market and Forest Kingdoms, they had failed to discover the identity of the felons.

It had originally been presumed that they must be residents of one of the many small, northern, coastal towns that fell under the control of the Sea Peoples. However, the Sisters themselves had fiercely appealed for information, only to be forced to concede that they were at a loss, for the pair seemed to be truly unknown among such communities.

The possibility that they had absconded from further afield, across the Great Sea, had not been lost on the Sisters, though the two stowaways must have been more successful in hiding their passage than their most recent sail, for all legitimate passengers were carefully recorded as per the

Laws of Commerce set down millennia ago by the Market People. The chances of them remaining concealed on a much longer passage were slim.

Well, it was a mystery but, the King reflected, a relief that the danger seemed to have passed. He had been so taken with directing the Forest's part in the investigation that he had barely had a chance to speak for more than a few moments at a time with Istreeth, let alone indulge in any real sort of social engagement.

He peered through the luxurious glass window in his meeting chamber. The sky had a bright grey tinge and he let out something between a grunt and a hum. Snow was on the way.

Eduerd, on the other hand, had been enjoying the past fortnight immensely. He had asked Ravar to spend a day with him and Hathsurst on their rounds and she had appeared to thoroughly enjoy the whole business. In fact, she had even asked whether she might accompany them again when time allowed.

It was normal for a courting pair to acquaint themselves with each other's everyday work and responsibilities and there had up until now, been a serious imbalance between the Doctor and Tutor because of course Eduerd already knew Ravar's teaching role so well.

Eduerd had recognised immediately that Ravar was not in the least bit fazed by the variety of ailments that he faced and treated. Her intelligent mind had no difficulty detaching her sympathy with the sufferer in order to carefully consider the best remedy. Equally, her natural ability to size up a character and adapt her tone and manner accordingly, meant that she was a hit with even the most difficult patients. One even asked if she could come again next time.

He had also noticed that, owing to her sharp eye and ear, Ravar often had a sense of when a patient was holding something back or understating a particular symptom. She had a careful way of drawing the whole picture from those who were frightened or embarrassed. Eduerd had told her with absolute sincerity that she possessed the makings of a Healer of the Mind. This was an area of medicine which was beyond the reach of most, not only because of its sheer complexity, but also because this Craft required a calm adaptability and compassion in the face of illogic that it was an impossible prospect for many.

To his great surprise, Ravar had nodded and confessed that she had been making a study of Eastern approaches to the Craft and had hoped to spend some time at the Hospital of the Silent Wind in the summer.

Eduerd made quarterly visits to the place in the Eastern Forest, where those with mental sickness could stay short- or long-term in tranquillity and under the care of its Master Healers. Ravar never ceased to amaze him.

*

Ravar had enjoyed a splendid start to the Dancer's Sixth Year. Eduerd had shown her a little of his life as a Doctor, introduced her to all manner of new and interesting books and artefacts and had even arranged for her to be able to borrow a friend's fine horse so that they could ride together on the cold winter mornings.

Having grown up on the Plains, Ravar and Amalin were considered something of disappointments to have only reached silver as Riders. However, in Forest circles, this was considered quite splendid and Ravar felt good to be in the saddle again. Eduerd, his choice of profession and living in comparative isolation having necessitated him becoming a good horseman, was an excellent riding partner. He had also generously given up the use of his own horse for a day so that Ravar and Amalin could ride up to the plateau to the West of the city and race along the flats.

Things at the School were going well too and the recent announcement that security measures by the Palace were to be relaxed meant that the curriculum could now be extended as planned.

It was while Ravar watched Lethan hoisting two thrilled students in a harness up to a lower branch of a Stoutburr tree, that the King surprised her with a visit. The students had been learning about the ten per cent rule that applied to most of the common trees of the Forest. In order to maintain the natural balance and avoid over-weakening the wild varieties in the Eastern Woods, the law stated that only this proportion could be taken from the trees within ten cycles. Although plant life grew with astonishing speed in this Kingdom compared with others, the Forest Folk had long since learnt the hard way that felling with abandon was folly.

'Will you be climbing today as well, Master Ravar?'

Ravar spun around at the King's voice. 'Good afternoon, Your Majesty,' she said. 'Perhaps, if there is time. As you can see, there is a long queue of those wanting to give it a try.' The King looked over fondly at the Nearage on the ground, staring up enviously at their peers.

'How is it that you are not cold?' he asked, regarding her attire. Ravar was clad only in a smock over a thin long-sleeved body suit. Ravar glanced down at herself and shrugged. 'Well, many will envy you in the coming weeks, My Lady, for I think that we shall see snow before long. I suspect your northern blood will welcome it.' He smiled.

Ravar glanced up suddenly. Her face was a picture of wide-eyed amazement. 'Snow?'

'Aye, snow!' the King laughed.

'I have never seen snow, Sire,' she said, breathlessly. 'But I have always desired to know it.'

The King's astonishment abated as he recalled that she had lived nearly her whole life on the Plains, where snow fell perhaps once or twice in a constellation. Even so, Ravar had spent time away from the South before now.

'But you have toured Marketdawn,' he protested. 'Their winters are as harsh as in the Northern Forest.'

Ravar smiled, sadly. 'Yes, and it was I who requested the tour during the summer months so as to escape the heat of the Plains.'

'Ah.' The King smiled. 'Then, I do not believe you will have to wait long to live your ambition.' After a pause, he said, 'My Lady, when it *does* snow, you must come to the Palace Gardens. Do not tell the Gardeners I have said so, but I believe they are at their most beautiful when painted white.'

He left Ravar trying to picture the scene and when she turned to look for him he had slipped away among the trees. Had he come just to tell her that? She had not seen him for more than a few moments in weeks and this cameo appearance made her realise that she had missed his company. So now there was another reason for hoping he was right about the weather.

*

The snow began to fall, first in small, slow flakes, then in large fluttering chunks during the night before the following rest day. Amalin's squeals of delight as she peered through the shutters brought Ravar to the front of the house and the two women stared with eyes like saucers at the outside world transformed before them.

Bursting out of the house, Amalin took up a great armful of soft, powdery snow and marvelled at its brightness. She spun round to advise Ravar gave it a try but was checked by the vision before her.

Ravar was standing, head thrown back and staring in fascination up into space. The still-falling snow brushed her face and settled on her hair. She held her arms out to her sides, the wide sleeves of her gown falling back so that the cold flakes landed on her bare skin. In all the lifetime together they had shared, Amalin had never seen her Soul Friend look quite as thrilled as this. The snow, of course was part of Ravar's element, and until now she had never even beheld it.

A surge of joy coursed through Amalin. Ravar had followed her everywhere she had ever been. Now, she thought, finally they were come to a place that was more truly her Soul Friend's than her own.

'Ah good, you are up and about!' roared a voice from a distance. The women turned in its direction and spied the unmistakable large form of the King, bounding through the deep snow in huge, confident strides. Without standing on ceremony, he opened their front gate, heaving it like a plough through the snow and said, 'Come on! Up to the Palace! We are hosting a snow sculpture competition on the lawn!'

Ravar and Amalin needed no further inducement and hurried to follow him. Amalin picked her way carefully, using the trench left by the King to find a way through the uneven clumps beneath the leafless branches of the trees. Ravar, however, did not seem to need to look where she was going. In fact, her eyes shot from side to side and up above her as she took in the cold stillness and muffled noises of the frozen landscape.

The Palace grounds were indeed transformed into a magical and unrecognisable place by the snow. Ravar revelled in their beauty. On the open lawns she saw many of the Palace staff, as well as Armick and his wife, Princess Istreeth and a hoard of the town's children. All were huddled into small groups and deep in discussion.

'Ah, we are just in time,' the King said, rubbing his hands together. 'Istreeth!' he called across to his sister. She scurried towards them, smiling.

'About time!' she admonished, nodding greetings to the two women.

'Now,' said the King, grinning excitedly, 'we have our team and we must decide what to create. We have until the next chime of the Palace Clock to complete our sculpture.'

'Who judges the winner?' asked Amalin, looking about.

'Why, Grandmaster Dethir of course!' replied the King. 'And he will not come out in the cold so we have to make our display big so that he can see it from the tower.' The party looked up and saw an outline of a figure standing at the large first-floor window. The King waved but received no reply.

After deciding upon the form of a snow castle, there was much activity between the four of them. The King attempted to direct proceedings but Amalin found it very funny how, in actuality, Istreeth always quietly undermined his orders and controlled the construction effort.

The King was in the middle of showing Ravar how to pack snow into hard blocks for the crenulations when a huge, soft snowball exploded on the side of his face. His eyes widened in mock fury and he spun around, knees bent like a hunter searching his prey.

While Ravar watched, amused by his expression, she too was stuck by a big, soft, frozen powder missile. In her case, however, there could be no mistaking her assailant, as Amalin could not control her laughter and was already reaching for another handful.

The King, meanwhile, had spotted the perpetrator of the first projectile in the form of Istreeth, who was taking cover behind their incomplete structure but peering around it to enjoy her victim's reaction.

The snowball fight began in earnest, several other groups getting involved after being caught in the crossfire, or simply because they didn't want to miss out on the fun. Ravar could not remember ever having such a wonderful time. Exhausted, panting hard from the running and ducking, she let herself fall backwards into the deep snow, feeling it cushion her landing and staring up at the still-falling flakes trickling down from the sky.

The King trudged over to her and looked into the little snow-lined pit where she lay. Her silver hair sparkled with the icy blanket surrounding it, her pale skin seemed to glow in sympathy with the glistening white. And as she looked up at him and, for just a second – had he imagined it? – her eyes flashed lilac.

*

When they finally arrived at home, Ravar and Amalin were tired, hungry and happy. They had thrown off their wet outer clothes and they fell upon the sofa together. Amalin snuggled up against Ravar, pulling a blanket over them. Ravar put her arms around her friend.

'That was fun,' Amalin said, smiling.

'I have not the words,' said Ravar, her eyes glazed. Amalin regarded her carefully. She was sure that Ravar's mind still danced in the snow.

'I think the King grows on you a little?' she chanced.

Ravar blinked slowly. 'Perhaps he does,' she said.

CHAPTER 14

Forestfyth, Sixth Year of the Dancer, early thaw.

Eduerd had found it difficult to interest Ravar in anything outside the classroom which did not involve snow while it had lasted. During the coldest snap of the season the Palace lake had frozen sufficiently to allow the city folk to skate on its surface and this had proved another attraction to which Ravar was magnetically drawn.

It was not that the Doctor disliked snow. In fact, he himself had introduced Ravar to sledging down the steep slopes of the forest to the west of the city. The problem was that the best places for most of the winter sports fell within the Palace grounds and therefore in the personal realm of King Aislyth. Eduerd had not enjoyed the way Ravar seemed to look at him now, or the relaxed, playful manner of the King around her, to which most people were wholly unaccustomed.

At last he had observed with relief the white heads of the spring Starflowers peeping up at the base of the trees in the forest. The temperatures had risen above the freezing threshold and, although there was a lot of rain, it washed away the snow and winter was over. With this happy thought, he rode to the School of the Nearage.

Ravar now allowed Istreeth the lead in half of the formal lessons at the School which freed her up to help plan and assess more of the project and community work. Thus, the Master Tutor was sitting in an empty workroom writing detailed annotations on an assignment in front of her. She looked up at a knock on the door and smiled at the Doctor standing in the doorway.

'I was not expecting you here today, My Lord,' she said, pleasantly.

'Well I have come for you, not the Nearage.' Ravar did not know what to say, so she kept silent.

'I believe we are due a clear spell over the next rest period,' he continued. 'I was wondering if I could tempt you to a little star gazing.'

'I should like that very much, Eduerd!' said Ravar, keenly.

'Good,' Eduerd managed, surprised but pleased by her enthusiasm. He cleared his throat. 'The best views,' he said, cautiously, 'I may say without bias, are from my house. You could bring Amalin…'

'Do not fuss, Eduerd,' said Ravar, quickly. 'I really do not need a chaperone and Amalin wouldn't like sitting out in the cold. I would rather come alone.' She paused, a wry smile forming on her lips. 'Unless you think me in danger of your impropriety?'

'No, of course not My Lady!' said Eduerd, mortified.

Ravar stifled a laugh. 'Then it is set. Will you pick me up on the evening of the first rest day?'

*

North-West of the city, the King had arrived after a long day's ride, at an isolated store barn. Standing outside it were a stricken-looking elderly couple, two Forest Guards and two Sea Guardians. All wore severe expressions. The King met these with a dark look of his own.

He had received the report at first light. A family who lived on the border of the Highturth and Forestfyth regions had gone to one of their outbuildings where they kept part of their winter store, only to find that a substantial part of their food stocks had been stolen.

Further, what remained had been roughly handled so that salted meat layers had been exposed to the elements. Broken crates had also meant that mice had made off with most of the dried goods. In addition, upon more careful investigation, it been discovered that some fleeces and pelts were missing.

The King had already arranged for food stuffs to be delivered to the unfortunate family from the central reserve. However, there was a much more sinister part of the report.

The Kingdom guards who had first arrived on the scene following the appeal made to the governor of Highturth, had made a thorough search of the outbuildings. There, they had found evidence that more than one person had been bedding down within one of them for several weeks.

As the King scanned the fetid scene inside the small barn with his own eyes, he was forced to conclude that the suspicions of the Guards might well be true. His previous belief that the men on the run from the Sea Guardians had met their end in the cold was erased as he took in the makeshift beds of straw and sacking. A charred circle revealed that a fire had been in regular use and there was a sour stench of unwashed flesh hanging about the place.

The King stalked out into the fresh air and inhaled deeply. The burly figures of the uniformed men came to stand before him, awaiting his orders.

'See to it that Guards are placed on the city outskirts of Highturth *and* Forestfyth,' he said. 'It would appear that these men have made away from this place. Perhaps they heard the approach of the owners and made haste. Ask trackers to go over the area and see if they can ascertain the direction in which they have headed. I shall meet with the Governor and then return to the Palace.'

'All that you have said will be done, Your Majesty.' The Lead Guard paused a moment and then puffed his chest out and looked his King firmly in the eye. 'But Sire, you must not travel unaccompanied.'

The King sighed impatiently but nodded. 'Then arrange for an escort and get to it.' The Lead Guard bowed to him, turned and began issuing orders.

News spread so quickly that by the time the King had returned to the capital very late on the following day, the place was buzzing with alarmist gossip about the discovery at the store buildings. He was compelled to hold another Assembly to reiterate the warnings he had made back in the winter. He then had to endure a multitude of meetings and questions from officials of a wide variety of Guilds and Kingdom Projects.

He wished that he could give more news and reassurance to these people but the fact of the matter was that, despite the men's trail having been picked up initially, it had been lost again at a nearby river and they appeared to have gone to ground once more.

The King turned it over endlessly in his mind. Where could they be hiding? It was still cold at this time of year and the spring yielded little in the way of sustenance. Unless, of course, they had had enough time to pack sufficient supplies from the store barn to take with them.

The last signs, about two miles south of the pillaged barn, indicated that the felons might even be heading in the direction of the capital. Heavens knew what their intentions might be. Ordinarily, he would have assumed that they would be inclined to travel westwards into the wilder part of the

Great Forest. This area was largely unpoliced and had become home to a strange community of outcasts and wanderers. There was an unspoken agreement that, as long as they refrained from causing trouble and contributed a prescribed quantity of, (mostly botanical), produce to the Kingdom Guard by way of Service quarterly, they could remain there unmolested.

Criminals pursued by the Kingdoms Guard could not expect such a fate, but he had nonetheless thought that it must be where they were headed. Instead, it appeared that they might be coming towards him and his immediate community. How could he ensure that his people were kept safe?

*

The startling revelation had not deterred Ravar from taking up Eduerd on his offer, nor encouraged the Doctor to take heed of his better judgement which said that riding through the Eastern Forest alone to fetch her, might be unwise.

Happily, they were not attacked by vicious criminals and had, instead, enjoyed a rather ethereal night together in the branches of the old Broadbirch above the cottage in the woods.

Eduerd had brought star charts, painted in an ink which glowed in the dark, up to the roof and the pair poured over these before climbing up to search for the constellations in the night sky.

Eduerd did not know the stories behind all of the major figures but was able to point out all of those for whom the calendar markers were named. The Dancer was only early into her ascendancy and so the Athlete still shone strong. Ravar was particularly taken by the Protector, the most complex of the major constellations. The stars formed a large figure in whose arms lay the sleeping form of a babe. It was colloquially often referred to as the Child Embraced and there was something soft and comforting about it, especially if one knew one's history.

Ravar had explained to the Doctor that the constellation had replaced the Hunter in the Calendar after the final Peace Accord had been reached at the end of the Great War. The change was to serve as a symbol of a new mind set amongst the Peoples of the Six Kingdoms.

Although he could not satisfy her hunger for the tales of the people in the stars, Eduerd had been able to fascinate Ravar by going over the elementary calculations by which one could track the movements and phases of some of the heavenly bodies. He had started by explaining the uneven movements and phases of the Near Moon and Ravar had delighted in working out some of the ways in which its orbit differed from that of its brother, the Far Moon. Further lessons held the promise of more complex computations in order to discern the speed of movement and the manner by which various bodies might be classified.

Ravar's head spun as she tried to take it all in. Her thirst for knowledge almost pained her because everything new that she learned of the mysteries of the Heavens presented a hundred more questions that demanded answers. She and Eduerd both knew that she would be straight down to the Palace Library for astronomical volumes the following day.

Eduerd also knew that this science was so vast that Ravar would not be able to master it with her usual speed. For now, he was just thrilled that, as he had suspected, the subject had captured her interest. At last, he had someone with whom he could really share his passion. And, of course, it was a bonus that this was also the person with whom he would rather converse on any topic over any other.

In fact, Ravar could talk about little else, much to the dismay of Amalin who, despite enjoying her own taste of star-gazing, had no interest in the complicated science that governed the skies. She was grateful to get out for walks and musical events with Lethan, who was equally unfussed about such academic pursuits.

Their best outing had been to a big concert in Highturth, to which they had been accompanied by Fiance. Fiance had arranged for them all to stay at the Falthson residence and it had been a spectacular performance.

Amalin had been recognised by some of the esteemed Musicians who had played with her in Marketdawn. She was immediately invited to sing with the famous Forest Choir and had bounced up to the stage, overjoyed to lend her voice to their seven-part harmony.

She had met a great many talented performers, composers and directors including a Sky Dweller who played paper drums. How she would love to go east one day and listen to the hundreds-strong percussion bands of the mountains. Ravar had read to Amalin accounts of their summer celebrations where drummers played in relay from different peaks so that the audience in the valleys heard the beats in sequence from different directions. How such a feat was even logistically possible, Amalin could hardly understand, but the Sky People were famed for their obsession with administration and organisation. She supposed that such displays were part of their culture of striving for discipline and thinking on a large scale.

Lethan seemed to feed off the same wonders as she did and they talked endlessly about movements, rhythm, interpretation of scores and sounds. In the home of Falthson it had been crowded, as the party from Forestfyth were not their only guests. In the late evenings everyone had to cram together into the limited number of sofas and chairs. She had, more than once, been squashed against the ever-smiling Carpenter. It had been wonderful. *He* was wonderful.

Now that the King had prevented non-urgent travel owing to the renewed hunt for the fugitives, there would be less opportunity for such exciting excursions. Amalin did not care. Lethan was, in fact, obliged to remain close for the foreseeable future.

CHAPTER 15

Forestfyth, Sixth Year of the Dancer, thaw.

After a week of what seemed to be an endless stream of Palace visitors and late-night conferences, Istreeth looked at the tired, strained face of her brother.

She had persuaded him to sit down with her for supper and been somewhat relieved to see him shovel in everything on his plate. Even by his usual standards, she had ensured that he was given a large helping. He had looked like he needed it.

'Brother, is there anything I can do?' she asked.

The King gave a weak smile. 'No, sister, beyond what assistance you have already given as an excellent diplomat with so many visitors.' He stood and walked round the table to her, planting a kiss on her forehead. 'Thank you for giving me the opportunity to eat a decent meal too.'

Istreeth smiled. 'Are you likely to be overwhelmed still tomorrow?'

The King blew out his cheeks. 'I think slightly less so, but I am probably to be confined to the Palace again.' He grimaced. He felt completely stir-crazy after days without a proper spell outdoors.

'Why do you not invite Ravar to join you?'

'What?' The King pulled a face of incredulity.

Istreeth replied calmly. 'As a suitor you are expected to give her a taste of your daily occupation and Crafts. You are a King and the safety and concerns of the Kingdom are yours. Let her see how you work.'

'But I am dealing with a major predicament!' he said.

'Exactly. Let her have a taste of being Queen.'

'Oh yes,' he said, sarcastically, 'and put her off the idea forever?'

Istreeth sighed, impatiently. 'Brother, do you know the Lady Ravar at all? Does she not thrive on challenge and complexity?'

The King worked his jaw, thinking. He slowly met his sister's eye. 'How is it that you have always been so much cleverer than me, Istreeth?'

The Princess relaxed back in her chair, sipping from her cup.

*

The missive from the Palace delivered to the cottage the next morning simply read: *If your duties at the School allow, I would be grateful for your clear thinking at the Palace Administration today. Aislyth.*

Ravar re-read it and gave a smirking frown. It seemed very strange to receive an informal note from the King and it being signed off simply with his name. What was all this about? She knew things at the Palace had been fraught this last week since the announcement in the town Assembly.

As she stood outside her front door re-folding the paper, the Princess came to the gate. 'Good morning, Master Ravar,' she said. 'I see you have my brother's note. I am happy to take the first two classes alone today if you so wish it? Masters Eduerd and Amalin have the afternoon slots.'

'Are you sure? I would not want you to think I am neglecting my duties.' Ravar did not want to appear as keen as she really was to see the inner workings of the Palace.

'No one would think that. Please give your assistance to the King. Indeed, I think he needs it. He is quite inundated with panicking and curious officials while trying to see to the everyday running of the Kingdom.'

Ravar laid a grateful hand on Istreeth's shoulder and thanked her. She had often tried to imagine how the King conducted business and now she had the opportunity to see for herself.

She decided against making straight for the Palace. If the King was receiving important dignitaries she should look the part. She went back into her house and donned formal attire, ensuring her sash and its contents were immaculately pinned. As she checked her appearance in the mirror, she added a sparking brooch to her waist tie and a matching ornament to her hair. There was nothing wrong with looking *good* either.

The King was in his private meeting chamber with his Chief

Councillor who was running through the order of proceedings for the day. Those requesting an audience comprised a dauntingly long list, including emissaries from the Governors of Westarm and Waterfyth, representatives from the Kings of the Plains and Marketdawn *and* two Leaders of fresh contingents of Guardians. He wondered if Ravar would come. Heavens knew he could survive weeks of meetings if she was there to accompany him.

As if the skies had heard his prayer, the door opened and in trotted a guard who bowed before giving his message. 'Your Majesty, the Lady Ravar is here. She says she has come at your request.' The King leapt to his feet, straightening out his sash.

'Please send her in.'

Through the gap swept a vision in smart, dark blue. About her exquisite, formal, long robes, she was adorned with glittering ornaments which set off her moonbeam hair and pale sash. Who would be able to witter on during discussions in the face of that? For his part, he could hardly find words to speak.

'May I be of assistance, Your Majesty?' she said before bowing. The King strode over to her, smiling, and made a bow in reply.

'I would be most grateful, My Lady,' he said, honestly. 'I am barraged by demanding officials from no less than four Kingdoms, *five* when I consider that the Sea Peoples send their own envoys. Please, will you help me to keep my sanity and lend your way with words to mine in calming the tension among them?'

'I shall do my best, Sire,' Ravar replied.

The King gestured for her to take a seat beside him at the end of the room behind a large oak desk. As he took his own place, he exchanged a glance with the Chief Councillor, who gracefully lowered himself into a chair at his other side.

The King turned to the wiry secretary seated apart from them at the side of the room. 'Please ask all those with updates relating to the investigation to come in first. The lead representatives from provincial Governors and the other Kingdoms can come and listen to the reports.' By way of explanation he said quietly to Ravar, 'That way no one can complain that they have been kept in the dark and I do not have to repeat the findings over and over.' She nodded her agreement.

In trooped five uniformed men wearing the garb of senior Forest, Sea and Marketdawn Guards. They stood in a line before them and made a synchronised bow with rigid precision. Ravar followed the lead of the others in the seated panel and rose to return the courtesy.

Behind the Guardians, a rather incongruous assortment of decorated men and women, their sash emblems denoting them variously as Emissaries or Administrative officials. Their clothing and physical appearance gave away the origin of most of their number, though one only had to look to the top of each sash for the symbol which denoted the Kingdom to which they swore loyalty.

'Master Ravar!'

The woman wearing the horse rampant pin that was the ancient image of the People of the Plains had blurted this from across the chamber. She was now flushed with embarrassment. Even one of the Guardians had turned to see the source of the outburst.

The King was quick to smooth things over. 'Ah, you must recognise your former countrywoman, My Lady,' he said with a smile. 'I do hope that you will have an opportunity to exchange your good wishes and news, informally, later in the day.' The woman gave him a grateful bow.

The King spoke to the room at large. 'For those of you who are unfamiliar with the woman beside me, let me introduce you. Lady Ravar is a Master Tutor and a woman of intelligence and logic without equal as far I am sure anyone who has ever met her is concerned.' The King looked to the Plainswoman who nodded vigorously. 'Therefore I have asked her to lend her wisdom to the problem we face. Stars know we need it.'

Ravar's heart fluttered from the heady praise and the elegant bows of acknowledgement that she received from the assembled conference. However, now was not the time for coquettishness so she gave a small nod and turned back to the King as a sign that business should continue. The host panel took their seats.

'Your Majesty, there have been sixteen possible leads since yesterday's report,' began the Lead Sea Guardian. He approached the table and handed the King a neatly laid out ledger. While he gave a summary of the reported incidents, Ravar cast her eyes quickly down the entries.

Reports ranged from possible sightings to a disturbed outhouse and chicken coup, to a wood den that might have been used as a shelter. As she zoned back in to the words of the Guardian, she heard him confirm what she had been thinking.

'The difficulty with nearly all the reports, Your Majesty, is that none can be considered concrete evidence. For example, no chickens were actually taken from the coup, the den could well just be a relic of children's games or an old hunter's shelter. Even the sightings do not tarry with one another. In some cases only one individual was spotted, two sightings claim one of the pair had a limp and the geographical spread and timeline tell us that they cannot all be the men we are looking for.' He set his teeth in frustration.

'Thank you, Captain,' the King said, feeling equally thwarted. 'Tell me, are there any leads that the Guard feel are more credible than others? Perhaps we should start there.'

The Leader looked to his sides, inviting any among them to speak, should they have an opinion. One stepped forward.

'Sire, I know that the absence of theft from the chicken coup makes it appear a false lead, but I examined the place myself and I am convinced that one or more persons bedded down there for the night.'

'It was *slept* in?' the King asked sharply. Ravar referred to the written report. There was no mention of this, only a disturbance.

'Yes Sire, I have only just returned from the place. The hutch is large. It's just that, well…'

'Speak your mind,' urged the King.

'I cannot think that any right-minded person would bed down in the filth, unless they were desperate. On the run perhaps?'

'Indeed,' said the King, thoughtfully. His eyes narrowed in thought. 'It was slept in two nights ago?' he asked.

'Yes, Sire. The owner checks the hutch twice a day and would have noticed.'

'But, Your Majesty,' cut in another Guard. All eyes turned to him. 'The other more credible sightings and incidents of the same timeline take place so far from the location of the hen house that it does not make the overnight stay possible!'

'They are only reports,' pointed out the King. 'Their accuracy cannot be verified.'

Ravar interjected. 'Your Majesty, may I have access to a detailed map that spans the areas where sightings and so on have been reported?' The King turned to his secretary and the man made off at once to fetch one.

'You have an idea?' he asked.

'I wish to see if there is a pattern, Your Majesty.' She turned back to the Guardians. 'You are sure that no chickens were taken?'

'We double-checked with the owner, My Lady.'

'Yes, this is curious given the reports of theft of food stuffs elsewhere,' put in the King. 'What do you make of it, Master Ravar?'

'A chicken shed must be an unpleasant place, but it is warm,' she said, ponderously.

'No more so than a good encampment, which we have seen used elsewhere,' said the King.

'Unless one had little time or chance to build one before the cold of nightfall,' Ravar suggested.

'What could have prompted the rush?' said the King. 'All the other evidence tells us that the men are patient and stealthy to the extreme.'

At that moment the secretary returned and smoothed out a large detailed map before Ravar. Two guards stepped forward to point out the location of the shed. 'Thank you,' Ravar murmured, thoughtfully. 'Please could someone plot the location of each reported incident on here for me? I think that we will all be better able to make sense of this once we can visualise the possible movements of these men.'

The Guards looked to the King for permission to take the map and ledger from the room to complete this task and he nodded. He then stood and addressed those at the back of the room.

'Can we pick this up in an hour?' All made their bows and hurried off to write up what little had been learned.

During the following hour, Ravar watched with great interest, the way in which the King quickly ran through a series of administrative and economic documents and reports that were each presented with a brief summary, by his secretary. Some required authorisation, such as permission to make changes to buildings or to export large quantities of produce to other Kingdoms.

Ravar approved of the systematic and careful approach of the King, who asked questions where necessary and always checked that requests had been signed off by Masters of the relevant Crafts in terms of safety and quality control.

Before she realised, an hour had passed and a Scribe entered the room to inform them that the map was fully annotated and the officials were waiting outside to re-join them.

As everyone crowded around the map, trying to see a pattern, Ravar held up a hand, begging their silence so that she could concentrate. It must be infuriating for the King to always have to be so transparent that he was never able to have quiet for his thoughts. Her natural authority from the classroom meant that she was obeyed without question. The King glanced around in wonderment. Perhaps he should employ her as a Guard.

'The two sightings where one man was reported to have appeared injured,' Ravar stated carefully, 'take place within relative proximity of the chicken shed. *And* they take place within the day it was slept in.'

'You think that they were forced to use this shelter because the injury was recent and prevented further travel?' surmised the King.

'I consider it a possibility.'

'But, Master Ravar,' said one of the Guards, 'we have food taken from a farm house twenty miles distant a day later. Surely a man, injured so badly as to necessitate sleeping in the hutch could not travel so far in that time.'

'True,' conceded Ravar. But she was looking carefully at the locations and cross-referencing them with the timeline of the other later incidents and not really paying attention to the ongoing discussion. The most recent supposed sighting was, once again, back in the vicinity of the shed. A group of travelling merchants claimed to have seen a man running along a high ridge some way north-west of the capital the previous day.

Her mind was working quickly, trying to visualise an order of events. Could it be that, after one man was injured, the other made the decision for them to camp in the chicken shed? Building a shelter after the exhaustion of supporting an injured comrade would perhaps not be in him. Having the next day found a nearby safer place to make a shelter, the fit man would need to leave the other in order to seek food and water, which would explain the sightings of a single person after this time.

It would also give a reason for the seemingly back-and-forth sightings, as the men could not make steady progress while one was having to leave and return to his lame friend.

Cautiously, Ravar presented this theory to the others. The King considered it. 'It is certainly possible,' he said slowly. 'Guardians.' The uniformed men jumped to a sort of attention as they recognised the tone of a man about to give orders. 'Concentrate your search once again in the area of the farmstead with the chickens. Be on the lookout for a single man and think about places which would offer good concealment. Let us run with the principle that at least one of the fugitives is relatively stationary and that the other will be travelling to and from him.'

'Sire?' Ravar cut in. 'If one of them is hurt, they must be getting fairly desperate. Could we not try to encourage them to come forward with the promise of medical treatment and a fair hearing?'

The King sighed. 'I cannot promise leniency, My Lady. The case is only under my jurisdiction at all because of where they have run. Their crimes are to be judged by the Sea Peoples.'

'I am aware of that,' Ravar said gently. 'But, Your Majesty, the search has so far proved most difficult and even criminals are entitled to basic care and dignity. They may have committed terrible deeds but we do not understand the path which has led them there. Perhaps we should appeal to them with compassion and hope that an offer of help will urge them to come forward.'

The King thought about this for some time. 'Very well, it can do no harm,' he said, tiredly.

He addressed the Lead Guardian once again. 'Place notices throughout the area that King Aislyth guarantees the fugitives medical attention and fair treatment if they turn themselves in to the Kingdoms Guards.' The Guard nodded his understanding.

The King looked around the room. 'Does anyone else have anything that they would like to say?' He was met by a sea of shaking heads. 'Then please relay your reports to your superiors and we will reconvene tomorrow morning.'

The King did not have a chance to discuss the matter further with Ravar, for there was a large backlog of everyday work that required their full attention. Firstly, a housing dispute between two residents in the Western Forest had been referred to the Master Law-Scribe in Waterfyth and the judgement required the stamp of the King to make it final. Then there were the rotas for Kingdom service which had to be signed off, statistical compilations from the orchards and large farming districts to be examined and some early end-of-quarter reports from projects to be read through and approved. After this he would have to hear the private and local petitions from his subjects.

Ravar found it all fascinating. The King had to know so much about so many things! She had never taken him for a particularly scholarly man beyond his knowledge of Written Works. She reflected that, in this respect, she had done him a grave injustice.

She also admired his seemingly endless patience and genuine concern for the well-being and happiness of his people. He brushed aside a tear with the news that a baby had been born to a family south of Westarm.

He had even hand-written a note of congratulation to be sent by Kingdoms Post with a small lantern by way of a gift.

The King also heard the heartfelt plea of a Bee-Keeper from the city begging to be allowed to travel to Highturth, despite the restrictions owing to the fugitives. The poor woman was desperate to visit her elderly and frail sister after receiving news that her sibling had taken ill. The King had readily accepted Ravar's sensible suggestion that she might travel with the next rotation of Guards posted to the region the following week.

Yes, thought Ravar, it was unsurprising that the King's sash was so heavily and unusually ornamented. In addition to his Mastery in two areas, he sported an array of gold through to bronze emblems, the Crest of the Kings of Marketdawn and the Plains and even a Pearl of one of the Sisters of the Sea. The latter pins were awarded as marks of thanks by rulers to those people who had performed the highest services to their Kingdoms.

Ravar did not know when or what King Aislyth's assistance to any of them had been, but she could well believe him capable of such feats. He understood the things that mattered to all manner of people. It was always said that the Way of the Bard was for those men and women who were able to guide the Souls of whole communities in the right direction. If that was the case, she thought, then the King had long since begun to travel that road.

CHAPTER 16

Forestfyth, Sixth Year of the Dancer, Thaw.

A week later and the Guardians' trawling of the Northern Forest had still failed to produce results. The King had to endure the increasing frustration of the Lead Guardian in his daily reports and do so without the benefit of Ravar's insight.

As much as Ravar would have loved to continue to sit in on the King's daily schedule, she had her own responsibilities at the School of the Nearage. However, at her request, the King had kept her informed of developments, or lack thereof, via runners carrying reports from the Palace.

In truth, she was surprised that the wanted men had not come forward. The Guardians' only lead had been the uncovering of a makeshift camp in a deep cave under an overhang that hugged a small river. It had been out of use for at least three days but there were bloodied rags left behind which seemed to be evidence of poor attempts to bind a serious wound.

The Healer of the Sea Guardian contingent had needed little time to draw the conclusion that the wound was infected and would be causing incredible pain. Yet, despite the Forest being positively littered with small paper copies of the King's offer of medical assistance, the wanted men had melted into the landscape once again without trace.

Ravar sat in the School gardens after her last class going over it all in her mind. How could the able man who obviously cared enough for his friend to put himself at greater risk by sticking with him, be prepared to ignore the offer of treatment? At the very least he could arrange for the injured man to be found while he made his own getaway.

Ravar tutted to herself at such pointless speculation. Given that the men had *not* come forward, how far could an injured man realistically travel in the Forest? Surely the Guards would have discovered them with such a narrowed search field. Unless… A thought suddenly struck Ravar as she recalled the topography of the map that she had asked for at the Palace.

When Amalin came out following the late class, she found Ravar still seated on the bench in the School Grounds. She knew the distant, narrow-eyed look on her friend's face all too well and crouched down in front of her with a stern expression.

'What have you in your head, Ravar?' she asked, suspiciously. 'I know you too well not to recognise when you have concocted some dangerous idea.'

There was no point in trying to lie to Amalin and so Ravar looked her friend in the eye and said, 'You are right. And you know that once such an idea has taken root, I will not be perturbed for seeing it through.'

Amalin sighed. Well she knew this. 'Then I will aid you,' she said, lightly.

'No!'

'Yes!' Amalin returned fiercely. 'Or I will report to King Aislyth that you are bent on some foolish plan.'

'No, you can't!' cried Ravar, quickly.

'Oh, Stars, then it *is* to do with the hunted men!' she exclaimed, horrified. 'No! Ravar, you mustn't—'

'I have to try! One is wounded and likely to *die* of infection if he is not soon found.'

'That is not your problem, Ravar!'

'Actually, it is!' snapped Ravar defiantly. As if she had let something terrible slip, her face suddenly took on a frightened look and she bit her lip.

'What?' Amalin demanded. 'What does that mean? What are you not telling me? Ravar? Ravar!' Amalin was fearful and angry now.

'It… It is only an idea, Amalin,' Ravar said, slowly. 'But, Amalin?' Ravar looked up pleadingly.

'But you think you are right,' Amalin finished the sentence for her.

She huffed, raised her eyes to the heavens crossly and then sagged. 'In which case, you *are* probably right.' Amalin hated this. 'But I meant what I said. Whatever you are up to, I will not let you face it alone. Do not argue!'

*

The next day Ravar and Amalin set out in their travelling cloaks, each carrying a large pack filled with food, camping apparatus, medical supplies and blankets.

Ravar had been obliged to share her theory with her friend and they had discussed her 'plan' late into the night. As Amalin had pointed out, it was not a very good one. In fact, it was vague, potentially very dangerous and likely to bring down the wrath of just about everyone they knew and loved upon them.

Nevertheless, Amalin knew that Ravar would not be moved and so had steeled herself to help her see it through.

The women made their way at first light to the Palace courtyard, where several wagons, a group of four traders and the Bee Keeper who had petitioned the King the week before were awaiting the ten-men-strong contingent of Guardians who would be travelling north-west to replace those who had been on duty for the past fortnight.

Having seen Ravar in her capacity as personal advisor to the King during the previous week, no one questioned her calm instruction that they were to escort her and her companion to Highturth. She and Amalin took places in the back of a cart and the group set off as the morning bell tolled in the Palace tower.

Ravar brought out the map of the area that she had carefully annotated from her pack. Amalin looked down at it anxiously. Her sense of direction had never been any good and even Ravar, whose was, had no real experience of the region.

Ravar attempted to quell her concern. 'There are several notable landmarks on the main Northern road, Amalin,' she said. 'We will be able to spot these without difficulty. She pointed an annotation on the map. We will make for this part of the river.' Amalin nodded without enthusiasm.

On the afternoon of the second day's travel, the two women slipped soundlessly from their slow-moving wagon. They had made sure that they had taken places on the vehicle at the back of the line so that their departure would not be noticed. The convoy's habit was to make a last, long push after the midday meal, using all of the remaining light. Ravar was counting on this routine to ensure that their absence would take some time to be realised. Even then, she hoped, the majority of the group would be forced to continue to Highturth.

They set a fast walking pace and Ravar found the spot on the river which she had been looking for quickly. They split up, Ravar fording the water to the other side, and they followed their respective banks downstream, each keeping their eyes peeled on the surrounding scrub.

After four exhausting hours of hiking, Amalin gave a yelp of excitement. 'Here!' Ravar waded through the cold, thigh-deep current and joined her. Camouflaged in the bushes was a small, rather battered rowing boat and one paddle.

'They did not get very far,' observed Amalin.

'Nor could they in this craft,' said Ravar dryly. 'One must have had to bail all the way.' She pointed to a narrow slit in one of the back panels.

'Now what? They could be anywhere,' said Amalin, looking about the endless woodland surrounding them.

'No, I do not believe so. Remember that one is badly injured. They will be hiding out within a mile or two at the most.'

'And you expect them to just come to us?' said Amalin, unhappily.

'I do,' said Ravar.

'I see,' said Amalin, in bad temper. 'And what is to stop them from attacking us, stealing our food and leaving us for dead?'

Ravar looked at Amalin. She could see that her friend was tired and frightened. She took her hand in her own. 'If I am right, all that is required is a softer approach than has been tried thus far. We have come all this way, Amalin. Can we really abandon the plan now?'

Amalin looked up into the calm, gentle face of her friend and grimaced. 'No, of course not,' she said, grudgingly.

They made their way about half a mile into the wood from the river. There, they made a small fire and set some meat and dough balls to cook on a bed of strongly fragrant herbs. After a while Ravar took a deep breath. 'The smell will travel well today. Let us hope the wind takes it in the right direction. But in case it doesn't we must employ our second tactic. If I start will you follow? We can take turns and save our voices?' Amalin nodded unhappily.

It was then that the forest underwent the most bizarre transformation of being filled with the soft but carrying tones of alternating female voices. Set to a simple tune that was often given to children's lullabies, Ravar and Amalin sang out into the forest. Ravar chose her words carefully and Amalin followed suit.

'Our names are Ravar and Amalin.
We are alone, without weapons.
We seek the two men,
So tired and hungry,
Who run from the guards.
We bring you food and medicine.
We will not harm you.
Let us heal your wounds.
Come to our fire.'

Ravar's singing voice was generally held to be reasonably good. She always sang in tune and had good tone and diction. However, even or perhaps especially, in the open stretch of the Forest, the beauty of Amalin's melody was so moving that the whole place seemed to fall under a spell. Ravar was counting on it being impossible to ignore.

It was well over an hour later, when the light was just starting to fade and Amalin was enchanting the air, that Ravar thought she caught the scent of sweat on the breeze. The fire itself was producing the fragrant smells of cooking and wood smoke so it was hard to be sure but once again there was the sharp tang she had noticed before.

Motioning for Amalin to continue singing a little more quietly, she placed a calming hand on her companion's shoulder, before relaxing her body to remain perfectly still, listening intently.

Still hearing and seeing no movement when Amalin came to the end of the refrain, Ravar did not take over. Instead she called out in a gentle voice.

'We know you are there.'

Only silence answered.

'By now you know that we sang the truth,' she continued. 'You can see that we have come alone and are unarmed. We will step away from the fire now. Come and take some food.' She and Amalin, firmly grasping each other's hands stood and walked slowly from the fire. Still there was no sound or movement. Amalin began to think that Ravar must have been mistaken.

'There is medicine in the brown bag,' Ravar called out again, undeterred. 'Will you let us try to heal your friend and take away the pain?' A twig snapped. Ravar put her arm around Amalin, whose shaky breathing gave away her nervousness.

Suddenly, a haggard and dirty figure emerged sideways from behind a tree near the fire. He was so filthy and dishevelled that he might have been taken for some Tree Imp from the old stories and the women flinched when they caught sight of them.

He had been able to get remarkably close without them noticing, thought Ravar. Upon closer scrutiny she guessed that he must be around the women's own age, though short by Forest standards. He was very thin and had a wild, terrified look about him. He had long, dark and matted hair and what she thought were blue eyes, though it was very difficult to tell in the greying twilight. He was bearded and clothed in makeshift garments of tied sacking. Ravar clenched her jaw hard, resisting the urge to say anything, lest she scare him off.

Never taking his eyes from the women for a moment, the man slowly approached the fire, where the joint of meat they had set to roast was now well-browned and giving off a wonderful aroma with the herbs. When he reached it, he seemed unsure of what to do. The food was burning hot and he had no way to carry it. His eyes flitted towards the brown bag containing the medicine.

'You need our help,' said Ravar, firmly. 'Let us prepare and wrap the food for you and take the medicine to your friend.'

The man tensed and shot her a look of anger but the flash of malice had no effect on the serene Tutor's features. His face suddenly sagged and his expression morphed into agonised look. Amalin thought he might cry.

'What is your name?' Amalin called over, gently. 'I am Amalin.' She flashed him a wonderful, warm smile. 'This is Ravar, my Soul Friend.'

The transformation in the man before them was astonishing. It was as though he had never seen a smile before. His mouth opened as if to say something but nothing came out.

'What is your name, friend?' repeated Amalin.

'My—' The man's jaw quivered. 'I am Soren.' He gasped, horrified by his own admission.

'Hello Soren,' said Ravar. 'Will you let us help you and your friend?'

Soren flinched. 'You are not like others!' he blurted, nervously.

Amalin and Ravar looked at each other, unsure of his meaning. 'We are not seeking to capture or hurt you,' said Ravar.

'Your hair—' Soren cut himself off in mid-sentence.

Ravar forced a little laugh. 'Oh, you are not the first to be unaccustomed to my silver locks. My mother was of the Snowseal Kingdom in the far North. She gave me my hair.'

'I have heard the masters speak of this place,' the man murmured, frowning.

'Did he say *the masters*?' whispered Amalin. Ravar had a terrible feeling.

'Will you let us help you or not, man?' Ravar said, in the carefully enunciated tones she sometimes used in the classroom when she wanted something done quickly. 'Your friend is hurt and if you do not let us treat him soon, he will probably die. We have come all this way and have taken considerable risks to find and help you. Will you run from us too?'

The women could almost see the conflict in the man's mind. He looked back over his shoulder as if seeking permission from an invisible friend and slumped into a mournful resignation. He met Ravar's eye and cried in desperation. 'Please hurry! Thalsay will not wake today and his skin burns like fire!'

The women quickly doused the fire and grabbed their packs. They slung the joint of meat and hot rolls in a cloth and hurried after Soren who was jogging ahead of them. Amalin's head whirred with emotion but Ravar seemed to have settled into the clear, detached thinking of one managing an emergency.

Before long, they came upon a huge, upturned tree whose immense root structure was half erupting from the ground. Within its dirt-encrusted talons, a well disguised camp had been formed with the use of sticks, leaf mould and other detritus from the woodland floor. Ravar wrinkled her nose at the sickly stench of infection as she knelt down beside the man who Soren had called Thalsay. He looked much like his companion in that he was emaciated, dirty, and slight in build and of a similar age. However, his brow was caked in beads of sweat and his clothing soaked in the same.

Ravar removed the pelt covering his lower half and could not mask her horror at the state of the poor man's leg. The wound had been wrapped, inexpertly, in filthy rags which were soaked through with blood and pus.

'Help him!' Soren pleaded.

Ravar shook her head in dismay. 'Your friend needs a Master Healer,' she replied.

'No! You said you could help him!' Soren said, angrily.

'I did not know how bad his wound was!' she argued. 'You must come with us. We will take him to Master Eduerd. He will know what to do—'

'No!' Soren cried. 'We will not go back! He… We would both rather die!' He had a hunted, deranged look about him and he swayed slightly.

Ravar stood and took his arm. He shuddered at her touch but allowed her to guide him down to be seated by his friend.

She cast Amalin a quick look and said, 'Amalin, our friend Soren is exhausted and half-starved. I will see what I can do to clean his friend's wounds if you will prepare some food.' Amalin immediately set about gathering dry wood for a small fire, glad for something to do. Once it had been lit she began taking items from her pack. She passed plates and forks to Soren who seemed puzzled by the utensils. He held the shining metal implement up to his eye in the dark.

Ravar, who had been gently unfolding the wrappings around the other man's leg glanced up and saw this. Amalin saw Ravar's mouth set and a dangerous flash of anger in her eyes.

'How did you come by the marks on your wrist, Soren?' Ravar's voice was strained and tinny. Soren grasped the band of scarred skin with the other hand as an automatic reaction. The movement served to reveal the same painful looking marks on the other arm. Amalin regarded them in shock.

'Thalsay bears such a mark on his left ankle. Do you?' Ravar's voice was only just steady.

'We could not go on!' wailed Soren, almost childlike. He leant forward to Amalin and grasped her hands. 'Please! Do not let her send us back!' Amalin took the man's head and turned it back to face Ravar, speaking softly in his ear.

'Listen to me,' she said. 'It was Ravar who guessed what you both had been through. It was also her that insisted that we come out to find and help you. And here we are.' He looked from Ravar to Amalin. Each of the women gave him a smile. 'Neither of us would ever do you harm. Do you understand?'

'No. I do not understand,' said Soren, rather pathetically.

'We will do our best to explain,' said Ravar. 'For now, you must eat. I can clean this wound and give Thalsay medicine to calm his fever. Then we shall have to get some rest. We can discuss what we will do next in the morning.'

*

A long distance northward, the travelling party from which the women had absconded had discovered their absence. It had been a full hour after pitching their camp and near darkness when it had been noticed that Ravar and Amalin were nowhere to be seen. At least half an hour had been spent conducting an equally fruitless search of the immediate area as the night drew in.

Stoney-faced, the Lead Guardian had told two Forest Guards to set off back down the trail and make top speed for the capital to inform the King. They grimaced at the idea of being the ones to bear such news.

In addition, three more from the party would begin a slower, more thorough search effort at first light. No more men could be spared as they were needed to protect the remaining travellers, not to mention at their destination.

*

After a fairly fraught night due to the tossing and turning of their feverish patient, Ravar and Amalin had insisted that Soren went to wash himself in the river. It gave the women a chance to talk.

'Have you seen the way Soren claps the arm of Thalsay?' asked Amalin.

Ravar nodded. 'It is reminiscent of the Soul Embrace.'

'Do you think they are joined?' asked Amalin. Ravar shook her head, but in frustration rather than a clear negative.

'I do not know. I wondered if they are brothers. There is a physical likeness.' Amalin nodded her agreement. 'But then,' Ravar went on, 'they are both so small and thin that it is difficult to tell. They cannot have had anything like a good meal in decades.'

'Can they really have been kept from the world so long?' Amalin was holding back tears.

'Any sort of *civilised* world, certainly,' Ravar said, the anger giving her words an acid barb.

'Then,' Amalin said, hardly believing her own words, 'you were right.

Heavens know I wish you were not. How can such a thing have been allowed to happen? How can it even have been made possible? Someone must know…'

'Aye, someone knows,' Ravar spat. 'Someone or, more likely, some *people* who have kept Soren and Thalsay chained up so long that it has permanently marked and deformed their limbs.' Amalin let out a sob.

'No wonder they did not come forward,' she murmured.

'I have been thinking about that too,' said Ravar. 'There is one of the King's notices offering medical assistance by Thalsay's side in the camp. Soren must have actually picked one up.'

'If they are so used to unkindness it is not surprising that they shunned the offer,' suggested Amalin.

'I think it is worse than that,' muttered Ravar, but before Amalin could question her further, they heard running back towards them.

He was looking pale and anxious until he saw that all was as it was when he left.

'When will you trust us, friend?' asked Ravar, gently.

Thalsay moaned in his sleep. Soren rushed to his side.

'His fever is down!' he exclaimed happily.

'It is,' Ravar said cautiously, 'but Soren, he needs proper medical attention. I have cleaned out the wound in his leg but I do not have the tools or skill to stitch it. In time, it will fester again and who knows what damage has already been done that I cannot identify. He has lost so much blood and—'

'No! They will take us back!' Soren cried desperately.

'I will not let that happen!' barked Ravar. Her fierceness took Soren by surprise. Amalin too, looked shocked. 'I will *not* let that happen, Soren,' she repeated, more quietly, though no less emphatically. 'The King of the Forest knows me. He will listen to what I say.'

'What can you say? We have stolen, we… we hurt a man!' He burst into tears.

'You did not steal a chicken, though you had the opportunity,' Ravar said calmly.

The statement caught the young man off-guard. 'What?' he said.

'You stowed Thalsay away in a chicken coup for the night and yet you did not take one of the birds,' Ravar elaborated.

'The birds in the wooden house?' said Soren, frowning in confusion. 'Why should we take one?'

'You eat meat, Soren, do you not?' Ravar asked.

'We were not often given meat at the caves,' said Soren, still frowning.

'No, I had guessed not,' said Ravar. 'Tell me, did you prepare your own food in the... *caves*?' Ravar internally recoiled at her repetition of Soren's term.

'The Masters gave us our food,' said Soren, impatiently. 'What has this got to do with anything?' he cried, his voice rising to a crescendo. 'We have defied the masters. When they catch us we will be...' He broke off in a sob.

Ravar took a deep breath and picked up the small paper notice lying before him. 'Soren, look at me.' He did so, blinking back tears. She held the notice us to his face. 'Where did you find this?'

Soren looked bewildered for a moment, then replied quickly, 'But they are everywhere! You must have seen them? They are pinned to trees and scattered on the trails. If I have done wrong I did not mean to—'

'Soren what do these mean to you?' Ravar interrupted.

'Mean?'

'Yes, what do they say?'

'Say?' Soren looked fearful and confused.

Ravar cast a meaningful look to Amalin who just shook her head sadly.

'They say,' Ravar said gently, that the King himself is offering you medical assistance and a fair hearing if you come forward.'

'I do not...' He halted mid-sentence. 'How do I know you are telling the truth?'

'You will have to trust what your experience of us so far. Have we failed to keep our promises?'

'No, but—'

'Do you think I will not keep my word to speak to the King on your behalf? I am a Tutor among our People.' Soren stared at her blankly. 'It means that I take charge of those who cannot yet fully represent themselves.'

'Your People?' asked Soren, frowning.

'The People of Forestfyth, of the Forest Kingdom. *Your* Kingdom if your colourings are anything to judge.' Soren looked amazed.

'The Forest? Thalsay speaks of the Forest sometimes…' He cast another worried look at the unconscious form beside him. 'I have only ever known the Sea Peoples.' He spat and his face contorted into bitter hatred. 'I should be glad if you are right and I am not of that evil race.'

Ravar and Amalin exchanged glances.

Amalin came forward. 'Not all Sea People are bad, Soren,' she said, earnestly. 'How many have you ever actually met?'

'Enough!' he said, emphatically.

'Well we will *not* let them take you,' said Ravar, firmly. Amalin shot her a warning look. It was hardly the sort of promise that could be kept given the charges against the pair. Ravar, however, did not seem at all fazed.

Soren was fiddling with an edge of the frayed piece of cloth that he had wrapped into a large poncho that cloaked his upper half. 'Can your people really save him?' he asked quietly.

'I believe so,' said Ravar. 'But we must not wait much longer.'

'How are we to move him?' asked Soren.

This was a problem which Ravar had not considered. They were a very long way from anywhere significant and neither she nor Amalin possessed the strength and stamina required to carry Thalsay, even if they could fashion some sort of stretcher. She knew that Soren would never consent to part with Thalsay and that equally, she would not leave Amalin in a wood with a dying man or allow her to travel alone with Soren, however non-threatening they might now find him.

'We shall have to think about that,' admitted Ravar. At least he now seemed to be on board about coming out of hiding, she thought. It was a shame that she had no idea how to proceed from here.

CHAPTER 17

Forestfyth, Sixth Year of the Dancer, thaw.

It was the third rest day in the Forest and Doctor Eduerd was waiting anxiously in the Palace courtyard. He had called on Ravar the previous day only to find her absent from the cottage and her regular haunts. Thinking little of it, he had returned today to find the same and was surprised that no one seemed to know where either she or Amalin might be.

Having called on Lethan earlier that morning, his surprise had turned to concern as he found out that Amalin had failed to meet the Carpenter as planned for lunch the previous day and had sent no word.

Despite his conversation with King Aislyth back at the Winter Ball, Eduerd hardly felt comfortable going and asking him if he knew where they were. However, Lethan had no such compunction and had agreed to make the enquiry today if the women's whereabouts was still unknown.

As Eduerd paced between the pillars, the King came striding out of the main doors, looking agitated. Lethan jogged along after him.

Without preamble the King addressed Eduerd directly. 'I had assumed that Ravar had been with you yesterday, for I called and found no one at home.' He looked worried.

'No, Your Majesty,' said Eduerd. 'I confess I had come to hope that she might have been with you. But it appears that both she and Amalin have not been seen since their last lesson at the School on the final work day.'

'Stars, this is no time for them to go missing!' said the King, his voice filled with a mix of anger and fright.

'Sire,' interrupted a voice from across the courtyard. The men turned to see a Groom clad in overalls. She had set down a huge bale of hay, bowed and was now nervously looking up at her King. 'I am sorry but I could not help overhearing. You are looking for Masters Ravar and Amalin?'

'You know where they are?' demanded the King.

The woman nodded vigorously. 'I saw them set off with the travelling party two days ago at first light.'

'What?' chorused three alarmed voices in unison. The woman regarded the three men nervously.

'They had big packs with them, Sire,' she added.

'The group headed to Highturth Province?' demanded the King, urgently. The woman nodded and the King thanked and dismissed her.

Lethan looked relieved. 'Well then they are probably visiting friends in the city.'

'No,' said the King, gravely. 'That is not where they are headed.'

'But—'

'Ravar has gone in pursuit of the hunted men,' interjected Eduerd through gritted teeth. The King nodded, breathing hard.

'What? Why? You cannot be serious!' cried Lethan, appalled.

'Ravar has put her mind to nothing else this last week,' said Eduerd, angrily, shaking his head.

'Ye Stars, it is my fault,' muttered the King, devastated. 'I should have known that she would not be able to let it go.'

'We cannot stand here wasting time!' said Lethan, his voice raised.

This broke the King from his misery. He swiftly looked about him and began to shout frantic orders to the Guards at the Palace gate. All at once a hundred instructions seemed to be being issued by hordes of Palace staff. Eduerd and Lethan watched in amazement as they became caught up in a sea of urgent activity.

Eduerd had his own horse with him but the Palace stables supplied one for Lethan, as well as riding gear. In a matter of just over an hour, they and an escort of nearly twenty additional men were hurtling north-west from Forestfyth.

*

The fast riders should have made it back to the capital by late afternoon. Stopping only to rest the horses and relieve themselves, the two Guards had made excellent progress, unhindered as they had been during the previous two days by slow wagons which had to use the winding main roads. In fact, they were spared the dreaded task of having to break the news of the women's disappearance at the Palace because they were met, ten miles outside the city limits, by the King himself and a huge group of Guardians.

Their sovereign's face and words had been thunderous, as had been those of Doctor Eduerd and Lethan the Carpenter who rode at his side. The only saving grace had been that none of them had been in the mood for halting their progress any longer than was necessary and, after getting a clear idea of the last place the riders could be sure that the women were still with the travelling party, the King and his party had all rode on, kicking up the dirt in a fast gallop.

*

Out at the camp in the woods, Ravar and Amalin had spent the best part of the day trying to gather materials to construct a makeshift stretcher. The trouble was that none of them really possessed the requisite skills to fashion such an object and they were making very poor headway.

'If only we had Lethan with us,' Amalin moaned, as a stick she was attempting to use to bind two larger pieces together snapped. Ravar sighed and threw her own materials down in disgust.

'Lethan?' enquired Soren.

'He is a Carpenter,' explained Amalin. Seeing his blank expression, she elaborated. 'One who works with wood.' Soren nodded in comprehension.

'Perhaps we could carry Thalsay on a blanket?' Amalin suggested. Ravar considered whether they could make a hammock to be suspended from a long pole but none of the sheets they had brought were large enough.

The sun was starting to fall and long shadows were cast through the woods. 'We should resign ourselves to bedding down for the night,' said Ravar. 'By now there will be a search party looking for us so perhaps we should concentrate on helping ourselves to be found rather than making our own way home.'

Soren's eyes had widened in alarm but when he looked at Ravar, she seemed to have pre-empted his thought process and held him in a piercing gaze to remind him of her promise.

He was too tired and too desperately worried about his friend, who had failed to regain consciousness all day, to argue in any case. Amalin had managed to get some water and honey down him by painstakingly administering small drops to his mouth and watching for restless swallows. Ravar had been redressing his wounds and adding medicine into the water which Amalin had been giving him. However, the fact remained that he was not showing any sign of recovery.

*

The King had stopped the search party once they had reached the vicinity of the cave by the river where the escapees were believed to have made camp. Ravar had been interested in this place and he reasoned that she might have come here as a starting point. Guards with good tracking skills fanned out to look for evidence of the women having been in the area.

Little had been said between the three suitors, all of whom were doing their best to control their mixed emotions. They were exhausted from hard riding and were out of their depth when it came to tracking. Yet, here they were all stood together, suddenly forced to remain still and hand over to the expertise of others. Their horses drank gratefully at the edge of the river and it was Lethan who broke the silence.

'You are not to blame, Your Majesty.' Both the King and Eduerd cast him a look that clearly said they begged to differ, but Lethan snorted irritably. 'By the Stars, did we not all choose to set our hearts upon these tumultuous women with passionate natures? Who among us would ever be able to master them? I, for one, would not want to do so in any case. Would you?'

There were fervent defensive mutterings from the others.

'Of course none of us would,' summarised Lethan for the three of them. 'This situation is the fault of Amalin and Ravar alone.' There were murmurs of agreement and some loosening of tense shoulders as the men transferred some of their anger from themselves and each other to those they sought.

Eduerd suddenly shook his head and gave his own thigh a gentle slap. 'No. We must not hold this against them either.' He ran his hand through his hair and stretched his sore arms. 'If we find them and greet them only with berating words I fear that it shall be we that find ourselves burnt.'

'You are right,' nodded the King. 'Let us try to keep cool heads and, if we bring our beloveds safely home, attempt to be satisfied that they have not come to harm. Dear Stars,' he added, his own words having struck him, 'let us hope they are unharmed.'

At that moment a shout went up and they hurried towards the sound of raised voices some way down the river. One of the trackers was standing over a patch of bank and pointing to a boot print. It was pointed towards the water and already another guard was wading, almost waist-deep, across the current to the other side. 'There are signs of disturbance here too!' he called.

'Then, they crossed the river?' asked Eduerd.

After further investigation the Lead Guard came to report a summary of their findings. The far side of the river was muddier and gave several traces of someone journeying alongside it. However, the trackers were certain that they could only make out one set of boot prints. The party split into two groups, each carefully tracing the depressions in the mud and signs of disruption which continued downriver.

After a couple of hours the night was falling and the light fading. The King reluctantly agreed to pitch camp. Although he and his two companions barely slept they had no choice but to wait for morning and the light to be able to resume their search.

*

Ravar and Amalin had rustled up a reasonable supper which Soren devoured as if he had never tasted anything so good. He sat for some time next to Thalsay, clasping his arm in the strange way that Amalin had noted the day before.

'He is your brother?' Ravar only put a hint of the questioning tone in her statement. Soren glanced only briefly at her and gave a single nod. 'Your elder?' Again, a nod. 'Did he look after you while you were young?'

Soren sighed. 'He did his best.' He made a choking sound and Ravar suspected that he was fighting back tears Fortunately for him, the gathering darkness helped to hide his face. 'He would always give me a part of his ration, even though he was also hungry.'

Ravar had to steady her breathing. *Ration, hungry,* she repeated inside her head. She did not want to push Soren to talk of things that might unduly distress him at this time, but she was anxious to get as full a picture as possible so that she might be able to protect him better when the time came.

'Thalsay must love you very dearly. When you clasp his arm, do you feel it?'

Soren looked shocked, as if she knew a great secret. 'We... it is... I cannot fully explain…' He cut off, frowning.

'We understand,' said Ravar softly. She moved around to where Amalin had been following the conversation in silence. 'We are Soul Friends. It is like being sisters and we feel something when we embrace.' Soren looked from one to the other in something like wonder. 'When Thalsay is better we can show you how to feel each other's emotions as we can.'

Soren watched in fascination as Ravar and Amalin slowly placed their hands on each other's hearts and smiled sadly at one another. Their desolation was because they shared their common feelings of anger and pain at the now unravelling story of these two men.

'I should like that,' said Soren, lamely.

'How old are you, Soren?' asked Amalin. Ravar gave her a slight nod, approving of the question.

'Old?'

'How many cycles of the seasons have you lived?' she prompted.

Soren shrugged. 'I do not know. Thalsay says I was three when the masters took us.' Amalin winced at the latter part of his reply.

'I see. I should think you are probably of a similar age to us then, about one hundred and seventy, perhaps?'

Soren pulled a face. 'Perhaps. We did not count.'

'Well perhaps now you may start to count the happier days of your freedom,' Amalin suggested, feeling it was a rather pathetic reassurance. To her surprise, Soren nodded fervently.

'They have already been the best of my life,' he said.

It was too much for Amalin, who thought of what the past few months must have consisted of for them. She got up and walked away, making the excuse that she needed to relieve herself.

Once Amalin was out of earshot, Ravar resumed her careful questioning. 'Tell me, Soren, what did your masters ask of you and your brother?'

Soren grunted. 'We made ropes and nets, sorted and shelled fish, mostly. Others were trained to sort the sea treasures.' Ravar had to swallow hard.

'There were others?' she said, forcing herself to breathe.

'Aye, though fewer now than before.' Soren fell silent and Ravar vowed she would press him no more.

Instead, she pulled him over to the fire. 'Among the people of the Forest,' she said in an airy, smiling voice, 'we tell stories at the fire.' Soren turned to look at her silhouetted face in the firelight. 'I would like to tell you the story of the Songbird.'

*

Amalin had returned to hear the end of the tale and Soren looked like a child with stars in his eyes. 'Thalsay is the Snow Cat!' he whispered.

'Yes,' Ravar whispered back. 'And I will be your Stubborn Camel.' Soren looked at her eagerly, anticipating another story. He was to be disappointed though, as Ravar said, 'But that is a tale for another night. Let us build up the fire, get some sleep, and hope that we are found tomorrow.'

*

Ravar and the others woke with a start as her and Amalin's names were barked by a harsh man's voice. Jumping bleary-eyed to their feet, Soren screeched as they realised that they were surrounded by a group of ten armed, uniformed men. Three began to step forward to seize the young man.

'No!' Ravar roared with the fierceness of a wild cat. So taken aback were the guards that they actually step back a pace.

'Ravar! Amalin!' came a chorus of cries as none other than the King, Eduerd and Lethan broke through the edge of the group. They had obviously had to catch up with the party of Guards that had found them as they were flushed and breathless. Amalin reflected that a Master Painter would have his work cut out trying to accurately capture the expressions of abject relief, concern and, she thought, supressed anger among them.

Catching sight of Soren, the King growled, 'Seize him!' However, before his escort could do any such thing, Ravar flung herself between them and the cowering man. She held out her arms out to shield him and wore a face so dangerous that she reminded the King of a snarling Forest Pig. Such animals had been known to maul a person to death if they had accidentally disturbed a litter.

'Do not touch him!' she said, menacingly.

The crowd before her stared at her disbelievingly but the King would not be so easily deterred. 'Master Ravar,' he said in a dangerous, low voice, 'Step aside.'

190

He was met with a furious glare. 'I will not!'

The King was struggling to keep his cool and continued through gritted teeth. 'This is a wanted man, Ravar. There is a warrant for his capture and arrest.'

'I will not allow it,' Ravar said, her voice and eyes full of fire. She stood up to her full height and took a step forward. 'I invoke the common law of the Kingdoms and take the place of Protector of these runaways. They may not be subject to arrest or trial.'

The King, Eduerd and Lethan all gaped at her.

'Protector?' Lethan spluttered, looking again at Soren. Eduerd seemed to have broken out of his trance. For some minutes he had been preoccupied, peering into the camp to the prone form of Thalsay. His Healer's instincts were strong, but Ravar's words had pierced through his concentration.

The King had lost patience. 'Ravar, what can be the meaning of your words? You cannot stand as Protector to two men who must be close to your own age.'

'Indeed they are, Your Majesty. Yet, they are not men. They are *children.*' There was something deeply dangerous in Ravar's tone now.

'Wh—' The King did not have a chance to speak.

'You will not arrest two persons who have known little but unkindness all of their lives and have never felt the full power of the Soul Embrace even as blood Kin.' Seeing the shock and confusion in the men before her, she hastened to continue. 'Aye, My Lords, taken from their homes when still in single figures and kept as prisoners and forced to work.' There were gasps of horror but Ravar's momentum was unstoppable.

'Ill-fed, ill-used, uneducated, unloved,' she went on. '*Unhappy* are we to live in the Third Age where such crimes continue to be perpetrated.' She spat the last words, a cruel alteration of the King's own phrase, used in his first ever fireside tale.

The King looked visibly shaken. He took in a deep breath and closed his eyes for just a fraction longer than a blink, as if he were listening to the Forest itself. He glanced from side to side, where he met the bewildered expression of Lethan, and Eduerd's straining posture, for the Doctor had returned to trying to see beyond Amalin into the shelter where the sleeping man lay.

Seeming to make up his mind, he motioned for the Guards around him to lower their weapons and looked at Ravar. 'From what you have said,' he said slowly, and purposefully, 'I am forced to accept your invocation to be recognised as these persons' Protector. As King of the Forest People I will submit to the law which shields those not of Age from arrest and interrogation in their own right. Until the full facts of the matter may be established I grant them amnesty in my Kingdom and the necessities of man's dignity.' Ravar breathed a slow, emotional sigh of relief.

The King nodded in the direction of Thalsay. 'Is the one asleep in need of a Healer?'

CHAPTER 18

The open desert, Sixth Year of the Dancer, summer.

The merciless sun baked the soft, seemingly endless dunes with increasing ferocity as it moved towards its zenith. Surrounded only by the monotonous swooping rise and fall of the Sands, two unlikely travellers had fallen into a shared, steady pace.

The boy, about twelve cycles in age, was trudging slowly. He sported a small traveller's pack on his back and a defiantly determined look. He had done his best to ignore the silent man who had come to walk beside him but could take it no longer.

'Do not try to stop me!' he said crossly, without looking at his companion.

As if noticing the boy for the first time, the elderly traveller turned his head only a fraction to look down at him. The child had a resolute way of moving in perfect methodical steps. He reminded the man of some of the wonderful clockwork toys that were produced by the Craftsmen of the Burning City.

Because he had received no reply, the boy looked up to study the man beside him for the first time. What he saw amazed him, for the stranger was so very old, clad only in a white tunic and carried *no* travelling pack. The boy clenched his fists angrily and came to a stomping halt.

'So this is how I am to be brought back!' he snapped, angrily.

The old man, who had continued to walk glanced back over his shoulder and stopped. 'Brought back?'

'Yes. You have been sent out with no provisions so that I will have to accompany you back to safety.' The boy sighed angrily. 'Come on then!' He swivelled round and waited for the old man to join him.

However, after a time he realised that his wait was in vain as he remained standing alone. The boy was forced to turn, once again, in the direction of his original intention to scowl at the old stranger who had continued to pace forward for several steps, but had now stopped and was looking back at him. He wondered if the sun had already addled the ancient's wits, for the man was gazing at him with something like a fond smile.

'Look—'

'It is a most kind thought,' the old man interrupted. 'I believe your family and Teachers would be proud to know that you put the safety and welfare of others before your own desires. However, you are mistaken that I have come for you.'

'Oh,' the boy managed, looking confused. He kicked at the sand beneath his feet. 'Then what are you doing out here?' he asked.

'Why, I am running away!' the old man said, jauntily.

'You should not run in the Desert,' the boy admonished. 'You will dehydrate and waste energy,' he intoned, no doubt quoting the wisdom of his elders.

'That is very true, my good fellow,' said the old man, sagely. 'Indeed, I am not running. But I am going away and I do not wish to stop, lest a search party find me. So, if you will excuse me…' And with that, the man resumed his journey. The boy hurried back to take up his place at the old man's side once more.

'What are you getting away from?' the boy asked curiously.

'Many things,' replied the man. 'My family, for one, who are forever telling me what I can and cannot do.'

'It is the same with me,' frowned the boy, sympathetically.

'And then there is my work which is tiresome and limiting.' Once again, the boy nodded, seemingly understanding.

'And I have had to preside over a most difficult and distressing case where I had to argue against the consensus.'

'Did you win?' asked the boy.

'Eventually, yes I suppose so. Though I am not sure there was any real victory.' There was a weariness in the old man's voice.

The boy grunted approvingly. 'I shall also prove myself right,' he said, thrusting his chin forward and puffing out his chest as he walked.

'Good for you,' said the old man, and the pair walked on in silence.

The King of the Sands felt a deep sense of relief to find himself in the company of such a person. In his experience, children were infinitely wiser, and less complicated by adult triviality than their older counterparts.

He had spent an exhausting two months travelling to, and taking part in the extraordinary court case held at Eastarm. The Sea Sisters had asked him to sit as one of the independent judges required by law to oversee important cases which had implications for more than a single Kingdom.

The trial of the six individuals identified as having kept no few than fifteen Forest People captive since childhood had been a harrowing process. The Merchants involved had taken advantage of those suddenly orphaned by the Sleeping Sickness, sweeping them from their homes before their Kin or the Kingdom Administration came to check the more remote areas. Some of those taken were no more than three years old. The King shuddered at the thought.

The first-hand testimony of the grievously mistreated captives had brought many a tear to the eyes of those gathered to decide upon the fate of their captors. Particularly poignant had been the story of two men named Soren and Thalsay who had escaped and been pursued halfway across the Forest Kingdom. The horrible truth coming to light and the justice that followed might never have been possible without the extraordinary intervention of a remarkable young Master Tutor who had accompanied them to the trial in capacity as their Protector.

The Old Man of the Sands had eyed the strangely beautiful woman with careful scrutiny and was under no illusion that the calm and captivating face she presented was nothing more than a mask for the iron-strength of her conviction.

Nor was he blind to the immense trust in which she was held by, not only the two men she had discovered and defended from no less than a large, armed party of Guardians, but *all* those in the party from the Forest who were called to the trial. Indeed, King Aislyth himself could not seem to take his eyes from her. Then there was the chestnut-haired woman of the Plains who he guessed must surely have been the Lady Ravar's Soul Friend. Even the Forestman Doctor who had taken charge of the escapees and worked with them at the hospital of the Silent Winds as part of their initial recovery seemed always to be drawn to the woman. He wondered where her destiny lay.

The greatest difficulty of the case had been deciding the penalty for the perpetrators of so great and unusual a crime. His voice had been the strongest of those arguing for comparative leniency.

The King of the Sands had regarded the criminals with no less disgust than the others. Nonetheless, he had lived long enough to know that no good ever came of brutal or harsh punishments that led only to bitterness and infamy that then leaked strange ideas into the heads of others. He had suggested that these unfortunates must, themselves, be in need of healing of the mind to have been able to perpetuate such a hideous operation for so long.

It had eventually been agreed that they were to be transported to the Eastern Desert, where they would be separately incarcerated and be made to work the same tasks, if not under the same inhumane conditions, to which they had subjected the children they had abducted. Healers of the mind would work closely with them and monitor them, the hope being that, in time, the men and women would come to realise and regret their own crimes. Perhaps they themselves were best placed to suggest their own paths to reparation and forgiveness.

The King of the Desert had also taken time and care to go over the proposed programme of care, education and integration of the newly freed Forestfolk back into society. All of the twelve surviving men and women had elected to take up residence in the Kingdom of their forefathers. It was, after all, the land of their much-loved Master Ravar, and the revered King who had led the operation to find and free those captives that the escapees had been forced to leave behind. There, in pairs, they had been adopted into volunteer families of the capital and surrounding areas. A special class had been formed at the School of the Young to accommodate their unusual needs which would be led by a team of Teachers and the greatly respected Grandmaster Onwosito, a Healer of the Mind from the Sky Kingdom.

Who knows when and if all of them will be able to come of Age? he thought, sadly. At least it was quite clear that they had all been spoiled with love, food, comfort and every care by those that had taken them into their homes and city. Thank the Heavens for such kindness to counter cruelty.

Drifting back into the present, the Old Man of the Sands regarded the stalwart little creature beside him. 'Where are we headed?' he asked casually.

'We?' he retorted.

'I wish to join your caravan. May I?' asked the King.

'I suppose so,' said the boy, airily. 'I am Yizyn, by the way.'

'Thank you. So, Yizyn, where are we going?'

'To the Lost Bird Oasis.'

'I see,' said the King.

The boy looked at his companion in wonderment. 'You are not going to tell me I am wasting my time?'

'Why should I?'

'Because my mother and father and Teachers all say that it doesn't exist,' said Yizyn.

'Do they now?' said the King, narrowing his eyes and smiling.

'Yes. And I am going to find it and prove them wrong.'

'Ah,' replied the King.

'I *am* going to find it,' said Yizyn.

'I did not say anything to the contrary,' said the King.

'My grandfather told me that he had once been there and how he found it,' the boy continued, obviously still determined that the King did not believe him.

'Good,' said the King, simply. 'I shall help. I think that I also remember the way.'

The boy stopped in his tracks. 'What?' he gasped. 'You have been there?'

'Not for a long time,' the King said. 'It is little more than a rocky hollow and the water is hidden deep within a cave.'

The little boy's eyes sparkled with glee. 'That is how my grandfather described it!' He exclaimed. 'He said that people always missed it because they did not bother to look for it.'

'I think your grandfather and I might have got on,' said the King.

'But what will you do without a flask?' asked Yizyn.

'Oh, do not worry about that,' said the King, kindly. 'The desert and I are old friends. She does not burn me unless I have done something to deserve it.'

*

When they returned six full days later, the Burning City had fallen into utter chaos. The Palace staff were fraught with fear and exhaustion. Endless searches and enquiries had been made, messengers sent to neighbouring towns and settlements, and excuses and platitudes given to visiting dignitaries to hide the fact that the King of the Sands had gone missing.

The six Princesses who still resided in the capital were particularly worried. It was not unusual for their father to disappear for a day or even two days at a time. He had a bad habit of taking himself away without warning when he became truly fed up with the demands and pressures of his office. However, he had never been away for *this* long.

The women wondered whether the ghastly trial in Marketdawn had taken its toll on their frail father. Neither of the two of them that had accompanied him on the voyage had been allowed to sit in on the hearings or discussion but he had emerged from each looking sapped of strength and full of woe. In the few days since he had been back in his beloved desert, he had been quiet and listless. And now, he was nowhere to be found.

The Desert Guards had yet another, perhaps even more worrying problem: a young boy had also been reported lost. Children were no less revered and treasured in the Sands as elsewhere in the Six Kingdoms. The only son of a respected pair of Masons, his family and neighbours were distraught and wracked with guilt, for their final words had been ones of derision regarding some historical oasis. It had never occurred to anyone in the city that the two missing people's cases were related.

The King and Yizyn surveyed the buzzing activity at the outskirts of the city sceptically.

'We are going to be in really big trouble,' Yizyn remarked, unhappily.

'I fear that you are right, my friend,' agreed the King. 'I wish to retrieve a few articles that I hid in safety before I left. If you will be patient, I shall come back shortly and we will brave the reprimand together.'

Returning as promised a quarter of an hour later, the King had donned a fresh tunic and carried a small bag in which, Yizyn assumed, was his sash.

As the pair of them made their way through the main street of the capital, it took some time before they were noticed and identified. However, after an excited shout from a Guard who recognised them both, it was only a short while before they were surrounded by cheering spectators.

A man and woman broke desperately through the crowd and threw themselves on Yizyn, showering him with kisses. When they caught sight of the Old Man of the Sands they threw themselves at his feet and thanked him for returning their son safely to them.

The King tried to calm the crowd and ask for quiet. Not succeeding, he reluctantly took his beautiful sash from his bag and roughly clipped it to his shoulder. This had the desired effect as the crowd remembered who stood at their centre. A hush fell over them as they waited for their sovereign to speak. He clasped Yizyn's hand and drew him close to him. The boy looked up in awe and wonder as he realised the identity of the man with whom he had shared his recent adventure. The Old Man of the Sands winked at him and raised his voice to his subjects.

'Listen with open minds and open hearts!' All around him, there was a muffled sound of collective confusion as everyone recognised the traditional form of the opening of the telling of a Bardic Tale. The King waited for silence before continuing in a carrying, if gravelly, voice.

The Stubborn Camel won its name long ago, when the Desert was already old, but the Peoples of the early Kingdoms had not yet found their feet in its sands.'

The People of the Desert kept their ears trained to the voice of the Bard. They did not know the meaning of the impromptu tale, but it was a Kingdom favourite.

'He alone of all the Desert creatures could traverse the arid and ever shifting plains between the oases, confident in the knowledge that, even if he were to find himself lost, his body would hold water enough to prevent him from dying of thirst.

'The other animals that roamed the land envied his freedom, matched only by that of the soaring birds that could fly from place to place, their destinations not hidden from view by the ever-changing landscape.

'It was not long before the Camel gained a following among the many-shaped scuttling and plodding creatures who lived in the few watered spots within his domain. They knew that he had knowledge of the places beyond their reach and told wonderful tales of the other waters and green spaces and lifeforms of the sands.

'The Camel would travel from place to place, traversing the sun-baked open spaces between them alone. He dearly wished for a companion to keep him company on his long treks, but even the birds of the sky could not afford to dally with him at his slow pace.

'He thought of how wonderful it would be if the separate realms and communities of those he loved could somehow meet and be united, enjoying the freedom to come and go as he did. As the image formed and burned harder and clearer in his mind, the more determined he became to turn his dream into reality.

The Camel trekked to the furthest oasis in the Southern Sands where, remote and unknown to any but those who lived there, a great lake sparkled under the Desert sky. Its water was the coolest and freshest of any he knew and was surrounded by palms and teeming with life.

He spoke to the ancient, scaly, waddling beasts whose home the lake had been since time began. He asked them to share with him their knowledge of the place, passed down from parent to child. Where could so much water come from and where did it go? How could the fast current below the surface simply be swallowed up by the ground at the northern end of the lake?

The Crocodiles laughed at the Camel's question, which they found stupid in the highest degree. "Why, it disappears under the sands, just as you say," they cackled.

"Does it return to its source where it gushes up in the South?" the Camel asked, undeterred by their scathing replies. "What drives it?"

"Why would water turn in such a circle?" one of the smiling lizards replied. "The water rushes to the surface, driven by the very heart of the earth beneath us. There is nothing here on the surface mighty enough to drive it down again."

"Then where does it go?" the Camel persisted.

"Go? Who knows?" replied the crocodile. "We do not care where the underground water strays."

So the Camel left them and made his own way to the northern edge of the pool where the glistening treasure of the Desert sank away beneath him.'

The Old Man of the Sands paused to look around the nodding faces of his subjects. The story was well known by all the Desert People and they waited for the weight of his next words which he intoned slowly and with meaning.

That day the Camel began to dig.

To the bewilderment of all of those who inhabited the great lake, the Camel kicked the sand at his feet, tossing it up at his sides.

Despite the jeering of the crocodiles and the indignant outcries of disturbed birds and insects, the Camel continued to dig. His hooves became scuffed and sore but still he kept on kicking up the sand from beneath his feet until, after a whole day, he stood in a narrow channel. And at the bottom of this channel, his hooves were cool. He had dug so deep that he had skimmed the sand near the top of the underground channel where the lake's water was carried away.

'As the Camel slunk back, exhausted, to the shade of the palms, many desert creatures came to peer over the sides into the mucky hole that he had left behind. It was an ugly deformity at the edge of their home and none of them had been able to prise from the Camel what he had been hoping to achieve by his labours.

'When the sun began to rise the following morning, the lake's inhabitants found the Camel in his channel once again, digging still deeper in the sand until the underground river rose about his feet.

'As the sun was setting, the Camel climbed up onto the bank and peered down at the shimmering water. The chattering desert birds flew in to his chasm and whipped their wings through their reflections. Other animals perched at the side of the little extension of the lake and looked from it to its creator. They asked the Camel once again why he had done this but the Camel's only reply was that his work was unfinished.

'As the days and weeks and months passed, nothing would deter the Camel from his endless excavation, bringing the river to the surface of the sand. In time, the camel's stubbornness became less of an enigma and more an ordinary part of the way of life at the lake. The other animals even aided the Camel in his efforts, clearing the sand, widening the trench and encouraging the plant life of the lake to spread along the banks of the water.

'Seasons passed and the Camel would not relent.

'Cycles turned and the Camel would not relent.

'The Acrobat passed the Seeker in ascendency and the Camel would not relent.

'The Camel grew impossibly old but still he would not relent.

'Until one day. On this day the creatures of the river channel were stunned to see a mysterious, unknown bird fly over them from the north.

'She had flown to the southernmost reaches of her range for her eagle's eye had spotted something strange down on the land. As she came closer she did not understand what she saw, for an ancient and grizzled beast, surrounded by smaller animals of every shape and size were burrowing in the ground before a shining river that cut through the sand behind them.

'The bird flew back to the oasis further north and told all who would listen about what she had seen.

'They would not believe her story until they saw the slow and extraordinary progress of the Camel and his people with their own eyes, but sure enough, they stubbornly continued to scratch the river from the earth. The animals of the oasis, seeing the aim of his design, began their own efforts at the southern extent of their own pool and the two communities raced to meet one another.

'It was a glorious day when the waters from two ends of the channel met, and the underground river which had always secretly linked the lake with the oasis was united at the surface.

'The Camel had carved a waterway through the dry desert that all living things, in time, would be able to follow. There were great celebrations as the creatures of the

Southern Lake met their distant animal brothers for the first time and all vowed to continue the ongoing efforts to secure and sure up the width and banks of the river that joined them, lest the river were ever lost again.

'But the Camel's work was far from done. For, the very next day, he began to dig again.

'The Camel would journey endlessly northward, bringing the life-giving water with him with every forward step he was able to take. Scores of communities of wildlife became one as the river snaked out behind him and the Desert became a Nation.

'The Camel had succeeded in his dream to never again condemn an animal to travel alone. He had brought the knowledge and wisdom of the Desert creatures together. He had traversed the Sands from its last inhabitable extreme and brought its people to lay their eyes upon the land's edge.

'Only when he was able to gaze at the tributaries of his grand work flowing into the Middle Sea did the Stubborn Camel know that his work was done and take his final slumber at the water's edge. He would be remembered by the Sand Dwellers through each generation, who would repaint his story along the rocks at the river's side and tell their children the tale.

'They would say that he brought the Great Rapid to the surface of the Desert so that even Man, one day, could cross it and live at its side. And we now repeat the tale in memory of the Stubborn Camel that gave the People of the Upper Face a place in the fiery Sands. We acknowledge what a single being might achieve by determination alone.'

There was a reverent silence as the King finished his tale, though everyone was wondering why exactly he had chosen to tell it.

After about a minute the King sighed, clapped his arm on the back of his young friend and spoke again.

'I am very sorry that, between us, Yizyn and I have been the cause of so much worry and exertion these last few days.' He looked all about him, to ensure that all knew his apology was truly meant. A few guards exchanged exasperated looks. The King's definition of a 'few days' evidently did not tally with their own.

'I left the city because my old heart felt weak and broken by the sad realities which the Peoples of the Six Kingdoms must, it seems, still face.

The crowd of dark and head-dressed faces surrounding the King looked saddened and shamed, for there was not one among them who had not heard of the shocking revelations from the Western Lands.

The King smiled warmly at Yizyn. 'I had to be reminded by this excellent young Sand Wanderer that I too must strive to be determined and strong as the Stubborn Camel, who never ran away from his task.' Yizyn grinned broadly and threw his arms around his King.

Looking a little embarrassed, the King gave the child a not too grudging embrace. The Guards exchanged more glances. This was so far from protocol that they could do nothing but endure it.

'Will the Teachers and family of Young Yizyn please step forward?' the King called out to the crowd.

Nervously, a small number of men and women shuffled to the front. They stood before him uncertainly.

'Good afternoon, Kin and Teachers of my newest friend!' he said. He made a point of straightening up and gently touched the solid gold Seal of the Desert at the top of his sash, the mark of his sovereignty. It bore the geometric stylised image of a lizard, sparkling emeralds set in the design for its eyes.

The King's subtle action had the desired effect for, suddenly remembering their places against the rank of the personage before them, the assembled party who had stepped forward bowed reverently.

Turning to Yizyn, who was regarding his family and teachers curiously, the King said, 'Present your findings.'

Yizyn opened his small pack and from it took a stoppered leather water pouch. He handed it to his puzzled parents.

'Inside this bottle,' the King announced in a booming voice so that all the crowd could hear, 'Yizyn has captured a sample of the water from the Lost Bird Oasis!'

There was a slight intake of breath across the crowd.

'Your King standing before you attests to this, for I witnessed this boy fill the vessel from its diminished waters with my own eyes.' Yizyn beamed proudly while his elders gaped.

'In recognition of the determination of this young man, whose labours reaped reward, and whose innocent childish wisdom brought a King to his senses,' the Old Man of the Sands continued in a regal, carrying voice, 'I award Yizyn of my People the Seal of the Desert.' There were loud gasps. 'When he has earned his sash may he wear it with pride so that all will know of the service he did to our common understanding and to his King.'

Yizyn slept soundly that night, having been tucked into bed by his adoring parents, happy and grateful that he had returned to them.

The Old Man of the Sands sulked on the steps of his Palace. The lectures from his daughters proved that his own household were far less understanding.

CHAPTER 19

Forestfyth, Sixth Year of the Dancer, high summer.

The end of spring and entry into the much-favoured summer in the Forest had not brought much joy to Ravar or many of her acquaintance. After the whirlwind weeks that followed the arrival of Soren and Thalsay in Forestfyth, she and Amalin had been required to present evidence before a regional judge at the Marketdawn hub.

Thalsay had recovered from his wounds sufficiently within this time to be able to corroborate Soren's story, though he was not able walk for over a month. Even then, he required the use of a crutch for some weeks.

The journey, hearing and constant dedication to her role as a Protector had exhausted Ravar. The young men were also understandably curious and eager for understanding of an endless number of customs and legal procedure, while still flinching at the slightest unknown quantity. It was a near impossible task to keep up with their need for both knowledge, and reassurance.

She had been grateful that the King Aislyth was obliged to attend the three-day process, during which the escapees had been acquitted of their crimes. The sailor who had been attacked had even formally requested the dropping of the assault charge of his own accord, once he had heard their story.

The ball had also been set in motion for the tracking down of the criminal operation in which they had been held for most of their lives. The King seemed to exude a sort of unerring confidence and determination in his quest for truth which no one could question.

Although meek before the giant, Soren and Thalsay had gradually lost their fear of him. He had taught them a couple of counter games on the journey in which they were swiftly becoming proficient and Ravar was glad of his attempts to keep them entertained.

The King had parted ways with them at the end of the hearing, taking a contingent of Forest Guardians to meet with three times their number of Sea and Market Guards to the port city of Northarm, from where the search for the slavers would be coordinated.

Ravar shuddered at the thought of the grim look the King bore on his return, nine weeks later, accompanied by ten more wasted and wide-eyed young men and women. The only happy part of this occasion had been the joyful reunion of the newcomers to the capital with Soren and Thalsay.

*

Doctor Eduerd had immediately requested that he be allowed to accompany all of the victims to the Hospital of the Silent Wind where they would stay for at least the remainder of the spring season. There they were joined by a much-revered Grandmaster Healer of the Mind who had travelled all the way from the Sky Kingdom to oversee their care. Ravar had visited the place on rest day breaks and had been treated as a sort of exalted hero by all.

When finally it was time for the trial of the six culprits of these people's misery, Eduerd came as an expert witness to comment upon the impact of the group's imprisonment and mistreatment before the judges.

The Doctor had read the formal diagnoses of all the Healers concerned with the twelve victims to the Court. These lengthy analyses consisted of those of the experts at the Hospital as well as his own assessment of the long-term impacts of malnutrition, brutality and inadequate sanitation and living conditions.

Eduerd had had to steel himself to get through some of the wretched contents, especially having spent two months in close contact with those concerned. Seeing and hearing, first-hand, the impact of their confinement, served only to catalyse his horror that living, feeling beings could be so misused.

At the end of the trial in Marketdawn, he had stayed on at Desledair's lodgings for two full weeks. His Soul Friend's drainage project was finally at an end and the Architect had refused to leave the Doctor's side until he began to show signs of recovery from his own trauma and exhaustion.

Desledair had needed to rely on his brother for a fuller account of what was being said and decided during the trial. The Market King was prohibited from sitting in judgement on a cross-Kingdom case which concerned his own realm but, like King Aislyth, was allowed to observe its proceedings. Renowned for his fierce temper which was most commonly directed at himself, King Rasaltin had been unusually demure on the subject. He admitted to his brother his abject shame that such a crime had been committed by subjects of his Kingdom.

Deeply affected by both his Soul Friend and brother being in such a bad state, Desledair had written to Fiance who had made haste to join her Kin. She had initially hidden her own distress from Desledair which stemmed from a very different aspect of the saga. However, Eduerd had revealed with fierce pride and commendation the part she had played in the recovery of the escapees.

It was agreed between them that they would make the journey back to the Forest together and that Desledair would stay for the remainder of the summer and into the autumn with Eduerd.

It was on this journey that Desledair had the chance to speak to Fiance out of earshot of Eduerd, who had ridden on ahead to speak to Hathsurst in advance of the others' arrival.

'Tell me, Fiance, where does Eduerd stand with regard to his suit?' Desledair asked bluntly.

Fiance regarded him askance. 'Such things have hardly been first and foremost in the minds of those concerned, Desledair,' she said with a note of censure.

Desledair huffed, crossly. 'Of course I appreciate that, my good Fiance. But Eduerd has spoken little of Lady Ravar, despite her heavy role in this whole business and if she has rejected him in addition to the other misery he had experienced this last season I would at least know of it.'

Fiance's hackles dropped. She had somehow forgotten that Desledair had been so distanced from events in the Forest. She patted him lightly on the arm. 'Rest assured, My Lord, that the Lady Amalin still bears Eduerd's feather upon her sash.'

Relief came over the Architect. 'As well as that of the King?' he asked.

Fiance sighed. 'Aye, as well as that.'

Desledair nodded to himself. 'Does Ravar show Aislyth much favour?'

Fiance shrugged. 'In truth I cannot tell. I believe she finds charm in both her suitors.' She allowed herself a coy smile. 'Indeed, who would not? The woman has the Serpent's choice.' Desledair smirked at Fiance's reference to the old Market tale of the snake who was forced to decide between two lucrative trades, each of which would bring a different sort of wealth to his fortune.

'Then we must lend our efforts to our Kinsman's quest,' said Desledair. 'If anyone can break Eduerd out of his melancholy I suspect it is the Lady Ravar.'

'Quite so,' said Fiance, in agreement. 'And that girl is in need of cheering up too. I have never seen her so grave and worn. There again, it is hardly surprising when you consider her own past.'

'Her past?' Desledair frowned his lack of understanding.

Fiance heaved a sigh. 'The Healers at the Hospital of the Silent Wind concluded that by far the most damaging part of the children's captivity was their lack of access to the normal Soul Embrace of their blood Kin during immaturity.' Fiance's voice became hollow. 'Even Soren and Thalsay, as brothers, were never taught how to join hand to heart.' She sobbed. 'I was there when Ravar first guided one hand to the other.' Tears now poured freely down the normally so robust woman's face. 'She told them…' She struggled to speak the words. 'She told them that they would now know the true love of another. The love they had always had but never fully known.'

Desledair leant over and hugged Fiance, the unsteady shuddering of the wagon over the uneven road masking her convulsions.

Yet, it occurred to him that Fiance had not directly answered his question. He thought back over what she had said and then it struck him: Ravar had been removed from her family as a babe. While her adoptive family had, by all accounts taken her in as one of their own, they would not have been physically able, no matter how willing, to join their hearts to a child not of their own blood. Ravar must have grown up in the same solitude, if not the neglect or cruelty, as the unfortunates she now protected.

*

The formal proceedings of such a court case had left no opportunity for Ravar to give her own views. However, she had forced herself to maintain as much poise as she could muster and put her talent for public speaking to good use. She owed it to those to whom she stood as a temporary guardian.

The legal process was complex and difficult to follow, so she had insisted on having everything explained in minutiae by the Advocate standing for the victims. It was an area of learning in which she felt sorely lacking in expertise and she vowed to dedicate some time to its study in future seasons.

In the courtroom itself she had been fascinated by the penetrating eyes and questions of the esteemed judges. They were headed by none other than the much-famed King of the Sands who lived up to his reputation as somewhat of an enigma. He was ancient yet energetic, fearsome and yet careful and compassionate. She found it hard to hold his gaze, as if he exuded some sort of power in his expression. The King of the Sands had been called upon, alongside Princess Fel from Snowseal and Fenso, a Grandmaster Scribe from the Sky Kingdom, to decide upon the miscreants' fate. She did not envy any of the judges their task.

The victims themselves were formally represented by the formidable and striking Advocate Osami, the first of his kind that Ravar had ever met in person. She was humbled by the sheer force of his presence and, even more strikingly, his command of language made her feel like a novice.

It was also the first time she had been in the company of her mother's people, whose colouring and build were so similar to her own. The two men accompanying the Lady Fel were tall and slender, their silver hair worn long and plaited, just as that of their Princess. Their only significant differences from Ravar lay in their peculiar purple eyes and these were framed by silver eyelashes and brows, where hers had taken the darker form of the Forest people.

Princess Fel had extended an invitation to visit the Kingdom of her ancestors at any time of Ravar's choosing and she fully intended to take them up on the offer, perhaps during next year's summer break.

Now, with only six weeks of this year's long rest period left, Ravar found herself gradually trying to get back into routine. The end of the academic year at the School of the Nearage had been hugely disrupted, closed early because its two principle Tutors were twice required away from the capital for extended periods. Ravar was determined that she would make up for the loss in the autumn.

There was also the matter of her two suitors, both of whom were finally returned to their own normal way of life now that the arrangements had been made for the new citizens of the Forest. Each man had made tentative visits to the cottage, trying to sense whether it might be appropriate to resume their courtship.

Ravar had not had any objection. Indeed, she had been reminded of the need to move away from melancholy by the ever irascible and practical Lady Fiance.

It had only taken the knowledge that Soren and Thalsay had been consistently underfed during their captivity to drive her like a storm in fury to the Palace to insist that she be allowed to adopt them into her household as a temporary measure after their arrival in her home city.

Never had Fiance had the pleasure of two such willing and grateful guests at her table and never had her generosity of spirit and love shone more bright. Upon their return from the Hospital of the Silent Wind, the two men had shyly called on her, after seeking Ravar's advice, to ask whether she might consider offering them permanent residence. Fiance had cried for nearly an hour with relief and happiness as she took her new sons into her family.

The formidable woman would have no careful wording or awkward silence about their former mistreatment. She referred to their previous existence in a matter-of-fact, almost throwaway way, saying that there was no point in trying to erase the past, only to pave a better present and future. This was advice that Ravar was determined to take to heart. And so, her breakfasts at the Palace and night walks with Eduerd had recommenced.

*

From swimming in the Palace lake and trying to ignore the racing of her blood at the sight of the King's exposed muscles, to an extended trip away to Woodsedge with Eduerd, Amalin and Lethan, Ravar had enjoyed a whirlwind of excitement and romance as the days began to shorten once more. Theatre, concerts, an archery contest, night-walking to spot the rare night creatures of the Forest, parties… The summer hosted colourful and happy days and nights for the Master Tutor. It more than made up for missing the Spring Dance which had been cancelled in light of more pressing concerns.

The summer equinox on the other hand, had been doubly celebrated and the King had called for it to take the form of the Autumn Feast so that all, including the new citizens of the city could partake in the festival. Dancing all the common dances, Ravar had stepped, skipped, turned and clapped, arm in arm with all those she loved and respected. Both Eduerd and the King had, by mutual agreement, agreed not to press their suit. The night was one for unity, not competition.

As the new term loomed close and Ravar met with Amalin and

Istreeth to draw up the lesson rota and discuss the input of local Craftspeople into this year's curriculum, Ravar stole a moment to look back upon the year. With stoicism that might only have been rivalled by Grandmaster Dethir, she determined that the balance was weighted to the good, even if the road to such an outcome had been hard going.

Amalin had no need to philosophise about such things. Even before the Summer Dance she had written to her parents to confide in them her intention of accepting Lethan's proposal in the autumn. It would be highly irregular to do so before at least then, as a courting couple were supposed to consider each other through the changes of each season before making a decision. In fact, it was not uncommon for a courtship to last several cycles and even then the outcome could be an agreement to cease consideration of marriage.

The Songstress was somewhat put out that she had received no reply from home and, sharing her irritation with Ravar, had wondered whether there had been some delay or problem with the Kingdoms Post. After all, their parents were not usually tardy in their replies.

Surely, Amalin wondered, they could not disapprove of her choice? They had not met Lethan, she supposed. Perhaps she should see whether a meeting could be arranged? This would probably be impossible before the winter when the Plains agriculture was at its low point and that Kingdom took its extended rest period. *Stars*, she did not want to wait that long.

With just a week to go before the start of the new Nearage semester, Ravar and Amalin were discussing this very problem when there was a loud knock at their door.

Ravar stretched and padded over to the heavy wooden door, tiredly. Such was the way with Soul Friendship that she could not help but share in Amalin's melancholy.

However, as the door creaked open, all her cares were gone in an instant as she flung herself at the bronzed, ruggedly attired man before her. Standing to see who it was, Amalin let out a yelp of delight.

'Father!'

CHAPTER 20

Forestfyth, Sixth Year of the Dancer, summer's end.

Osharm of the Plains embraced both of his daughters tightly on behalf of all of the family and friends back in the Rivermare Province who were unable to join him on his journey north. He had travelled to the Forest three times before in his younger life but this trip was the most fascinating and strange of all. Although their regular letters had allowed him in his mind's eye to form a picture of how his beloved children lived and worked, it was no match for what he was able to observe with his own eyes. Their house alone, crooked and weaving like the trees that surrounded it was a rich and complicated sort of beauty that contrasted markedly with the whitewashed and sun-baked brick buildings of the Plains.

Having received Amalin's letter earlier in the summer, he and his wife had been determined that at least one would be able to make the journey to meet the man who had won her heart. It was not unusual for family members to be parted for long periods of time unless the bonds of Blood Kin were also by the Soul. It was a big world after all and the lives of its Peoples were long.

Nevertheless, it had been a hard wrench to lose both daughters to another Kingdom and at the same time. Osharm took in the contrasting features of his two girls. Amalin was all excitement while Ravar held her familiar cat-like grin and flashing eyes. He was glad that some things at least, did not change.

*

Upon hearing of his arrival, the women's father had been inundated with

212

invitations to meet and dine with their friends. Their suitors had been even more anxious to make a good impression and Osharm had been rather overwhelmed to receive a personal call from the King of the Forest on the morning following his arrival.

Pleasantly surprised by his energy and humour, Osharm had taken to the man seeking his adopted daughter's hand. King Aislyth possessed many of the qualities held in high regard among the Plainsfolk: strength, spirit and musical talent. And yet although, (admitting paternal bias), her father could see precisely why he should be so taken with Ravar, Osharm was surprised that his daughter would consider his proposal.

Unlike her sister, Ravar was such a studious and unusual character. That was not to say that she did not have an electric way with people and a wicked wit, but he had always imagined her taking some Scribe or Master of Written Works for a husband. In many ways he was delighted that the King seemed to have brought out a more gregarious spirit in her. He parted from a morning's tour of the capital by Royal escort by firmly embracing the tall and imposing man.

In the evening he joined his daughters for a supper given by their astonishing friend, the Lady Fiance. The woman's house seemed to consist of one giant kitchen and dining area on the ground floor. Fiance was larger than life in more than one sense and it had taken some time to recover from the embrace he received from her upon arrival, let alone the more fervent one to which he had been subjected at his departure.

However, the supper she had given was significant, for she was Kin to both Lethan and Eduerd, the other men courting his daughters. Naturally, these gentlemen had been invited to the dinner and Osharm had plenty of opportunity to get to know them. In fact, Fiance might as well have locked them in a room together, so careful was she to ensure that no one else was able to interrupt or join in their conversation. Osharm did not mind. He could see that she was a woman who did her best for her Kin and that was a commendable virtue.

It was easy to like Lethan. It was even easier to see that he was the perfect match for Amalin and that the bond between them was already obvious and secure. As the evening wore on, the simple kiss he planted on Amalin's forehead was enough to tell his daughter that her father gave his full blessing to the match.

Far more complicated was his introduction to Master Eduerd. By any stretch of the imagination he was an impossibly handsome man and he seemed to be possessed of intelligence that could give even Ravar a serious run for her money. Osharm had tried in vain to recall any man, so young, whose sash was as decorated. The Doctor was also polite, dry humoured and clearly most popular. It was a problematic situation for Osharm not because he in any way failed to understand Ravar's attraction to him, but because he recognised the worth of both men courting her favour. He was glad he would not have to make the decision.

*

On the final evening of Osharm's stay, an outdoor party was held by his daughters in their pretty little back garden. Into the late hours, the friends of the hosts talked and sang and even enjoyed a short tale, courtesy of the King at the behest of the guest of honour, whose entreaty he could hardly refuse.

The last to leave were Lethan and Eduerd. They were tired and happy in their cups, sitting by the outdoor hearth in which a dying fire radiated heat from glowing ashes. Osharm wandered over to join them and the three men enjoyed a few moments of silence, broken only by the crackling logs.

'It has been a pleasure to meet you both, My Lords,' smiled Osharm at his younger counterparts. Waving their immediate replies that that they felt the same, he continued. 'I have no influence over my strong-willed daughters of course, but should they choose to accept you as their own, I for my own part would be happy to call you my Kin.'

Eduerd and Lethan, who did not know how to respond to such an unexpected and warm sentiment, simply beamed. Osharm thought back to the same smile, accompanied by a humble bow that he had received from King Aislyth just half an hour earlier when he had spoken the same words to him. Osharm did not envy the man who might take a second place, should Ravar decide to marry one or the other of her suitors.

'Lord Osharm, you do us a great honour by your words,' Eduerd suddenly blurted out. Before Osharm could say anything, the Doctor went on, hurriedly. 'However, I wish to tell you of the great indebtedness so many here in the Forest, and no doubt back in the Plains are to your good self and your family.'

Osharm regarded him in surprise, as did Lethan. 'Ravar may have told you that I resided with the rescued Forest People at the Hospital of the Silent Wind during their stay there,' Eduerd continued, quickly.

'Aye, she did, My Lord,' began Osharm uncertainly. 'She was most glowing in her report—'

Eduerd cut him off, almost irritably. 'The healers of the Mind there had much to say on the damaging effect of children brought up without the comfort of the Soul Embrace.' Suddenly, Osharm began to understand where this was going. He glanced over at Ravar, standing by the gate, deep in conversation with Amalin.

'Such love and care you must have given her, that she became all that she is,' Eduerd croaked, his voice failing him. He got to his feet and made a bow.

Osharm sighed and rose to lay a hand on Eduerd's shoulder. When the Doctor rose and met his eye, the elder man gave him a strange, sad smile. 'Lord Eduerd, when we took Ravar in, she was only a babe. We vowed we would give her everything that we would to Amalin and that we would never make the distinction between them.' He paused, shook his head sadly, and sighed again.

'Alas, we were never to be her Blood Kin. We could offer as much love and affection as our outward actions would allow but, try as we did, we could not pass our affections to such an immature child through hand to heart. As you know it is impossible outside family tie without the maturity of each to accept and understand.'

'I know, My Lord, which is why...'

Osharm held up a hand to silence him. He gestured for Eduerd and Lethan to be seated again and they complied. 'You misdirect your thanks My Lord Eduerd and I should like to tell you the truth of it.' He glanced, a little guiltily at the women, still talking at the gate. 'But it is a truth that both of you should know, I think.' He took a deep breath and began.

'When Ravar arrived with us, Amalin was only six years old. We had worried that the addition of a second child, a competitor for her parents' love and attention might cause her some resentment and difficulty.' He smiled. 'Happily, it was never so. Indeed, from the moment that Ravar became part of our household, Amalin would not leave her side. It was as if she loved her straight away. We would look for Amalin sometimes, only to find her endlessly rocking her sister in her crib and stroking her silver hair. She only discovered to the world her voice because of singing Ravar to sleep.' Osharm wiped a tear from his eye. When he resumed his account, he did so with a sad, weary expression.

'When Ravar cried, Amalin would come to me and her mother distraught. "Why does she cry?" she would ask, over and over. "Please Mother, Father, make her stop. I cannot bear it!"

'We would tell Amalin that all babies cry, and that we were new to her, and that she would be happier in time. Ah, but Amalin would become hysterical. She would beg us to comfort the child as we would her. She would pull us over to Ravar and try to press our hands to her chest.'

The memory brought pain to Osharm's face, but he carried on. 'We had to explain to her that it was not possible, that our bodies would not allow it between those not of the same blood before they are full grown. Amalin raged against the injustice that prevented her sister from knowing such love and comfort. We would catch her time and again desperately placing her own hand to the babe's heart in the hope she could defy the years.' He looked up and saw both Lethan and Eduerd struck with looks of horror and pity.

'As time passed, Ravar grew into such a clever and striking child,' Osharm continued. 'Oh, but children are cruel. At the School of the Young the others would tease her about her strange appearance and question her place in the Plains. And when she came home, sometimes she would cry.' Osharm set his lips hard, to keep control of the emotion he felt.

'Ravar would acknowledge rather than be truly comforted by our words of solace and it was an agony not being able to do more. Amalin would become incensed on such occasions and clasp her sister in such a tight embrace and with such a look of defiant protectiveness that even we, as her parents would back away.'

Osharm had paused again. Eduerd and Lethan studied his face, which had now lost its sadness. There was a sort of strange smile forming on his lips. 'And then,' he at last continued, 'it happened. They do not know but I confess that I saw it with my own eyes for I came to stand in the doorway when I heard their crossed words.'

'What?' Lethan demanded, unable to help himself.

Osharm smiled. 'I heard Amalin pleading with Ravar. "Sister, please do not cry, do not cry!"

"'I am ugly and strange! I do not belong here!"

'Ravar was sobbing, but Amalin told her, "You *do* belong here! You are our family, no matter what anyone else says. And you are *not* ugly! You are *beautiful!* Do you hear me? I will make you see how beautiful you are to me!"

'I saw Amalin reach out her hand to her sister, but Ravar batted it away, saying, "You cannot, Amalin! You know that you cannot. We are too young. You have tried many times and it does not work."

'Amalin, of course, did not listen. Instead she replied, "I do not care what anyone says!" Amalin spoke with a steel which, until then, I had not known her capable.

'I watched as Amalin placed her hand on Ravar's heart and leant forward so that their foreheads touched. "Everyone says that you are the cleverest child the province has ever known, Ravar," she whispered. "Surely you can open your heart to mine? Surely you will let me in?"'

Osharm leant forward, his voice almost a whisper. 'My Lords, I witnessed my daughters join in Soul Friendship when they were but thirteen and eight years old.'

Eduerd and Lethan were staring at him, their jaws dropped. 'How is such a thing possible?' said Lethan, frowning in disbelief.

'It is possible,' said Eduerd, his eyes staring into the distance. 'It is extremely rare but I have read of such cases. By the Stars, I had no idea that...' His voice trailed off.

'So now, My Lord, you will perhaps direct your gratitude toward the person who truly deserves it. After all, Ravar surely knows to whom she owes her wellness of Soul. Why do you think she has followed Amalin everywhere she has ever gone and always bowed to her wants and judgement? Ravar's first memory and sure knowledge of how beautiful and loved she was in another's eyes came from Amalin. It was Amalin who made her.'

Osharm rubbed his face with both hands, tiredly. Through them, he murmured, 'Two daughters. One to save the other.'

Lethan nodded slowly. 'She is the music,' he murmured.

CHAPTER 21

Forestfyth, Sixth Year of the Dancer, the Autumn Equinox.

All had eaten and drunk their fill. Surrounded by a crowd of their Nearage students, Ravar, Amalin and Istreeth were receiving great baskets of produce. The traditional harvest gifts were well received and the three principal Tutors of the School received a small round of applause from those near enough to see what was happening.

King Aislyth grinned at his sister. He was so glad that she was considered such an able and committed teacher that she was now treated to the same respect and honour as the School's official Masters. Istreeth had been awarded the mark of Silver by Ravar the week before, the latter knowing that her student would not appreciate a public display at the Feast. Aislyth watched his sister touch it subconsciously as she made her way back over to the dais.

It had been a wonderful couple of months, the season living up to its reputation as a time of bounty. The orchard crops had been exceptionally plentiful and the King had received report after report of favourable assessments of Kingdom Projects. It was as though the Forest were reaping a sort of cosmic reward for putting right a great wrong earlier in the year.

Then again, perhaps his excellent mood had more to do with the company he had been recently keeping. Ravar had not only responded to nearly all of his invitations to spend time together, she had twice been the instigator.

He remembered the time that she had leant into him as they sat side by side at the top of the ravine, west of the city. It was probably no more than a contented and tired action, resting her head against his upper arm after a long morning's ride. But he was filled with hope that, if she could relax in such a way around him, her heart might be open to a life together.

*

In fact, Ravar hardly understood her own feelings. She could not deny a tremendous attraction to the King, in whose company she seemed to find a way to wind down and be still. It was as if his immense size allowed her to carve out a quiet space in his shadow, his strength being enough for the both of them. He made her laugh and was always quick to catch and counter her teasing. He was also rather wild and bound to the Forest in a mysterious and earthy sort of way. When he walked he would brush the tips of his fingers over the bark of the trees as he went, and he would whistle the cries of the birds overhead, seemingly without even noticing he was doing it.

And then, there was Eduerd. She found that, out of his company she thought of him less often than the King. Yet, when they were together, there was a sort of lightening-like current that seemed to run between them.

Eduerd had a way of firing Ravar's mind into explosions of intellectual delight and curiosity. There was also something heady and addictive about his steady, precise dialect and perfect gentlemanly charm that could make her swoon.

The Doctor's Kin were also a great attraction. Desledair's prolonged stay in the Forest had meant that he and Ravar had quickly become fast friends in their own right, sharing a love of dark humour and a critically analytical approach to most things.

As for the others, Ravar got on well with them all. With Amalin shortly to announce her intention to become part of that Kin circle, Ravar had to admit that she too would be happy to make her home within it.

It was becoming an impossible and almost painful choice. Although there was no pressure to make up her mind for at least a cycle yet, Ravar found that she did not enjoy the prospect of making both men compete and wait so long. The crux of it was that she now held a torch for both of them and did not want to send either away. It was selfish, she knew. But it was also the truth.

A trumpet blast signalled the time for the celebrants to crowd back to the dancing area for the King's final words and the awarding of honours.

Ravar was surprised to find Amalin wandering over to her and taking her arm.

'Where is Lethan?' Ravar asked. Amalin had been stuck to him like glue all night and it had been her intention to find an appropriate moment to give him her acceptance of his suit during the celebration.

'I do not know,' Amalin said, looking around and frowning. 'He disappeared while the Nearage were giving us the Harvest gifts. So much for my happy plans!' There was more than a little annoyance in her voice.

Ravar was prevented from replying to console her friend by the resounding voice of the King, giving his customary thanks to those who had prepared the feast and opening the floor to those in the crowd wishing to recognise the achievements of those apprenticed to them. After two such awards in silver and bronze were bestowed by Masters of Forestry and Earth Craft respectively, a hush drew in as everyone waited for the King's final address.

Instead, the King stepped back from the stage and gestured to the man who had been seated at his right throughout the Feast. His Kinsman, the huge Grandmaster Falthson rose to take the centre stage. Ravar and Amalin shot each other a surprised look.

'Surely, it must be!' whispered Ravar, quickly.

'But he never said anything!' Amalin exclaimed.

The only reason for a Grandmaster to take the stage at such a time could be that a Craftsman of the Gold Level wished to present his Masterpiece. And the only Carpenter of the Gold Level that Ravar and Amalin knew of in Forestfyth was Lethan.

'Joy to you all this at this Autumn Feast!' shouted the great hulking form of Falthson from the stage. His whole face was a beaming smile, his nose and cheeks flushed and his forehead shining by the light of the candles and fire.

The crowd, many of whom had reached the same conclusion as Ravar and Amalin, surged forward excitedly, shouting back merry greetings. No one had questioned the presence of the Grandmaster at their autumn celebration, whose ties by marriage and Kinship often brought him and his wife to the capital from their home in Highturth. Now they were all excitedly waiting to see the piece which he had deigned of a high enough quality to award Mastery to its creator.

'People of the Forest, I, Falthson of the Forest People, Grandmaster of my art, present to you Lethan of the same People!' A roar of applause, led by Fiance whose enormous hands beat together over her head sending her many folds wobbling beneath them, greeted a shyly grinning Lethan as he stepped up to the stage. The King clapped him on the shoulder as he passed.

'Lethan, I have judged your work presented to me this very morning to be of exceptional merit,' Falthson boomed, for the benefit of the people before them. Another applause rose and fell. Amalin and Ravar jumped up and down, squealing with delight.

Falthson turned and intoned in a solemn voice, 'Do you accept the responsibility that befalls a Master of his Craft?' Lethan bowed to his master, bent to one knee and looked up at the enormous, beaming man.

'Then…' Falthson leaned forward to pin the beautiful metal pin depicting an auger, plane and chisel overlapping one another at the centre of Lethan's sash. The crowd panted in anticipation, waiting for the coming words. 'Rise, Lethan, Master of your Craft!' The thunderous cries of celebration erupted from the People in an instant and Lethan was embraced by all the personages on the stage. He was then hauled down by Fiance, who had practically picked him up by his feet and made to endure one of her lung-crushing hugs.

"I *knew* it!" she cried, victoriously.

The Cook only let him go when she saw Amalin appear at their side and presented the staggering, winded man to the woman who meant more to him than any accolade for his Craft. Amalin's big green eyes brimmed with tears and she took his hands, gripping them hard and bowed to him. Astonished and embarrassed, he pulled her back up and said gently, 'Do not bow to me, My Lady. Why, you have not even seen my Masterpiece and after all, it was meant for you.' There was an intake of breath as those near enough to have heard his words began to look about them.

Lethan led Amalin, the crowd of spectators following keenly, to a dark corner of the hall. No one had noticed a large, covered object, draped in sacking cloth standing there in the shadows. Candles were promptly lit, revealing a tall, squarish silhouette, narrow in depth.

Shushing the crowd by putting a finger to his lips, Lethan, still holding Amalin by the hand, led her to the hidden object's side. 'Grandmaster Falthson has proclaimed my work worthy of Mastery.' He smiled at Amalin. 'I say its worth may only be judged once we have heard it played.'

'Played?' Amalin repeated, almost stupidly, just before Lethan flung down the cloths.

An impressive collective gasp rippled through the crowd. At the back, the King's eyes danced as he beheld the imposing yet graceful form, whose transportation and situation within the Hall, he had personally supervised earlier that day.

"A great harp!" Amalin breathed in disbelief.

The workmanship was difficult to take in all at once. Lethan had fused red and dark woods together seamlessly to create a spiralling pattern all along the column of the harp. Its head and neck were a labyrinth of beautifully carved circular rings and ridges, so that it looked as though the wood had been looped and plaited as easily as leather. The thick, pale strings were fitted into immaculate bronze sockets and its tuning pins that shone no less brightly than the highly polished frame.

Eduerd came to stand behind his friend, clasping his arm in congratulation for, although he had known of Lethan's long labour in its construction, he had never been allowed even a glimpse of the actual instrument.

However, unlike the rest of the admiring onlookers, Amalin had walked over to the instrument as if in a trance, like a moth to the light. Ravar came to stand at Lethan's side where he was gazing upon Amalin who circled the instrument, taking in its every feature without blinking.

'Oh, Lethan, what have you done?' Ravar taunted him, looking pointedly at Amalin. Before he had a chance to reply a great clap broke the chattering of the crowd and all turned to see the King, whose hands were still held aloft.

'Grandmaster Falthson has declared this beautiful instrument a Masterpiece,' boomed the King, smiling broadly. 'But surely we must beg our Master Musician to put it to the test?' He extended his arm, palm face up towards Amalin who was tentatively running her forefinger down one of the strings.

His suggestion was met with clamours of agreement and Amalin sank without hesitation on to the little stool, gently pulling the levered strings towards her.

Nearly a year of absence had not dulled Amalin's feel for such an instrument and her newly acquired talent for the fiddle had at least kept fingers of one hand hardened enough to negotiate the taught bands without difficulty. The people of Forestfyth marvelled at the hauntingly beautiful sound which emanated from its strings and Amalin swooned with delight as she conjured the melody.

When she abruptly brought her play to an end and stood, walking straight towards Lethan, she seemed completely oblivious to the applause for her skill that filled the hall. Ravar alone knew her mind and came to stand at her side before the Carpenter.

Silence fell as the whole gathering surrounded them, those further back straining to see and hear what was passed between them. Even Fiance had gone quiet.

Amalin had stars in her eyes as she smiled up at the man to whom she had given her heart. 'Lethan,' she spoke softly, 'know that, even before I had seen you ascend into Mastery, long before I had played your Grand Harp, your sash was always destined to be adorned with a new mark tonight.'

As Lethan's eyes widened in surprise she turned to Ravar and gently plucked the feather from her Soul Friend's shoulder. There were excited intakes of breath from the crowd and she turned to pin it to the upper portion of Lethan's sash, the gold side facing up. It was the mark of a suit accepted. Her own feather would be pinned during the marriage ceremony.

Lethan reached out and grasped Amalin, his strong hands pulling her gently closer to him. 'Mastery be damned!' he whispered in her ear. He took her hand and brought it back to the top of his sash. 'This is the only pin that matters.'

*

The wedding was set for the second month of winter when the families of both Amalin and Lethan would be able to make the journey to attend. Amalin and Ravar busied themselves with the arrangements for the ceremony which was to be celebrated in the open form, witnessed by the whole city.

Naturally, Fiance had taken charge of most of the practical arrangements. Amalin had been careful to ensure that her request that the Master Cook provide the victuals for the occasion was put in quickly. Fiance had swelled with pride though the Heavens knew that she would not have countenanced the idea of anyone else being allowed the honour.

Master Armick had the rare privilege of being commissioned to make a wedding gown for Amalin. Given her personal disposition against all things needlework-related, she had given the Tailor total free rein and he had selected shimmering bronzes and maroons for a long, trailing dress with leaf-like, gold patterning.

The only task which fell to Lethan was to choose his Soul Giver and ask someone to conduct the marriage. The former was an easy choice: he did not want to choose between his brothers and, in any case, Eduerd was close to both Amalin and the women who would be giving her away in his own right. As for the latter, he would go with the traditional option and ask the King. After all, he too was a personal friend of his future wife, sharing many of the same musical interests. He would also be well qualified to lead the sung version of the ceremony, which was the obvious choice given how they had met and spent much of their time together.

In the midst of invitations sent, garments made, decisions taken and excitement building, life in the Forest had also had to continue as usual.

The School of the Nearage demanded most of Ravar's attention. In addition to their regular lessons, a Goldman Trainer had been employed to take the students through their paces, giving regular instruction on health and fitness which was being met with varying degrees of enthusiasm.

Ravar herself had set a theme of composition for the term and had been directing and discussing the efforts of the Nearage in all manner of art forms from poetry, to the direction of theatrical performance. Her idea was that these labours would culminate in a great celebration performance at the Palace in the spring and the King had expressed a desire to organise the event.

As for Eduerd, he had moved onto teaching about the symptoms and diagnosis of long-term conditions. Although it could hardly be thought of as a cheerful topic, the subject matter was challenging and required precise knowledge and understanding. There were several among the class to whom this held great appeal and one student had even started to volunteer at the city hospital, where such maladies were treated. Ravar looked on his lessons with ever-increasing approval. The Nearage continued to be drawn in by the same compelling quiet enthusiasm and intellectual fervour as she was.

With all the talk of Amalin's upcoming nuptials, Ravar could not avoid considering her own ongoing dilemma. She found that she could actually form a picture of an everyday life with either man at her side that would make her happy. To put her imaginings in such terms might appear rather mundane to some, but Ravar had tried very hard to separate her thoughts from the surges of physical attraction and the times where it had seemed that her very Soul had taken flight in each man's company. She was young for marriage and conscious that Soul Joining was a life-long commitment that was almost impossible to break.

Therefore she had to consider the day-to-day that she might live with each of her suitors.

Eduerd offered a heady, intense mix of intellectual passion and entertainment. Together, she was sure, they could conquer all the Crafts of the Mind. Perhaps they would travel the Way of the Mathematician hand in hand. She would become part of the very Kinship circle that Amalin was soon to share and join in with the laughter and jokes and parties and songs in the strange little cottage that was lost in the woods.

By contrast, she might stand at the side of the King and help to govern a whole people. She could revel in the pleasures of the daylight hours, walking and playing games in the Forest, rather than staring up at the glittering stars. The King's circle was rich with life and action. The challenges of the mind were real, with tangible consequences. And instead of Lord Desledair as a brother, she would gain Princess Istreeth for a sister.

CHAPTER 22

Forestfyth, Sixth Year of the Dancer, early winter.

The Palace Hall was lit by hundreds of candles and garlands of dried and winter flowers wound around every pillar. Every resident of city had turned out to watch Lethan and Amalin wed in the festive, open form.

Standing before the couple who stood shoulder to shoulder on the dais, the King sang the old words of marriage, recalling the first union of Souls at the start of time. Married pairs in the congregation held each other tight and fingered their gold feathers, recalling their own memories of the day that they were joined.

For the final part of the rite, Ravar and Eduerd stepped forward and the bride and groom turned to face one another. Ravar took Amalin's right hand in hers, smiling over at Eduerd who had taken that of Lethan.

The couple spoke the final vows, their voices in unison: *Queen/King of my heart, I will love you forever. I give you all of the joys of my life. Amalin/Lethan, to you my Soul is open. Every toil and every burden my body and mind will help you endure. Every path we shall travel together until death forks the road.*

With the greatest joy, Ravar guided Amalin's hand to Lethan's heart, just as Lethan's was pressed to hers. In the profound silence that followed as the whole gathering bowed to the Souls meeting for the first time, Ravar wept. She did not need to join her own hand to Amalin's heart to know how full it was.

And yet, there was a twinge of pain within her too. Tonight she would return to an empty house as Amalin made her new home with her husband. Amalin of course, was hardly going to abandon her – she knew that. And Lethan would, she was sure, never begrudge his wife time with her Soul Friend. But Amalin was embarking on a path of her own and forging a new existence and family. It would be different for her and Ravar now.

Looking up, Ravar saw Amalin and Lethan still frozen, their eyes closed and heads drawn in, resting against each other. She dared a glance beyond them where the King stood and found that she did not flinch in the weighted gaze in which he held her.

How long he had been staring at her? She did not know. And, she thought, she did not care. She looked back into his deep, blue, penetrating eyes that were filled with strength and warmth. And she looked out at the stars through the great glass window beyond him, haloing his form.

And Eduerd watched Ravar, his heart folding in pain.

*

The Doctor kissed Amalin on both cheeks. She was now part of his Kin and he delighted in Lethan's glow of happiness as he walked his wife back to his home near the Carpenters' workshop. Ravar was standing, looking after them, a torn expression clouding her features. Eduerd started to make for her but the King materialised like a great shadow from beyond her and laid a huge hand on her shoulder. Looking up, Ravar took his proffered arm and they walked away in the opposite direction.

So that was it, thought Eduerd, emptily. He was a good man, the King. He would walk her home and he hoped he would be able give her comfort. But comfort to Eduerd in this moment, nothing could bring.

*

As Ravar and the King slowly snaked their way back to her cottage, they maintained a steady conversation. It was strained on her part, as she tried not to think of her destination, already emptied of most of Amalin's things.

'I am for Marketdawn tomorrow,' the King was saying.

'Kingdom business?' Ravar asked.

The King sighed and nodded. 'I will hopefully only be gone a few days. I shall look forward to my return all the more knowing that I shall see you soon?' He scanned her face in the darkness.

'I would like that,' she replied. But Ravar's mind was elsewhere. She knew they were nearing the cottage and she kept her eyes trained to the floor as if to put off having to see the place which was now, for the first time, hers alone.

However, as they rounded the last trees on the path and the cottage came into few, the King let out a small, 'Ha!' which caused her to look up.

Ravar did not understand what she was seeing, for she saw bright light emanating from the windows and could hear women's voices raised in song. A bewildered smile formed on Ravar's lips and she looked questioningly at the King who merely shrugged his shoulders and opened the gate.

As they stepped through it the door to the house was flung open and the bright light within was eclipsed by the enormous, multi-coloured, ribboned, bejewelled and tasselled form of Fiance.

'Ah! The Lady of the House has returned!' she cried, grabbing Ravar and making batting gestures at the King as if to sweep him away back to the Palace. The King had no intention of arguing with her and so gave a waving goodbye to a gawping Ravar before turning on his heel.

Barely over the threshold, Ravar was seized by what felt like an octopus' wealth of arms and brought to the centre of a circle comprising Fiance, her sister, Doctor Keldair and several more of Fiance's friends.

'Well?' Fiance scolded indignantly, having taken in Ravar's astonishment. 'You did not think that this Kin circle would abandon you on such a night?' Ravar was humbled by their kindness.

'Thank you all,' Ravar said, with feeling. 'I was not looking forward to spending the first night without Amalin alone.' The women around her smiled. It was late and they were happy and full and tired.

Keldair yawned. Fiance shot her a cross look but Ravar laughed and pleaded with her guests to make themselves comfortable and to get to bed if they so wished.

Ravar, having given over her own bed as well as the spare, huddled up under one of the mountain of blankets Fiance had brought with her on the long sofa. It gave a menacing creak as Fiance daintily lowered herself onto it next to her.

'My own sister was married not a year ago,' Fiance whispered kindly. Ravar smiled sleepily and laid her head in her friend's lap. 'I know a little of the feeling of loss. But I was told of the way of it with you and Amalin. Ah, me, so young to have found your Soul Friend.' She yawned.

Ravar opened her eyes suddenly. How did Fiance know of this?

Fiance stroked her hair and shushed her. 'Our Kin would never allow a distance to form between you. And when you must be parted, you may always count yourself one of our Circle's number.' Ravar held back a sob and buried herself in the warm, voluptuous folds of blankets, garments and Fiance.

*

The following day Ravar set out early for the House of Amalin and Lethan. They had insisted that she accept, in advance, their first hospitality as a married couple and was looking forward to seeing them at breakfast.

Lethan answered the door looking tired, almost dazed with joy and with the dishevelled appearance of one who has not long been awake.

Stifling a laugh, Ravar said that she could return in an hour or so but Lethan grinned, looking a little sheepish, and was adamant that she came in.

Amalin bounced down the stairs looking wide awake and more or less jumped into Ravar's arms. Ravar thought she looked stunningly alive. Her beautiful rich brown hair flowed, untied around her face which was full of colour, her eyes bright. So this was marriage, she thought.

While Amalin crashed around the unfamiliar kitchen, finding things for breakfast, Lethan invited Ravar to take a seat and offered her a cup of steaming tea.

'Are you well, My Lady?' he asked quietly, his eyes flitting to the kitchen where Amalin was clumsily rummaging in a low cupboard. 'Amalin worried about you last night. You must know that you are always welcome under this roof. I have told Amalin that she must stay with you at least one night each week if you both wish it.'

Ravar took his hand and clasped it in both of hers. 'Thank you, Lethan. You are very kind. But Amalin had nothing to fear last night as I am sure you reassured her?'

'I did my best,' Lethan replied, unconvinced. There was a pause before Ravar spoke again.

'Are your Kin joining us?' she asked, thoughtfully.

'Alas, no. Desledair journeyed directly to Woodsedge this morning with Credain and Keldair. He has gone to Marketdawn at the summons of a delegation from the Sky Kingdom. He believes that the Emperor wants to commission him for some huge undertaking.'

'Heavens!' exclaimed Ravar. Desledair's reputation had evidently traversed the Middle Sea.

'Quite so,' chuckled Lethan. 'I thought that Fiance would be taken up with fussing over her boys and Eduerd snuck away last night before I had the chance to invite him.' Lethan held his arms up in mock despair. 'Therefore, you are our only guest!'

Ravar smiled, but her eyes narrowed as they often did when she was deep in thought.

She remained quiet over the morning meal and Amalin was sufficiently concerned to hustle Lethan from the room after they had finished eating to have it out with her.

'Ravar? Are you alright? What is going on in that head of yours? You are worrying me!'

Ravar looked up from her bowl where she had been slowly stirring the dregs of her porridge for some time. She looked Amalin full in the eye and smiled broadly. 'You have nothing to worry about, my dear, wonderful Amalin. Your happiness brings joy to my heart beyond measure.'

'But then—'

'However, I am afraid that I must demand a great favour which will disrupt your married bliss.'

'A favour?' Now Amalin was truly curious. 'Ravar, you know I would do anything!'

Ravar got up and walked around the table to her Soul Friend. She drew from Amalin her hand and pressed it to her own heart. Seconds later Amalin leant back, eyes round in surprise.

'You have chosen!' Amalin whispered.

'Yes,' Ravar smiled.

'Oh Ravar, I did not think anything could make me happier!' Amalin's words poured out of her like a fountain. 'I did not think you were close to deciding! How things have come together for us! But,' suddenly a thought struck her, 'when will you tell him? What would you have me do?'

Ravar gave Amalin a hug and got up. She reached for her cloak. 'For now, await my return I suppose. I must go to Marketdawn.'

When Lethan cautiously re-entered the room some time later he was surprised to find Amalin sitting there alone.

'Ravar is gone?' he asked. Amalin nodded. 'Is she all right?'

Amalin stood, walked over and kissed her husband. 'Everything is just right, Lethan. You will see.'

CHAPTER 23

The Eastern Woods, Sixth Year of the Dancer, winter.

Eduerd slumped at his desk. He had been trying to distract himself in his books but it was no use. After bidding Desledair farewell two days ago when Keldair and Credain had stopped on their way to pick him up, the Doctor had been left on his own to brood. Two days on and he was restless, lonely and in dark spirits.

He had told his Soul Friend about what he had seen between Ravar and the King at the wedding and, rightly, the Architect had berated him for his self-defeatism.

However, he had ridden into the city yesterday with a fresh resolve to call on the Lady, only to find her house unoccupied. After much enquiry, he had eventually been told that she had travelled, alone, to Marketdawn.

And so Eduerd had returned to his house in the woods, made up the fire and shut himself up with his work and studies. But no matter how he tried to concentrate on all manner of tasks, the same image haunted his mind: Ravar, staring up into the eyes of the King.

Sighing in frustration at his own melancholy, he heaved himself up and wandered over to the mirror. He pawed at his shadowed face and resolved to have a shave. Although it was already nearing the end of the day, Eduerd was naturally fastidious about his appearance and disliked the idea of being called upon by a late patient looking such a state. In any case, it would give him something to do and he would be forced to pay attention to the task if he did not want to be himself in need of a Healer.

Having accomplished this, Eduerd changed into a clean shirt and waistcoat and walked through to the Den where he stoked the fire. He checked the hour and, deciding that it was sufficiently late in the afternoon to justify calling the day at an end, fetched a bottle of Forest Warmth from the pantry and poured himself a cup. He was just about to take a swig when there came a knock at the door.

Surely it couldn't be... Eduerd knew the three firm knocks only too well and opened the door to see a strangely jolly looking Desledair standing before him.

'Stars what are you doing here?' exclaimed Eduerd.

Desledair set his teeth in disfavour. 'A fine way to greet your Soul Friend after a long ride.' He said, grumpily.

'I am sorry!' demurred Eduerd, beckoning him in and taking his cloak. 'But you yourself said that you would likely not be back until next week.'

Desledair ignored this and surveyed, with distaste, the table in the Den upon which the heady drink and cup were laid. As Eduerd brought over an additional mug he felt the hard stare of unusual scrutiny as Desledair appeared to look him over.

'Were you planning to drink yourself senseless in my absence?' said Desledair, accusingly. Eduerd flushed a little. He looked into the cup he was holding and pushed it away from him back on the table with disgust.

'I think I was, friend.' Eduerd admitted. He sighed, ran his hands through his hair and threw his head back.

Desledair raised a disapproving eyebrow. 'And what, pray, has turned you towards such a poor course of action?'

'You can guess,' Eduerd said, snappishly.

'Ah,' said Desledair.

'She is gone to Marketdawn,' said Eduerd.

'Really?' murmured Desledair.

'Yes, Desledair. *Marketdawn.*' Irritated, Eduerd elaborated, 'Where the *King* is.'

'Is that so? I was not aware. And you are sure that Ravar has gone to meet him?'

'What other purpose can she have in going there?' asked Eduerd, morosely.

'Many, I should think,' said Desledair, frowning at his friend. 'Now look here, Eduerd, go and fetch us something more reasonable to drink.

And find something to eat. *You* may be intent upon suffering through the evening in unpleasant fettle but I had hoped for a happy evening in good company.'

Eduerd grunted but got up to comply with the request. 'You never know, Eduerd,' Desledair said airily, 'perhaps the evening will turn out brighter than you suspect.'

Eduerd returned to give Desledair a disparaging glance over. 'Since when,' he said incredulously, 'did you become the voice of optimism?'

Desledair looked eminently pleased with himself. 'Since you became so bleak.'

Just as Eduerd was flashing him an even more cynical look there was a rap at the door. He groaned.

'Well, answer the door, man!' said Desledair, as Eduerd remained seated.

Eduerd grimaced. 'I am in no fit state to treat patients.'

'What kind of talk is that from a Healer?' admonished Desledair, getting up to answer the knock himself. Eduerd took a bite of the bread he had brought over to the table and chewed it sulkily. He almost spat it out again as he heard the cheerful greetings from the doorway.

'Ah, Ladies Ravar and Amalin! What a pleasant surprise!'

'Thank you, Lord Desledair!' sounded Ravar's voice. 'It is very good to see you! I hope that we are not intruding?' Eduerd jumped up and raced to the entrance hall.

There, looking fresh and lovely as ever was the Lady Ravar, resplendent in a dark purple cloak with matching ribbons in her hair. Amalin bobbed about beside her, looking cold, despite being clad in a hooded fur coat.

'Ravar, Amalin! Do come into the warmth,' Eduerd stammered. He tried to avoid meeting Desledair's eye for he would be intolerably smug, having just suggested that the evening might take a turn for the better. However, as he ushered the ladies in and Desledair took their coats, Eduerd caught the look of absolute triumph on his Soul Friend's face. Eduerd groaned inwardly and Desledair saw it in his features. That made it even worse.

Ravar and Amalin had seated themselves comfortably in the Den and were unloading their packs which were filled with good food. Desledair assumed that they must have begged from the larder of Lady Fiance.

'You have come well-prepared, I see!' said Eduerd, chuckling. 'Are we to enjoy a feast?'

'Indeed,' grinned Ravar. 'It is nearly the end of the rest period and we wanted to finish this happy break in good company and with a good supper.'

Eduerd's transformation was instant and absolute, marred only by Desledair's ever more sickening gratification. He did not even try to unravel the whys and wherefores of this unexpected turn of events because he was simply too delighted to have Ravar here in his company.

When several hours of merry festivity had passed, it was Amalin who peered out of the rounded window into the darkness without.

'Stars it is late!' she exclaimed. 'We should get going Ravar, for it is a long walk home.'

'You *walked?*' said Eduerd in surprise. He had assumed they had borrowed horses at this time of year. But then again, Ravar at least did not seem to feel the cold.

'We are not afraid of a little exercise, My Lord,' smiled Ravar, though Eduerd thought Amalin looked less keen.

'Well you certainly shall not walk home alone in the dark,' said Eduerd. Desledair went immediately to fetch his and Eduerd's coats.

Setting a moderate pace, Amalin and Desledair took the lead and Ravar and Eduerd fell into step behind them. Ravar linked her arm through his. Eduerd could smell the spiced scents she wore and feel the heat of her hand through his cloak and garments on his arm.

'Your visit this evening was much appreciated, My Lady,' said Eduerd. 'You helped to save what looked likely to have been a rather sombre night.'

Ravar looked up, quizzically. 'Oh?'

'I confess I was rather melancholy. I thought all those I cared to see were gone to Marketdawn.'

Ravar nodded. 'I had heard that Desledair was there.'

'And you, My Lady.'

Ravar turned sideways to look up at him. 'Yes,' she said. There was a silence between them, where Eduerd was not given any more elaboration. At length, Ravar cleared her throat.

'I too recently feared a somewhat lonely and depressing night,

Eduerd.' She fixed him with a meaningful look but did not give him a chance to say anything as she continued. 'However, it seems that the women of your Kin circle thought even of my wellbeing on the day of their Kinsman's wedding.'

'I am glad that they brought you comfort,' said Eduerd, softly.

'Oh they did, My Lord,' Ravar said evenly. 'Fiance told me that your circle understand the particular bond I share with Amalin, that I am vulnerable without her.'

'Oh, Ravar, I am sure no offense was—'

'Hush, Eduerd!' Ravar interrupted. 'Fiance was right. How he came by the story I know not, but Lethan it seems told Fiance that perhaps I should not be left alone on the night he took Amalin from my home. It was a kindness I shall never forget.'

Eduerd smiled a little in the anonymity of the dark.

'It was so kind in fact,' she went on, with a strange lightness in her voice, 'that I meant to thank Lethan for the thought when I breakfasted with him and Amalin the following day.' She paused a moment. 'Only – and it was the strangest thing – I would swear that he knew nothing of the arrangement.' Eduerd remained silent.

'And so, My Lord Eduerd, I realised that the idea had not come from Lethan. And I knew it had not originated from Fiance, for she spoke openly of the thought of her Kinsman.'

Ravar stopped walking and took Eduerd's hands. 'Thank you,' she said.

Eduerd's heart soared. 'I would never want you to be unhappy,' he said.

'I know,' she said.

Suddenly a little self-conscious, Eduerd looked about. He saw that Amalin and Desledair had stopped just ahead of them and were watching with interest. Before he could think of anything else to say, he frowned and looked more carefully about him. This was not the path they should be on to make their way back to the city. They were at a sort of small clearing, the moonlight shining through the leafless branches of a relatively young Great Oak.

'Desledair, where the blazes have you taken us?' he gasped, wheeling round to try to get his bearings.

Desledair and Amalin walked over to him. They seemed to share a strange, enigmatic smile – as if they knew something that he did not.

'Exactly where we are meant to be, I think,' Desledair said, lightly. He smiled at his friend.

Eduerd frowned even harder. Were they playing some sort of joke on him?

'*Witnessed by one who precedes and will succeed us,*' intoned Amalin, looking up at the giant tree.

Eduerd spun to face her, his mouth gaping.

'*And the timeless lights of the sky.*' This time it was Ravar who spoke. Eduerd moved to face her, almost in slow motion. He knew the meaning of these words. They were the simple prerequisites of the ancient marriage rite, the mysterious and most closed form of the Six Kingdoms. A pair could make their vows in the presence of these two witnesses alone and the Soul Bond would be as unbreakable as any other.

Eduerd stared carefully into the face of Ravar, the moonlight making her hair glow. She merely smiled and nodded to Amalin, who stepped forward. Ravar unpinned the single feather from her friend's sash and neatly fixed it to Eduerd's. No one had even noticed that, for the whole evening, Amalin had only worn one bronze token.

'Now?' asked Eduerd, gently. 'Here?'

'Under these skies that you and I shall master together,' said Ravar. Eduerd looked at the sparkling heavens above him and them to the sparkling eyes before him.

'Yes.' Suddenly he caught her hands and leant forward. 'Ravar, you are sure? I thought that...'

'I am sure.'

Eduerd smiled. He looked up at Desledair, whose eyes were dancing. So that was what Ravar had been doing in Marketdawn. He pointed an accusing finger at his friend.

'You were in on this!' He whirled around at Amalin. 'And you too! Stars, is this what my life is to be from now on? All of you ganging up on me?' He was laughing now. They all were.

After the solemn rite, Amalin and Desledair melted into the darkness. Ravar and Eduerd remained in the Soul Embrace for so long, that by the time they stood back to look upon one another as husband and wife, they had lost all sense of their surroundings. It was only then that they realised they were alone.

Only they would understand what had passed between them, but the understanding was absolute. They made love under the stars and walked home to the house in the woods hand in hand. In the crooked walls of the Healer's cottage, Ravar and Eduerd fell asleep in each other's arms, watched over by the Dancer and her fellow stars above.

CHAPTER 24

The eastern woods, Sixth Year of the Dancer, winter.

Barely had the sun risen the following day when there was a banging at the door. Eduerd held Ravar closer to him, screwed up his eyes and willed the noise away. More knocking. His wife's body shook with giggling.

'You will have to answer, Eduerd,' whispered Ravar. 'What if it is a patient?' Eduerd responded by grabbing a pillow and throwing it at the bedroom door.

'It will have to be an emergency to tear me away from you.' But the words were barely out of his mouth when a much more frantic rapping ensued.

With much groaning and some surprisingly bad language Eduerd hauled himself out of bed, throwing a robe about him and descended the winding stairs. He opened the door a crack and peered out.

'Desledair!' The Doctor rolled his eyes, aghast, and spoke quietly through gritted teeth, refusing to open the door any further. 'Of all days, friend, I thought that you might appreciate that I really, *really* do not wish to be disturbed!'

Desledair returned his eye roll and replied irritably. 'Indeed Eduerd, do not presume that I am not painfully aware that you would rather not be interrupted.' Desledair peered back over his shoulder as if looking for something. He turned back to his friend and continued hurriedly. 'It is with this precise knowledge in fact, that I have made the fast ride here directly.'

Eduerd pulled a strained sort of face and opened the door a notch further.

'Eduerd,' Desledair continued, insistently, 'the Lady Fiance came to call upon Ravar this morning, only to find the house empty. She made her way straight to the house of Lethan where I answered the door...'

'Stars! You told her?' Eduerd was horrified as it dawned upon him what Desledair meant by his visit.

'Eduerd, you know she is not a woman from whom secrets are easily kept!' Desledair pleaded.

'How long?'

'I believe she must be less than an hour behind me.'

With more cursing, Eduerd bustled Desledair inside.

*

Fiance arrived with Amalin and Lethan in tow. Once she had berated everyone sufficiently for not including her in the previous night's proceedings, she then moved on to congratulations.

'Why we are *all* Kin now!' she cried. 'What a fine circle we make! Today I shall send word to all our friends, for you will *not* escape a fitting celebration,' she added sternly, pointing a forceful, fat finger at Ravar and Eduerd.

'Now,' she went on, composing herself a little, 'I have brought provisions for I know that Eduerd *never* has anything decent for breakfast and I daresay that you newlyweds are in *particular* need of adequate refreshment! Ha!' She chortled at the blushing faces of Ravar and Eduerd.

The newlyweds bid farewell to their friends at midday, having made arrangements to follow them to the city later to collect Ravar's possessions and stop by the administration offices to register their marriage. It felt appallingly mundane and the pair felt a mutual lack of enthusiasm for the venture. Because of this, they were later setting out than they had planned. Darkness was already creeping in and Ravar suggested that they should stop over at her own house that night. They were just fringing the outskirts of the city limits when urgent shouts broke the silence of the forest.

Automatically steering their horses towards the commotion, Ravar and Eduerd caught up with a frantic man who was running towards the city centre.

'*Fire!*' he cried, his eyes wide with fright.

'Where?' Raver and Eduerd demanded in unison. Fire was the great enemy of the Forest People, even in midwinter, for almost everything in their communities was built of wood.

'At the Grapple Tree Hamlet!' The poor man cried.

'Go!' Eduerd ordered him. 'Fetch more help!' And he began to run. Ravar could not keep up with him but knew the way. Grapple Tree was a small row of neat two- and three-storey houses, comprising dwellings that doubled up as workshops. Ravar did not know the families there well, but Eduerd had been present at the births of no less than four children born to the tiny community within the last five years. The youngest, twins, were only eight months old. He had to make sure that they were safe.

By the time Ravar came, sweating and panting, to the small opening in the trees, the scene that met her eyes was like something out of a nightmare. The two end buildings blazed in full fury under the now darkened sky and the light wind was fanning the flames.

Already the next two buildings had caught alight and about twenty paces in front of it, three coughing forms were gasping for breath, crowding around a prone figure whom they must have rescued from within.

Eduerd was nowhere to be seen, while a pitifully small number of people were desperately drawing water up from a well and passing buckets down a line.

Ravar could see that their labours would be off little use, but lent her services to the effort nonetheless. There were shouts and, to her absolute horror, Ravar looked over to see Eduerd emerge from the fourth building, spluttering and covered in ash, with another man. Between them they carried the unconscious form of a woman and they laid her down near the other casualty. Eduerd knelt over her and began to administer to her as best he could.

With a sudden jolt, the woman, her dress charred and face dirtied by blood from several cuts, struggled against Eduerd who was appealing for her to remain still.

'The *children*,' she rasped. All those in earshot turned to look at the agonised features of the woman who, even now, was trying to get up, her arms flailing wildly in her attempt to escape the grasp of those holding her back.

'They are upstairs!' she wailed, her voice breaking into a choking coughing fit. All eyes turned to the awful blaze that had now fully engulfed the third building and had already caught the ground floor of the fourth in earnest.

Time slowed as Ravar realised with dread, that Eduerd had broken away from his patient and grabbed a bucket of water from the line. He wrenched off his cloak and doused it in the water, flinging it back on over his head and face.

'No!' Ravar screamed, against the noise and confusion all about her, but two people threw themselves at her and held her fast.

Eduerd had run headlong into the wall of fire that now served as a doorway to the woman's house. There was a loud crash as something within the building gave way, ejecting a puff of smoke, ash and sparks from the flaming entrance. The crowd of onlookers fell silent. Ravar felt her heart thudding in her chest.

What seemed like an eternity later, the top-storey shutters were suddenly flung open and Eduerd's head appeared through the window. He howled down to the people below, 'The stairs are fallen in. You must catch them!' and he disappeared again from view. The people in the bucket line surged forward. Ignoring the fierce heat that emanated from the building, they came to stand as close to the house beneath the window as they could.

Presently, Eduerd appeared once more, holding a wrapped bundle. He flung it out from the flaming lower walls and it was caught, with cries of fear and relief by the crowd below.

Eduerd disappeared once again from view, returning seconds later, and threw the other baby to safety.

How is he to escape? hammered the voice in Ravar's mind. The window was too small for him to climb through, even if he could survive the fall, or be cushioned without killing someone on the ground below. *How is he to escape?*

People around her were having the same thoughts and there was panic in the voices of those calling up to the Doctor.

They did not have long to give themselves to such thought, for the building gave a terrible groan. It was as if the house itself had let out a terrible gasp of agony and there was a lurch in its outer structure.

The crowd in front of it flinched, before instinctively turning on their heels. They managed to run only a couple of paces away from it before the the whole thing came tumbling down in an explosion of flames, sparks, splintered wood and thick, dark smoke.

Amidst the turmoil, a maddened wraith-like woman surged through the people, her mind wandering in chaos. Thoughts streamed simultaneously, without beginning or end: pain as a wave of heat and smoke and ash scorched her eyes, strong arms and hands that clawed at her and ripped her dress, a deafening wail that split her ears. Was it her own? A sinking heaviness that dragged her down. And then an icy hand reaching within her, tearing at her heart. Pulling, pulling and then ripping it in two.

And then the grey. The grey of nothingness, the dull ringing in her ears, the empty space in her chest.

CHAPTER 25

Forestfyth, Sixth Year of the Dancer, winter.

'The ancient writers had a name for men such as Eduerd.' The King paused, taking a long breath to steady his voice. Never had such numbers flocked to the city. And never in such sadness. He found the hollow-looking face of Desledair who was standing at the front of the congregation and met his eye. To lose a Soul Friend was to lose a part of oneself. He must find the strength speak the words for him.

'Star Born.' He let the beauty of the words rest in his people's minds for a moment. 'Eduerd of the Forest devoted his life to the remedy and care of others, choosing as his profession the great Craft of Care for which so many of us are indebted.' There were solemn nods among the crowd and more tears shed.

'The old stories,' the King continued, 'describe the Star Born as Souls that descend to the earth on the back of falling stars. They become the people who are destined to perform the ultimate acts of good among the Peoples of our world.' He breathed in deeply. He cast a sad but proud smile at the crowd. 'In so doing, the writers say, their Souls earn their places to be elevated once more to the Heavens to shine for us all until they are needed again.' He beckoned at the stars above them.

Heads turned skywards in the cold. The funeral, at the King's own suggestion was being held in the open air of the Palace grounds, under the night sky that Eduerd had loved.

Ravar stood at Desledair's side, unsteady on her feet and being supported by Amalin. The King had not been able to see her since the day of the tragedy, for she would admit no one to her home but the two people at her side. She herself had not left the house.

The King had to force himself to remain focused on his task as a ruler to honour the life of such a man. But it was hard when the woman he loved stood, so gaunt, so expressionless before him.

Arriving far too late to make any difference, the King had raced to Grapple Tree Hamlet having heard the news on his journey back to the capital. By the time he entered the clearing, the smoking blackened shells of the buildings were all that remained. He had been led to the makeshift shelter where the injured had been taken and where the body of Master Eduerd had been carefully wrapped. When he asked to view the body to pay his respects he had been assured that there was nothing within that he would wish to see.

And then he had been taken to Ravar. Stars knew what she had been doing at this terrible place but the locals said that she had fought like a warrior to enter the blaze herself when the building had fallen in, taking Eduerd with it.

He had approached the trembling, unseeing, unhearing figure which better resembled a petrified animal than the woman he knew. He had taken her unresponsive form in his arms and carried her to her home, where he sent a messenger and waited for Amalin to come. That had been the last time he had seen her.

And now here she was, standing before him once again. Only, it was not any Ravar he recognised, for she was trance-like and seemingly uncomprehending, a contrast to the stricken faces either side of her. He was appalled that she appeared no better than when he had taken her from the hamlet.

The King took another breath and steeled himself. The Master Doctor deserved to be honoured.

'Eduerd of the Forest People was Star Born.' His voice rang out with emotion. 'He gave his life to save not one, but *two* of our number.' He gave a sad smile to the weeping parents who stood near the front of the gathering, each holding a child close to them.

'Two children, but babes in arms,' he repeated. 'Because of his sacrifice, they live. Because of his selflessness our People lost only one in number rather than two.' Desledair's shoulders shook up and down and he bowed his head.

The King's voice, faltering slightly, finished his piece. 'Eduerd of the Forest was a *hero*. He was the best of us. Let his body rest in the earth with the oaks and let his Soul return to the Heavens.'

*

When the last of the Forest People had left, the King and Istreeth had returned to their seating chamber and sat together at the hearth in sombre silence.

A cautious knock at the large doors prompted an irritable response from the King but he quickly apologised when he caught the chastised look upon the woman's face.

'I would not have disturbed you, Your Majesty. Truly I would not,' she said, quickly. 'Only, it is Lord Desledair and Lady Amalin.' The King immediately got to his feet.

'Yes?'

'They request an audience, Sire.'

Both he and Istreeth made their way to the audience chamber at once. Entering through the side-door, they took in the scene. Desledair stood before the raised platform, bolt upright, Amalin clinging to his arm. As the King took his seat, the Architect and Musician each made a formal bow. The King acknowledged this and spoke.

'Lord Desledair, Lady Amalin. I understand that you have requested a formal audience. You should know that, today of all days, such formality is unnecessary. Lord Desledair, may I offer my most sincere sympathy. Eduerd was…'

'I thank you, Sire,' Desledair broke in. 'I apologise for my abruptness, but I find I can scarcely hold back the storm which thunders in my mind.' His dark eyes and brows seemed to darken further, casting a sort of shadow down through his face. The King waited in silence.

'You spoke well of my friend this day, Your Majesty.' He swallowed and grimaced. 'For this I thank you.' The King nodded gravely. 'However,' Desledair continued, 'I find that there is no peace for me among even those with the kindest of intentions. How can there be when all I desire is the company of the one man whose presence I shall never again enjoy?' He sniffed angrily, though his ire was not directed at anyone in particular.

'Alas, I am a wretched companion and shall be until the time when I do not loathe and wish to cast away anyone and everyone for the simple reason that they are not my Eduerd.' He paused again and the King waited.

'Sire, I have been offered a long commission to design a sky garden on the Plateaus of High Cloud,' he said.

The King balked, slightly. It was an astonishing honour for an outsider to be entrusted with such an undertaking. The Sky Kingdom was notorious for its belief in the superiority of its own Craftsmen. There again, Lord Desledair's reputation was already widespread and he had worked with Sky Engineers on a number of his projects. No doubt they had reported on him favourably.

'And you will take the commission?' asked the King.

'I will. It is my hope that the distance between me and this place of Eduerd's may help me to come to terms with his departure from my life.' Desledair straightened himself and continued with quiet conviction. 'I shall build the sky garden in his name.'

The King held his gaze. 'A fitting tribute,' he said.

'It will be my finest Masterpiece,' said Desledair.

The King nodded. 'Then,' he said slowly, 'I wish you well in your task, My Lord. But tell me, why have you requested this audience, for you need no leave from me to journey across the Middle Sea?'

Desledair turned to Amalin and something painful and difficult passed between them. When Desledair returned to meet the King's eye, he spoke quietly.

'I wish to take Ravar with me.'

The King's eyes rounded and his jaw dropped. 'Ravar?' he repeated, not understanding.

'Yes, Your Majesty.'

'To the Sky Kingdom?' The King's voice was raised.

'Yes.'

'But why? You cannot take her with you!' The King's words fell from his mouth in quick, anxious succession. 'She is needed here! This is her home!'

'No, Sire.' Desledair countered, still calm and quiet.

'But—'

'Have you seen the Lady Ravar recently?' Desledair interrupted, a dangerous edge to his voice. 'She does not know her home anymore! I believe she hardly knows any of us either.'

'She is grieving!' the King protested. 'Surely you can see that?'

'She is lost, Your Majesty,' said Desledair. 'Let me take her away to try and find herself once again.'

247

'Find herself?' the King cried. 'How is she to do that a thousand miles from what she knows?' Receiving no reply, he came over to Amalin and pleaded imploringly.

'Lady Amalin, surely you are not a party to this mad idea? You would not be so long parted from your Soul Friend? She is grieving, she needs her People, her home!'

Amalin looked up. Her face was streaked with tears but her eyes and voice were sharp and defiant. 'Do not presume to tell me how I should feel and think about Ravar!' she spat. She struggled through gasping breaths while the King stared at her, quite taken aback. He glanced over at his sister who shook her head a fraction.

'I am sorry, Your Majesty,' sobbed Amalin, her crumpled form now half supported by Desledair. 'But Desledair is right. I do not know what else to do!' she wailed.

'Then let her stay here with you, with all of us!' said the King, quickly. 'We will help her to heal, to recover from her sorrow.'

'It is not grief!' Amalin cried. 'Your Majesty, it is not grief, it is something worse. She gave her Soul to Eduerd's and less than a day passed before they were ripped apart!'

The King let out a long breath to mask the pain that surged through him as he realised the full meaning of her words. He stepped back and slumped into his chair.

'She chose Eduerd,' he breathed, staring into nothingness. Istreeth stifled the desire to run to her brother and hold him in her arms.

'Aye, Your Majesty,' Amalin replied, grimly. 'She chose Eduerd and then he *left* her alone!' Desledair let out a yelp of protest but she pushed him away from her.

'It is the truth of it, Desledair! I truly sorry that Eduerd is gone for I had come to call him one of my Kin and I will miss him. But he *is dead!* He is gone while Ravar remains! Only, *what* of her remains? I have tried so hard to break through the awful wall with which she surrounds herself but I cannot.'

She swung about, alternating her piercing glare between the two men. 'Do you know what I hear in her Soul when we embrace?' she shouted shrilly. Without waiting for a reply, she said, 'Nothing! There is *silence!* Do you hear me? *Ravar* – our wonderful Master of words – her heart is silent! When Eduerd died it is as if her Soul went with his and I for one cannot find it to bring it back.'

She wiped the tears roughly from her face and once again addressed the King. 'Let her go, Sire. I will let her go in the safe company of the only other who understands the loss.'

The King cast about for anything that he might yet be able to use to persuade them against this. 'But the School...'

'I will take on Master Ravar's duties,' came a quiet voice from behind him. Istreeth had risen and glided soundlessly towards the others. She laid a gentle hand on her brother's shoulder.

'Sister! I..." The King faltered as she moved her arm around him.

'Let her go, brother,' she said softly. 'Let the Mountains heal her.'

'But what will we do without her?' the King rasped, his voice faltering.

'Ah, that will be the hardship, Aislyth,' said Istreeth. 'We will bear it together.'

He looked up at her delicate, pointed features. Her eyes were wide and sad but the hand she still rested on his shoulder was warm and strong. He knew that she was right. She always was. He drew in a deep breath and looked at Desledair.

'When will you depart, My Lord?'

'In the New Year, Sire,' said Desledair.

The King nodded, regaining his composure. 'And how long do you intend to remain at High Cloud?'

'I should think four seasons, Your Majesty.'

The King swayed. *'Four?'*

'Yes, Your Majesty.'

'And then?'

'Then,' said Desledair, 'if we are ready, we will return.'

The King sat in silence for some time, upright and alert. Amalin could see his mind whirring. At length, he murmured, 'Ravar must not be silent.'

'Sire?' said Desledair.

'Ravar is no Architect, Desledair. And she is no Botanist either. Take Ravar, but allow me to send her away not empty-handed.' Without waiting for an answer, he bowed, thereby dismissing Amalin and Desledair. They watched as he turned on his heel and stalked from the room without so much as a backward glance. Istreeth gave an apologetic bow of her own and scurried after him, leaving Desledair and Amalin alone in the chamber.

'What was that about?' said Amalin.

'I don't know,' said Desledair, honestly.

'By the Stars, I hope you are right in this,' said Amalin.

Desledair sighed. 'So do I.'

CHAPTER 26

East Arm, Seventh Year of the Dancer, late winter.

The Sky Kingdom had provided a most luxurious carriage for the Master Architect and his companion. It was all Desledair could do to insist that he be allowed to walk alongside it twice a day to stretch his legs and get some fresh air. Ravar had accompanied him at his pressing but if she was there in body, she was not with him in spirit.

Desledair observed that the Lady was running on a sort of automatic, functional level. She would eat and walk and dress and do as she was prompted, but her independent mind had departed to some distant place, far beyond the reach of those around her. Perhaps her Soul danced and talked and laughed with Eduerd's still. He would have been envious had he not to confront daily the ghostly form of the once so lively woman gliding through the world beside him.

At the bustling Marketdawn city of Eastarm, the pair were to stay two nights in the comfort of its finest rest house before taking the short voyage by sea to the Sky Kingdom's principal port.

It was over breakfast, for which neither showed much enthusiasm, that the travelling companions were notified that an express Kingdoms Post Messenger had arrived with a package for Ravar. Ravar acknowledged this by putting down the spoon with which she had been nonchalantly stirring her food and looking up at Desledair.

Frowning, he got up and went to the door to take the parcel. It was a small wooden box, bearing the mark of the Forest Kingdom. He placed it in front of Ravar, who eyed it with dislike.

She broke the seal and undid the elegant clasp to reveal a scroll bearing the royal seal and a letter within. She took up the letter first.

To the Lady Ravar of the Forest, Aislyth, King of your People sends greetings.

Your position as a Master of your Craft demands that you continue to give service to your Kingdom during your seasons beyond the Middle Sea.

You are hereby commissioned to represent the Forest in the court of the Sky Emperor. Additionally you will serve as a personal advisor and Tutor to Princess Amosono, the Emperor's daughter who is of Nearage.

Enclosed are the official documents and Kingdom Seal that all may recognise your status. Go east and serve your King and yourself well by teaching its people the song of the West.

The letter was signed off on behalf of the King with his seal in the official manner by the scribe. Ravar recognised the hand of the King's friend, Master Ralgon. However, there was a note at the bottom in the King's own hand.

When your task is done, remember the Forest. Remember your People and come home.

'What is it?' asked Desledair, seeing the unmistakable surprise in Ravar's expression. It was the first time he had seen any reaction in her features for almost a month.

Ravar handed him the letter and he read it quickly before passing it back and regarding her thoughtfully. He took the scroll carefully from the box.

'This will be a salutation to the Emperor of the Sky Kingdom, bearing your introduction to the Royal Court.' He raised a sardonic eyebrow. 'Your credentials.' Ravar wore a slight frown, her eyes darting slightly from left to right, as if reading an invisible script.

Desledair leant over the box again. 'Open the bag,' he said, nodding to a dark red velvet pouch at its bottom.

Ravar obeyed and pulled the neatly tied strings of the bag. From it she drew the beautifully cast, large bronze brooch from its pouch. Cut into its surface was the silhouette of a Great Oak, the symbol of the Forest

Kingdom and the insignia of its King. Ravar stopped dead, staring at it. Such an object marked its bearer as holding, not only the trust of their sovereign, but the power to speak and act as that ruler in another's realm.

'Well now, My Lady, there is quite a thing,' said Desledair, evenly. He came around the table and took it from her, opening its clasp and pinning it over the embroidered likeness at her shoulder.

Ravar peered down in wonder at the ornament that now crowned her sash. Desledair rose and stood formally before her.

The others in the small dining room had not failed to notice the mark of honour with which she had just been presented and they too had risen from their seats.

Desledair led all those present in a deep bow.

'Congratulations, *Ambassador,*' he said.

*

Across the Upper Face, the chosen men and women touched their hands to their marks. The Hidden Places were awake.

11170956R00152

Printed in Germany
by Amazon Distribution
GmbH, Leipzig